Deborah Challinor has a PhD in history and is the author of nine bestselling novels. *Behind the Sun* is the first in a series of four books set in 1830s Sydney, inspired by her ancestors — one of whom was a member of the First Fleet and another who was transported on the Floating Brothel. Deborah lives in New South Wales with her husband.

www.deborahchallinor.com

Also by Deborah Challinor

FICTION

Girl of Shadows

Tamar
White Feathers
Blue Smoke

Kitty
Amber
Band of Gold

Union Belle

Fire

Isle of Tears

NON-FICTION

Grey Ghosts
Who'll Stop the Rain?

Deborah
CHALLINOR
Behind the Sun

HarperCollins*Publishers*

HarperCollins_Publishers_

First published in Australia in 2012
This edition published in 2014
by HarperCollins_Publishers_ Australia Pty Limited
ABN 36 009 913 517
harpercollins.com.au

Copyright © Deborah Challinor 2012

The right of Deborah Challinor to be identified as the
author of this work has been asserted by her under
the _Copyright Amendment (Moral Rights) Act 2000_.

This work is copyright. Apart from any use as permitted under the
Copyright Act 1968, no part may be reproduced, copied, scanned, stored
in a retrieval system, recorded, or transmitted, in any form or by any
means, without the prior written permission of the publisher.

HarperCollins_Publishers_
Level 13, 201 Elizabeth Street, Sydney NSW 2000, Australia
Unit D1, 63 Apollo Drive, Albany, Auckland 0632, New Zealand
A 53, Sector 57, Noida, UP, India
77–85 Fulham Palace Road, London W6 8JB, United Kingdom
2 Bloor Street East, 20th floor, Toronto, Ontario M4W 1A8, Canada
10 East 53rd Street, New York NY 10022, USA

National Library of Australia Cataloguing-in-Publication entry:

Challinor, Deborah, author.
  Behind the sun / Deborah Challinor.
  2nd ed.
  ISBN: 978 0 7322 9298 0 (paperback)
  Female friendship—Fiction.
  Women convicts—Australia—Fiction.
A823.3

Cover design by Nada Backovic Designs, adapted by Alicia Freile, Tango Media
Cover images: Woman © Margie Hurwich / Arcangel Images; Rock formations
on beach © Simone Byrne / Arcangel Images; ship by tallshipstock.com; all other
images by shutterstock.com
Typeset in Sabon by Kirby Jones
Printed and bound in Australia by Griffin Press
The papers used by HarperCollins in the manufacture of this book are a natural,
recyclable product made from wood grown in sustainable plantation forests.
The fibre source and manufacturing processes meet recognised international
environmental standards, and carry certification.

5 4 3 2 1   14 15 16 17

This one is for my sister,
Anne Challinor

Part One

His Majesty's Hotel

One

November 1828, London

Friday Woolfe blew warm air onto freezing hands in fingerless gloves. Fog hung heavy over the street, deadening shouts and laughter from the nearby taverns and making a small yellow moon of the solitary gas light on the corner. It felt like it might soon snow.

'Feels like that cold's creeping straight up my fanny, Bets,' she grumbled to her friend.

Betsy Horrocks, her hands jammed in her armpits, stepped back and inclined her head. 'It is. Your skirts are all caught up at the back.'

They giggled madly as Friday reached around and rearranged her clothing: that'd teach her to squat in alleyways. She adjusted the angle of her straw hat with its silk rose, though she'd left her hair unbound as its bright copper colour never failed to attract the cullies.

God, when was the bugger going to come out? They'd freeze out here if he didn't show his face soon. And he'd seemed so likely, too: waving his glass around, expensive claret slopping over the rim, haw-hawing drunkenly in the tavern's parlour with his friends. He wasn't a nob but he was certainly throwing his money about, him and his yellow ivory false teeth that didn't fit right. But she and Betsy had caught his beady, hungry eye before the publican had tossed them out. Friday knew very well they had.

Perhaps they should have set their sights higher tonight. Gone after the young toffs — the 'quality' — swanning about Covent Garden Piazza, fancying themselves as intellectuals and wits, lording it loudly and drunkenly in the taverns, casinos and coffee houses around Drury Lane and the Bow Street theatres. But if they went for the big spenders the competition would be fierce, and who could be bothered with that?

Covent Garden in the 1820s had become a bustling marketplace offering an eclectic mix of flowers, vegetables, whores and entertainment and attracting thousands day and night. Friday and Betsy, never short of customers, found it just as easy, and equally lucrative, to work the peripheral streets that ringed the precinct, such as Bedford and Southampton, York and Brydges, or trawl Long Acre Street, on the northern side of which lay notorious Seven Dials.

At last Betsy spotted him: a small, middle-aged man weaving on bandy legs through the tavern doorway and out into the shadows of Henrietta Street, his shirt tucked in all crooked and his topper at a silly angle. God, what a ninny. 'Here he comes,' she murmured.

Flicking open the fastenings on her worn velvet jacket and feeling the usual sharp, almost vicious sting of anticipation, Friday stepped out to intercept him.

'Good evening, fine sir,' she said brightly. She tossed her head, knowing her hair would fan out beneath her hat and catch the light from the nearby street lamp. 'Might you be looking for company?'

She stood close, her hip bumping his suggestively, hoping her uncommon height of five feet six inches wouldn't intimidate him, but confident that the sight of the unfettered bosoms beneath her virtually transparent shift would have the opposite effect.

'I most certainly am not!' the man spluttered with affected indignation, the heels of his shoes scraping on the cobbles as he lurched backwards.

Friday followed him. 'Oh, I think you are,' she purred. 'What's your name?'

'John Smith.'

She smiled. They were *always* interested when they gave a false name. This one had a fat purse, too, they'd seen that earlier. And a heavy watch chain the muggins had on display for any light-fingered dip to covet, and a fine walking stick and good, well-made shoes.

A black cab clattered past, its cloak-shrouded driver almost invisible on his tiny seat high at the rear. The vehicle's iron-clad wheels sent a wash of filthy, freezing water from the cobbles across the lower portions of Mr Smith's trousers.

Friday leapt out of the way — her boots were near new — but Betsy flitted to Mr Smith's other side and caressed his arm. 'Never mind, love. We've got somewhere nice and cosy we can go. All three of us. Together.'

Mr Smith swallowed audibly, looked from Betsy to Friday, who had sidled back to him, then, as though he couldn't help himself, at Friday's voluptuous chest again. Small clouds of condensation hung before his face in the cold air as he breathed rapidly in and out. 'I don't usually do this sort of thing, you know.'

'Of course not,' Betsy agreed.

'How much?' he asked.

'A quid.'

'*A pound?!*'

Two men ambled past, smirking. 'Good weather for highway robbery,' one remarked to the other.

Mr Smith tugged the brim of his topper down over his face.

Tars, by the look of them, Friday thought. She grinned. 'Fancy some yourselves, do you?' She turned back to Mr Smith. 'That's for the both us, mind. Twice the fun. And that includes books for you to look at ... with *lovely* pictures.'

He rubbed his chin, as if calculating how much he could afford.

Friday stifled an irritated sigh and pulled at the ribbon holding her shift closed. It really was freezing and when the fabric slipped off her breasts her nipples sprang up into tight little marbles.

'Afterwards,' Mr Smith said quickly. 'I'll pay a pound, but afterwards.'

'That sounds like a fine idea, Mr Smith.' Friday snatched her jacket closed and slipped an arm through his.

Betsy, with a quick prayer of thanks for her friend's attributes, took his other arm and they marched him round the corner towards Maiden Lane, where they'd rented a room for the evening in a boarding house.

Wreathed in shadows, Maiden Lane appeared, to Mr Smith anyway, to recede into darkness forever. They weren't too far from the Thames here, only a few minutes' walk, though the clamour of the traffic on the river also seemed flattened by the fog-thickened night. There were no gas lamps lighting the streets this far from the theatres, and Mr Smith had the eerie feeling he had stepped back in time at least a hundred years. In this area of London he could easily be assaulted and even murdered, his lifeless body hurled into the river's putrid depths, not to be revealed until the ebb of some future tide. Nervously, he struggled to focus his smoke- and alcohol-reddened eyes and stepped clumsily around a pile of evil-smelling refuse on top of which sprawled a dead cat, its teeth bared in a feral, needle-toothed snarl.

'This isn't some sort of nefarious scheme, is it,' he said suddenly, 'whereby I'm about to be robbed?'

'Don't be a silly billy; of course not.' Betsy cupped her hand around his scrawny buttock and gave it an encouraging squeeze.

They helped him up the rickety steps to the boarding house's second floor and at last ushered him into the chamber they'd secured for the night. Its meagre furnishings consisted of an iron bedstead, a lumpy mattress on which sat a folded but threadbare blanket, and a single wooden chair. The temperature inside the room was almost as arctic as that outside.

'This'll warm us up.' Friday knelt, reached into the far corner beneath the bed and produced two bottles of gin.

Mr Smith made a disparaging sound and said pretentiously, 'I don't drink Blue Ruin.'

Having unwound his muffler and removed his hat, leaving the greying hair on his head sticking up like errant feathers, he perched himself on the chair like a skinny little bird sitting on a gutter, its legs dangling improbably over the edge. Now that he was here he didn't seem at all sure of what to do.

Bloody airs and graces, Friday thought, and from someone probably no better than a grubby little shopkeeper. 'Well, you'll have to. It's all we've got.' She turned a bottle so he could inspect it. 'It's proper distilled.'

'It's not what I'm accustomed to,' Mr Smith said stubbornly.

Friday eased out the cork and took a swig. 'You're welcome to it, but suit yourself. Freeze to death then, go on.'

Betsy glanced uneasily at Friday: she'd been drinking all day and was turning sharp-edged now with the liquor. If Mr Smith carried on like this, she'd be likely to belt him one and really hurt him; she was a big, strong girl and lost all her tolerance on the jar.

But just as Betsy opened her mouth to diffuse the situation, Mr Smith himself piped up. 'I understood we were going to ...' He gestured vaguely at Friday and Betsy. 'Also, you mentioned books.'

Relieved, Betsy teased in her sweetest voice, 'Lord, you're a keen one, aren't you?' Loosening the kerchief at her throat she sat on the sagging mattress and slowly raised her skirts so Mr Smith couldn't fail to see the curve of well-turned ankles above laced boots. 'But me and her always have a few gins first. This is *special* gin, y'see. Makes us feel extra loving. Doesn't it?' She turned to Friday for confirmation, hoping she was still in the mood to play along.

Friday took a huge swig of gin and stifled a burp. 'Not just us, either. Our customers swear it gives them a cockstand 'til nigh on sun up.'

She felt the sneer of disdain begin to form as soon as she'd said it but suppressed it with practised ease. They loved it when you came out with dirty words, but it made her sick. Not the words — she could swear like a lobsterback and often did — it was the fact that they were so predictable and so easily manipulated. Say this and they'll do this, touch that and they'll do that. Like starving dogs.

Mr Smith went red to the roots of his fluffy, receding hair, but managed to gasp, 'Distilled, you say?'

'I swear on my mother's life,' Friday insisted. 'None of your flavoured rubbish for *our* customers.'

'Perhaps just a taste, then.'

Mr Smith had more than a taste. Half an hour later he passed out and slid bonelessly off his chair. Friday dumped him on the bed, pleased they wouldn't even have to lift their skirts to get what they were after. She and Betsy relieved him of his gold watch and chain, his purse and its twelve pounds, his walking stick, his fine linen waistcoat and his shoes. They also took his muddy trousers, to slow him down when he regained consciousness, which hopefully wouldn't be until the morning. They did, however, cover him with the blanket.

Neither worked as part of a crew nor belonged to a flash man so they divided the swag between them — Betsy took most of the money, the vest, trousers and shoes and Friday the watch and chain and the walking stick. Betsy headed home but Friday went immediately to see her fence and sold the watch and chain, as always for a lot less than it was worth. She kept the walking stick, though, as she'd taken a fancy to the snake's head that formed the handle. The glinting green eyes weren't emeralds, just cut glass, but they were very pretty.

She rose early the next morning, her stomach growling, and made her way to the ordinary she favoured on Skinner Street, dodging drays and wagons and holding her shawl over her mouth and nose against the greasy, eye-watering stench of freshly slaughtered meat as she cut through Smithfield Market. It was a journey she made most days and it never smelt any better, though in a way she loved it. Her streets were always vibrant, always teeming with butchers and livestock vendors and stallholders ready with a greeting or a ribald comment. The area had been a marketplace for livestock for centuries, and every morning as the sun rose the thoroughfares and streets — some of London's narrowest and busiest — were jammed with thousands of lowing, bleating, squawking, squealing, shitting animals on their way to be butchered and dozens of shouting, whip-cracking drovers. By mid-afternoon the five-acre marketplace would be awash with blood and shite and heaped with tons of raw fat, much of which would be rendered for tallow, and great piles of hooves and bones and guts, which would eventually find their way into the Thames or be left in place to rot. The hides would be sent to nearby tanneries to be made into leather goods, rendering the air in the vicinity so foul as to be almost unbreathable, and the feathers from fowl sent to stuff quality pillows and mattresses.

Smithfield Market wasn't the most unpleasant of her daily encounters, however. Ahead was something even worse, though it had long since ceased to turn her stomach. Exiting the market, she entered a narrow street and, in preparation, withdrew a handkerchief anointed with oil of cloves and bunched it beneath her nose. Nodding genially to passersby with similarly muffled faces, she hurried along until she came to the wall of an old churchyard from between whose bulging bricks oozed a thin, reeking brown liquid that formed a shallow puddle on the street. The wall was four feet tall and the ground within had been raised over the centuries by burial after burial to almost level with the top row of bricks.

At the lychgate she paused, as something interesting was happening inside. Near the church itself, these days looking as though it had been built in a pit, a pair of gravediggers were hauling up half-decayed coffins from a large hole and dumping them willy-nilly on a piece of oilcloth. The headstones had been wrenched up and pushed aside and now the men were clambering back into the pit to retrieve more bodies, urged on by the arm-wavings of a supervising sexton.

It was common knowledge that bodies at the paupers' end and in the cheaper plots of this churchyard had been layered and shuffled around for hundreds of years to accommodate incomers — that was so in all London churchyards. But it wasn't expected regarding plots closer to the church, for which people paid a lot more to lie undisturbed after they'd gone to their long home. Obviously it *should* be expected, Friday thought, watching a coffin flying out of a hole and bursting open as it hit the ground, disgorging a half-rotted corpse with long hair and a decaying shroud tangling in the split wood. She herself had money put aside so she wouldn't have to be buried 'on the parish', but if this is what you got being buried in the toffs' area she might change her mind.

As the morning breeze shifted she pressed her handkerchief closer to her face. It was tragic, really. The relatives of whoever these rotted wretches were would turn up one day to have a good grieve, and there they'd be, weeping their hearts out over the wrong graves, their dearly departeds reburied twenty yards away. If they'd been reburied at all. It had long been rumoured that half the bodies disinterred weren't even in churchyards any more, more likely to be found in the foundations of new roads or nourishing the market gardens of Kent. But her loved ones weren't in this churchyard. They were elsewhere in bolted, solid lead coffins that had cost her the earth, safe from greedy sextons and the Resurrection Men, so what did she care?

Unable to bear the stink any longer, and aware of the irate looks from the sexton squelching around in the putrid mud in a pair of filthy leather Hessian boots, she walked away. Occasionally she thought about finding new lodgings on the western side of the market and closer to where she worked, but someone very wise had once told her that a smart animal didn't shit in its own nest, and she had to agree.

A number of the whores who worked around Covent Garden actually did live in the theatre district, though not all by any means. There was an unofficial but strict hierarchy within the capital's bustling sex industry. At the very top of the heap were the courtesans, women kept by men of wealth for unrestricted and exclusive use. These women unashamedly appeared in public with their beaux, glittering with jewels and bristling with lace and feathers, and would scratch the eyes out of any other demi-monde daring to bat her eyelashes.

Below the courtesans, London's whores separated into those women — and men and boys — who either worked the streets, or those who operated from brothels of one form or another.

Of the streetwalkers, the elite wore the latest silk and taffeta fashions and took their quality cullies back to their own smartly furnished apartments around Bow Street and Drury Lane. The rents were astronomical so to pay them they charged high fees and worked long, hard hours.

Next came the whores who serviced their customers in far less salubrious rooms rented for the night or by the hour, and beneath them were the worn-out judies who'd been treading London's cobbles for years, followed by those so unattractive or destitute they charged little more than a shilling for a hurried coupling against a wall in a dark alleyway. At the very bottom of the streetwalker ladder were the wretched park whores, often badly diseased or in thrall beyond redemption to Blue Ruin or the poppy, who would take sixpence in exchange for five minutes in the open air. Though they were objects of pity, whores of all other stripes looked down on them.

There were several elegant and exclusive bawdyhouses, to which the watch turned a blind eye, in the Covent Garden precinct; but no matter how sumptuous their cages' interiors, the girls employed there worked when they were told to and handed over at least half of what they earned to the madam.

Just beneath these stylish and well-patronised salons came the single private rooms funded solely by the earnings of the prostitute who occupied them, whose ultimate goal was often to become one of the pampered courtesans seen on the arms of their benefactors at casinos, the theatre, the races and in the shops of Regent and Bond streets. Such a goal made sense: many noble benefactors took their responsibilities to their dependents seriously; they either passed old mistresses on to their peers or pensioned them off when their charms faded.

Below these hopefuls came the brothels to which any man with money in his pocket and an erection in his trousers had access. Some were clean, bright establishments; others less so. Then there were the groups of prostitutes who banded together, often sharing clothes and food costs, to rent rooms in houses around Covent Garden and operate unofficial brothels, until the watch broke them up or the girls moved on, more often than not with several months' back-rent left unpaid. Weeks later they would find new premises and set up once again.

Last and definitely least of the 'indoors' category were the women who worked out of their own homes, sometimes with their children unavoidably in attendance.

There were child prostitutes — both boys and girls; mollyhouses where men could enjoy sex dressed in women's finery; beautiful coffee-skinned whores from Jamaica and stunning girls from Africa with skin as black as Whitby jet; flogging brothels with all manner of whips and devices; discreet salons for ladies who preferred the smooth curves of female flesh; and in Holywell Street off the Strand were close to fifty shops selling dirty books. Friday herself had posed several times for illustrators of such publications — it paid quite well.

Life as a streetwalker suited her. She didn't occupy a particularly lofty position in London's hierarchy of whores and didn't care to. She didn't have to pretend she was something she wasn't, she worked when she wanted to and, if she didn't like the way a man looked, she could walk away. She had a good wad of money put aside now — she wasn't dependent the way a lot of whores were — and when she and Betsy worked the caper with the drunks there was always extra. And if sometimes she felt like sitting in the ordinary or the tavern drinking gin with her friends instead of walking the streets, she could. It wasn't the life most mothers would have wanted for their daughters, but hers had been a prostitute herself, and a drunk, and she'd been dead seven years anyway.

Friday swallowed the last of her bread and cheese. She sat for a moment, then shaved off a sliver of tobacco, tamped it into her pipe and lit it, drawing up the smoke and expelling it from the side of her mouth in short, regular puffs until the tobacco caught properly. As she coughed and reached for her ale, the sound of raised voices drew her attention.

To her alarm, she saw a bilious-looking 'John Smith', a pair of trousers far too big for him hauled up over his bony shanks, standing near the ordinary's doorway accompanied by a grim-faced constable.

Her heart thudding with panic, she rose, grabbed her things and ran for the door at the end of the bar that opened onto a lane behind the ordinary.

'*That's her!*' Mr Smith shouted. 'With the red hair! Stop her!'

Friday ran, but the constable was too quick and too strong. He darted across the room and grabbed her wrist as she lunged for the door latch.

'I thought it might be you. God's truth, girl, did you not learn your lesson last time?' the constable said as he guided her firmly back towards Mr Smith.

'Don't know what you're talking about,' Friday muttered as she struggled to free her arm.

Mr Smith, fizzing with righteous wrath, wrenched his walking stick out of Friday's hand and hit her across her shoulder with it. 'That's *my* cane! Thief! Dirty, whoring *thief*!'

The ordinary's morning patrons let out an 'aaah!' of appreciation at this unexpected entertainment.

Friday's mouth fell open in astonishment. 'Oi, you little shite, watch who you're thumping!' And she struck out with a closed fist and punched Mr Smith in the side of the head.

The small crowd cheered lustily and someone threw a bread roll.

Mr Smith staggered, then, his hand cupped protectively over his ringing ear, demanded of the constable, 'Did you see that? Thievery *and* assault!'

'Settle down now,' the constable said to him wearily. 'You'll get your day in court.'

'She's a thieving whore! She took my watch and my money and my shoes!' Mr Smith was almost spitting, he was so beside himself with indignation. '*And* my trousers!'

Hoots of laughter from the breakfast crowd.

'And there was another one, with dark hair. I insist she be apprehended as well!'

The constable raised an eyebrow at Friday. 'Who might that have been then?'

'Dunno,' Friday responded automatically. 'I don't even know what he's talking about.'

The constable knew very well that she did and he also knew he would never get her accomplice's name out of her, because Friday Woolfe had a rare sense of honour among the canting crew — she had never been known to rat on a colleague. Her accomplice would no doubt get away with it, unlike Friday. Pretty, buxom, cheerful Friday Woolfe was headed for Newgate Gaol and then, like as not, this time the boat.

Harrie Clarke rubbed the lustrous rust-coloured silk between her fingers, imagining she could feel the exceptional quality of each individual thread against her skin. Then, as she always did, she sighed hopelessly and let the fabric fall; never in her life would she be able to afford to buy anything like it, not on the pittance she was paid as an assistant sempstress to Mrs Lynch. If she could just manage to save enough to make two or three demonstration gowns, featuring her original lace and embroidery patterns to show customers how lovely they were, then she could take orders, buying the materials she would need with the deposits.

A skilled 'first hand' in a dressmaking salon in Regent Street could earn up to sixty pounds a year — a fortune — personally measuring ladies for dresses and cutting patterns. Apprentices, who sewed sleeves and bodices, earned less, but still a lot more than the wage Mrs Lynch paid Harrie — and Harrie, all modesty aside, knew herself to be very good at what she did. But at least she hadn't been reduced to skirt work, which was sent out to teams of piece-workers who lived in the garrets of Carnaby Street and worked all through the night during the Season, ruining their eyesight and their backs for as little sixpence per piece.

But even though what she earned barely covered her family's living expenses, Harrie dared not leave her position with Mrs Lynch. It was tedious and soul-destroying but her mother was ill constantly now, coughing up her lungs night and day, unable to earn an income but at the same time refusing to allow Harrie's half-brother Robbie and half-sisters Sophie and Anna out to work. At eight and seven respectively Robbie and Sophie were old enough, but Ada couldn't bear to see them ruined at such a young age; she had sworn it would be another year at least before she let Robbie look for employment in the city's factories or markets.

But Robbie was courting ruin anyway, out on the streets ducking and diving, stealing food and telling Ada it had come from a neighbour. It worried Harrie enormously. She agreed that the children should be kept out of the factories, but the prospect of another year as bread-winner filled her with misery: she just didn't know if she could tolerate working for tight-fisted, slave-driving, mean-mouthed Mrs Lynch much longer. She was constantly on the lookout for something better, but jobs were scarce and she knew she was lucky to be employed at all. Some of her friends supplemented their incomes with casual prostitution, but she knew she could never do that, not even as a last resort. She just couldn't.

The linen-draper moved along his counter and conferred with his shop assistant. They both disappeared through a doorway into the back of the shop. Harrie drifted over to the counter and inspected some boxes of lace. Next to them were arranged half a dozen tapestry-covered compendiums containing spools of silk embroidery thread. One in particular caught her attention: a selection ranging from the palest blue to a startling turquoise to a deep, rich indigo — colours that would work into her latest embroidery pattern *perfectly*.

The hairs on her arms lifted and her skin prickled with goose bumps. Did she dare? She'd never stolen *anything* in her life. A vision flashed through her mind of well-to-do ladies ordering dozens of copies of her demonstration gown — it would be rust silk with stunning blue embroidery on the bodice — while her mother, miraculously healthy again, wrote down measurements in the order book. Inside her something seemed to swell almost to bursting, her hand reached out, and the compendium of gorgeous threads disappeared beneath the waistband of her skirt. Then, feeling as though she were walking in some sort of dream in which all the sound in the world was muffled by the thudding of her heart and the colours of everything were suddenly much, much brighter, she returned to the rust silk, slid the flat bolt up her skirt, clamped it against her thigh with her hand and walked out of the shop, the hot blood in her face surging in time with her pulse. She might get away with it, she really might; she had the sort of ordinary features and demeanour that allowed her to go about unnoticed so perhaps ...

Then someone shouted and she began to run: the bolt of fabric slipped down and tripped her, sending her sprawling face first onto the cobbles; she knew then she had just made the worst mistake of her life.

November 1828, Newgate Gaol

Looming on the corner of Newgate and Old Bailey streets, just outside the former western wall, or 'bailey', of the city, Newgate had been home to London's debtors and felons, and those awaiting trial or execution, for more than six centuries. It had burnt down twice, once during the Great Fire of London, and been demolished and rebuilt many more times in an attempt to obliterate the pestilence and disease that flourished within its high walls. This latest incarnation, completed fifty years earlier, incorporated a 'common area' for prisoners with no money and a 'State area' for those whose personal finances afforded them a superior standard of accommodation. Female prisoners, however, were all housed together in the same wing. No improvements had been made in those fifty years; facilities had not been maintained, and there had been no proper effort to clean the wards or rid them of vermin.

It was common knowledge that many of Newgate's wards stood deliberately empty because the governor liked to save money by crowding inmates into half the prison's available space. Harrie's ward was loathsome. Twenty-nine females were crammed into a space thirty feet by fifteen, with one barred, unglazed window too small to admit enough breeze to stir the damp, fetid air inside, but big enough to let in the biting cold. A perpetual chill crept through the ward's oozing stone walls and floor, which were filmed with the accumulated slime and grime of fifty years, and seemed to permeate everything it touched. Everything dripped, everything remained continuously damp — clothes, blankets, hair and even skin wouldn't dry. Rats scuttled across feet and sniffed around faces at night, and centipedes and slugs curled and writhed wetly under anything left on the flagged floor.

The inmates slept on a barracks bed, a wide wooden platform built inches above the floor and lined with rope mats, each covered with a threadbare rug, though Harrie's rug had been stolen. It didn't much matter, however, as bodies were crammed so tightly together they drew warmth from each other. At times during the day they went out into the courtyard onto which all the ground-level women's wards opened. Those who wanted to wash, and as far as Harrie could tell most didn't, could do so at a pump in the yard. For calls of nature, there were two profoundly noisome water closets off the yard, and a bucket in each ward for use at night when the doors were locked.

At the time of Harrie's incarceration, there were about one hundred and fifty female prisoners in Newgate, from bright-eyed young girls of eleven or twelve to toothless crones bent almost double with age, all jammed into five wards. Some women had little ones with them and infants still on the breast; many of these children would remain with their mother for her entire sentence, perhaps years. There was no separation at all of inmates — tried were mixed in with untried, debtors with felons, minor offenders with murderers, the insane with those awaiting transportation.

During her first six days in Newgate, Harrie had spoken to almost no one. Though a member of the class referred to as the labouring poor herself, she considered her station to be above the women with whom she was sharing a cell, albeit by only a couple of rungs, and she was shocked at their crude and rough behaviour and by the utter squalor of the environment. Her cellmates appeared almost accustomed to living in such horrible conditions; indeed she was discovering some of them had been inmates of, or in and out of, Newgate for years.

This morning, crouched on her mouldy rope mat, she clamped her hands even more firmly over her ears. Mad Martha was in full flight: on and on it went, the old woman's cackles and moans and off-key singing echoing off the cell walls, a constant irritant to all but Martha herself, who was oblivious to the agitation she was causing. The wardswoman had already belted her once and now Harrie felt an overwhelming urge to do the same.

She poked her fingers so far into her ears it hurt, but it was hopeless. Someone would murder Martha soon, she was sure of it, and when it happened she wouldn't be sorry at all.

At a great rattling of keys Harrie stood and moved towards the door, desperate to escape out into the courtyard, but when it opened the turnkey wasn't alone — beside her stood the big red-haired girl, whom Harrie hadn't seen since she'd been taken away four days ago for kicking and swearing at a warder.

'Morning all!' the girl announced, her cheerful face glowing as though she'd been up with the lark and out for a morning perambulate around Hyde Park, followed by a hearty breakfast of pork sausage, fried potatoes and batter pudding.

'*Eeee!*' Martha shrieked, her filthy hands flying up in the air. 'The red devil!'

'Get your things, Martha,' the turnkey said, her plain face wearing its perpetual scowl. 'You're being shifted.'

'Shifted! Shifted! Shifted!' Martha spun round, the rags of her dress flicking out around her scabby, bare legs. 'No, I won't be! I won't be shifted! Martha likes it here!'

The turnkey sighed. 'Come on, Martha, you need some time in solitary. Before someone does you a proper injury.'

'No!' Martha thrust a dirt-encrusted finger at Friday. '*She* wants to steal me place.' She turned again and pointed towards an empty corner. '*And* me fine things. The *king* give me that card table, you know!'

'Right, Martha, that's enough.'

The turnkey moved towards Martha, who retaliated by whipping up her tattered skirts to display straggly grey pubic hair above the sagging, blue-veined skin of her emaciated thighs. A hideous rotting fish smell wafted from her, making Harrie gag.

Grasping Martha's arm, the turnkey yanked her towards the door. The old woman began to scream and kick, in the process knocking over the bucket they'd all been peeing in during the night.

'You know she's got the women's cancer,' someone said as Martha was dragged outside. 'Be dead soon.'

Someone less kind remarked, 'Good riddance. Stinking old bag o' bones.'

Harrie waited until Martha and the warder had gone, then escaped out into the pale, cold sunlight, hugely relieved to exchange the fetid miasma of the ward for the sharp, smoke-tainted morning air. She crossed the yard to the pump, worked the handle and splashed freezing water over her face. Desperate for a proper wash but too embarrassed to undress, she held open the neck of her blouse, cupped water in her hand and had a go at her armpits, soaking herself in the process.

'Poor old bat, thinks I'm the devil incarnate,' a voice said.

Harrie turned around; it was the girl with the copper-coloured hair, a small leather pouch clamped under her arm and a tin in her hand. Opening it, she took out a cake of tobacco and sliced off two slivers with a small knife, realised she didn't have enough hands, swore, and crouched, setting everything on the ground.

'I'm not,' she went on, addressing the dirt, 'despite what some people say.' Crumbling the tobacco flakes until they'd achieved a satisfactory consistency, she poked them into the bowl of her clay pipe, then rummaged around in the pouch. 'Bear with me. Won't be a mo'.'

Harrie watched, fascinated.

Producing a tiny compendium, the girl stood, took out a Congreves match and struck it against the attached strip of sandpaper. The flame flared hugely, singeing her hair. Managing to swear roundly and light her pipe at the same time, she drew on it and coughed until her eyes watered. She coughed again, then hoicked and spat.

'Beg pardon. I'm Friday Woolfe. And you should cheer up, because it could be worse. And don't bother with the bathing, love. Everyone in here stinks to high heaven.'

'How could it be worse?' Harrie said, a little more rudely than she meant to. What did this girl know about her situation? She was clearly all right herself, if she could afford to buy tobacco and proper matches.

'Well, you could be swinging on the end of a rope.'

Harrie looked at Friday Woolfe. She was a good four inches taller than Harrie, with strong, round arms, a neat waist and full breasts, pale, lightly freckled skin and glorious, wild, copper-coloured hair. 'That's not a very nice thing to say. And I don't mean to be cheeky, but Friday's quite an odd name.'

Friday Woolfe looked contrite and uncomfortable, as though the first were an emotion she rarely bothered with. 'Sorry. It's my mouth. Sometimes it opens and things just come out. It is odd, my name, isn't it? It's after St Frideswide.'

Harrie, absurdly relieved that someone was actually being civil to her, said in a rush, 'I stole a bolt of cloth and some embroidery thread from a shop. Do you think I *will* swing?'

Friday gave her a long, contemplative look. 'You've not been up before, have you?'

'Up where?'

Friday rolled her eyes. 'Well, that answers my question. Up in front of the judge.'

'No, never.'

'Then it's hard to say what you'll get. But you won't go to the gallows — not for shoplifting. Not since about five years ago, anyway. What's your name?'

Harrie felt faint with relief. Her toes were going numb and she stamped her feet. 'Harrie. Harriet Clarke.'

Friday laughed, a loud guffaw of amusement. 'Harrie. I like that. Well, like I said, it's hard to say, and I couldn't guarantee anything, but you'll probably get sent to New South Wales. You must know about that?'

Harrie nodded. Her father's older brother had been transported in 1817.

'Unless you've done a murder as well?'

'A murder? God help me, no!'

'Then it's likely to be the boat.'

They moved aside as a fight broke out between three women arguing over a pack of cards.

'You don't think I might just get a year in here? Or in Brixton, perhaps?' Even to Harrie's own ears the question sounded hopelessly naive. And it didn't matter where she was incarcerated, of course — her mother and the children would still be deprived of her income. But at least if she stayed in England she might still see them occasionally.

'Sometimes it'll all just turn on whether the judge had a good dinner.' Friday drew hard on her pipe, creating clouds of unpleasant smoke. 'I'd be hoping for the boat if I was you. A year in an English prison'll wring the life out of someone like yourself the same way hanging will, only a lot slower.'

Harrie wasn't sure if she'd just been insulted or not. She didn't think so, but said anyway, 'What do you mean, "like yourself"?'

'Well, look at you. You're not exactly flash mob, are you? I'll bet you've even got a nice, proper job. I can tell: you've got really clean, smooth hands.' Friday looked down at her own — not dirty, but rough, and with fingernails bitten to the quick. Harrie saw there were three small stars tattooed on the web of skin between the thumb and forefinger of her right hand.

'Are you?' Harrie asked, surprising herself. 'Flash mob, I mean?'

Friday gave an ambiguous shrug. 'Yes and no. I'm not in a crew. I work for myself but everyone needs contacts. I'm on the town,' she added, anticipating the question.

Harrie wasn't shocked. It wasn't against the law. 'But why are you in here?'

'Oh, I robbed a customer,' Friday said breezily. 'I'll be on the boat for sure. For life, I expect.' She laughed again. 'This isn't my first offence.'

Harrie stared at her. 'How can you laugh about it?'

'Because you have to, don't you?' Friday scratched her armpit. 'So what *do* you do, when you're not thieving?'

'I'm an assistant sempstress. Or I *was*. I did a bit of fancywork, too. Lace and embroidery and the like.'

'An orrice weaver? See, I was right, wasn't I?'

'No, I don't make the lace; that went out to piece-workers. I just design the patterns. I do all the embroidery, though. Well, I *did*, before this.'

But Friday seemed to have lost interest in Harrie's specialist skills. 'You fixed for everything you need in here?'

Harrie shook her head, acutely conscious of her face turning red. She had nothing. She had left everything behind for her mother.

'Money?'

Burning with embarrassment now and struggling to blink away hot tears of self-pity and bitter regret, Harrie looked up at the sky. It was low and a bright, dirty white and it made her feel dizzy. She wondered if it might snow.

Finally she admitted, 'I was the only one bringing anything into the house.' Here it comes, she thought, she's just going to laugh again.

After a while, Friday said, 'I'll see you right.'

Harrie's mother came to visit her after ten days, bringing her a fresh bap and two cold saveloys Harrie knew she couldn't spare, but she ate them anyway, she was that desperate for something tasty.

'The food's awful, Ma,' she said through the railing in the visitors' passage. 'There's usually enough of it, but it's stirabout and hard bread and smelly, fatty mutton soup.'

'Then you eat them saveloys now, love,' Ada Clarke said. 'They'll only be stolen if you don't.'

That was true.

As Harrie ate, Ada watched, her eyes brimming with tears. She didn't want to ask but she couldn't help herself. 'Why did you do it, Harrie? Did you not think about getting caught?' The hard 'c' in the last word was too much for her raw throat; she raised her hand and coughed hackingly, wiping bloody phlegm onto a streaked cloth.

The lines that misery and pain had etched into her mother's pallid face were plain to see and Harrie would have given anything to erase them. But now, because of what she'd done, she'd only made them worse.

'I don't know, Ma. I thought perhaps ...' She trailed off: it seemed so pointless to be talking about her grand schemes now.

Ada waited, but Harrie remained silent. 'Have you heard when you're to go to trial?'

Harrie shook her head. 'I don't even know if the bill of indictment's been drawn up yet. Then it has to go before the Grand Jury. I'll get a trial date after that.'

'But only if it goes that far,' Ada said.

Wordlessly, they looked at each other; they both knew it would.

'Will you come? When it's time?' Harrie asked.

'I don't know, love. I'm not sure I could bear hearing it if, well, if it's to be the worst.' Ada slipped her bony hand through the rails and cupped Harrie's cheek. 'All you can do is pray. The little ones send their love. But whatever happens, you won't be coming home soon, will you?'

Not trusting her voice, Harrie shook her head again, kissed her mother's palm, and hurried away before Ada could see her tears.

Two

December 1828, London

'Ready?' Sarah Morgan asked.

Her colleague, Thomas Ratcliffe, peered through the displays in the window into the shop and nodded.

Sarah laid a gloved hand on Tom's arm and they entered the small, elegant haberdashery, the bell over the door announcing their arrival. The shopkeeper didn't even look up, too busy watching what he clearly suspected were three hoisters, milling about in front of his counter overtly eyeing a display of carved bone awls and needle cases, ivory thread waxers and gilded crotchet hooks. To one side stood a well-dressed, middle-aged woman carrying a beaded reticule and a wicker shopping basket, a look of consternation growing on her plump, pink face.

'Good morning, madam,' Tom said, doffing his hat to her.

The woman took in Tom's smartly cut trousers, coat of black superfine and beautifully folded starcher and Sarah's elegantly plumed hat and heavy velvet cloak, and her face sagged with relief.

'Oh dear,' she whispered hoarsely, and gestured towards the shop's other occupants. 'I think there may be some unpleasantness.'

'Stand back, please, madam,' Tom commanded, stepping between the woman and the ill-smelling, raggedly dressed wretches crowding the counter. 'Elizabeth?' he said to Sarah.

Sarah took the woman's elbow and drew her gently out of the way. Tom approached the counter, prodded the nearest of the three with his cane and said loudly, 'I'll thank you to leave these premises at once.'

'No, we're doing our shopping,' the young man replied, his hands thrust defiantly into the pockets of his filthy corduroy trousers. With him were another man and an undernourished girl wearing a grubby, patched dress and a shawl so worn the pattern was no longer discernible. Their sour unwashed smell filled the shop. Behind Tom, the woman with the shopping basket discreetly lifted a scented handkerchief to her face.

Tom raised his cane again, its silver knob glinting. 'I said get out! Go on, be off with you!'

The shopkeeper found his voice. 'That's right. Go on, clear off or I'll call the watch.'

'We've not done nothing,' whined the girl, her hair hanging around her face in greasy hanks.

'*Out!*' Tom roared, and lunged at them.

The three held their ground for no more than a second, then raced for the door, jerked it open and set the bell ringing madly. They shot out into the street and disappeared.

'Lord above, the *cheek* of them!' the woman said, fanning her face weakly with her handkerchief. 'I feel quite faint. I was *convinced* I was about to be robbed!'

Sarah took her hand and led her to a chair near the counter. 'You rest awhile. You've had a dreadful fright. We all have.'

'I'm still reporting it,' the shopkeeper grumbled. 'Damned beggars and thieves, coming into my shop bold as you please. Begging your pardons, ladies.'

'Yes, quite right. It's thoroughly unacceptable,' Tom said. 'In fact, allow us to do that for you. Come, Elizabeth, we'll go straight to the watch house now.'

'Thank you,' the woman said. 'Lord only knows what might have happened if you hadn't arrived when you did.'

If the shopkeeper was offended by the implication that he couldn't defend his own premises, he knew better than to show it. He inclined his head at Tom. 'Aye, thank you, sir. Much appreciated.'

'You're welcome. Good day,' Tom replied, and held the door open for Sarah.

They walked swiftly along Bond Street, turned into Brook Street, ducked across Hanover Square, then onto Oxford Street where they hailed a cab. The driver baulked at the Seven Dials address, but reluctantly agreed after Tom bunged him an extra two shillings.

Inside the cab, Tom said, 'So? Show me.'

Sarah looked at him, debating whether to risk concealing any of it from him. Probably not this time: none of it was worth it. He didn't trust her and was watching her closely, but that was all right because she didn't trust him. She didn't trust anyone. She loosened the cords on her reticule.

'Her purse, which has —' she opened it and had a quick look '— three ten-pound notes, maybe six five-guinea coins, some silver and a few coppers.' She closed the purse and dug deeper into her bag. 'Two rings, one engraved gold and one set with a sapphire. It's small, but it's a nicely cut stone. And a silver snuff box with a topaz set into the lid.' She eased it open. 'With a broken hinge. Perhaps she was on her way to a silversmith.'

'Not bad,' Tom said with grudging appreciation. He extended his hand. 'I'll hold on to all that. 'Til we divvy it up.'

Sarah dropped everything back into her reticule. 'I think it's safer in here. At least until we meet up with the others.'

Tom stared at her, his hard, dark eyes under their heavy brows giving nothing away. He was a handsome man in a swarthy sort of way, but he held no appeal for Sarah. She knew him far too well. She stared back until finally he looked away. It might have been petty, but it felt to her like a tiny victory.

They rode in silence until they reached Earl Street and the driver rapped on the roof of the cab; Sarah and Tom had barely alighted before he cracked his whip and urged the horse on again. Sarah didn't blame him, Seven Dials was no place to loiter, it being an extension of the dreaded St Giles rookery. She would be safe with Tom, however — no one ever got away with stealing from him. Not in the long run. And Seven Dials was her home; she knew its people, its rhythms and moods, and its dangers.

Thousands of people — the unemployed, criminals, low-class prostitutes and the poverty-stricken — lived crammed into the crumbling, rotting tenements of Seven Dials and St Giles. The tall houses, jammed together and divided into as many rooms as possible by unscrupulous landlords, resembled beehives, galleries added on front and back over the years to accommodate more and more tenants, windows broken and stuffed with rags or covered with boards, one water closet and one hand pump per hundred residents. Outside every door lay stinking pools of human waste thrown from carelessly aimed pisspots. Narrow alleys and wynds bored through the buildings like wormholes, undermining already decaying foundations and trapping filth and smells, terminating in nothing more than walled courts deep as wells and filled with decades of accumulated rubbish and ash. Hundreds of dogs roamed freely, defecating everywhere and feeding on refuse, and countless skinny, scrofulous cats crept silently about or perched on walls and window ledges in the thin winter sun. The lodgers themselves rarely strayed from the rookeries except to buy whelks and oysters, or watercress, or pennie-pies and baked potatoes from street vendors, there being no cooking facilities at all in the tenements. At all hours talking and shouting and laughter could be heard — and screams and drunken swearing and the slamming of rickety doors.

Here Sarah was anonymous, and that was the way she liked it. No one asked where she had come from and no one cared what she did with her time. The rent was cheap, her neighbours personable if rowdy and, if trouble followed her home, she could disappear into the warren of tenements like one of the millions of rats that scuttled incessantly through the hallways and galleries.

They crossed the crowded circus with its traffic and stalls and vendors to St Andrew's Street, then turned into a cold, narrow alleyway, the sun completely occluded by tenements leaning in on both sides. The sparsely laid cobbles underfoot were slimy with moss and filth overflowing from an open drain trickling through the alley and, as always, Sarah watched where she placed her feet. They ascended a set of dilapidated steps and entered the first floor of a soot-encrusted brick and stone building. Sarah unlocked the door to the room she'd been renting for the past three months; Tom pushed past her, sat down on one of two mismatched wooden chairs and made himself comfortable.

'They could be hours,' he grumbled as he removed his hat and threw it at Sarah's bed.

The room was dark. The glazing in the window had long gone and Sarah had paid someone to fashion a wooden shutter over the empty frame; this she opened to let in some light and air to chase away the ever-present smell of mould and decaying plaster. It was a miserable little space but at least she could afford it to herself. On her left two families lived in one tiny chamber and on her right were an extended family packed into a room no bigger than her own. Sarah was aware that the matriarch, Rosina, supported the household by illegal coining — at night the air was sharp with the telltale smell of hot metal — and the noise of her neighbours on both sides talking, laughing, squabbling and generally going about their lives was barely dampened by the disintegrating walls.

Rosina's family, she also knew, were in trouble. They owed three months' rent and when the youngest child had died three days earlier, the bailiffs had come and seized the body and would not release it until the debt had been paid. The hallway had been tainted with the smell of heated lead and pewter ever since.

'I wouldn't think so,' she said. 'They'll be wanting their pay.'

'Empty your bag,' Tom said, gesturing at Sarah's reticule. 'I want to count that money.'

Sarah tugged off her gloves, found the woman's purse, rings and the snuff box, and laid them on the blanket covering her mattress. While Tom was greedily examining everything, she removed her pretty hat and placed it carefully in its box, making sure the ostrich plume wasn't bent or crushed, and slid it beneath the bed. She'd paid for the hat box but not the hat. That had been damned tricky to pinch and had involved house-breaking, of which she wasn't fond, and she didn't fancy stealing another one. She took off her cloak with its detachable, sable-trimmed winter hood, sponged a few patches of mud off the hem, and laid it out on a wide length of muslin. This she rolled into a large sausage and draped over the vacant chair. She must get a good leather suitcase one of these days for storing her nice things — rookery rats ate anything. Beneath the cloak she wore a skirt and bodice of slightly lesser quality, bought from the tallyshop.

She glanced at Tom, who was attempting to force the sapphire ring onto his little finger, swearing as it jammed against his knuckle.

She rinsed a fresh cloth in cold water from a jug and stood in front of a small looking glass on the wall. Aware that Tom was watching her now, she wiped away the powder on her face until the scar on her cheek was revealed. She knew he was smirking — she could feel it — and her stomach clenched in a spasm of loathing for him so intense she felt momentarily sick. He had laid into her one night in a fit of rage, after discovering she'd kept something back after a day's work. It had been a tiny opaline perfume bottle, a pretty little piece she'd fallen in love with, but despite its value Tom had broken it just to spite her; he had hit her so hard the ring he wore on his right hand had split her cheek. His mark would be on her forever and she knew he took a quiet, proprietal pleasure from that. More than once since then she'd imagined killing him, just so she wouldn't have to look at his mean, smarmy, handsome face again. Instead she focused on doing extra jobs on the quiet and keeping the profits for herself.

She stared at her reflection in the glass, at the sallowness of her skin and the shadows beneath her eyes, then sighed and rinsed out the cloth, the rice flour clouding the water. If Tom hadn't hit her she wouldn't have to trowel the stuff all over her face every time they pulled one of their 'toff' capers, but real ladies, women of breeding and manners, didn't go about with ugly scars on their phizogs, so cover it she did.

Behind her Tom said, 'They should be here by now. I don't think they're coming.'

Sarah ignored him. They would come — they needed the money as desperately as she did. She had to get out of this business, she really did. She'd already done six months in Newgate and knew very well if she was to be picked up a second time no judge would be so lenient. She was seriously considering going back up north. Not back home, not back to Leeds and her father, especially not now that her mother had gone. But perhaps to Birmingham, where she was sure she would find work. And far enough away so that this time Tom wouldn't find her. She'd slipped away before but had only gone to Spitalfields, which, looking back now, hadn't been very far at all; and he'd come after her and convinced her to return to work for him with promises of more money. She'd been so stupid. There hadn't been any more money, of course, and he'd beaten her again and kicked her so hard he'd broken one of her ribs. But that was before she'd done time in Newgate. She'd learned a lot in Newgate.

She had a trade, a good one, though she hadn't been able to find employment in London since she'd lost her first job. But the fact she'd completed a skilled apprenticeship might encourage someone to take her on at something, even if it wasn't what she'd trained for. She would have to lie about her time in gaol, though. Most importantly, she had to save enough money to actually get away from London and Tom, which she almost had. She thought about the jar of coins and notes hidden in a cavity in the wall near the door, careful not to let herself even glance in that direction for fear that Tom might read her mind. He could smell money, she was sure of it. There was a lot there already, but she wanted more than just enough to get by on until she found work — she wanted enough to make her feel *safe*.

She crossed the room and emptied the bowl of dirty water out of the window.

'Here they come,' she said, spotting three ragged figures traipsing along St Andrew's Street.

Tom gave an uninterpretable grunt. A few minutes later Sarah let them in.

'You took your time,' Tom said.

'Unlike yerselves,' the older of the two men remarked pointedly as he unwound the tattered scarf from around his neck. 'Some of us didn't have the brass to get no fancy cab.'

Tom took his booted feet off Sarah's bed. The swag had disappeared from it before she opened the door. He dug into his jacket pocket, retrieved some of the stolen money, and tossed six one-shilling coins onto the blanket.

Sarah hated this part. It was so demeaning. They all worked for Tom — no one had any illusions about there being any sort of partnership — but why he couldn't hand his colleagues their pay like the toff he pretended to be, she was never sure. Humiliating the decoys — and her — gave him a sense of power, she supposed. He relished being the flash man because he thought it set him apart from the rest of them, though it didn't. His hands were just as dirty.

The girl in the shawl, whose name was Maisie and who Sarah knew to be a hopeless opium inebriate, collected her two shillings in silence, tucked them inside her bodice and left quickly.

The men pounced on theirs, complaining as always about the paltry sum, and eventually departed with bad grace. Sarah had picked the pockets and stolen the rings of the woman with the shopping basket while Maisie and the men diverted attention. It was a caper they used occasionally and often with great success. All you needed was an unaccompanied, well-heeled woman who believed she was in danger of being robbed, an accomplice or three to manufacture that threat, and then you robbed her yourself. No one was hurt, Sarah and Tom took most of the risk, and all the victim lost were a few valuables and her pride. Sarah had become so skilled now at picking pockets and relieving marks of purses, rings, bracelets and even necklaces she could lift almost anything off anyone, and it made no difference to her whether she stole from someone in a store, the markets or walking down a crowded street.

Tom had also coerced her into breaking into houses and shops now and then and, on rare occasions, she shoplifted as well, though like all professional pickpockets and cracksmen, she looked down on shoplifters: there wasn't enough skill involved to consider it a craft. She, Tom and their crew stole mainly money, silver and jewellery, swag that could be easily spent, fenced or broken down and remodelled. Tom took most of the proceeds, of course, but he paid her more than he paid anyone else, which was something, she supposed. But so he should: he'd be lucky to find anyone else with her unique combination of talents.

He paid her enough to live moderately comfortably without starving or having to go on the town. But she wasn't living comfortably: she was living in Seven Dials squirrelling away her money because she'd finally decided he didn't pay her anywhere near enough to put up with him, or to risk rotting in gaol for the rest of her life.

Tom Ratcliffe left Sarah's mouldy, rat-infested lodgings, stopped to buy a baked potato and a mug of hot elder wine from a street-seller, then walked along the busy thoroughfares towards his own lodgings at the Drury Lane end of Short's Garden. 'Garden' —

that's a joke, he thought as he stepped around piles of animal dung and refuse. Nothing green's grown here for decades. Christ, now he had some sort of shit splattered on the hems of his good fawn trousers.

He trudged up the stairs to the pair of rooms he and his family lived in and pushed open the door. His wife, Caroline, looked up from the mean little hearth where she sat stirring a pot of something that smelt like it might be his supper.

He set his hat on the table and slumped onto a chair, looking around at the shabby furnishings, the lumpy mattress on which his three children slept, the mess they'd made of their things left lying all over the place — all the dross collected by a family who couldn't afford cabinets or bureaux or robes to put it in. You'd think he'd be a relatively wealthy man by now, all the loot his crew had stolen over the years, but times were hard, his gambling debts were huge, and the dollyshops weren't paying as much now as they once might have. Too risky, the fences said, take it or leave it. Nothing had been the same since Ikey Solomon had disappeared from the scene.

And he'd heard just a few weeks ago that his man, who had been so good at turning one fat old dowager's ear pendants into a necklace that some other rich heifer just *had* to have, had been nabbed and was now in Newgate and looking at fourteen years minimum. He'd thought briefly about getting Sarah to rework the pieces they stole — he knew she could do it — but he had a nagging, uneasy feeling about her, and it wasn't going away. She'd changed since her six months in Newgate. She was … less biddable. And sometimes when she looked at him he couldn't fathom what she was thinking, whereas in the past he always could. It really bothered him. Bloody women.

He reached down and retrieved a crust his pet ferret had chucked out of its cage, his stomach lurching queasily as he spotted what looked like a dirty nappy on the floor beneath the table. 'Jesus, woman, can you not clean up after those bloody chavies? There's a shitty clout on the floor here.' Caroline was such a slattern sometimes.

His wife, her face shiny and red from the fire, turned to look at him. 'You clean up after them, Tom Ratcliffe! I'm cooking your supper.'

Tom glared at her; she glared back. They had ceased being interested in each other long before the birth of their third child and, since then, the indifference had turned into outright animosity. But she wouldn't leave him, Tom knew; she was too stupid or too lazy — he couldn't decide — so he'd have to be the one to eventually go. Which suited him.

'Where are they?' he said.

She waved a wooden spoon vaguely towards the door. 'Outside somewhere.'

He frowned; Phoebe was only eighteen months old. But he supposed the others would be looking out for her.

Caroline turned back to the pot, then said over her shoulder, 'The watch were here.'

Tom felt his heart quicken nauseatingly. 'What?'

Caroline faced him again, swivelling her bony arse on the stool. Tom noted she didn't sound half as perturbed as she should. 'The watch. Two of them. Looking for you.'

Tom half rose, panic bubbling in his chest. 'When?'

'Not long before you got in.'

'Did you tell them I was away?'

'Told them you weren't in.'

'What else?'

'What else what?'

Tom exploded. 'Don't be so *bloody* stupid! What else did you tell them?!'

Caroline looked at him for a long time, then a tiny, vengeful smile appeared at the corners of her mouth. 'I told them you'd be back soon.'

Tom grabbed his hat — he'd deal with her later — but he was too late: a heavy fist banged on the door. He glanced at Caroline, who shrugged. So, not stupid then. Just a bitch.

He briefly considered the window but dismissed the possibility — they were three storeys up. He paused, thinking. Perhaps he could do a deal; he had other names after all. His mind racing, he opened the door.

Friday and Harrie watched the new girl unenthusiastically slosh soup around her basin with her spoon. They were eating, as they always did, sitting on their mats in the ward. The other women were all too busy slurping and complaining about their food to pay any attention to them. The girl had a slim, wiry build, hair the colour of jet, and wary dark eyes. Her skin was very slightly olive but had an unhealthy pallor and her right cheek was marked by a curved silver scar.

She looked up and scowled at them. 'What are you staring at?'

'That scar on your phiz,' Friday responded brightly. 'Just wondering how you got it.'

'How do you think?' The girl stabbed a lump of potato and inspected it closely.

'Dunno.'

'Fighting someone who asked me nosy bloody questions.'

Friday laughed. 'What's your name?'

The girl gave an irritated sigh. 'If I tell you will you go away?'

'No.'

After a moment's consideration, the girl said, 'Sarah Morgan.'

'What are you in for?'

Sarah propped her spoon with deliberate care against the rim of her basin and gave her full attention to the two girls regarding her. She'd been watching *them* for several days now. The redhead, whose odd name she already knew was Friday Woolfe, was a whore, and mouthy and quick-witted, and seemed to wield a fair bit of power because of it. She wasn't at the top of the heap in here — those who were, Sarah knew from her own associations, were already well-established flash mob — but the Woolfe girl was giving them a run for their money.

The smaller one looked like she wouldn't say shoo to a goose. She had a pretty figure, nut-brown hair, hazel eyes and a sweet, open, freckled face with hardly any pockmarks.

'What are *you* in for?' Sarah asked her. 'And what do they call you?'

'Me?' The girl flicked a questioning look at Friday Woolfe. Friday nodded and the girl said, 'I'm Harrie Clarke, arrested for stealing a bolt of silk and some embroidery thread.'

'Shoplifting.' Sarah snorted derisively. 'Up the skirt?'

Harrie nodded.

'And you?' Friday persisted.

'Breaking the law,' Sarah said. 'Been tried yet?'

Friday shook her head. 'Indicted, waiting for the Grand Jury, both of us.'

To Friday, Sarah said, 'First or second offence?' Hoisting a bolt of cloth was so obviously Harrie Clarke's first offence she wasn't going to bother to ask.

'Third for me,' Friday replied. 'You?'

Sarah wondered how much about herself she wanted to reveal to this nosy, garrulous girl. What purpose would it serve, really?

'She's done a stretch before,' wardswoman Maryanne Marston said, eavesdropping. 'I remember her sour bloody mug.'

Sarah gave her a filthy look. Maryanne Marston was a long-time inmate and controlled everything that happened in the ward, which gave her the power to demand and receive a regular payment from every prisoner. The system was almost as old as Newgate itself and known as 'garnish', and those who couldn't pay it were deprived of food, drink, eating utensils, a place on the barracks bed and even physical safety. Payment could come from legal or illegal sources, but inmates who had recourse to neither found their time in Newgate even more insufferable than expected. Maryanne Marston was universally hated but, not unexpectedly, had her share of toadies. During her first prison sojourn, Sarah most certainly had not been one of them.

Forced now to admit it, Sarah said to Friday, 'I did six months here about a year ago.' She turned to the wardswoman and snapped, 'And you can keep your bloody nose out of my business, you old tarleather.'

Maryanne's eyes narrowed. 'Watch your tongue, you, or you'll find yourself with no food, no drink, no nothing.'

'You watch yours,' Sarah shot back, 'or I'll cut it out one dark night.'

There was a mutter of consternation now among the other women in the ward, as everyone suffered when Maryanne was in a bad humour, but she merely glared at Sarah, then returned to trawling through her own watery soup.

Sarah had no fear of repercussions from Maryanne Marston. She'd already discovered that the woman was due for release very soon: she wouldn't do anything to jeopardise her chances of walking out of Newgate. Unlike Sarah, who wouldn't be walking anywhere. When her time came to go up before the judge, she'd be sentenced to transportation. The same fate would no doubt befall Friday Woolfe.

'Has there been talk yet of a transport?'

Friday shrugged. 'You hear the rumours. We've heard April, we've heard May, but who knows?'

'There are a hundred women here already sentenced to New South Wales,' Harrie added, 'so surely a ship must go soon?'

'Don't bet on it,' Sarah said, who knew of prisoners who'd languished in Newgate for over a year waiting to be transported.

Friday gave her soup a last disgusted swirl and set her basin on the ground. 'Anyone you know in here?'

Sarah put her own basin aside, leaving most of its contents untouched. An oily film floated on the top, with bits of stringy mutton rising through it. Her stomach clenched and saliva filled her mouth. She pushed the basin away with her foot. 'A few faces,' she said. 'No one I'd call a friend.'

'You can be our friend,' Harrie offered.

Sarah looked away. She wasn't very good at making friends and never had been. 'I'll think about it,' she said tersely, then regretted it the moment she saw the expression on the other girl's face.

Friday also caught her mate's hurt look. 'Don't bother,' she snapped, taking Harrie's wrist and hauling her up and away. 'We're fine as we are.'

Freezing sleet fell for the rest of the day, keeping everyone huddled inside the stinking, damp cell. Sarah kept to herself, as much as anyone could in a ward built for ten inmates and crammed with almost thirty. That night she took a place on the barracks bed as far away from Harrie Clarke and Friday Woolfe as she could manage.

She couldn't sleep, with the cold and people snoring and farting and whispering and having nightmares and crying out and breathing rank breath everywhere. Her rope mat was no better than a sugar sack and she was sure she could feel the very grain of the bed's hard planks pressing into her hip and shoulder. Last time she'd been in Newgate there had been talk from Mrs Fry and her Ladies' Newgate Committee about getting straw-stuffed mattresses for the women's prison, but that clearly hadn't happened.

What a barmy pair those girls were, asking her if she wanted to be their friend, as if they were all five years old and playing some silly little game in the lane! Mind you, Harrie Clarke might be a bit cracked, but that Friday Woolfe was a lot sharper. She'd have to watch out for her.

She tried to turn over and found she couldn't, everyone was that tightly packed together; someone must have moved off the floor and crept onto the barracks bed. She eased herself half onto her back, covering her face with her arm so she wouldn't have to breathe in the smell of the woman next to her.

When she was in Newgate last time she'd waited three months for her trial then served a six-month sentence, which lucky for her had included her period of remand. It had still felt like eternity. She'd been told then she was lucky to have waited only that long to go to trial — some people marked time in the wards for up to a year before they saw the judge. But the word this time was that they were pushing people through the courts as fast as possible to clear a backlog, so with a bit of luck she wouldn't moulder in here too long before her day came.

She wondered why Harrie Clarke had made such an open offer of friendship, especially as it appeared she was already friendly with Friday Woolfe. It had been ... unexpected.

She'd not made any friends in here last time either. It was the same as on the outside — you didn't have friends if you worked with a crew, you had *acquaintances*, and you didn't trust anyone. Her neighbour Rosina had been obliging, though, very happy to accept payment generous enough that she could retrieve the body of her dead child in exchange for smuggling in Sarah's precious cache of running-away money. Sarah was loathe to dip into it but she had to now, for garnish and for the other things that would make life in gaol bearable. It was hidden somewhere no one would ever think to look.

Sarah was the first to admit she didn't look the sort of person to make a likely friend. She had a sour face marred by an ugly scar, she didn't smile enough and she was often in a bad mood. She hadn't always been this way, but since she'd lost the job she loved and gradually descended into a life in the underworld, her good humour had also slipped away. Those early months when she'd lived like a muck snipe sleeping on the streets and eating discarded scraps from the markets had been very, very hard. She'd not sold herself, but she'd come very close.

Then came the day she'd tried to pick Thomas Ratcliffe's pocket on Regent Street and he'd caught her, but instead of dragging her off to the nearest watchman as she'd feared, he'd made her an offer and so had begun her second apprenticeship. For the next two months she'd practised picking the pockets of an empty coat with small bells attached to it until the bells stayed silent. She then progressed to picking Tom's pockets and relieving him of his watch and rings until he judged her proficient enough to go onto the streets. When it became clear she had a talent for stealing, he taught her the craft of the cracksman, or house-breaking, and presented her with her own set of skeleton keys. Because she was small — barely five feet tall and slender — she could break into houses and hide there, if necessary, until it suited her to let herself out again.

The people she met during this apprenticeship had almost all been flash mob and she hadn't liked them, and it had taken her some time to admit to herself that she was flash now, too, whether she cared for it or not. She had come a long way since she'd last been legally employed, but very much in the wrong direction. She was very good at what she did now and it kept her from starving and off the streets, but it didn't make her happy and it had soured the way she looked at the world. Friends would be nice, but friends weren't for the sort of person she had become.

She felt a sharp, stinging sensation on her breast and dug into her bodice, her fingers closing over something tiny and hard. Carefully, she withdrew her hand and dropped the offending flea onto the sleeping body of her neighbour.

Harrie Clarke shouldn't be in Newgate Gaol, that was obvious. Her first effort at pinching something and she'd been nabbed! That only happened to either really incompetent sneak thieves, or the completely naive. Harrie Clarke was clearly the latter. She really was quite likable — very chatty and friendly. No artifice, which was very refreshing. But no nous and not a hint of slyness or duplicity, either, so she would never manage in here on her own. Perhaps that was the reason Friday Woolfe had befriended her. If so, Friday must be the proverbial whore with a heart of gold. Sarah smiled in the darkness. She'd never met one herself and very much doubted they existed. So was there something specific Friday wanted from Harrie?

Friday could be a useful ally. She was smart, physically and mentally strong, and savvy in a way that could work in their favour should the three of them find themselves together on their way to New South Wales. And to be honest, Sarah had to admit, she admired the girl, with her big mouth and rowdy laugh and irreverent attitude.

She yawned, and realised with a little jolt of shock that she was actually considering accepting Harrie Clarke and Friday Woolfe's offer of friendship.

Except she had rather ruined that opportunity.

Harrie had been chosen by Maryanne Marston to assist with fetching the morning's bread and gruel. While she was gone from the ward, Friday sat down on the edge of the barracks bed next to Sarah.

'I want a word with you.'

Sarah regarded her warily, then nodded.

'You didn't have to be such a bitch to Harrie yesterday. She was only trying to be kind.'

Sarah said nothing.

Friday leant menacingly towards her. 'I think you should say sorry, don't you?'

Sarah scowled, but Friday got the feeling she wasn't as discomposed as a person told they had to apologise should be.

Looking her squarely in the eye, Sarah said, 'You don't frighten me, Friday Woolfe.'

'I expect I don't. I expect you're as hard as ruddy nails. But Harrie isn't, so I want you to tell her you're sorry.'

'All right,' Sarah agreed. 'I will.'

Friday blinked. 'When?'

'After what passes for breakfast in here.'

They sat in silence for a minute as the women in the ward talked and called out and milled around them. Sarah's heel tapped rapidly on the filthy flagstone floor, as though her leg had too much energy and couldn't help itself. She didn't seem to notice.

She said, 'I like your jacket. Velvet, isn't it?'

Disarmed, Friday nodded. 'Cost me a fair penny, too.'

Was the dark girl toadying? That didn't seem likely, from the little Friday already knew of Sarah Morgan. Or was she trying to make amends for her rude behaviour, without actually saying sorry? That felt closer to the mark.

'You're a toffer?'

'Streetwalker,' Friday corrected. 'Can't be bothered with the swells. I do all right.'

'Flash man?'

Friday made a derisive face and shook her head. 'You?'

'Yes, and may he rot in hell.'

Friday said nothing, sensing there was more to come.

'We worked together. Posed as nobs and ran capers.'

'He was your man?'

Sarah's top lip curled, revealing good, sharp teeth. 'He was *a* man. Not mine. Took most of what we made. There were six or seven of us.'

'Unlucky, just you being nabbed.'

'No, it was Tom who was caught. He sold the rest of us up the river. Some of the others got away. I didn't.'

Friday fiddled with her woollen scarf, rewinding it around her neck so the ends were the same length; she knew if she waited long enough Sarah would finally tell her what line of work she was in.

Eventually she did. 'I'm a dip and a crackswoman. Well, screwswoman, really: I specialise in keys.'

Friday's copper-coloured eyebrows shot up. She was impressed: a pickpocket, yes, but you didn't hear of many women skilled in the arts of house-breaking and lock-picking. 'And you've always done that?'

Sarah's heel ceased tapping; her face had softened and her eyes glimmered with something that might be regret.

'No, only for the last few years. I'm a qualified jeweller. I did an apprenticeship in Hatton Garden, with a Jew. He had a son, ten years older than me, who'd bought himself a commission in the army. Just after I'd finished my apprenticeship, the son sold his commission and came home to work in the shop.' Sarah's heel started tapping again. 'He wouldn't leave me alone. I complained to his father, who disbelieved me and told me to leave. Bloody smouses, always stick together.'

Surprised, Friday said, 'I thought *you* were a Jew.'

'With a name like Morgan?'

'You've got that skin; it's not very English. And Morgan could be short for Morgenstern or something.'

'For God's sake, my grandparents came from Wales.'

Friday shrugged; she didn't particularly care what Sarah's ancestry was. 'So did you leave?'

'I was dismissed in the end. But I couldn't find another position as a jeweller. Or anything that paid a decent wage.' Sarah's face turned hard again. 'So instead of making beautiful things, I stole them. And here I am.'

Friday was silent for a moment. It was a hard-luck story, but everyone had one of those. 'What about your family?'

'What about them?'

'Could you not have gone to them after you lost your job?'

'What for? They don't have any money. My mother's dead and I'm not bothered if I never see my father again. Why didn't you go to *your* family instead of walking the streets?'

'If you must know, my ma's dead too and I don't know who my father was. Neither did Ma.'

'Anyway, it's none of your business,' they both said at exactly the same time, which made them smile.

Friday noticed that when Sarah smiled properly, and meant it, the corners of her mouth turned up quite charmingly. She said bluntly, 'It wasn't my idea to offer you the hand of friendship, but if you want it, that's all right by me, as long as you don't do anything to hurt Harrie. You have to promise that.'

Sarah looked at her unwaveringly. 'I'll only promise if you tell me why you're so fond of her.'

'Well, for Christ's sake, look at her! She shouldn't be in here!'

Sarah silently agreed, and waited. She knew a bit about listening herself.

Friday inspected the toes of her boots, then retied one of the laces. 'And she reminds me of someone I used to know. Someone I cared about.'

Sarah knew what it was to have secrets; she let it go. 'All right, I promise.'

'If you do hurt her,' Friday warned, 'I'll give you a right dewskitch. I'm not joking, I'll beat the shit out of you. And I don't trust you yet, all right?'

The expression on Sarah's face told her the feeling was mutual.

Three

By the following morning the rain had stopped, leaving the courtyard's cobbles dotted with miniature lakes frozen at the edges, icy doilies around water turned a scummy brown. Harrie trod on as much ice as she could on the way to the pump, something she had done with much glee as a child. She felt her bowels cramp but ignored the discomfort, having learned to hold on for as long as possible in an effort to limit her visits to the dank, reeking, vermin-infested water closets. The gruel made it difficult, though. And the farting!

She worked the pump handle, rinsed her basin and spoon, then splashed freezing water over her face. Finally, she rubbed a finger over her teeth and gums, worrying at a back tooth that felt a little loose, hoping it wasn't going to give her trouble.

She backed away from the pump and stamped squarely on someone's foot.

'Beg pardon,' Harrie said.

'Just me.' Sarah Morgan pulled her shawl tightly around her shoulders over her jacket; in the pale sun and crisp air her face looked washed out, her scar more obvious. 'I've something to say. About yesterday.'

Harrie glanced around the courtyard, saw Friday leaning against the far wall, smoking her pipe and watching a handful of sparrows fight over something on the ground.

'I was feeling out of sorts,' Sarah declared. She paused, then sighed with ill-disguised irritation. 'I'm sorry if I sounded rude. It wasn't my intention.' Another pause. 'Well, it was, but you shouldn't take it personally.'

Harrie could see the apology was costing Sarah a great deal. This was Friday's doing, she was sure. But Harrie had never been one to hold a grudge and didn't particularly need an apology.

'I just thought you might want someone to talk to. A friend or two.'

Sarah inclined her head in Friday's direction. 'She looks out for you, doesn't she?'

Harrie nodded. 'I don't know what I'd do without her.'

'And what does she ask for in return?'

'Nothing. Luckily, as I don't have anything to give her.' Harrie frowned, then her heart thudded with shock as she realised what Sarah was implying. 'Oh! What a thing to say!'

'I'm *not* saying it; I'm just wondering. Well, you know, in a place like this. I think I *would* like to be friends, if the offer's still open, but not if you and Friday are ... together. That wouldn't suit me.'

Harrie's cheeks flamed. 'Well, it bloody well wouldn't suit me either!'

Sarah burst out laughing. 'You should see your face.'

'I'm not inclined that way at all!' Harrie went on, her voice sharp with indignation, 'And neither is Friday. She's just very generous and kind, which you'd know if you got yourself a really tall ladder and climbed down off your high horse.'

Sarah laughed even more heartily. 'You look like an angry squirrel.'

'And you look like a cackling old crone,' Harrie shot back. She picked up her basin and marched off.

Sarah grabbed her sleeve. 'No, wait.' She wasn't laughing now. 'I meant what I said before, about being friends.'

Harrie stopped.

Sarah said, 'But I have to warn you, I'm not a very easy person to like.'

Harrie regarded her for almost a minute. 'Friday made you come and apologise to me, didn't she?'

Sarah nodded.

'Would you have done it anyway?'

'Probably,' Sarah said after a short pause. 'Eventually.'

'Why?'

'Because of the look on your face when I said I'd think about it. You looked like I'd slapped you. I felt … well, I felt mean.'

Harrie smiled. 'Then I'm happy to let bygones be bygones.' She extended her hand. 'Friends, then?'

Sarah shook. 'Friends.'

They glanced across the courtyard at Friday. The sparrows had gone and she was in shadow now, but her nod of satisfaction was as plain as day.

January 1829, Newgate Gaol

Sarah had wished them both luck. Harrie knew the wish had come from a place inside Sarah that no one saw very often, so it was quite precious.

She wasn't the same girl these days. Oh, she was just as sly and sharp and prickly with the others in the ward, and certainly with anyone who crossed her, God help them, but Harrie knew she and Friday were privileged to know another side of her.

For a start she was unexpectedly generous. She had money — her 'running away money' she called it — and wasn't averse to sharing it, though she had it secreted away somewhere. Which was very sensible, Harrie thought, given their current situation. To date she hadn't told Harrie or Friday where and neither had asked, but at regular intervals cash would appear to supplement Friday's reserves, which Friday always carried on her person for safe-keeping and used to pay the garnish for both herself and Harrie and to buy luxuries like soap, tobacco, gin and extra food. Harrie, to her never-ending shame, had no money at all, but one day Sarah presented her with a small package of needles and assorted thread and after that she assumed responsibility for mending and patching their clothes, which were rapidly turning to rags in the harsh, damp gaol conditions. It wasn't much, but it helped her feel as though she were making a contribution.

They were all three firm friends now, though sometimes Friday and Sarah bickered and argued and when she was in one of her moods Sarah was prone to silence for hours on end. Friday couldn't keep quiet if her life depended on it. Then it was up to Harrie to smooth things over as best she could. And it wasn't just because she relied on Friday and Sarah for the things she needed in Newgate, it was simply because she hated to see the people she cared about upset.

Now, on the day she and Friday were to face the judge, stumbling through the dank passageway that linked Newgate Gaol with the Old Bailey courts, she felt sick to her stomach and watery-kneed with fear. Beneath the flagstones in the passage lay the bodies of murderers executed outside Newgate and she was sure she could smell the stench from their rotting remains wafting upwards, taunting her, even though she knew she wouldn't be facing the gallows. The Grand Jury had declared 'true bills' for both herself and Friday, meaning that sufficient evidence had been presented by the prosecution to justify sending the bills of indictment against them to court and putting them on trial. Today they and four other Newgate women would learn their fate.

Harrie was second in line. She and the others were ordered to sit on wooden stools in a small antechamber and wait to be escorted into the courtroom proper when their turn came. Normally they would wait in the underground cells beneath the courtroom, but as a large number of men were also being tried today, the cells apparently were full. Harrie could not afford the prohibitive cost of private counsel and was to defend herself, though she had been offered the services of a state-subsidised dock brief yesterday afternoon. Sarah had offered to pay the fee, but everyone in Harrie's ward, including Sarah, told her not to bother, as it was common knowledge that dock briefs were notoriously young and inexperienced and therefore as good as useless. Gilbert Wilton, the linen-draper from whom Harrie had stolen, however, probably was in a position to engage experienced counsel to act on his behalf. She wondered if he had.

Friday was called first. At the sight of her the clamour from the crowd in the jammed public gallery started almost immediately; her voice rang out clearly above the din. She was deliberately encouraging them, Harrie was pretty sure. Fascinated, her own fears temporarily stifled, she shuffled her stool along so she could see better through the doorway, earning a scowl from one of the turnkeys.

Her name, Friday was informing the courtroom, was Friday Woolfe, she was eighteen years old and, yes, her occupation was in fact correctly recorded as being 'on the town', a declaration evidently meeting with approval from the public, who clapped and whistled. The judge, the Right Honourable William Thompson, Lord Mayor of the City of London, barked for quiet.

A clerk stood up and read out the indictment against Friday, while she leant in the dock with her arms crossed, gazing at the domed ceiling in a deliberate display of contempt. The clerk sat down again and several foot-shuffling, throat-clearing minutes passed before a bewigged man in a black gown rose and began asking her questions about where she was on a certain night and so forth, then called on a rather insignificant-looking gentleman named Hector Slee to give evidence. Mr Slee, Harrie noted, was managing to look both embarrassed and indignant at the same time, so she guessed it was he who had been cuckolded and robbed. The way Friday had recounted the story had made the victim sound like a vainglorious little seek-sorrow. Harrie had assumed this was to make the yarn more amusing, but she could see now Friday hadn't been embellishing.

Friday gave Mr Slee a withering look and announced that given the amount of 'amorous encouragement' likely to be required, she would have charged a lot more than a quid to lift her skirts to him, therefore it couldn't have been her who stole his watch and walking stick.

The gallery roared and Mr Justice Thompson was forced to call the room to order again, this time warning the accused to watch her tongue.

The turnkey poked Harrie on the arm and told her to move away from the doorway, obscuring her view of the proceedings. She could hear quite clearly, though, when the judge pronounced sentence a short while later because the public gallery had fallen into an anticipatory silence — fourteen years' transportation to New South Wales.

When Friday was brought back through the antechamber, Harrie saw that beneath the smattering of freckles across her nose and cheeks her skin was parchment white. Her mouth, however, was set in a little smirk of triumph: Harrie knew she'd half expected a life sentence. Fourteen years was nothing compared with that. She sent Harrie a quick wink.

Then it was Harrie's turn. The turnkey prodded her off her stool and led her up the steps into the dock, and by the time the little wooden gate had clicked shut, closing her in, all Harrie's stomach-clenching fear had flooded back. She desperately needed to sit down but there was no chair, so she leant her elbows on the rail, feeling dizzy and sick.

'Stand up straight, prisoner!' the turnkey ordered in a terse whisper.

Harrie straightened, but kept one hand on the rail to steady herself. Below the dock sat counsel for the prosecution at an expansive green baize table, beyond them the Clerk of the Court and, above him, directly opposite her, Mr Justice Thompson in his scarlet robes and long white wig. The Lord Mayor of London, Harrie thought as her face flamed and her very innards shrivelled with shame. The Lord Mayor of London himself is to pass judgment on my sins!

On her right sat the jury in two tiered rows. At one end stood the witness box and above both ran the packed public gallery. Her stomach rumbled at the smells of vinegar, fried fish, spice cakes and hot nuts wafting down from the crowd. She was amazed she could feel hungry at a time like this. On the opposite side of the courtroom, on her left, sat the reporters, several members of the watch and various other official spectators.

The clerk read out the indictment, then returned to his seat. Harrie knew this wouldn't take long — she had already indicated she would plead guilty, so it was simply a matter of what her sentence would be. She glanced up at the gallery, but fear had blurred her vision and she couldn't pick out her mother's face in the crowd. She hoped she hadn't come after all.

Counsel for the prosecution called Mr Wilton and all eyes were upon him as he mounted the creaky steps to the witness box.

'Mr Wilton,' the barrister began, his voice booming out across the courtroom, 'can you tell the court in your own words what happened on the afternoon of the event in question?'

'I most certainly can,' Mr Wilton said pompously, leaning back, his hands gripping the lapels of his best black coat. 'I was in my drapery, working hard as an honest man does, when I asked my shop assistant to step into the back room with me.'

There was a titter from the gallery at this, which earned a stern look from the judge.

'There were three or four customers patronising my establishment at the time,' Mr Wilton went on, 'including that girl there.' He thrust an accusing finger in Harrie's direction. 'I had my suspicions from the outset, I did. She was fingering the Chinese dupioni like she couldn't wait to get her hands on it. We were only gone a minute or two and when I returned I immediately noticed that the bolt of silk was missing. And so was *she*!' Mr Wilton pointed again. 'So I ran out to the street and there she was haring off like the devil himself was after her. I shouted and gave chase and was able to wrestle her to the ground and retrieve my stolen property. She had one of my compendiums, too, down her skirt. Good silk thread, six spools of it!'

The barrister consulted his notes. 'It says here in the arresting constable's report that the prisoner said she dropped the bolt of silk, then fell over it.'

Mr Wilton made a horse noise with his lips. 'That's her story!'

'Thank you, Mr Wilton. You may be seated.'

Mr Justice Thompson enquired of the counsel, 'Do you have any more witnesses, Mr Crawley?'

'One more, my lord. I call Mrs Maude Lynch to the witness box.'

Harrie felt fresh apprehension prickle at her already clammy skin as her ex-employer made her way from the witnesses' waiting area and entered the box.

'Mrs Lynch, you are Harriet Clarke's employer, are you not?' Mr Crawley asked.

'I *was*,' Mrs Lynch replied haughtily. Her mouth took on the appearance of a drawstring purse pulled very tightly indeed. 'She's no employee of mine now.'

'And what can you tell the court about her character, Mrs Lynch?'

From the public gallery, someone cried out in a high, reedy voice, 'Thief-taker!'

This was a gross insult, as individuals known as thief-takers used their knowledge of the underworld to inform on those who had committed a crime to collect the rewards the state offered for their prosecution. As many of the unemployed and the labouring poor in London knew someone accused of criminal activity, or perhaps had even been in that situation themselves, thief-takers were deeply unpopular. They also weren't above blackmailing individuals wanted for crimes, in exchange for not informing on them.

To Harrie's ears it sounded like a child's voice. Very much like her half-brother Robbie's, actually. She suppressed a smile, then worried that Robbie, at only seven years of age, might have come to the Old Bailey alone. She squinted at the public gallery a second time, but again saw no one she recognised.

Mrs Lynch ignored the accusation and rearranged her bonnet ribbons so they lay flat over her shawl. 'I can tell the court that she was a sour-faced little thing at times — and slow to do as she was asked if she wasn't feeling disposed. An adequate sempstress, yes, but I never quite trusted her with money. Or my bits and bobs. I was often missing lace pins and what have you. And they're not cheap to buy, you know.'

Harrie gasped. Mrs Lynch had been enough to try anyone at the best of times and, yes, she had dragged her feet occasionally, but she had never stolen from her, never! And she'd always been trustworthy with money: Mrs Lynch had frequently sent her to the draper's and the haberdasher's and she'd *always* brought back the right change!

'Thank you, Mrs Lynch, I believe we've heard enough,' Mr Crawley said. 'You may step down.'

A low rumble of commentary spread through the courtroom as Mrs Lynch scuttled back to her seat.

The judge swept the court with a warning gaze then turned to Harrie. 'Harriet Clarke, do you have anything to say in your own defence?'

About the theft she'd committed she didn't, but Harrie certainly had something to say to Maude Lynch. She'd worked for the old shrew since she was fourteen, and never said a retaliatory word in three whole years, but now, it seemed, she had nothing to lose. She leant out of the dock so she could see Mrs Lynch sitting in the witnesses' waiting area and in a loud, clear voice said, 'Actually, Mrs Lynch, I think I'd have preferred to swing than carry on working for you. You paid slave wages; you're a carping, vindictive old bitch; I wouldn't be seen in a pauper's grave in one of your tatty gowns; and your ugly husband pinched my arse at least twice a day. I hope you rot in hell.'

The gallery burst into wild applause while Mr Justice Thompson went red in the jowls and shouted, 'Order! *Order!*'

When calm was finally restored, he demanded of Harrie whether she pleaded guilty or not guilty.

'Guilty, my lord.'

The jury was therefore not required to deliberate and the judge sentenced immediately.

'Seven years' transportation to New South Wales,' he declared, his mind on the roast beef he would shortly be having for his dinner.

The latest new girl lay on her side, sobbing. She was obviously destitute: she had only the clothes she'd arrived in. She'd eaten nothing for a day and a half, despite the orders of the turnkeys and a short-tempered telling-off from Matron — all she would do was hide her face and weep. It was getting on everyone's nerves. Since Mad Martha had been moved to the hospital the nights had been a little more settled, but now this girl had arrived and was upsetting everything all over again. Becky Hoddle, the new wardswoman, who was even more disagreeable than Maryanne Marston had been, was already muttering about 'sorting her out'. And as right-hand-woman to Liz Parker, ringleader of Newgate's flash mob contingent, she had every resource at her disposal to do so.

Finally Harrie, unable to bear the sound of such anguish any longer, crouched beside the girl. She tried to remove the grubby hands from her face but couldn't budge them.

'Go away,' a snot-thickened voice mumbled, and a slender, wool-stockinged leg struck out, its knee hitting Harrie's arm. Harrie didn't move.

The girl was delicately built and a good couple of inches under five feet. It was hard to tell, the way she was all curled up. Her unbound hair, lank and dirty, was straight and very light blonde, almost white, and her skin fair. Her wrists looked the size of a child's. Perhaps she *was* a child? Her clothes, though filthy and spotted with grease, were of reasonable quality.

'Come on now, that's enough crying,' Harrie murmured. 'Surely you've run out of tears by now?'

'Go to hell,' the voice replied. 'Leave me alone.'

Harrie considered how she'd best dealt with her little brother and sisters when they behaved like this.

'If you don't stop that I'm going to smack your arse so hard you won't sit down for a week.'

The sobbing slowed to a sniffle, then stopped.

'You can't say that to me,' the girl said.

'I can and I just did,' Harrie replied.

The little hands came away from the face. The girl's irises were a startling cornflower blue, at the moment framed by sclera turned dull red from copious crying. Her eyelids and lips were swollen and her nose raw and running, but even so Harrie could see she was extremely pretty.

'You can't cry forever.'

'Yes, I can,' the girl replied, and started again.

Harrie grasped her thin shoulders and sat her upright.

'What's your name?'

'Rachel.' The girl's face screwed up and her mouth wobbled ominously.

'Stop that,' Harrie warned. 'Rachel what?'

'Rachel Winter.'

Harrie settled onto the mat. 'Rachel, you do know where you are, don't you?'

'In gaol.'

'That's right. And in gaol there are plenty of people who will hurt you if you annoy them. So please, try not to cry any more.'

Rachel rubbed her face and pressed the heels of her palms against her hot, swollen eyes.

'Do you have family?' Harrie asked.

A nod.

'Do they know where you are?'

Rachel shook her head.

'Do you come from London?'

'Guildford.'

'And how have you ended up in Newgate?'

Sniffing loudly and wiping her nose on the back of her hand, Rachel said, 'I eloped.'

Eloping wasn't a crime, so something else must have happened between then and now. As tactfully as she could, Harrie asked, 'And where's your husband now?'

'We're not married yet. He had to go back to his regiment, but he's coming back for me.'

Harrie's heart sank. She wasn't the most worldly person, but even she knew that if she had a pound for every girl who'd been told by a soldier he'd be coming back for her, she could have started her own dressmaking business ages ago.

'Did he say when he'd be returning?'

Rachel's bottom lip wobbled again. 'He just said for me to wait.'

'But how did you end up in gaol?'

'Lucas — that's his name, Lieutenant Lucas Carew — paid for me to stay in a lodging house here in London, but he gave all the money in advance to Mrs Begbie, except she kept it and said he hadn't given her anything, and —'

'Just a minute, who's Mrs Begbie?'

'The landlady. Rotten cow. And I couldn't pay the rent so I sold everything I had except these clothes, then she accused me of pawning some of the things in the room, but I didn't, and she called the watch.' Rachel's face crumpled and fresh tears dribbled down her cheeks. 'And if Lucas doesn't get here in time I'll *hang*!'

'No, sweetie, you won't hang. Can you write to your family? Do they have any money? You're going to need some in here.'

Reluctantly, Rachel said, 'They've a little bit of land. My da's a farmer.'

'Well, send them off a letter today, right now. My friend Friday can get you some writing paper and I'm sure we can —'

'No.'

'What?' It occurred then to Harrie that perhaps the girl didn't know how to write, and she silently castigated herself for being so thoughtless. 'Or I could do it for you. Really, it would be —'

'I know my letters,' Rachel snapped. 'And I can read. I'm just not doing it.'

Harrie stared at Rachel in astonishment. 'Why not?'

'I don't care to communicate with them. They don't approve of Lucas.'

Harrie felt her normally calm disposition faltering and she briefly considered shaking Rachel until the pretty blue eyes flew out of her empty head. 'Well, I suggest you have a good look around! You'll freeze and you'll starve in no time!' She pointed at the ring Rachel wore on her wedding finger. 'And that will be gone before you know it. I'm amazed Becky Hoddle didn't have it off you the minute you came through the door.'

'It's a tidy piece of work,' Sarah said, returning from rinsing her basin under the pump. She leant in for a closer look. 'Pearl, enamel and some nice little diamonds. You're lucky you've still got your finger, never mind the ring. I could probably get you a reasonable price for it.'

'*No!*' Rachel snatched her hand away and tucked it into her armpit. 'Lucas gave it to me. And I won't starve or freeze. He'll be here soon.'

Sarah glanced at Harrie. 'Who's Lucas?'

'Her lover.'

'My *fiancé*,' Rachel insisted.

Reining in her irritation, Harrie asked solicitously, 'Rachel, have you actually told him where you are?'

Rachel stared at her knees. 'I can't. I'm not sure where his regiment's stationed.' She raised her face, swollen eyes alight with hope. 'But when he writes to me at the lodging house and I don't write back, he'll know something's wrong and come looking for me. I know he will.'

Harrie and Sarah regarded her in embarrassed silence. Harrie said, 'I'm sure you're right. But until then, why don't you send a message to your family? They must be very worried.'

A shadow of longing and regret flickered across Rachel's face, though she struggled valiantly to contain it. 'I can't. My da will beat the hell out of me.'

'Not from the other side of the visitor bars, he won't,' Sarah observed.

Harrie asked, 'Rachel, how old are you?'

'Fifteen.'

Harrie's eyes narrowed; she looked a lot closer to thirteen. 'Is that the truth?'

'I'm not lying, I swear. I've always been small.'

A possible complication struck Harrie. 'This fiancé of yours, did you and he —'

'Yes. But I'm not with child. I'm not completely stupid, you know.'

'Oh, no, love, I wasn't suggesting that,' Harrie said hurriedly, but she dared not catch Sarah's eye.

* * *

They were sitting in the yard, their backs against the wall and their bums freezing in spite of the blankets folded beneath them. A few feet farther along, Rachel Winter lay in the crumpled heap she'd slumped into when Friday deposited her after carrying her out of the ward for fresh air because she'd refused to walk out herself.

Pitching her voice so it contained just the right balance of conversational fact with a hint of not-too-earnest pleading, Harrie said, 'She doesn't have any clothes or money or anything. Not even something she can sell for garnish.'

'Oh rubbish, she's got that bloody great ring,' Sarah said.

That was the other reason they'd brought her outside; so they could see her and make sure she wasn't robbed. They had attempted themselves to take the ring off her for safekeeping but Rachel had screeched like a banshee and scratched and tried to bite them, so they'd left it on her hand, where it shone like a beacon at almost every inmate on the women's side of Newgate Gaol.

She'd snivelled her way through last night jammed, at Harrie's behest, between Sarah and Friday, neither of whom slept at all, and since daybreak she had been 'accidentally' manhandled by no less than a dozen women in an attempt to separate her from her jewel. She'd fought like a cat and managed to defend herself and her property, but Sarah had remained nearby in case her help had been required. Why, she didn't know, as she said to Friday — the girl was a spoilt little cow and deserved to be robbed.

'But that's her betrothal ring,' Harrie protested. 'Would you sell the last thing you had to remind you of your fiancé?'

Sarah said 'Yes' as Friday nodded.

'You're being silly, Harrie, and so's that precious little dollymop,' Sarah said, pointing at Rachel, now lying flat on the cold, wet ground. 'We're in gaol. If we don't pay garnish, we don't eat, and if we don't eat, we die. Princess Rachel, too.'

Harrie realised then that it was unrealistic, and rather childish, of her to expect either Friday or Sarah to pay for Rachel Winter, especially when she did actually have a means of paying for herself. They were already supporting someone — her. She felt ashamed at having even briefly entertained the idea. She stood up, wiped her hands on her skirt and approached Rachel.

She bent down. 'Rachel, get up.'

Rachel's bonnet had been left behind on their mat, which meant that by now it would have been stolen and sold to someone in another ward. Her dirty hair was spread across the ground, the ends lying in a puddle of muddy slush. Harrie noted, not for the first time, that Rachel had quite a flair for the theatrical. She pulled her into a sitting position, then hoisted her to her feet.

'Come on, love, we'd like to talk to you for a minute.'

'What about?' Rachel grumbled. Her breath was rancid from not having eaten for several days and she desperately needed a bath.

From the corner of her eye, Harrie caught sight of Liz Parker approaching across the courtyard and hurriedly pushed Rachel towards Friday and Sarah. At the last minute Liz veered away, giving Harrie a filthy look.

Harrie breathed a sigh of relief. Liz Parker was a big woman, shorter than Friday but considerably wider, who had managed to retain her bulk despite being incarcerated in Newgate for the past six months. Everyone knew she had most of her food smuggled in; it wasn't uncommon for her to dine on oysters, saveloys and pickled eggs for breakfast, potatoes and fresh or smoked fish from Billingsgate market for dinner, and meat pies from the pennie-pie vendor for supper. She also had a seemingly endless supply of coffee, tea, tobacco, salt, Coleman's mustard and gin, only a fraction of which she appeared to share even with her coterie. Anyone with a friend or associate on the outside could arrange to smuggle in food or gin, but those with less money at their disposal than Liz Parker, which was the majority of inmates, tended to rely on the garnish system for their food and spend the bulk of their money on gin and tobacco.

Parker wore gold hoop earrings no one dared steal from her and a fine silk kerchief at her throat, ran the card schools in the wards and was the most cunning sharp of the lot, and was very free with her fists. Her own nose had been broken several times and now sat kitty-corner to her lumpy face; her four top front teeth were missing; and healed nicks and scars further blemished her already heavily pockmarked complexion. A gang of about thirty inmates had declared allegiance to her and within that thirty was a coven, as Sarah had labelled them, of around a dozen zealously loyal women and girls who acted as her eyes and ears in the wards. She was a very powerful woman, almost as powerful as she had been out on the streets overseeing one of inner London's more successful flash mobs. She scared the living daylights out of Harrie. Every night during compulsory prayers, she thanked God Liz Parker slept in another ward.

'She nearly got you,' Friday teased as Harrie eased herself down on wobbly legs, her back against the wall again.

'Please, Friday, don't even make a joke of it. Honestly, I don't know what I'd do if it was just her and me.'

Friday patted Harrie's knee placatingly. 'Don't worry yourself, love. It's never going to be just her and you. I'll strangle the bitch myself before that happened.'

Vaguely mollified, Harrie turned her attention to Rachel, who was looking more alert now, gazing at the women sitting in small groups in the exercise yard playing cards, standing around stamping their feet, or trudging in a never-ending circle, wearing a track in the dirty slush.

'Back from the dead, are we?' Sarah remarked.

Harrie shook her head. 'Don't be mean, Sarah. Rachel, we have to talk about this ring of yours. It's causing trouble. Friday and Sarah didn't get any sleep at all last night.'

'I don't like it here,' Rachel said.

'No, neither do we,' Harrie agreed. 'But you could make things better for yourself by selling that ring. You could buy food and a basin and spoon and a blanket and we could even get you things from outside.'

'All right,' Rachel said abruptly. She slid the ring off her finger and handed it to Sarah. 'What do you think you can get for it?'

There was a short, stunned silence as Friday, Harrie and Sarah stared at her.

Friday said, 'You were screaming blue murder about giving it up last night! You said it was your last link to your fiancé!'

'I know, but it isn't really.' Rachel pushed a muddy strand of hair off her face. 'He didn't give it to me; I stole it from Mrs Begbie. She was such a trollop, accusing me of pledging her tatty linen.'

'You little cow!' Sarah exclaimed, and slapped Rachel's leg.

'Ow! What was that for?'

'For lying to us!' Sarah replied, then added quickly when Rachel's face crumpled, 'Oh for God's sake, don't start that again.'

Rachel swallowed and took a deep breath. 'I *wanted* it to be from Lucas, but he said there wouldn't be enough money for a ring after he paid for my lodgings. That Begbie woman said it all had to be paid in advance or I couldn't stay there.' Her voice took on a note of defiance. 'It was a nice lodging house and I refused to stay in a hovel.'

Friday slid her skirt up her leg and inspected a boil developing on the inside of her knee. The area was swollen, red and hard and, as soon as pus appeared, she was going to attack it with something sharp. It would hurt like buggery, but the poison would be far better out than in. They were all getting sores: Harrie had one on the corner of her mouth and Sarah cursed every time she sat down.

'Well,' Friday said, pressing the swollen lump and wincing, 'you've ended up in one anyway.'

Sarah, thoughtfully examining the ring, said to Rachel, 'If you stole this off the Begbie woman, why have you still got it?'

Rachel shrugged. 'How should I know? Perhaps she hasn't missed it yet.'

'So you weren't arrested for stealing this?' Harrie said, confused.

'No, I *told* you, she accused me of pawning her sheets.'

'And did you?'

'No, but she told the watch I did, to get rid of me so she could keep the money Lucas had given her and let my room to someone else. Wait 'til he finds out!'

'So when did you steal the ring?' Sarah asked.

'When she was out fetching a constable. I didn't know what she was up to but I had a funny feeling and I thought I might need some insurance.'

Sarah gave Rachel a look that was nearly but not quite one of admiration. 'We'll have to go outside to get the best price for this. Do you want to fence it or sell it to a private buyer?'

'Which is quicker and which will get me the most money?'

Not so silly after all, Harrie thought.

'A fence would be quicker, but you'll get a better price privately.'

'A fence then. It's money for nothing anyway, isn't it?'

Friday and Sarah exchanged sour glances, recalling the sleepless night they'd endured protecting Rachel's precious 'nothing'.

'But how can you get it out?' Rachel asked. 'What about the turnkeys?'

'It'll go out like everything else comes in and goes out,' Friday said. 'With a visitor. Sarah, do you have anyone in mind?'

'I do. I'll have to get a message to her. She'll collect it, fence it, then probably be back with the money the same day. The day after tomorrow, perhaps?'

Rachel clapped her hands, which made her look about ten years old. 'I'm going to buy a comb and some soap. I want to look my best when Lucas comes.'

Harrie's heart felt as though it were being squeezed. What a strange girl — half child, half woman. 'Sweetheart, you don't think you should be writing to your family? They'll be desperate to know where you are.'

Rachel's pretty, mud-smeared face clouded over. 'No! I said no and I meant it.'

'Do you have a favourite pig on your farm?' Friday asked kindly. 'Won't it be missing you?'

Harrie stared at her. What an odd thing to say.

'It's dairy, not pigs,' Rachel replied, scowling. 'Still stinks, though. All that shite! You can just about smell it from Guildford!' She held her nose.

Harrie, suddenly catching on, said, 'Really? You can smell it in Guildford?'

'Well, no, probably not. Only if the wind's coming from the north. I do miss my dog, though. He's called Shannon. It's Irish and it means ancient river, though he's only six years old. I didn't want to leave him but Lucas said I had to.'

'What regiment is this man of yours with?' Friday asked.

'The 31st East Surrey.'

Friday nodded: the Huntingdonshire — they were fairly local and not uncommon on the streets of London when they were at home. 'And you don't know where he is?'

'No. But there isn't a war on, is there? He can't be far away.'

'He'll be as far away as he can get by now,' Sarah whispered to Harrie.

Rachel heard. 'He will not! He had to go back to his regiment! He wouldn't have left me if he didn't have to! Don't be such a harpy. I don't think I want to talk to you any more.'

'Good,' Sarah said, getting up. 'Because I don't want to listen.'

Four

Sarah's neighbour Rosina fenced Rachel's ring for enough money for Rachel to pay the garnish Becky Hoddle demanded, buy the basic things she needed and, to their collective surprise, give Friday, Harrie and Sarah a half-sovereign each for helping her. She also purchased a pack of cards, telling the girls she intended to make regular contributions to the kitty with winnings from the card school held in the exercise yard.

Sarah and Friday laughed, though Harrie didn't, worried about hurting Rachel's feelings.

But as usual she seemed immune to insults. 'I'm good at cards. Watch this.'

Shoving her sleeves up to her elbows, she shuffled the new pack with lightning speed, cut the deck and somehow recombined the two halves with just a flick of her thumbs, then raised the pack high in one hand and let the cards fall in a perfect, continuous cascade into the other.

Friday and Harrie grinned with delight, but Sarah said, 'Very clever, but it's not broads, is it?'

Rachel pulled a particularly childish who-cares-what-you-think? face. 'Come and watch me play, then.'

They trooped out into the exercise yard after her and waited until she'd found enough women to start a game, which wasn't difficult.

'If she really can play cards, why didn't she do it before?' Harrie asked.

Sarah replied, 'Well, if she actually does know what she's doing, which I doubt, she probably didn't want to play with someone else's deck.'

'Why not?'

'It'll be marked, so the owner can cheat.'

'Oh. Are Rachel's cards marked?'

'I hope so.'

They gathered around as Rachel and three other women, sitting cross-legged on the ground, began to play. The game was Twenty-One, and it soon became obvious that Rachel really did know how to play cards. After an hour she had won five games, taken the entire pot of four pounds, two shillings and four pence — thus cleaning out her opponents, who were left confused and not a little irritated by having been taken in by Rachel's initially naive and somewhat vacuous demeanour.

'Where did you learn to play like that? Did you cheat?' Sarah asked, deeply impressed in spite of herself, as Rachel handed her the entire winnings. 'No, not all of it. Keep some for yourself.'

Rachel took a few shillings. 'No, I didn't cheat. I've been playing cards with my da and brothers since I was five years old. Not in front of Ma, of course; she thinks cards are the devil's work. I can play better than all of them now.'

'You could make a good living at that,' Friday remarked.

'I said that to Ma once and she whacked me with the wooden spoon.' Rachel tucked the shilling coins down her front. 'I was supposed to be wedding the son of the farmer who owns the fields next to ours, then spending my life shovelling shit for him and having babies. I told Ma I'd rather go out in the world and earn my own money playing cards than do that.' She smiled a little sadly. 'I said to myself when I turned twelve, that's not the life for me. I want pretty things and lovely dresses and cakes and a fine house with a garden full of flowers.'

'Well, that won't happen now, will it?' Friday said. 'Not now that you've run off with a soldier. *And* you're a canary-bird.'

'Lucas won't mind about me being a canary. He'll know it was because of Mrs Begbie.'

Will he? Friday thought; he obviously hadn't noticed the Begbie mot was crooked. And he *will* mind about her being a canary. 'Rachel, what if you're found guilty?'

'I won't be because Lucas will get me out before then,' Rachel said matter-of-factly.

Friday felt her patience leach away. 'This bloody Lucas cove of yours! How's he going to do that, eh? Look, love, no one gets out of Newgate unless they've served their time, or they're on their way to a transport somewhere, or heading for the gallows. And if he actually does come looking, and he won't — I'm sorry, love, but I'm willing to put money on that — he could be standing outside those gates for a bloody long time. Do you honestly think he'll wait for you?' Rachel looked so dismayed Friday immediately felt horribly mean-spirited. 'I'm sorry, really, but trust me, I know what men are like. Once they get what they're after they're gone.'

Rachel rallied. 'Not my Lucas.'

Friday gave up. 'What will you spend your money on?'

'Not going to.' Rachel patted her hidden winnings. 'I'm saving it to bribe my way out of here.'

'I'm not sure that's going to work,' Friday said, laughing.

Rachel gave a mock scowl. 'Damn it to hell. I was sure it would.'

Friday laughed even more uproariously. 'Did your brothers teach you to curse as well? You'd better not say that in front of your ma when —' She shut her mouth. Sod.

'When what?' Rachel demanded, her lovely face suddenly ratty with suspicion. 'When *what*, Friday?'

Friday sighed. 'We wrote to your family and told them where you are.'

'But you don't know where I live!'

'We sent it care of Winters' dairy farm, north Guildford.'

Stamping her foot like a child, Rachel shouted, 'You bloody cows! You had no right to do that! That's *my* business! I *told* you I didn't want them to know! I especially asked you *not* to!' She glared at them a moment longer, then turned on her heel and marched off.

Harrie and Friday gazed after her. Eventually Harrie said, 'I don't think it's that she doesn't want to see *them*. I think she's frightened that they won't want to come and see *her*.'

But they did. Mr and Mrs Winter arrived at Newgate Gaol a week later. When the turnkey passed on the message that Rachel had visitors, she asked Harrie to go with her. As soon as she saw her mother and father beyond the railing of the visitors' passage she burst into tears.

Mrs Winter, Harrie observed, was a small, fair woman with a sweet face that had probably been close to beautiful before she'd married a man who'd asked her to raise a family of five, run a house and tend cows in all weather for the next twenty-five years. Mr Winter was taller than his wife, broad in the shoulders and a little bandy, though still a reasonably fine figure of a man. His cheeks were as ruddy as his side whiskers. They both wore good, plain clothes, if not their Sunday best, which made them stand out from the other mostly ragged visitors. They were small-scale but no doubt hardworking farmers and, if they did have money, Harrie suspected, it wouldn't be much.

'Ah, Rachel, me love, what have you done to put you in here?' her father asked, sliding his hand through the rail to grasp hers.

The turnkey saw but looked away: if there was contraband being passed she would make sure she got her cut later.

So Rachel told him her story, becoming increasingly animated the more she realised he wasn't going to drag her through the bars and beat her senseless. All the while her mother hung back, the hands clutching her reticule white about the knuckles and her lips pressed tightly together.

Finally, ignoring Harrie, she stepped forwards. 'What were you thinking, child? Moses Stemp will never have you now, not after you've thrown yourself at the first redcoat as trotted past. And we never even met him! You just ran off. Why?'

'You could have met him, Ma!' Rachel retorted.

Mr Winter said, 'Keep your peace, Flora. I know you're bothered, but we've more to worry about than that now. Rachel, have you had the indictment yet?'

Rachel looked at Harrie, back at her father, then at Harrie again. 'I don't know. Have I?'

'Who are you?' Mr Winter demanded.

Harrie thought he was being quite rude, even if she was on the wrong side of a set of prison bars. 'My name is Harriet Clarke,' she said in her best voice, 'and I'm a friend of your daughter's.' She stuck her hand through the railings.

Mr Winter regarded it suspiciously for a moment, then shook it. 'Edgar Winter, Rachel's father.' He cocked his head. 'Her mother, Flora.'

'We've not seen a bill of indictment yet, Mr Winter,' Harrie said. 'But she's been here ten days now, so it should be soon.'

Flora Winter clutched her husband's arm, hope illuminating her face. 'Then we've still time to speak to the governor!'

'Bugger the governor, beg pardon, girls,' Mr Winter growled. 'If there's been no indictment yet, I'm off to talk to the Begbie woman, see if she'll take money to withdraw her prosecution.'

Rachel and Harrie shared an uneasy glance; Mrs Begbie surely would have discovered that her ring was missing by now.

Mrs Winter tugged on her husband's sleeve. 'Edgar, please, can we not deliver our letter first? He might give her a reprieve anyway. Or he might let her out on bail. I don't know how these things work. But we can try, can't we?'

Mr Winter looked down at the tears blurring his wife's tired, swollen eyes. 'Aye, you're right, we can try.'

'Have any letters come for me?' Rachel asked hopefully.

'Who the hell from?' Edgar Winter exploded.

'Lucas. He might have written to me at home if he didn't get an answer from the lodging house.' Rachel stared at her father, who glared back, his face a picture of irate exasperation.

Rachel had the sense to lower her gaze first. 'Is Shannon missing me?'

'Been moping from sun up 'til sun down,' Mr Winter said with a deliberately cruel edge. 'Lying under his tree not earning his keep.'

Rachel blinked hard. 'And the boys?'

'Roger and Noah are minding the cows, and I've sent Nathaniel and Peter out to look for lover boy. The 31st are still at home, far as I know. He got you into this mess; he can marry you. No one else will now.'

'You don't have to look, Da. He'll be coming back.'

March 1829, Newgate Gaol

Sarah was convicted of picking pockets and sentenced to seven years' transportation to New South Wales. Rachel was indicted for pawning two bed sheets that didn't belong to her, that is, the property of Mrs G Begbie of Marchmont Street, London, and of stealing a pearl, diamond and enamel ring from same. The Grand Jury decreed that the bill was true and Mrs Begbie's counsel was expected to be ready to assist his client in her prosecution by the April sessions. Edgar and Flora Winter continued to campaign for their daughter's release, but their hopes were fading at approximately the same rate as their funds and they began to talk about when Rachel 'came back', not 'when they got her out'. Neither hide nor hair of Lucas Carew was seen by anyone and the 31st East Surrey moved out of the area for training exercises. The only positive news during the freezing and dismal months of winter was that it appeared Rachel had avoided becoming pregnant during her brief time with her lover.

They were sitting on the ground outside their ward, waiting for their supper to arrive. The stink that had built up inside over the coldest months was only to be borne when absolutely essential and the late afternoon was cool but fine. They'd spent the hours after the midday meal in the courtyard anyway, standing around while one of do-gooder Mrs Fry's ladies led them singing hymns, which almost everyone enjoyed. Rachel certainly did; she loved singing and knew she had a pretty voice.

Halfway through a song she'd felt a familiar tugging sensation low in her belly. Hoping it might just be a guts ache from the breakfast stirabout she went inside to check, but when her finger came away smeared with fresh blood she knew her courses had started. She wondered whether she was sad or relieved. She was very disappointed for Lucas, who had mentioned several times his desire for children. She had nothing with her so she'd had to ask Harrie, who had given her some strips of cloth. Now her rags, too, would be added to the line of stained and tatty little flags flapping across the courtyard.

It would have been nice to have Lucas's baby and he'd have been delighted, she knew he would. But Newgate Gaol — what a place to be expecting! Not for long, though. Her mother and father hadn't been able to get her out, but she knew when he came back, Lucas would.

She wished she knew where he was. Some days lately she was starting to wonder if she'd imagined him, but she couldn't have, because if she had, she wouldn't be here in gaol, would she? That first ever time she'd seen him he hadn't seemed real he'd been that lovely, just like an angel or a prince or a knight, or perhaps all three together. The day had been cold and foggy and she'd had her woollen scarf tied over her head to cover her ears, trudging along the side of the road on her way to see if the berries were out yet on the mistletoe growing on the poplar tree halfway along the ditch. It had been at the behest of her mother, who had decided it would be a good idea if Rachel were to be standing under some mistletoe when the Stemps arrived to pay their Christmas visit in a few weeks, so she hadn't been in a very good mood.

As usual Shannon had been with her. It was useful having four older brothers because they spoilt her, but often they treated her as though she were a silly little girl. Shannon didn't; he never told her to grow up. Well, he couldn't — he was a dog. When she wasn't busy with her chores she would go for long walks across the fields with him and talk to him about everything. He knew all her secrets and dreams. He was supposed to be a farm dog and had a kennel outside under the big tree, but sometimes she sneaked him upstairs to her attic room and he slept on her bed, though not that night because he'd rolled in a dead hedgehog.

Someone on horseback had come trotting down the road behind them, the mount's hooves squelching in the muddy gravel, and she'd stepped aside to avoid getting splattered. But as the rider had passed she'd looked up just as he had glanced down and, when their eyes met, she felt a jolt of something so strong her knees had almost given way. He'd reined in, whirled his horse around and touched his hand to his shako in *such* a dashing manner. Vanity had made her slip the scarf from her head so her hair swung free. She knew of course from his uniform he was a soldier, but it was his beautiful face that snatched her breath away. Oh, he'd been so handsome, his red jacket making such a bright splash in the grey day, his blue eyes sparkling and his black horse tossing its head and snorting clouds of vapour.

And that's how it had started. He was on three weeks' furlough from his regiment and they met every day for a week in the woods near her family's farm, until her mother demanded to know where she was sneaking off to. So she'd told her and her mother and father both said she would marry a soldier over their dead bodies, even if he was a junior officer: she was from farming stock and on the land was where she belonged. When she crept out to meet Lucas the next day she had a bag with her and after she asked him to take her away, he did.

They had two wonderful weeks together in London, then he'd had to leave. But he'd promised he would come back. He had, he'd promised. She remembered that very clearly, even if everything else concerning their time together in the city was turning into a bit of a muddle in her head. And she knew he'd find her, even here.

She missed him horribly, but she knew she'd feel even worse if she didn't have Harrie and Sarah and Friday. Harrie was kindest. Harrie was like her mother, on the rare occasions when her mother was in a calm, loving mood, but she'd come to like and appreciate Sarah and Friday very much, too, even though she annoyed them. Yesterday she'd overheard — because you overheard everything in here — Sarah telling Friday that she, Rachel, was spoilt, which was true, she supposed. But it wasn't her fault she was the only daughter in a family of lads and her father doted on her — and she was doing her best. She'd won nearly seventeen pounds now playing cards and put just about all of it in the kitty. Pretty well the only person she hadn't played was Liz Parker, and that was because she was terrified of her. She was tough, nasty and very unpleasant. Friday and Sarah were tough, too, but each was generous in her own way, though not quite as generous as Harrie, who would give you everything she had if the others didn't stop her.

Rachel had her back against the wall and her knees bent, using her skirt as a barrier so no one could see what she was doing behind it. She'd arranged for Rosina to buy her some plain white linen handkerchiefs and, as a surprise, was embroidering Harrie's,

Friday's and Sarah's names on them. She was quite good at needlework; better at that than shovelling cow shit anyway.

'What are you hiding?' Friday asked.

Rachel eyed her. Her cheeks were ruddy and her eyes bright, which meant she'd got in some gin. Not always a good sign. Gin tended to make Friday a bit ... unpredictable.

She pulled her skirt up over her lap. 'Nothing.'

Friday shrugged. 'I meant to ask you, what did you use?'

'What did I use for what?'

'To stop getting knapped.'

Harrie said, 'Is that not Rachel's business?'

Rachel thought that was nice of Harrie, but she didn't mind Friday asking. 'I didn't do anything. I wanted a baby.'

Friday shook her head in frank disbelief. 'You're bloody lucky you didn't fall. Imagine that. In here!'

'Watch out,' Sarah warned.

Liz Parker and a handful of her acolytes were approaching, doing a circuit of the courtyard. Liz's hoop earrings glittered in the pale sunshine. It was rumoured she had Romany in her blood, but Friday told everyone who would listen her skin was dark because she'd never, ever had a wash.

'On the rag, I see!' Liz called gaily, pointing between Rachel's legs.

Rachel quickly dropped her knees and covered herself with her skirt.

'Be sure to let me know when you're off.' Liz stuck out her tongue and waggled it. 'Partial to a tender bit of corned beef, I am!'

Shocked, Rachel felt her face flame and her skin crawl. What a completely revolting thought!

Friday jumped up, fists clenched. 'Fuck off with yourself, you dog-faced baggage.'

Liz stepped forwards. 'What did you say?'

'You heard.'

Liz launched herself at Friday, who swung her fist at Liz's head. Liz ducked and only partially avoided the blow.

Rachel scrambled to her feet but Sarah gripped her arm. 'Where do you think you're going?'

'To help.'

'Don't be so stupid. Look at the size of the cow. Get over there with Harrie.'

It was true: the top of Rachel's head didn't reach Liz's shoulder and Liz was possibly three times her weight.

A shouting, cheering circle immediately formed around the sparring pair. The turnkeys came running.

Liz hit Friday in the jaw; Friday staggered backwards, stood on the hem of her skirt and fell on her backside. Sarah dragged her to her feet and lashed out at Liz. In seconds more women joined in the mêlée, Friday managing to rip an earring from Liz Parker's ear, leaving a trail of blood down the woman's neck and shoulder.

Rachel and Harrie watched from the safety of the ward doorway as more turnkeys arrived, males this time from the men's prison, to break up the fight. In minutes it was over, the women herded back to their wards, Friday led off to a cell in solitary and Liz Parker, shouting and cursing, to another.

Friday returned five days later, with a bruised face and complaining of a sore, loose tooth. 'See?' She opened her mouth and with a finger wobbled a molar in her upper jaw.

Harrie's stomach lurched: she hated things to do with teeth. Thank God her own had settled down.

Sarah had a look. 'It stinks, too. You should get it pulled.'

Harrie gave a tiny, sour-tasting retch. 'I'd avoid the hospital. Liz Parker's in there. Her ear's gone rotten.'

Friday smirked. 'Dearie me. You can do it, can't you, Sarah?'

'I suppose. Rachel's got some news. Well, we all have.'

'My trial's next week,' Rachel said glumly. 'And —'

'And they're saying there's a transport leaving for New South Wales at the end of April,' finished Sarah.

'They've been saying a transport's leaving since November,' Friday said dubiously.

Harrie, looking miserable, shook her head. 'No, it's true. Matron told us yesterday, after prayers.'

Friday's eyebrows went up. 'Just women?'

'Seems so.' Sarah picked at a scab on her wrist. 'She said about a hundred and ten of us from Newgate, which will clear the place out, won't it? But nothing about any men prisoners.'

'Unless we're picking them up on the way,' Friday said thoughtfully. 'But if it's just us it won't be a big ship, so not a big crew.'

'Working out how much money you can make on the side?' Sarah said slyly.

'It's all right for you. I haven't been able to work for the last four months.'

'Neither have I. How many pockets do you think are worth picking in here?'

Harrie waved an irritated hand. 'Stop that, you two. Rachel needs to know if she should plead guilty or not guilty.'

'Guilty,' Sarah said.

'Not guilty,' Friday said.

They looked at each other.

'She did steal the ring,' Sarah said.

'But she didn't pawn the sheets,' Friday argued in a muffled voice as she prodded her tooth, 'so she might as well plead not guilty to everything.'

'But then she'll get the jury and they'll mark her a barracks hack for running off with a soldier and pass a guilty verdict anyway. And the judge will be a bigger prick than usual because of her pleading not guilty when the jury's decided she is and give her a heavier sentence.'

'But if she pleads not guilty the jury might decide she isn't. Look at her; look at her face. She looks like a child. You can say you were seduced, can't you?'

Rachel nodded and massaged the back of her head. She was getting another headache. She wanted the trial to be over and she wanted Lucas. She still hadn't heard anything from him and she was so sure she would have by now.

Why hadn't he come for her?

Rachel was sentenced to seven years' transportation. In the public gallery Flora Winter cried out, then fainted. Her beautiful, beautiful daughter, banished across the seas, ruined and branded forever as a common thief.

Rachel had stopped listening to anything once she was certain Lucas wasn't in the gallery. She'd seen her mother and father and two of her brothers, then turned to face the judge and let her mind wander off. She didn't even hear Mrs Begbie deny ever having met Lucas Carew. When she was asked a question she answered, but afterwards couldn't remember what she had said. Her father told her she'd pleaded guilty.

The morning after Rachel's trial, Sarah returned from the water closets in a fury and threw herself onto the ground outside the ward beside Friday.

Momentarily distracted from examining the split ends of her hair, Friday stared at her. 'What's the matter with you?'

'Some fucking cow's stolen my money! *Our* money.'

Harrie gasped and leant forwards to hear better. 'What? Oh *no*! Where was it?'

'In the bog, hanging down the side of the pit on a string.'

Harrie made a disgusted face.

'Oh for God's sake, it was in a bloody jar!' Sarah snapped. 'And now it's gone.'

'Bloody hell, how much was left?' Friday asked, aghast.

'Twenty-three pounds of my money, and Rachel's seventeen.'

'But who could have taken it?' Harrie said.

'I don't know, do I? But whoever it was must have stuck their entire bloody head down the crapper because the jar was completely out of sight.'

Friday groaned and swept her hair back off her face. 'Jesus Christ. Well, that's us buggered, isn't it? I've got a bit left but it won't last forever. We'll have to get it back. Ah shite, what does she want?'

Liz Parker and half a dozen of her girls swaggered up. Liz's earrings were uneven, the hoop in her left ear sitting much higher now that the lobe was missing.

'Bugger off,' Sarah said, in no mood for Liz Parker's antics.

'Mornin', ladies,' Liz said, smirking. 'Enjoying the sunshine?'

No one answered.

'I am. I've had meself a lovely morning. A *lucky* morning, ya could say. That reminds me, I think this might belong to yous.' She fumbled about in a pocket of her voluminous skirt and pulled out an empty jar. 'Reckernise it?'

Friday launched herself up off the ground, but Sarah grabbed her ankle before she could reach Liz. Friday landed on the hard dirt on her hands and knees, cursing.

Liz cackled. 'That's right, best keep ya dogs tethered.' And she and her crew laughed themselves silly as they walked off.

Friday slapped angrily at Sarah's hand. 'What did you do that for?'

Her voice shaking with suppressed rage, Sarah said, 'What was the point? She won't have it on her; it'll be hidden somewhere.'

'Somewhere safe like down the bog, you mean?'

'It *was* safe. How was I to know she'd go crawling down it?'

'She's a bloody pig of a woman,' Friday shot back. 'She's probably one of these types who has to admire their own turds and saw it then.'

'Well, that's not my fault. I can't —'

'Stop it!' Harrie ordered. 'Just stop it!'

Friday and Sarah stared at her.

'We need that money. Stop bickering, both of you, and work out how we're going to get it back.'

Harrie and Rachel were dismayed now that their departure from England, perhaps forever, had actually been confirmed. While there had only been idle talk and rumours of a transport setting sail for New South Wales, it had been easy for them both to pretend it might not happen, especially Rachel, who had demonstrated a tendency to ignore the things she didn't care to know about.

Newgate was a loathsome place, but in Harrie's mind it was better to be incarcerated there where she could still receive visits from Ada and the children. She had been making a little money of her own for a few months now, artfully mending clothes for the women in the wards, and was no longer quite so dependent on Friday and Sarah. She had even managed to pass a little to her mother. But when she was transported to New South Wales, there would be no one to give Ada and the children anything. They would have to rely on outdoor relief — virtually nothing these days. It was making Harrie sick with worry, though she tried to hide it. She wasn't the only one; everyone would be leaving friends and family — husbands, lovers, children, siblings, parents — and no one knew when they would meet again, if ever. A heavy pall of gloom and nostalgia was settling over the women and they'd not even left Newgate yet. What would it be like when they finally arrived in Australia?

Rachel was anxious about the fact that the farther she went from London, the more difficult it would be for Lucas to find her. And she would miss her family, too, she had finally admitted. They came to see her when they could, visits that often resulted in tears and bitter, quickly regretted words on both sides of the railing, but all hope of a reprieve or a pardon had evaporated after Rachel's guilty plea. Her mood was brittle and prickly and she flipped between the expectation that Lucas would gallop up Old Bailey Street and hammer on the great gates of Newgate Gaol at any moment and lying on the barracks bed weeping inconsolably because he hadn't.

Sarah, however, was not unhappy about leaving England. Matron had confirmed that the ship would transport female convicts only: men awaiting transportation would be moved from Newgate onto the prison hulk HMS *Retribution* at Woolwich. Which meant, Sarah knew, that Tom Ratcliffe — who had blithely exchanged the names of his associates for his own freedom but had himself been played the crooked cross by the watch — would be left behind to rot in a dripping, disease-ridden, rat-infested skeleton of a navy ship on the river Thames, while she finally began a new life far away from him. The prospect of his fate pleased her immensely, even though she would be at the beck and call of a master or mistress for quite possibly every month of her seven-year sentence. She had heard, however, that if a convict girl kept her eyes and ears open, there were opportunities to be had in New South Wales — far more than in London. More perhaps than in all the British Isles. And they said the sun shone more days there than it rained, the rivers were clean and you could eat the fish from them, the air was sweet, the streets were wide and a convict's money was as good as anyone else's.

And leaving Newgate had a more immediate advantage. She and Friday had not been able to get anywhere near Liz Parker's ward, so clearly their money was hidden in there somewhere. They'd paid some girls a shilling to stage a fight in the yard to get Liz's crew to rush outside and that hadn't worked; they'd tried fighting their way in and been beaten black and blue for their efforts; and they'd bribed one of Liz's crew to hand over the money and had themselves been double-crossed. The bloody money was more secure in Liz's ward than it would be in the Tower of

London! They'd likely have a better chance of getting it back on the transport, Sarah suspected, where there would be even less privacy and fewer hiding places. If not, she would personally rip it out of Parker's filthy hands coin by coin.

Friday, too, wasn't overly perturbed about leaving England, as she had also heard stories about better times to be had across the seas, even while a convict girl was serving her sentence. She had no intention of curtailing her money-making activities when she arrived there and, in fact, would have to go back on the town in the very near future as she had eroded her savings quite severely. As Sarah had remarked, she could attend to that problem on the transport. Men were the same everywhere, whether walking foggy London streets, sailing a ship, or working beneath a southern sun — they would all hand over money for a fuck if they wanted one. And Friday wouldn't be leaving much behind, really: only the filthy streets of London and a few graves she hardly ever visited any more. She would miss her old mates, but she'd always made friends easily. And she had three now who, day by day, were becoming closer almost than her own family had been.

Harrie, mending a rip in the armpit of Friday's jacket after yet another fight, severed the thread with her teeth, licked her fingers and rolled a knot into it. She pulled on the seam, scrutinised the tiny, immaculate stitches in the candlelight and said with satisfaction, 'That should hold it.'

'Lovely,' Friday said, sitting in her shift, skirt and shawl. 'What do I owe you?'

'Don't be silly.' Harrie carefully wove the needle into a folded piece of cotton and placed it back into her sewing kit. It was a collection of very basic needlework tools she'd added to Sarah's gift by buying or barter and kept in a little tin box, but one day, when she could afford it, she would buy herself a proper sewing compendium with a needle case and all the things a dressmaker needed. She passed over the jacket.

Friday slid off her shawl, revealing tattoos on both pale, well-muscled arms. Along the inside of her left forearm the name 'Maria' was inked in uneven black letters. 'Just someone,' she'd answered vaguely when Harrie had first asked. On the same arm, above the elbow on the outer aspect, were a dagger stabbing a heart and a set of initials. The other arm featured an anchor and another set of initials. Friday insisted she couldn't remember who the initials belonged to. Lovers, Harrie assumed. Brothers? Though Friday had never said anything about having brothers. Harrie had been fascinated when she'd first seen them: men, she knew, were occasionally tattooed, sailors in particular, but she'd not seen many tattooed women. At least, not until she'd found herself in Newgate.

Friday put on the jacket, fastened the buttons, flexed her shoulders and grinned. 'Perfect. Fits even better now.'

'I let the darts out around the bosom. It looked a bit ... snug before.'

Friday snorted with laughter. 'It was meant to! It's a tool of the trade!'

'Oh.' Harrie looked around — the other women in the ward were enjoying a good giggle at her expense — and smiled ruefully. 'Should I take them back in again?'

'No, it *was* a bit tight. Squashed the hell out of my tits when I had the curse coming.'

At the mention of menstruation, Rachel began to blink hard.

Sitting next to her, knowing what would come next, Sarah warned, 'Stop that!'

'But he'll be so disappointed when I tell him,' Rachel said, her voice rising to a pre-weep whine.

Sarah hurled her dinner basin across the ward, scattering a trio of rats skittering along the base of the wall. 'For Christ's sake, Rachel! *When* are you going to face facts? He's *not* coming!'

'He is!'

'He *isn't*!'

Rachel punched Sarah's shoulder. 'He bloody well *is*!'

She pulled back her arm to do it again but Sarah grasped her wrists and held them. Rachel kicked out and caught Sarah's shin with her boot; Sarah held on, not looking at Rachel, staring impassively at the far wall.

'Let me go!' Rachel demanded, and bit Sarah's hand.

'No.'

'*Let go!*' Shrieking now.

Sarah shook her head. Everyone was watching.

Slowly, Rachel bent forwards, her silver-white hair tumbling over her face. She gave a long, low moan like an animal in pain and subsided with her head in Sarah's lap. Sarah let go of her hands.

Then the sobs started, Rachel's slight body jerking as they coughed out of her, deep and raw and ragged.

Alarmed at last, Sarah looked at Harrie, mouthing, 'Now what?'

Harrie, for once not being the one to calm or mollify, made a gesture indicating that whatever happened next was up to Sarah.

She did nothing for almost a minute while Rachel continued to sob, then, hesitantly, Sarah laid her hands on Rachel's head and began gently to stroke, one hand after the other, as though petting a cat. Harrie and Friday exchanged glances. The other women lost interest when they saw there would be no more entertainment. Gradually, Rachel quietened; and eventually she stopped crying.

A while after that she sat up. 'Will we all be together when we get to New South Wales?'

They had no idea, but Friday, Harrie and Sarah told her they were quite sure they would.

Rachel wiped her nose on the back of her hand. 'That's all right then.'

Part Two

Across the Seas

Five

April 1829, Woolwich Dockyard

Woolwich Dockyard had been Henry VIII's idea, the warships he built there insurance against possible attack from Catholic neighbours angered by his desire to divorce Catherine of Aragon. By the time convict ships were departing there for New South Wales three hundred years later, Woolwich was still a busy naval yard.

Gulls screeched and wheeled overhead and the tang of salt sharpened the air even though Woolwich was miles from the sea proper. The river smelt a little sweeter here, London's torrents of shit having either settled on the banks farther upstream or washed out into the estuary. It was almost as busy, though: several dozen deep-hulled civilian ships and those of the Royal Navy stood just offshore, their tall masts like denuded trees, tilting lazily as the river flowed beneath them. The dilapidated prison hulks HMS *Retribution*, *Prudentia*, *Bellepheron* and *Justitia*, mastless and crippled, squatted just beyond the navy ships, close enough for the convicts aboard to be ferried ashore each day for work, but too distant for them to swim safely to freedom.

Prison hulks had been moored off Woolwich for over fifty years, housing male prisoners awaiting transportation to New South Wales, though some unlucky men had served their entire seven- or fourteen-year sentences aboard the rotting shantytowns. Thousands had died of gaol fever, dysentery and any number of other epidemics that swept the dripping, weed- and rat-infested decks — more unsanitary even than Newgate Gaol itself — and from lack of suitable food and from overwork. Each day the prisoners were rowed ashore to labour around Woolwich Dockyard and nearby Woolwich Arsenal and put to work dredging the Thames to ensure the river's main channel remained clear, returning at dusk to the floating dungeons exhausted and broken. Banishment to New South Wales, even for life, was far preferable to a sentence served on the hulks, which was guaranteed to shatter a man's spirit if not his body.

The navy's dockyard extended along the right bank, its covered and uncovered slips, dry docks, mast and mould lofts with their towering roof-lines, manufactories, mast ponds, gun bastions, offices and massive workshops surrounded by a high stone wall, intersected by a single wide wooden gate and gatehouse. Great ear-splitting clangs rent the air; there was an underlying cacophony of hammering and shouting; laden carts trundled in a steady procession to and from the ships moored at the quay; and jacktars and civilian workers trotted about busily, like ants scurrying between their nest and some tasty discovery. It was a startling contrast to the Kent countryside rolling hazily off into the distance beyond the dockyard's walls.

The Newgate women had been left for some time in the closed carts that had brought them from London. Long enough for Friday's boredom to override their caution, at any rate.

'I'm not going anywhere in that,' Sarah said over her shoulder as she peered though a gap in the canvas covering their cart.

Friday folded the flap aside and, in silence, they regarded the ship moored alongside the quay as she heaved and dipped gently on the tidal swell of the Thames.

'But is that it?' Rachel asked. 'The one we're going on?'

'It says *Isla* on the side,' Harrie said. 'It must be.' Her eyes were swollen from crying and she had a dull, aching headache. Saying goodbye to her mother and the children, who could not afford to make the trip to Woolwich, had been the most upsetting thing she had ever had to do. She was leaving them to perish and it was her fault and she felt like lying down and going to sleep and never waking up.

'It *is* quite a bit smaller than I thought it would be,' Friday said, her voice notably bereft of its usual enthusiasm.

'Hey! You lot!' a voice bellowed. 'Put that flap down! And stay out of sight 'til you're told!'

Friday dropped the canvas a second before it was struck with something that made a flat, cracking sound. ''Til we're told what?' she shouted back.

'Less of your lip!' the voice responded. Boots crunched away over gravel.

'Have they got whips?' Rachel was shocked. 'We're not cows!'

'Yes we are, dear,' the woman sitting next to her said with fatalistic assurance. She looked to be in her fifties; her grey hair hung limply about her ravaged face and those of her teeth that remained were a transparent green, testifying to repeated doses of mercury, the treatment for syphilis. 'We'll be herded onto yon ship and sent across the seas and when we get to New South Wales we'll all be sold to highest bidder.'

Alarmed, Rachel looked at Friday, who said, 'Shut up, Matilda Bain. You don't know what you're talking about.'

'I do. My niece were transported five year ago and *she* were sold to highest bidder.'

'Ignore her,' Friday said, and peeked out under the canvas again. 'The front cart are getting out.'

It was almost five o'clock and they'd been sitting in the cramped carts all afternoon. Told not to attract attention by lifting the canvas covers, forty women from Newgate had been driven through the streets of London, roughly following the course of the Thames, until they'd come to Woolwich. Yesterday a small cavalcade had transported the first forty women from the prison, who were now aboard the *Isla*. Shortly they themselves would board; and tomorrow the remainder — those who had children with them — would be brought to Woolwich and the *Isla*'s captain could sign off her manifest.

They *had* attracted attention, though — and deliberately, following a tradition that had begun decades ago when men and women sentenced to the boat had been forced to walk the distance between Newgate and Woolwich in irons, at the mercy of jeering and missile-hurling crowds. The convicts had retaliated then by swearing, making vulgar gestures and baring their bottoms, and regardless of the carts — a recently introduced convenience — the latest lot had no intention of being deprived of a last swipe at a citizenry who viewed the convicts' position at the bottom of the social dung heap with total disdain. Friday had a stone bruise on her arse the size of an egg.

At last they were told to get out. Sarah was almost crippled by the need to empty her bladder. Wincing as she lowered herself from the cart, she hobbled away from the male turnkey's prurient gaze and squatted, grimacing with relief as urine hissed onto the stones. She glanced about, her mouth twitching as she realised that most of the cart's occupants were following suit.

'Bugger me!' Friday exclaimed loudly. 'The relief!'

She nodded sympathetically at Harrie, who was also squatting, staring off into the distance at nothing, her face scarlet. Rachel, on the other hand, was standing, the front of her skirt raised, legs slightly apart, directing a jet of urine at the cart's wheel.

'Brothers,' Sarah remarked.

The guard with the whip was staring at them openly now.

Friday gave herself a shake and stood. She rubbed her thumb and forefinger together. 'Oi! Where's your chink? Nothing's for free, you know.'

The guard laughed and spat on the ground. 'Whores, the lot of yis!' He pointed his whip at a line into which the women from the other carts were being herded. 'Get your belongings and hurry up.'

From the cart the girls collected the little they owned and trudged the short distance to join the line.

At its head, beside a gangway connecting the quay to the *Isla*, stood three men. The eldest, a short and stocky man with greying sideburns and ruddy, windburnt cheeks, appeared to be in charge. At his side stood a younger man holding a board onto which were clipped some papers. The third, tall and perhaps in his early thirties, wore a smartly tailored blue uniform coat and white trousers.

'Not a navy ship, then,' Friday remarked.

Rachel said, 'How do you know?'

'The only Royal Navy uniform is on that tall cove and I'm betting he's not the master. The short-arse will be. The tall one'll be the surgeon. It'll be a contracted ship.'

'Is that good or bad?'

Friday shrugged dismissively. 'Depends.'

'On what?' Sarah said.

'The surgeon. The master. The provisions. The weather. How should I know?' Friday snapped. 'I've never been transported before.'

Harrie suddenly realised that Friday was nervous — a very uncharacteristic state for her. 'What's the matter?'

'Nothing.'

'You don't like the sea, do you?' Rachel said.

Sarah and Harrie gaped at her; Rachel had not displayed much in the way of perceptiveness.

Friday said nothing for a long moment, then let out a resigned, irritated sigh. 'No, I don't. It scares the shit out of me. I've had nightmares about drowning since I was a little kid.' She swallowed. 'And it doesn't like me. I can't even cross the sodding Thames without spewing my guts out.'

There was another shocked silence at this: after all, the voyage to New South Wales would take months.

The turnkey with the whip chose this unfortunate moment to crack it in Friday's general direction. She strode across to him, snatched it out of his hand, hurled it on the ground and shrieked, '*Will you fuck off with that!*'

A hearty cheer erupted from the line of women. Friday, tackled immediately by several guards, was manhandled across the gangway and into the bowels of the *Isla*.

Harrie picked up Friday's sack of belongings and balanced it awkwardly on top of her own smaller basket, shuffling forwards in the line. When they reached the gangway they were brusquely told by the younger of the two civilian men to state their names, ages and sentences, were ticked off the ship's muster list, and ordered to go below and get squared away. The man in uniform also informed them that they would be receiving a medical examination the following morning.

Rachel said, 'What if we fail it?'

Harrie gave Rachel's ankle a little tap with her foot, to let her know she was pushing her luck. Rachel had already asked Matron at Newgate that question, and Matron had terrified her with stories of being left behind to rot in the blackest and most rat-infested of holes in Brixton or Newgate Gaol until she had reached the end of her seven-year sentence. *If* she reached the end of it. Matron had been a bitch, but she'd probably been telling the truth. But here was Rachel, having another go anyway.

The two men in civvies looked at Rachel blandly, as though this weren't a particularly original question.

'Would that mean we'd have to stay behind?' Rachel said, clearly gambling that Matron's threat had been an attempt to put her off playing the invalid card. 'You see, I've been quite poorly for a while.' And it was true, Harrie knew — Rachel had been feeling a little out of sorts.

'Aye, it would mean that,' the man with the grey sideburns answered gravely. He leant sideways and consulted the muster list.

'In Newgate or Brixton. For seven years. Not up to me, though, is it, being only the master? You'd have to discuss that with surgeon superintendent Mr Downey here.'

The surgeon gave her a stern and uncompromising look. Harrie watched poor Rachel's face fall.

'Move along,' the master growled. 'You're holding up the line. Collect your prison slops before you go below.'

'But I can't!' Rachel blurted, panicking now. 'My fiancé will be coming for me any time soon.'

'Move along,' the master repeated, not meeting her eye.

Harrie gave Rachel a gentle shove and they followed Sarah across the deck of the *Isla*, weaving past coiled ropes and teetering piles of crates and barrels and boxes. There wasn't much room, though even she, a complete sailing novice, realised that at least some of the clutter would be packed away by the time they sailed. But there would still be little deck space. At the bow was a raised foredeck, its boards forming the ceiling of the cabins that lay beneath, in the middle the lower waistdeck and at the stern a raised afterdeck. Companion ladders provided access to all levels.

On the afterdeck, just before the mizen mast, were the great wheel and the capstan. Above the waistdeck were suspended two upside-down longboats — surely not big enough to take them all should the ship sink? — and on the starboard side hung a smaller quarterboat, ready to be launched. Set into the waistdeck were four hatches. Three were about a yard square. One was open to the elements but covered with a sturdy wooden lattice with a canvas cover rolled neatly to one side, while the other two had timber covers, presently lying open. The larger hatch, its solid cover also currently open, suggested access to the hold. Nearby two small animal pens had been built, at the moment unoccupied. The small foredeck was relatively clear, access to the cabins beneath being from the waistdeck, except for the great beam of the bowsprit encroaching onto the deck space and down into the ship's gut, the anchor windlass, assorted piles of coiled rope, the casing housing the gleaming ship's bell, and the handgrips on the gunwale near the bowsprit forming the 'seat of ease', which Harrie privately vowed she would never use even if it meant she would die from constipation.

Everywhere — all along the gunwales from bowsprit to stern — were attached ropes and rigging and shrouds from the three masts, interspersed with arrangements of blocks and tackles for hoisting sails and moving equipment and cargo. Harrie peered up at the main mast, its tip appearing to scrape the clouds as they scudded past. The flags snapping at the very top seemed so high and so far away she felt dizzy and lost her balance, staggering slightly until a grinning sailor gave her a gentle shove towards a hatch, its open cover revealing a ladder descending into near darkness.

Before this stood a nervous-looking ship's boy with a bundle of clothing in his arms. He thrust it at Harrie and reached for another.

'Two, please.'

'Beg pardon?'

'I need two. One for my friend in the ...' Harrie couldn't think of what sailors called wherever it was Friday had been dragged off to. 'The prison bit.'

'The brig?'

'That's it.'

The boy looked doubtful. He was only about ten, Harrie thought, and probably suspected she was trying to trick him.

'It's true. She was rude to the guard and got carted off. She'll need prison clothes when she gets out.'

The boy looked across to an older crewman. 'What do I do, Mr Furniss?'

Second Mate Amos Furniss grinned, revealing stubs of tar-stained teeth. 'Could be true. Or maybe she's hoping to have the first lot ripped off by a lusty sailor. Which is it, eh, girlie?' He winked slyly.

Shocked, Harrie looked quickly down at her boots.

The second mate laughed, hoicked and spat on the deck. 'Give her what she wants.'

The boy handed Harrie another pile of clothing.

'Thank you,' she said with as much dignity as she could muster. 'What's your name?'

Turning red, the boy said, 'Walter Cobley, missus.'

'Thank you, Walter.'

'Ooh eh,' Furniss said, punching Walter on the shoulder. 'Walter's got a fancy piece.'

Walter coloured even more.

Awkwardly clutching her basket, Friday's sack and now a large double pile of clothing, Harrie gathered up her skirts and descended the ladder backwards, keeping a good grip on the rope that served as a handrail in case she missed her footing. At the bottom she turned and blinked. Where the sunlight spilled down through the hatch she could see floorboards and to her left and right vague shapes rising upwards, but beyond that she could barely discern anything. She could hear women talking, however, and sense their presence close by. It was hot and stuffy and smelled of damp, rotting wood and warm brine tainted with something else indescribably rank. Bilge water, perhaps, sloshing about in the very bottom of the ship? There was the sharp, acrid smell of water closets, too, which was a relief because it probably meant they wouldn't have to do their business over the front of the ship. And not quite disguised by the gentle creaking of the ship's timbers she was positive she could detect the sounds of scuttling, scratching claws. She felt panicky and claustrophobic.

'Sarah? Are you there? I can't see anything. I'm blind.'

'No, you're not. Just wait a minute.'

Harrie did and in a moment her sight returned. Sarah was there with Rachel, both calmly waiting for her to get a hold of herself.

'Better?'

Harrie nodded at Sarah, then looked around.

Down the length of the prison deck, in the centre, ran a long table six feet wide, through which half a dozen of the wooden pillars and posts bracing the *Isla*'s skeleton reached to meet the upper deck. The very large one in the middle was presumably the main mast. Flanking the table were long benches, and lining the hull on both sides were bunk beds six feet wide and perhaps five feet deep, one row on top of the other. The ceiling was low — barely five and a half feet below the heavy beams — and the space was cramped, especially when you considered that by tomorrow evening there would be a hundred and seven women and twenty-five children crammed into it. There were no windows and no ventilation except for a row of small scuttleholes in both sides of the hull, and the single hatch. Two oil lamps swayed gently from the ceiling, but pervaded the deck with a smoky haze and gave out only a dim, honeyed light.

Harrie peered at the women who had preceded them, busy laying claim to the berths. It seemed they were to share them, four to a bunk. 'Where's Friday?'

'I don't know,' Sarah said, sounding worried.

'I want that bed,' Rachel said, pointing into the dimness behind the ladder up to the hatch. 'Over in the corner, the one on the bottom.'

Sarah and Harrie looked, then Harrie cast her eye down the length of the cabin again and saw what Rachel had no doubt already noted: Liz Parker and her crowd, who had embarked yesterday, settled in at the far end, playing cards. She elbowed Sarah, who followed her gaze then raised her eyebrows in belated comprehension. Rachel clearly wanted to be as far from Parker as possible.

'Good choice, Rachel. Well spotted,' Sarah said.

It *was* a good spot and no one had claimed it yet: they dumped their things on the bunk. From here they would be able to see

Parker and her girls coming and going and, most importantly, when their possessions were left unattended.

'Come on then,' Harrie said, forcing a note of cheer into her voice. 'Let's try on our new clothes.'

Rachel unfolded a blouse and held it up. 'God, it's hideous.'

In each bundle were two calico blouses, a brown stuff skirt, a loose-fitting jacket and an apron of duck, a pair of woollen hose and a straw bonnet.

Harrie agreed, inspecting a row of stitching. 'And cheaply made.'

In spite of her misery, Rachel started to giggle.

Sarah frowned. 'What?'

'All my dreams about pretty things and dresses and cakes. It's just that, well, I'm not sure this is really the sort of thing I had in mind.'

Sarah and Harrie stared at her, then burst into wild laughter, Harrie feeling awful because she knew how much Rachel really did want those things, but cackling until tears ran down her face anyway.

Rachel removed her worn and mended top, revealing an extremely grubby shift, and slipped one of the stiff new calico blouses over her head. The neck opening was enormous, even with the buttons done up, and her fingers didn't even reach the cuffs. Pathetically, forlornly, she waved her hands, causing the stiff calico sleeves to bend emptily and lend her the appearance of some sort of bizarre little puppet. They all roared.

'What size did Friday get?' Sarah asked, wiping her streaming eyes and pointing at the bundle sitting on Friday's sack.

Harrie had no idea. She handed one of the blouses to Rachel: it sat on her a little better, but she was so small nothing was going to fit well. She and Sarah, on the other hand, had received clothing more appropriate to their sizes, though everything was stiff and would require some breaking in.

'I can put in a few darts if you like,' she said to Rachel. 'And take in the waistband on the skirt. Friday can have the bigger size.'

'*Is* it a bigger size?' Sarah asked, holding up the blouse Rachel had discarded. 'Or are they all the same? Surely they wouldn't have made them all the same size.' She nodded towards the far end of the prison deck. 'What about fat people like old gannet guts over there?'

By this time they were shouting to hear one another above the din. The cabin rang with curses, laughter and hoots of mostly good-natured derision as the newly arrived women changed into their slops and exchanged greetings and gossip with those who had settled in yesterday. The atmosphere reminded Harrie of a particularly busy day at Petticoat Lane market, and she sat and watched for a moment, savouring it and storing it away, because she suspected there would be few moments like this again.

Harrie woke early the next morning to the inharmonious clanging of a bell. She rolled over, stretched — and remembered there wasn't enough room to sit up. Next to her, Sarah slept on. Knowing how grumpy she was first thing, Harrie watched her for a moment, then gave her shoulder a shake.

Sarah jerked upright and banged her head. She rubbed her skull, scowling and looking as muzzy as Harrie felt. 'What the *hell* is that noise? Christ.'

'A bell.'

'I know it's a *bell*.'

Sarah felt around in her hair then inspected her hand to see if she was bleeding. She gave her thankfully intact scalp a good scratch, yawned, then rubbed her face. 'I haven't slept that well in months.'

'No, neither have I!'

Harrie was very pleasantly surprised. The mattress was thin and lumpy and smelt sour, but was the height of luxury compared to the barracks bed in Newgate, and last night they'd each been issued with a pillow — an actual pillow! — and a new blanket. And though the bunks were a tight fit even for three, these factors combined with the gentle rocking of the ship had sent them into a deep slumber in spite of the chatter from the cabin's other occupants.

Sarah gave Rachel a gentle shove. 'Wake up, sleepyhead.'

Rachel rolled over and peered at her, revealing swollen, red eyes. Harrie hoped this wasn't going to be one of Rachel's miserable, missing-Lucas days. The girl could be so ... mercurial. Was that the right word for her moods? She and Sarah shared a dismayed glance before Sarah said brightly, 'Come on, princess: put your brave face on.'

'Is Friday back?' Rachel mumbled.

As if in answer to her question, the hatch banged opened, letting in a shaft of early morning sunshine and a welcome waft of fresh air, and Friday herself bounced down the ladder, landing with a thump on the floorboards.

'God, it's dark in here. Sarah? Harrie? Rachel? Where are you?'

Competing with shouts of 'Shut up!' and 'Bugger off!', Rachel cried out, 'Here we are, Friday! We're over here!'

Friday turned and squinted, then waved. She looked dreadful, dark bags under her eyes suggesting she hadn't slept at all.

'Get through the lot of them, did you?' Liz Parker called nastily from her hive at the other end of the cabin.

Friday slapped her left hand over her right bicep and stuck up the middle finger of her right hand.

Rachel scrambled out of the bunk, her hair all over the place. 'Where've you been? We were worried. Are you sick yet?'

Friday made her way down the three-foot-wide aisle between the bunks and the long, central table. 'Not yet. They've got a couple of cells in the hold. Really tiny — I could hardly sit down.' Friday looked around. 'Good spot. In a corner so no one can sneak up, close to the hatch for the fresh air. Bloody hell, are they real pillows? Did you bring my sack? It's cramped in here, isn't it? God, the roof's low, I'll be sconing myself all day.' Her voice was rising, her eyes widening, reflecting fear. 'It's *really* cramped, isn't it? And dark.' She let out a strangled shriek and clapped her hands over her mouth. 'God, sorry, I didn't mean to do that. I'm not the best in small spaces.'

Harrie thought of all the time Friday had spent in the tiny, dank, pitch-black solitary cells in Newgate and felt a great, hot urge to weep. She'd never said anything, not once. Not trusting herself to speak, she indicated the gap under the bunk where they'd stored their possessions. Friday retrieved her sack, dug through it to an accompaniment of clanking sounds, pulled out a bottle of gin and took an enormous swig.

'God, that's better,' she said, wiping her mouth with the back of her hand.

Harrie had already guessed what was in Friday's things, but was glad now she hadn't tipped it out. Still, she had to say, as diplomatically as she could, 'Do you think we'll be allowed spirits?'

'Doubt it.'

'What will you do?'

'I'll hide it. Or drink it first.'

'And what about when you run out?'

Friday took a more genteel sip, then replaced the lid. 'Sweetie, who sails ships?'

Harrie felt better — this sounded more like the fearless, smart-arsed Friday she knew. 'Sailors do.'

'Yes. And what sort of refreshment do sailors like?'

Harrie realised where this was leading. 'You'll end up in that cell again.'

'Be worth it.' Friday pulled a hideous face and shuddered theatrically. 'I'd rather be dead than go on the dry for four months. While sailing the seven seas in a big leaky barrel of whores and thieves!'

Rachel started to laugh, her giggle rising infectiously until heads began to turn. Harrie was relieved that at least something had cheered her up.

* * *

Told in no uncertain terms not to get used to being waited upon as they would soon be responsible for managing their own rations, they were served a breakfast of oatmeal gruel with raisins and sugar made by the ship's cook, which they ate at the long table using the wooden bowls and spoons they'd each been issued.

The day passed surprisingly boringly. Access to the upper deck was curtailed while the *Isla* was still being provisioned and also as a precaution against escape attempts, though the surgeon superintendent allowed them up twice, in shifts, an hour at a time, for the fresh air. During their first turn on deck, he ordered each shift to bring up their civilian clothes, which he inspected. Anything he declared unfit to be worn again was thrown over the side, where it floated listlessly for a short while, then eventually sank, taking its cargo of lice, fleas and body odours with it. Harrie was called for her medical examination mid-morning, then Sarah, but Rachel wasn't fetched until three o'clock in the afternoon.

James Downey, of the Royal Navy and responsible for the health of all those sailing aboard the *Isla*, leant back in his creaky chair and massaged his tight neck muscles. He knew he took too long with this initial examination of his charges, but he'd been caught out during his first superintendency by convicts who'd insisted they weren't ill when they were and then died on the voyage, passing their malaise on to other prisoners, and had vowed not to repeat his mistake. During that trip, seven children under the age of five had died and he still had terrible dreams about their wasted, gasping little bodies. At the time he'd also put two prisoners off the ship who had convinced him they were ill when they weren't, which had earnt him a scathing letter from the governor of Newgate, testifying to the prisoners' glowing health. It hadn't done much for his self-confidence, or his reputation: by taking his time with the examinations he felt more assured regarding who really was sick and who wasn't.

So far he'd put four women off the *Isla*: two of such advanced age they clearly would not last the journey, and two approaching the final stages of death from consumption, which was vastly irritating as the prison was supposed to only release prisoners for transportation if they were fit for it. That is, hale enough to survive the voyage, then undertake physical employment when they reached New South Wales. He had also discovered that three women were pregnant, but hadn't been able to bring himself to turn them back, even though they would likely deliver at sea. To give birth in a hellhole such as Newgate would be a certain death sentence for any child and probably its mother. Nor could he put off the mothers still suckling infants, though it was against the rules for a woman to be accompanied by a child still on the breast. They tried to hide it, but the dampness of the fabric over their bosoms, carefully concealed beneath their shawls, was always a sure sign.

He was also still vexed by the fact that he had been denied permission by his superiors to perform his medical examinations somewhere suitable within the confines of Woolwich Dockyard, before his charges boarded the *Isla*. He was firmly of the opinion that at least some of the diseases he saw and treated on a regular basis were passed from one patient to another through actual physical contact, or at least the sharing of confined spaces, and did not have their genesis in the miasmas of the cesspit or the rubbish heap. It was a view that went against current medical wisdom and was considered by the majority of his medical colleagues to be seriously flawed, outlandish even, but his experiments with various medical treatments and remedies were furnishing his theories with considerable substance. It seemed to him that it would be far more sensible to examine the prisoners who were to be his charges — and the same could be applied to emigrants, for that matter — *before* they had a chance to mingle aboard the transport and spread any diseases they might be harbouring.

His greatest fear was typhus, also known as gaol fever, ship fever, spotted fever, famine fever and putrid fever. It was the curse of the military and prisons — in fact, of any group of people confined in unhygienic, crowded spaces — and every surgeon's nightmare. Symptoms were aches in the head and body, weakness, vomiting, fever and delirium, and a rusty-red rash that began on the torso but spread and worsened to gangrenous sores. It passed among the population rapidly and was very often fatal. Other convict ships had discovered typhus on board and the outcome had been disastrous.

Of course, these women, like all the convicts he had superintended, had been crammed together in prison for months and had quite possibly already contracted anything going around, but there was always a chance he might be able to spot particular symptoms and remove the carriers before they all boarded and set sail. He hoped so, anyway.

He had also wanted the women to wash and change into their new slops ashore, to avoid infecting the *Isla* with the vermin prison inmates always harboured, but no, permission had been denied for that as well, even though he knew there were several vacant buildings that might have been adapted for that purpose. He suspected it was because these prisoners were all female and the idea of one hundred-odd convict women, some of them whores, some of them mothers, milling about, distracting his men and befouling his lovely dockyard, had turned the admiral's stomach.

This was James's fourth appointment on a convict ship. He didn't enjoy the duty and wasn't aware of any Royal Navy surgeon who particularly did, but he did take a certain satisfaction from overseeing the passage of his charges from England to New South Wales in a reasonably healthy and fit state, some even arriving with better constitutions than that with which they'd embarked. They were a trial, though, and the women far worse than the men. He'd had to admit, if only to his wife, that he had felt some trepidation when he'd learnt that the *Isla* would carry only women.

He had dual authority with the ship's master in all non-nautical matters, which meant that the inhumane treatment of convicts during some earlier voyages, which he had not tolerated under any of his own watches, could not occur. He'd used this authority to ensure that provisions would be adequate, as per naval regulations, and the ship's hospital suitably furnished and well stocked. Located on the same deck as the prison, but to the stern and separated by a bulkhead, it had been fitted with six beds and two cradles, lockable cupboards, a work table and shelves with raised rims to prevent items sliding off in rough seas. The ventilation was *almost* adequate, too, the lattice-covered hatch being set above the centre of the cabin. He would need to choose two or three suitable women to act as attendants when the ship got under way. As well, he'd had a cubicle within the hospital curtained off and fitted out as an examination area with a small desk at which he could write his notes, so that the women could be afforded some privacy when speaking with him. The hospital, in fact, had been located at the expense of the crew's quarters, now squeezed into an even smaller space beneath the officers' cabins on the afterdeck.

It was true he'd had to lobby with some energy for all this, but James had concluded that the master, Captain Josiah Holland, was neither an unkind nor unpleasant man. He was flawed, however, in the sense that he seemed far more at ease with the ocean and the winds than he was with his fellow human beings. Still, James felt confident that he and his charges were in competent hands. Josiah Holland ran a tight and efficient ship, that was already clear; his sailing record must be reasonably unblemished for him to have won the tender to transport the convicts, and his ship sound to have passed the navy's inspection.

The *Isla*, an ordinary merchantman, was, at three hundred and seventy tons, not a particularly large vessel, her deck measuring ninety-seven feet in length and her beam twenty-eight feet. She was a barque, triple-masted and square-rigged. Her hold was deep and she sat low when fully loaded, depending on her cargo, but generally she rode the sea well, according to her captain.

On this voyage she carried a crew of thirty; her master, three officers, a carpenter, a sailmaker, a cook, twenty-one seamen and two boys. In addition, six 'free' passengers would also be travelling to New South Wales: a minister, his wife and their two young daughters, and two gentlemen bound for appointments in the New South Wales government. Which, including the twenty-five children under the age of seven allowed to accompany their convict mothers and the further thirteen prisoners they were to pick up at Portsmouth, gave James a total of one hundred and seventy-one potential patients. He sighed. It was a lot for one surgeon to oversee, but not enough to justify an assistant surgeon and, actually, fewer than he'd superintended on previous trips. Providing no truly disastrous event occurred — a shipwide epidemic or some such — he should manage.

At the sound of boots on the hospital's companion ladder he whipped his feet down off his writing desk and sat up as the third mate ushered a young girl into the room.

James felt his heart plummet. This was the girl who yesterday afternoon had declared she had been feeling poorly of late, but that wasn't the cause of his anxiety. 'Sit, please,' he said, indicating a straight-backed chair next to the examination bed. 'Thank you, Mr Meek.'

The girl waited until Third Mate Meek had gone, then sat down, her knees primly together and her eyes downcast.

James consulted the muster list. 'Rachel Winter, is that correct?'

She nodded.

'Aged fifteen?'

'Yes, sir.'

She looked up at him, and he knew for certain she was going to be trouble, or at least the cause of it. Her eyes were huge and the exact colour of cornflowers, her pale skin clear if a little anaemic-looking, and her hair thick and extremely fair. She was very, very pretty. And tiny. She had the appearance of a living doll and she would drive the men to distraction. He'd seen it happen before and had no doubt it would happen on this voyage, if he didn't keep a very close eye on both his charges and Captain Holland's men. He stifled another sigh.

'Do you have any illnesses, Rachel?'

He could see she was struggling with her answer. She looked reasonably healthy, except for some sort of sore on the side of her neck, but they all had them, these prison women. It was the profoundly inadequate diet and lack of exercise, he was convinced of it. He wondered if she might be a little simple, which would be a terrible shame, with such lovely looks.

'You said yesterday you had been feeling unwell for some time. Have you had a cough, or bleeding, or eruptions of pus or anything like that? Perhaps —'

'No,' she said suddenly, scowling at him. 'I lied. I've not been sick at all.'

Briefly he pondered what might have solicited such a cross outburst, then went back to his notes. 'You're not married?'

It paid to make sure, as some women declared they were when they weren't, wrongly believing that newly arrived female convicts were automatically assigned to their husbands and intending to pose as the wives of friends or colleagues already in New South Wales in the hope of gaining more freedom. This frequently caused problems when they lodged genuine applications to marry. Though some women, of course, actually did have common law or legal spouses serving sentences in New South Wales or Van Diemen's Land.

'I'm betrothed. My fiancé is a soldier.'

She said this with such defiance that James suspected there was much more to the story than he was ever going to be told.

'Is there a chance that you could be with child?'

She looked away. 'No, there isn't.'

'Would you please recline on the table so that I may examine you?'

He busied himself rearranging things on his desk while she climbed up on the table and lay down, her gaze fixed on the lamp that swung slowly from the ceiling.

'If I touch you anywhere that causes pain or discomfort, you must tell me, do you understand?'

She nodded. She was filthy and she stank, but they all did. He was accustomed to foul smells, of course, but the stink that clung to the inmates of England's prisons seemed to have an eye-watering intensity all of its own. He reminded himself to check that extra water barrels had been ordered aboard so they could all bathe thoroughly and launder what remained of their civilian clothing prior to sailing.

He began his examination. Palpating her arms and legs through the fabric of her clothing he found no evidence of recent or past broken bones, felt no telltale swelling of the lower belly that would indicate pregnancy, and saw no major abnormalities of the skin visible to him apart from gaol sores. Until he appointed female assistants who could act as chaperones he would not be carrying out examinations of an intimate nature and then only if expressly required. He had colleagues who had found themselves in deeply compromising situations due to attempts at blackmail, or simply as the result of malicious behaviour, and he had no intention of being caught in the same trap. It meant he could not initially examine for indications of syphilis or gonorrhoea, but to put off the ship women afflicted with those particular maladies would be to sail with the prison deck half empty, which would defeat the purpose of the voyage. He put his stethoscope to his ear, listened to her breathing and heard nothing untoward.

'Sit up, please.'

He looked into her mouth, noting that she had all her teeth and that her gums were reasonably healthy, in her ears and into her eyes. Then he paused.

'Blink, please.'

She blinked.

'Again.'

She did it again. He moved his face closer to hers, covered her left eye with his hand, then uncovered it. The right pupil was larger than the left and didn't change regardless of the amount of light it received.

'Has your eye always been like this?' He tapped her right temple.

'Like what?'

'The pupil seems to be fixed. Do you suffer from pains in the head?'

'I ... no, not really.'

'In bright sunlight do you find yourself squinting?'

'No.'

James peered into her eye a moment longer. Perhaps it was simply a congenital abnormality. He sat down at his desk. 'You appear fit and hale to me, Rachel. The boil on your neck seems to be on the mend. If it doesn't improve, come to me for a poultice.'

She slid off the table and straightened her skirts. 'Yes, sir.'

'Thank you. You may go.'

She left, disappearing through the curtains. He stared after her for quite a while. She might not be pregnant now, but he had a horrible feeling he could have the devil's own job making sure she remained that way over the next few months.

The last of the Newgate women arrived with their children late that afternoon. By the time they'd all embarked, come below, fought over the remaining berths, changed into their new slops, stowed their belongings, eaten supper, walked round the deck for the fresh air on which Mr Downey seemed so keen, been sent below again for the night, been told to shut up by the first mate, and tentatively settled in, it was nine o'clock. The children, however, all under the age of seven and either frightened or overexcited, could not effectively be kept quiet, which caused the majority of women without children to shout at those who had them, which upset the children further, which caused the master himself to storm down the ladder and threaten troublemakers with a night in the solitary cells in the hold. When he left, the women discovered that the hatch had been locked, and had been all along, which made Friday and Sarah laugh because they were, after all, in a floating prison. Friday began to bash the ceiling with her wooden bowl, daring Liz Parker to forget about playing bloody cards for once and get off her arse and show some spunk — there could be a fire in here and if they couldn't get out they'd all be burnt to a crisp. In less than a minute the aisles were jammed with women all banging on the roof and shouting to be let out, except for Friday, who had gone back to her bunk.

It wasn't long before Captain Holland reappeared, his face livid in the glow of his lamp, accompanied by several of his men bearing drawn pistols. Bellowing to be heard over the yells and hammering and catcalls of the women and the piercing shrieks of the children, he finally drew his own pistol and let loose a shot. The women scattered like rats to their berths, leaving Liz Parker, too heavy to move quickly, marooned in the middle of the prison deck. At a signal from the captain she was unceremoniously dragged up the ladder, swearing the air blue.

At the top she dug in her toes momentarily and screeched down at Friday, 'I'll get you for this, you scabby whore!'

Friday waved gaily and snuggled under her blanket.

Eventually, the cabin settled and the children, exhausted from such a long and eventful day, nodded off. The Thames lapped with an almost unbroken rhythm against the *Isla*'s hull and her timbers creaked as she rocked gently. The snores and somnolent mumbles began.

Harrie, lying next to Friday, whispered, 'Have you felt sick yet?'

'Not yet. Maybe I'm cured, eh?'

'Did you tell the surgeon?'

'What for?'

Harrie propped herself on one elbow. She could barely see Friday's face in the gloom, though her rich copper hair still gleamed softly. 'He might have something that will help.'

'Would he give me gin, d'you think?'

Harrie could hear the tease in Friday's voice. 'No, I mean real medicine.'

Friday put her arms behind her head and closed her eyes. 'Go to sleep, Harrie. Stop fretting. You're a terrible worrywart, you are.'

Harrie waited a full minute. 'Friday?'

'Oh, go to sleep, Harrie, will you?' grumbled Sarah.

'What?' Friday said on a sigh.

'Why do you hate Liz Parker so much?'

Friday's eyes opened again. 'Because she's a nasty piece of work, that's why. And a thief and a cheat and an intemperate gambler. And because she nicked our money, obviously.'

'Is that all?'

'That's enough, isn't it? Why? Why do you want to know?'

'I don't know. Because it upsets me.'

'Leave it, Harrie,' Sarah warned.

Carefully, to avoid connecting with the bunk above her, Friday sat up and hunched over her bent knees. 'If you must know, Madam Nosy, I hate the way she carries on with the girls. She tempts them with food and trinkets and says she loves them and she'll look after them. But she's not really ... one for the ladies. She's got a man and a litter of kids at home. She only does it because under all that flash mob shite she's weak and doesn't want to be alone. She's not honest. She's ... double-dipping.'

Sarah laughed. 'None of us are honest. That's why we're here.'

Friday lay down again and wriggled around until she got comfortable. 'I don't know. I can't put it into better words than that.

But she really gets up my snout.' She gave a little grin. 'Anyway, it's good sport. Like bear-baiting.'

Sarah eyed Harrie and said, 'Sorry you asked?'

Harrie made a face. 'I'm not sure.'

'Can we all be quiet now?' Rachel said, her voice muffled by the pillow clutched over her ear. 'I want to go to sleep. My head hurts.'

Six

After breakfast the following morning the entire contingent of convict women and their children were locked out of the prison deck and mustered on the waistdeck, squeezed among piles of provisions not yet stowed away, to listen to Captain Holland, who had donned his best coat with silver buttons and his passé but still splendid tricorne hat to add authority to his announcements. Beside him on the afterdeck at the *Isla*'s stern stood his officers and the surgeon superintendent. The remainder of the *Isla*'s crew lined the waistdeck's gunwales and the rail of the foredeck, vigilant against possible escapees and secretly hoping for some such spectacle. Overhead, shore and marsh birds wheeled and cried, clashing noisily with gulls over scraps from the dockyard and ships moored nearby.

The master began by castigating the prisoners for the previous night's minor riot. 'Behaviour like that will *not* be tolerated!' he exhorted, his voice competing with the mild wind coming off the Thames and winning easily. 'Let it not be forgotten that you are prisoners of His Majesty the King and for your crimes the courts of England have sentenced you to transportation to lands beyond the sea! For the purposes of this voyage this is a *prison* ship and Mr Downey and myself are authorised to administer punishment as we see fit. And rest assured we will!' He paused to let the gravity of the message sink in, scowling down at the women below him, then opened a journal and cleared his throat. 'Each day will be effectuated according to a timetable. You will break into messes of six and each mess will —' He looked up as the women began to shuffle around, finding friends, forming little clusters. 'Not *now*! When you have been dismissed!' When the women had settled again he continued. 'Each mess will elect a mess captain, who will draw the ration for her mess every morning and be responsible for overseeing the washing of bowls and eating utensils, the cleanliness of berths and the orderly conduct of messmates. Mr Downey will shortly select attendants for the hospital and draw up rosters for cleaning the prison deck and tending to the water closets. The ship's cook will prepare all meals in the galley; meals will be eaten below deck; *no* cooking will be permitted below deck. At sunrise the hatch will be opened and buckets placed on deck to facilitate prisoners' ablutions *daily*, providing the weather is clement.'

This drew a gasp from the women.

Ignoring it, Captain Holland carried on. 'Also daily, the deck will be swabbed and bedding rolled and brought up for airing, again providing the weather is clement. This must be completed by eight o'clock, when you will muster prior to breakfast. The prison deck will then be holystoned — dry, not wet — and the surrounds scrubbed. Those rostered to specific duties will attend to them. Laundry will be done twice a week, including that of the crew. Materials will be made available for those of you who wish to do needlework and a school for reading and writing will assemble providing suitable tutors can be found. Dinner will be at noon, supper at four o'clock. You will muster at five o'clock for prayers, after which bedding will be taken below again. On the recommendation of the surgeon superintendent there will then be dancing, games and exercise above deck before you retire. The prison hatch will be locked at seven o'clock. Below deck there will be no striking of lights, no smoking of pipes, no cards or dice, thieving or fighting. Severe punishment will be administered to any prisoner found to be fraternising with the crew. Foul language and insubordination will also be punished. There will be no contact with the free passengers when they come aboard. Due to unforeseen circumstances, we will be departing Woolwich in three days' time, briefly dropping anchor at Portsmouth, then leaving English waters and sailing south-west.' Captain Holland closed his journal with a snap and handed it to First Mate Silas Warren.

There was a brief silence as the women on the deck below him absorbed his final sentence, then rose a great wail of grief as they realised that for most of them there would no chance to say goodbye to family, friends and lovers. Other ships, they'd heard, had remained in port for up to three weeks before setting sail, so few had yet sent for their people.

Deeply disconcerted by such a raw outpouring of feminine distress, Josiah Holland glared down at the miserable assemblage before him, daring the women to overtly challenge anything he had said. But not a single one did, which amazed him and left him feeling more uneasy than if the wretches had railed at him directly.

This was his fifth and final charter transporting convicts to New South Wales, and he had only tendered for it because the cargos he was shipping to and from Port Jackson, plus what he was paid to carry the convicts themselves, made the voyage significantly worthwhile in financial terms.

The female convicts were always the worst. Of course it was unlucky to sail with women aboard ship: every sailor knew that. Also, they misbehaved, they ran around screeching, they lied, they scratched and fought, they jabbered all the time and laughed too loudly, they were lewd and dirty, they fouled his ship with their filthy female bodily emissions, they fraternised with his men and they gave him terrible, humiliating dreams. James Downey was convinced that the needlework, the school for letters and the exercise routines he had devised would keep them gainfully occupied, or at least too occupied to play up, but Holland had seen it all before and had considerable doubts about that. Downey had seen it before, too, Holland knew, and should damn well know better.

But he was the naval surgeon, and the navy represented the government, and the government was paying. And to tell the truth he wasn't really averse to sharing authority with James Downey, who seemed a decent enough chap, at least when it came to matters not concerning the running of the ship. The less he himself had to do with these women, the better. Last night Downey had gone ashore so it had fallen to him to sort out the fracas below deck and it had been like stepping down into *hell*.

Apparently now, thank God, the prisoners intended to limit their protestations to weeping and whining, so he stomped down the companion ladder from the afterdeck and into his cabin.

'Pompous bloody arsehole,' Sarah hissed.

They stood where they were, stunned by the captain's announcement regarding their early departure from Woolwich, until the first mate shouted at them to go below again.

Rachel threw herself onto their bunk and declared, 'Well, I'm not cleaning the bogs. I've had enough of shit.' She put her pillow over head and started to cry.

'I think we'll all be having a turn,' Harrie remarked, forcing false cheer into her wobbling voice. 'It sounds like everyone's going to be on Mr Downey's rosters.' She busied herself straightening a blanket, then she, too, began to weep.

For a fleeting moment Friday considered volunteering to take Rachel's place on the bog-cleaning roster, just to cheer her up, but there were limits even to her generosity. She felt desperate for her, though, as Rachel's family would certainly have come to Woolwich to see her off if they'd had the chance. Friday knew, too, that Rachel still believed somewhere down in the very core of her being that her soldier would come to save her at the last minute. But he'd better hurry up, because now he only had three days left.

Rachel and Harrie weren't the only ones weeping. Distressed murmurs then cries rose around them as the true impact of Captain Holland's announcement sank home; in only seventy-two hours the *Isla* would sail and most aboard her would never see England or their loved ones again. A great wave of grief seemed to engulf the prison deck as women keened and wept and tugged at their hair, so when a single voice screamed in terror, no one at first noticed it.

The scream resounded again, higher and sharper this time; the lamenting and anguished praying in the cabin faltered and the women one by one quietened. The silence disclosed a dreadful, low-pitched grinding noise emanating from the floorboards towards the bow.

Matilda Bain wailed, 'Lord have mercy, we're sinking!'

No one moved for perhaps two seconds, then fresh screams erupted followed by a panicked stampede for the ladder, which was immediately jammed with shoving, scratching, shrieking women. Those who reached the top became wedged so firmly in the hatchway that the sunlight was blocked. The grinding noise continued and the ship, horrifyingly, tilted slightly to port.

Friday grabbed Rachel, who, being so small, had found herself forced to the floor by the crush of struggling bodies, and hauled her along, her boots barely touching the deck, towards the hatch, violently elbowing others out of the way. Harrie and Sarah followed directly in her wake, doing their share of shoving and screaming, scared witless of not getting out before the ship went down.

A pistol shot rang out, sharply audible above the terrified weeping and cries for mercy. Suddenly silenced, the women crowding the ladder froze, there was a second's hiatus, then they awkwardly untangled themselves and backed down a step or two, followed by Captain Holland, silhouetted against the light.

'Get back to your berths, all of you, and remain there!'

'Have mercy, sir!' someone entreated. 'Please! Do not drown us!'

The master turned his attention to the deck above him, listened, heaved a great, vexed sigh, then retreated. Mr Downey appeared in his place and gently but firmly cleared everyone off the companion ladder.

Raising his hands in a calming gesture, he said loudly so everyone could hear, 'There is no need to panic, the ship is not sinking. I say again, *the ship is not sinking*! The noise you can hear is simply the sound of the anchor being raised. Captain Holland has ordered that the ship be towed a short distance out into the Thames for our remaining time here.'

'Bugger,' Sarah said in Friday's ear, 'if that's all it was we could have had a go at grabbing our money.'

'What for? Why are we being towed?' Liz Parker demanded in an attempt to re-establish her authority, having been one of the first to reach the companion ladder during the panic.

'To minimise opportunities for escape,' James Downey replied, clearly seeing no need for obfuscation.

Muttering and the beginnings of indignation and protest began as the women made their way back to their bunks.

'That's me buggered, then,' Friday said to Harrie.

Harrie gasped. 'Were you going to try to escape?'

Friday laughed at the look of shock on her friend's face. Laughing felt good and it helped to ease the terrible rate at which her heart still galloped at the thought of being trapped inside the ship as it filled with cold, murky water and dragged her down into the mud beneath the Thames.

'Doubt it. I'd go straight to the bottom with all that gin tied round my neck.'

James Downey treated one broken wrist, a severely sprained ankle, multiple cuts and bruises and two cases of hysteria after the anchor-raising incident. He also had a heated discussion with Josiah Holland in the privacy of the captain's cabin about his not having informed the prisoners that the *Isla* was about to be towed away from the quay. The captain, feeling guilty, argued that he shouldn't have to inform a cargo of convict women of every single order he gave; James countered by pointing out that probably not one of them had been aboard a tall ship before — of course they would panic if it suddenly rattled and rumbled and shifted beneath them. He also suggested that the women would more likely behave if they were made aware of what to expect, and when, rather than be subjected to frightening surprises.

'I told them what to expect,' Captain Holland insisted. 'You were there.'

'You told them what their domestic schedule is to be and what they are prohibited from doing.'

The captain made a hurrumphing noise. 'You speak of them as though they're first-class passengers I should be inviting to dine at my table. They are not, Mr Downey, they are convicted felons. Whores and thieves. No doubt both.'

James silently asked God to forgive him for evoking His name for advantage. 'Do you consider yourself to be a Christian man, Captain?'

'What?' Josiah Holland looked startled.

'*I* do, sir,' James went on earnestly. 'I know already from our short acquaintance that you harbour deeply Christian principles. You must forgive me for being so impertinent as to suggest this, and for suggesting it so bluntly, but you could demonstrate those principles handsomely by exhibiting a little charity. Think of Our Lord's example: He associated with the lowest of the low.'

The captain's already pink face flushed with indignation. After a moment, however, perhaps recalling that James had as much authority as he did on this voyage, he gave a long-suffering sigh. 'What are you suggesting, Mr Downey?'

'Just that they be treated with some small amount of dignity. This is, after all, to be their home for the next four months. And we are in fact departing Woolwich with uncommon speed. Many of them will not have had time to farewell family and friends and will be suffering because of it.' James raised a hand to ward off the captain's interruption. 'I'm well aware that the winds and tides are favourable and that we should take advantage of them. I am a naval man myself, you will recall. And obviously I'm not suggesting we consult the prisoners about every matter — you are of course the master of this ship — but if they know at least that they are in no immediate danger, they may feel less ... wretched, and therefore be easier to manage.' He hurried on as the captain again opened his mouth to interject. 'And yes, we must abide by the rules — yours and mine — and administer punishment when necessary. Christian charity can only carry us so far! We can't have individuals running amok, or cliques holding sway over the prison deck. But I'm convinced that given the opportunity, most of these women will respond to kindness and consideration.'

Clearly unconvinced, Josiah Holland raised his wiry eyebrows. 'And if they don't?'

James met his gaze steadily. 'Then at least *we* will have done the Christian thing.'

On the afternoon two days prior to the *Isla*'s departure from Woolwich, the women of Newgate received a small party of visitors. The women, allowed on deck for hours at a time now that the ship had anchored farther out into the Thames, watched as a wherry rowed by a straining waterman approached across the river's choppy surface. Seated in the centre were three women, heads bowed against the stiff breeze, hands gripping the brims of their plain grey bonnets.

'It's Elizabeth Fry,' Sarah said as she leant on the ship's rail. 'I thought we'd seen the last of her.'

'I didn't,' Harrie said, who had a lot of respect for Mrs Fry and the Ladies' Newgate Committee. 'I knew they'd come if they could.'

Sarah gave Harrie a sour look but said nothing. She didn't altogether trust Mrs Fry and her ilk. The campaigner was a

Quaker, and it was true that her work had improved conditions for women in Newgate Goal, but Sarah wasn't overly impressed with the price extracted for those improvements — endless bible readings, the singing of hymns and allegiance to a God she didn't have much time for. Harrie was quite religious and prayed every day and what have you, and Sarah didn't begrudge her that at all. Perhaps it was the praying that made her the cheerful, calm and persistently helpful person she was, but probably not; she suspected Harrie had been born with those qualities.

But it wasn't Sarah's cup of tea at all. Her mother and father had been extremely religious, but it had done her mother no good in the end and her father had made a complete mockery of it. She, Sarah, had prayed a lot when she had been younger. In fact, she'd prayed so much she'd just about worn the skin off her knees, but no one had heard her. No one at all. So why did God listen to some of his flock and not others? She'd thought about the matter at length and found it hugely confusing and demoralising. Either Christians were misguided, or it was all a great, festering heap of lies; an immense fabrication, designed to catch people like a spider traps insects in a sticky web. But did that make God a spider? Perhaps it did, because spiders did horrible things to the prey they caught and Sarah had certainly seen some horrible things happen to people in her time.

The waterman manoeuvred the wherry alongside the *Isla*'s hull and the bosun's chair was lowered. He drew in his oars, laid them safely in the bottom of the wherry and held the chair steady. From above the sight was somewhat comical as Mrs Fry slipped the ropes of the chair over her bonneted head and eased the narrow seat under her considerable bottom. But no one laughed, for she was generally respected among the women of Newgate, if not always appreciated, had gone to considerable effort to be ferried out to the ship and was putting herself at real risk using the bosun's chair. The women, hanging over the rail and cheering Mrs Fry on, applauded as the chair was hoisted up, sending her stout, cape-wrapped body twirling slowly and swinging from side to side like a roosting bat.

The rope was deftly snagged with the aid of a boat hook and Mrs Fry pulled in and deposited safely on the deck, nothing more askew than her bonnet, which she quickly straightened. Captain Holland greeted her with exaggerated courtesy, then stood at her side in silence while her lady friends were winched inelegantly up from the wherry. That achieved without incident, he rather stiffly invited them to his cabin for refreshments.

'Thank you very kindly, Captain,' Mrs Fry said in a refined but authoritative voice. 'Unfortunately I fear we cannot spare the time for social niceties. You sail on the morning tide, I understand? Then we would like to begin our work immediately. I'm sure you also have much still to do.' She gestured at the pair of trunks that had followed her companions up from the wherry. 'We have brought with us parting gifts for the women from the Society and we would like to deliver them personally. Just tokens, but we hope they will remind the women of all they have learnt under our tutelage during their time at Newgate.'

'Yes, of course. Lots to do. I understand,' Captain Holland said, relieved. He turned to his first mate. 'Mr Warren, get the prisoners below then see that Mrs Fry has everything she needs. Mrs Fry, would you care for Mr Downey to accompany you?'

'Thank you, no. Though I would appreciate a moment or two of your time, Mr Downey, before we depart, if I may?'

James touched the brim of his hat. 'Of course, madam, at your service.' He had a few things he wanted to ask Mrs Fry himself.

Sitting on their bunks, having been herded below by a bossy Mr Warren, the women watched Mrs Fry as, with some difficulty, she negotiated the companion ladder down onto the prison deck. Being a plain Quaker, her skirts were by no means full, but even so her costume was considerably more substantial than anything they wore and she hesitated on each rung, placing her smartly booted feet heedfully and gripping the rope tightly.

When she reached the bottom, she adjusted her cape, which had slid slightly sideways, and clapped her gloved hands twice, demanding and receiving attention.

'Good afternoon, ladies. I trust you have settled in?'

There was a chorus of 'yes, ma'ams' as she made her way down the aisle between the table and the bunks on one side of the deck, and back again up the other. Having done her 'rounds', she sat down. Above her a lamp swung gently, its smoky yellow light illuminating first one section of the cabin, then another. It also fell directly onto Mrs Fry's head, the shadow cast by her bonnet relieved only by the bright gleam of her eyes; the only clear lines the contours of her jowls and strong nose.

'You all know that some of you will not be returning to England,' she said frankly and loudly, her voice carrying to all corners of the deck. There were a few stifled sobs at that. 'But remember, the Lord goes with you, wherever you may travel, and wherever you may make your homes; He is your Saviour and is available to you every day upon this earth. But remember this, too: hard work, clean habits, honesty, moral fortitude and a contribution to society will encourage His spirit to work freely within you and to shine through you. A return to the poorly lit paths of yesterday, paths that have led you to this ship, which very soon is to take you far from your homes and loved ones, will surely see you once again lost in a spiritual wilderness and without hope. So, ladies, take these gifts we have for you, use them and enjoy them, and remember the lessons you have learnt.'

At that Mrs Fry's companions opened the trunks that had been laboriously hefted down the ladder by Mr Warren and his men and began to pass every woman a drawstring bag of black cloth.

Sarah looked inside hers. It contained a bible, several additional religious tracts, a comb, a piece of soap, and a square of felted wool folded over two needles, blue thread, white thread, a length of inexpensive ribbon and six buttons. She felt slightly annoyed by the gift, even though she could do with the comb and the soap. She would give the needlework things to Harrie, but had no intention whatsoever of opening the bible. She didn't take charity, had never asked for it and never expected it. She was also irritated by her response, which she knew was a churlish and ungrateful one.

Rachel peered over her shoulder. 'What did you get?'

Sarah showed her.

'That was nice of them, wasn't it?' Rachel sniffed her soap. 'What's that funny smell?'

'Palm oil,' Friday told her. 'It's marine soap. Lathers in salt water.'

'How do you know so much about being at sea?' Harrie asked.

Sarah laughed. 'Because she spends such a lot of time with sailors.'

'They talk to me,' Friday said. 'It's not all trousers down and skirts up, you know.'

'Oh, I never thought that,' Harrie replied quickly.

'Yes, you did,' Friday said, laughing herself now.

Sarah handed her sewing kit to Harrie. 'You know I'm not much use with a needle. If you do the sewing, I'll do the stealing.'

'S*arah*,' Harrie admonished.

'Har*rie*,' Sarah said back, grinning. She felt the weight of someone's gaze on her and turned to see Mrs Fry watching her. She smiled politely. No, she definitely wouldn't be opening her new bible.

The second trunk turned out to be crammed with pieces of cloth of various colours and lengths, with which, Mrs Fry informed them all, they could busy themselves during the voyage sewing clothes to wear when they arrived in New South Wales. She then asked them to join her in prayer and the singing of two or three spirit-raising psalms before she said goodbye to them all for the last time.

Sarah bowed her head, but she didn't pray. At her side Rachel did, mumbling away like the child she almost was and belting out the words to the psalms but staying nicely on key, enjoying herself. Harrie had a pretty singing voice, too. Friday didn't, and she sang — as she did everything — loudly. After a verse or two more, Friday's vocal efforts deteriorated even further. Sarah risked a quick glance at her; Friday stared resolutely ahead, refusing to meet her eye. Then came a wink so fleeting it almost wasn't there. The volume of Friday's voice increased a decibel or two and slipped off another half-key. Rachel began to giggle.

Mrs Fry's brows descended until they almost met in the middle, but she refrained — deliberately, Sarah suspected — from looking up from her psalm book. At the psalm's conclusion, Mrs Fry thankfully decided that two would suffice.

James waited politely until the waterman had struck out for the quay, then turned on his heel and returned to his cabin.

Mrs Fry had confirmed in general terms the impressions he'd already gained from his initial appraisal of his charges. The gaols only provided prisoners' basic details, such as place of birth, age, trade and marital status — and even the veracity of those plain facts couldn't always be relied upon — and a simple physical description of each prisoner, plus their crime, place of trial and sentence, so he appreciated any further knowledge he might glean from other sources. He would know his charges all too well by the time they landed at Sydney Cove, but it helped to learn as much as possible as *early* as possible.

He had first met Elizabeth Fry five years earlier, when he began superintending the ships transporting both female and male convicts. She had always been the person with whom to converse regarding the women, because of her frequent contact with them at Newgate. Not that they all came from Newgate — some were brought south from regional gaols and at least two ships per year sailed from Dublin — but many did.

She was a formidable woman, Elizabeth Fry, and without doubt an admirable one, though James was aware she had at times attracted criticism for wielding a political influence unbecoming to the fairer sex and for allegedly neglecting her duties as a wife and a mother. James didn't know whether her banker husband and seven children suffered from her dedication to charitable work or not, but he admired what she set out to achieve. She was a philanthropist and an evangelist and over the past twenty years had, among other things, introduced schooling to Newgate Gaol, scripture lessons, sewing and knitting, female matrons rather than predatory male gaolers, and these last-minute farewell gestures to transportees. She had also attempted to ban gaming, swearing, begging, drinking and anything that even hinted at immorality, issuing edicts that had not, as far as James could deduce by the time he encountered the prisoners, translated particularly effectively into reality. The schools, too, came and went, so did the handcrafts, though the matrons had remained a fixture.

Other theories about prison reform were finding favour now and these days Mrs Fry was facing troubles of her own. Her once wealthy husband had been declared bankrupt in 1828 and it was rumoured that the Society of Friends could no longer summon the charity to welcome the family. But her influence as an activist and a prison reformer had extended beyond the bounds of England, and she had published a book only two years earlier setting forth her opinions on the government of female prisoners, based on her experiences, so even if her social status had slipped somewhat in Quaker circles, she continued to be celebrated for her efforts, both in England and on the European continent. She would not be an easy woman to dislodge from the path she believed she had been chosen to follow.

He didn't consider himself to be a personal friend of Elizabeth Fry's, more of a colleague, but he had always found her forthcoming when it came to matters regarding the female convicts' welfare, which went some small way towards mitigating his herculean task.

This afternoon, for example, she'd had no hesitation in quite frankly pointing out which of his new charges might be expected to give trouble and which, in her opinion, could be helpful to him in various roles.

He unlocked the drawer in his desk and withdrew his copy of the ship's muster list, together with a foolscap journal. A gift from his wife Emily, it was bound in the new-fashioned cloth — fittingly, she had chosen a navy-blue colour — and stamped with his name in gold leaf. Initially he'd been quite reluctant to sully its pristine, cream pages with descriptions of boils and catarrh and diarrhoea, but he knew Emily meant him to use it in his work, and once he'd filled the first few pages with his admittedly not very legible handwriting, the spell had been broken.

He reached into the drawer again, retrieved his bottle of Indian ink, a steel nib and the carved bone nib holder that had also been a gift from Emily, and lined them up on his desk. Experience had proven that Mrs Fry was a sound judge of character, so when she said that Liz Parker and her coterie were likely to cause the most trouble aboard ship, having already succeeded in ruling the roost in the women's wing at Newgate, then they probably were. He opened the ink bottle, dipped his pen and wrote 'Liz Parker' on a fresh page. He wasn't surprised; the woman certainly looked the part. There was a particularly unattractive toby jug he'd recently seen depicting a character named 'Drunken Sal': a hefty, bulldog-faced woman sitting with her knees apart, a glass presumably of gin in her hand, her arm resting on her ample belly. James wondered only half in jest if the Parker woman had sat for Davenport, the makers.

He then penned the names of the prisoners he had observed keeping company with Liz Parker, and whom Elizabeth Fry had confirmed to be her closest associates: Louisa Coutts, Ruth Bowler, Beth Greenhill, Mary Ann Howells and Becky Hoddle. They were all, he recalled, young, whereas Parker herself was middle-aged. He checked the manifest — yes, she was thirty-five years old. He wondered what the attraction could be. Perhaps the younger women were in need of a mother-figure: if so, he doubted that

Liz Parker really was the most suitable candidate. Unsurprisingly, they had elected to mess together. He could attempt to split them up, he supposed, but to what real effect? They would only spread disorder among the rest of the prisoners, perhaps even managing to inspire rebellion. Or, away from Liz Parker's influence, would they settle down? It was a difficult decision. No, better to have them all together in one small group where he, and Josiah Holland, could keep a close watch on them.

He massaged the back of his neck, feeling the muscles there knotted beneath his fingers. Suffering tension already — and the ship hadn't even sailed out of the Thames! He was glad he had kept his hair short, though. He'd had to cut it during his last voyage after he'd caught head lice from the prisoners and had worn it that way since. Emily thought it very modern and said it made him look even more handsome, which made him smile, because he knew he wasn't a handsome man at all.

He rotated his shoulders to relax them and bent again over his journal. The other name Elizabeth Fry had given him was that of Friday Woolfe, which had also not surprised him. With her unusual height, buxom figure and that abundant copper hair, she was the sort of female a man could not fail to notice, but it was her behaviour that had really caught his attention. Mrs Fry had insisted that the girl's antics were every bit as disruptive as those of Liz Parker and her crowd, and they probably were, but James didn't think Friday Woolfe and Liz Parker really shared much else. Friday Woolfe was common and cheeky and very irreverent, but he could not see any malice in her. Perhaps he was being a fool.

In fact, he was. During her examination, he'd smelt gin on her breath and she had suggested to him, none too discreetly, that a deal might be struck in which he might have access to her personal charms throughout the voyage in exchange for medicinal alcohol. His face flaming, he'd declined her offer, which she'd apparently found very entertaining. He should have reported both matters to the captain — the alcohol on her breath and the offered bribe — but he hadn't. The girl had already suffered a night in one of the dreadful little cells in the hold and the ship hadn't even left Woolwich. If she was a habitual drunkard she had probably brought alcohol on board with her, but that would soon run out. The captain had decided not to search for contraband; after months of living in Newgate the women would be experts at concealment and to find it all would require virtually stripping the ship back to her framework. There would be the usual shenanigans when Friday Woolfe, and no doubt a number of the other women, attempted to elicit alcohol from the crew, but James expected this. Many prisoners he'd superintended had demonstrated an unhealthy fondness for alcohol, particularly the gin they called Blue Ruin, which, as far as he could determine, did in fact ruin them. But the crew had been threatened with severe punishment if they obliged and the hatch to the prison deck would be locked every night, so their attempts would be in vain.

Friday Woolfe had come aboard in a group of four and they seemed determined to maintain closed ranks to the extent that they had resisted the addition of two extra women to their mess and had only got away with it because the numbers had worked in their favour. But James expected that would change once the *Isla* reached Portsmouth and the Bristol prisoners embarked. Josiah Holland seemed very fond of his precisely calculated shipboard schedules — and they were, truth be told, the only way to maintain any semblance of order — and if he wanted six women per mess, James was confident there would *be* six women per mess.

Included in Friday Woolfe's quartet was Rachel Winter, so at least, in Woolfe, the young Winter girl would have a protector of sorts. The other two in the group were also interesting characters. During her initial medical examination, Sarah Morgan had struck James as somewhat sly — indeed, almost unnervingly intelligent. In fact, at the conclusion of the examination he'd been left with the uncomfortable sensation that *he'd* been interviewed by *her*, and it had been most disconcerting. She had very dark eyes and he had deliberately avoided looking into them — except for when he'd shone his torch at her retinae — because of an irrational notion that she would know what he was thinking. She was smart, very observant and, of the four, he suspected, most likely to be a professional criminal, a probability borne out by the fact that this was her second conviction.

She had been in reasonable health — undernourished and in need of sustained applications of sunlight and fresh air, but otherwise sound. The smarter inmates usually were the most hale. It was a sad fact that the mentally and physically unsound fared worst in the gaols, as often did the youngest, unless they found themselves a benefactor, as Rachel Winter had apparently managed to do.

Despite being felons, the prisoners he saw weren't all criminals, in James's opinion. For some, certainly, crime was a chosen way of life, but he was convinced from his dealings with both male and female convicts that not everyone who had the misfortune to find themselves in front of a judge had made a conscious decision to set out on a lifetime of criminal endeavour. The majority were ordinary labouring people, and many of them in ordinary — badly paid — employment. They broke the law because they couldn't manage the rent, or feed their children, or repay their debts, or because the interminable misery of their lives drove them to make bad decisions.

Harriet Clarke, he had decided, was an example of that brand of convict. Her crime had been to steal a bit of cloth and thread, but up until that point she had evidently been a law-abiding girl, supporting her family working for a sempstress and hoping only for a better life for them all. Or so she had told him, and he believed her. Why shouldn't he? She clearly didn't have connections to any underworld criminals, she spoke well, could read and write and had nice manners, and she seemed mortified by what she had done. It had been a stupid, impetuous act, but he knew she could never otherwise have saved the money to fulfil her plans and, despite being a pretty girl, she probably couldn't have married either — or, rather, co-habited, the arrangement many of the labouring poor seemed happy with — not with a sick mother and three young siblings in tow. Despite his natural distaste for her hopefully momentary lapse into sin, he felt sorry for her, which was why he had decided to choose her to be one of his hospital attendants. She struck him as being capable and steady; and the experience might boost her chances of securing a better assignment when she reached New South Wales.

James had also considered giving one of the positions to Rachel Winter, if only so he could keep an eye on her. The thought of what might follow should any of Holland's crew take a fancy to her really did make him feel uneasy. But, frankly, she was barely more than a child and had seemed so flighty when he'd talked to her he didn't think she would be suitable at all. He would have to rely on her messmates to look out for her. He had observed the way they hovered about her — like three mother ducks sharing one duckling — and suspected she would be as well chaperoned as she possibly could be.

In his journal he drew a line under Rachel Winter's name, rolled his blotter over the ink, waited for it to dry, then closed the cover. All that was left for him to do now was organise the prisoners' bathing and laundry session in the morning — it would be their first and last using fresh water, as only salt water would be available for bathing after they set sail — and check for the final time that the provisions had been stowed correctly and would not deteriorate during the voyage. Then he had to oversee the arrival and storage of his two special orders: one of medicinal leeches and the other of half a dozen bolts of coarse muslin for the women's menstrual needs. Tomorrow evening he would introduce himself to the handful of free passengers when they embarked and after that he would go ashore and say goodbye, once again, to his poor, patient, long-suffering wife.

Seven

On the day before the *Isla* sailed from Woolwich, three things happened: the women of Newgate were ordered to bathe thoroughly; two disembarked in a somewhat memorable fashion; and the *Isla*'s six paying passengers came aboard.

Although the ship's upper deck had still not yet been completely squared away, James Downey ordered that a framework of canvas be erected to screen off an area about ten feet square. Inside this enclosure Mr Meek and Amos Furniss placed two wooden tubs and sloshed into each six inches of water heated on the galley's huge cast-iron stove. Captain Holland then ordered all sailors to work below deck, after which James instructed the mess captains to bring their women up one mess at a time.

Standing within the confines of the canvas cubicle fully dressed, her arms across her chest as though she were already naked, Harrie squinted up into the *Isla*'s rigging, not trusting that there wasn't a sailor hiding up there, peeking down at them like a prurient, overgrown squirrel.

Friday, who already had her boots and stockings off, tested the water with her foot. 'It's actually warm! It's lovely.' Suddenly her smile dissolved. She turned to the others and said quietly, 'Don't undress. Don't move.'

Casually, she bent and picked up a scrubbing brush, stepped towards the edge of the canvas enclosure and hurled it over the other side. There was a thump and a clatter, followed by a barrage of swearing, then Friday ducked out of the cubicle and took off, her bare feet pounding across the deck.

She was back a few minutes later. 'That dirty bloody Furniss cove was peeking through the gap. I've told Downey. Furniss'll be up before the master — you'll see.'

'Are you sure no one else will creep up on us?' Harrie asked nervously, peering around at the cubicle screens as though expecting to see the entire crew lined up outside.

'I am,' Friday replied confidently. 'Downey's having a go at the tars now.'

She pulled her calico blouse over her head, yanked her skirt to her feet, wriggled out of her shift and stepped into the tub.

Everything about her was spectacular, Harrie thought enviously, trying not to look. Even her muscular tattooed arms had a garish sort of beauty about them and if her lovely white skin was marred in places by the purple smudge of healing sores, well, everyone had those. The pattern of fine silver lines on her gently curved belly, though, could only have been caused by one thing — Harrie had seen them often enough on her own mother's stomach.

Rachel shrugged out of her clothes. 'I'm having a good long soak. We won't be getting fresh water to bathe in after this, will we, Friday?'

'Wouldn't think so.' Friday reached for a square of soap left on an upturned bucket and energetically began to make a lather in her hands, her full breasts jiggling.

'You're not,' Sarah said, hands on hips. 'You're to get in, wash, then get straight out. The other messes have to have a turn yet.'

Rachel, one foot in the tub and one out, glowered. 'You're not my mother.'

'No, and thank Christ for that. But I am the mess captain — you elected me — so do as you're told and hurry up.'

Rachel put both feet in the tub and stood there, sulking. Her white-blonde hair, a few shades lighter than her sparse bush, fell almost to her waist above round white buttocks. Her belly was flat and her breasts small and upturned. She looked like some sort of grumpy little water nymph. Harrie, averting her eyes, passed her the soap.

'Come on, Harrie, hurry up and get in.' Sarah stripped off and stepped in beside Friday. 'Christ, it's not *that* warm. Not when you get your clobber off.'

'I'm not.' Harrie looked down at her boots.

'Not what?'

'Getting in.'

Friday stopped lathering her hair. 'Why not? It's your last chance of a decent wash for months. Not to mention your first. What's the matter?'

Harrie risked an overt glance at the nude bodies of her three friends and bit her lip. If they were animals instead of girls, Friday would be a tiger, Rachel would be a new fawn and dark, slender Sarah would probably be something like an otter or a mink. Harrie strongly suspected she herself might be a hedgehog. She'd never been naked in front of them before. She'd never been naked in front of *anyone*, except her mother when she was a small child.

'I don't really feel that grubby,' she lied.

'Well, you smell it,' Sarah said. 'Come on, we won't look. We promise.'

Harrie sighed: she knew she stank. She nodded reluctantly and waited until they'd turned away, then took a deep breath, undressed quickly and stepped into the tub next to Rachel. She looked down at herself, at her white body and her nipples sticking out like acorns because she was cold, and closed her eyes with embarrassment.

'Oh, Harrie, you've a lovely little figure,' Sarah said gently. 'Really pretty.'

Harrie's eyes flew open: they were all staring at her.

Friday grinned and handed her the soap. 'What's so special about you anyway, Madam Modest?'

Harrie couldn't think of a valid answer. She started to laugh, which turned into a squawk of alarm when the cubicle's canvas opening was whipped aside.

It was Matilda Bain. 'Yous are to hurry up. We want our baths,' she said, and let the canvas drop again.

It took almost four hours and twenty tub refills for all the women and children to bathe — longer than James Downey had expected. Those who refused had to be threatened with suspended rations until they succumbed. Once at sea, the prisoners would perform a quick, daily ablution on deck using a bucket of sea water, but he'd insisted they bathe properly this once to rid themselves of the filth and vermin of the gaol before they set sail. Laundering of their civilian clothes would have to wait now until they were underway as Holland's crew could not put to sea tomorrow with the deck festooned with drying washing, and it could not be taken below in a wet state, where it would immediately sprout mould.

Much to their disappointment, the women were sent to their berths when the last of the *Isla*'s passengers were rowed out to her mooring, hoisted aboard via the bosun's chair and installed in the four available cabins. James Downey, however, and an inwardly grudging Captain Holland, who couldn't care less about paying passengers as long as they *did* pay, were on deck to receive them.

The Reverend Octavius Seaton, a minister with the Church Missionary Society, came up first. A fleshy man of medium height with red cheeks that looked scraped rather than shaved, he dismounted inelegantly from the chair and staggered about briefly in response to the rolling of the *Isla*'s deck. Taking pity on him, James held his elbow in a steadying grip as they waited for Mrs Seaton to appear. She was even more stout than her husband, and required the assistance of two crewmen to get off the chair, though James noted that for such a round woman she had an improbably neat waist. This was surprising as he had always assumed that vanity — including the overt use of corsets — was frowned upon among clergy in the CMS.

Reverend and Mrs Seaton's daughters followed: two rather attractive, cinnamon-haired girls of thirteen and eleven, each spinning around in the chair and giggling, much to their mother's disapproval. Introduced to James and the captain as Eudora and Geneve respectively, they stood on the deck, the brims of their bonnets catching the wind, eyes bright, gazing excitedly about.

Next to board was a young man who swung agilely off the bosun's chair and offered a hand first to Josiah Holland then James, introducing himself as Matthew Cutler. He was smartly if not flashily dressed in light-coloured trousers, white shirt and a well-cut frock coat with matching waistcoat; he looked, James thought, vaguely uncomfortable, as though the whole outfit were new and he wasn't accustomed to wearing it. He had rather exuberant sandy hair, bright blue eyes and a ready smile. James liked him immediately.

The final passenger to board was Gabriel Keegan, the last entry on the ship's manifest. At twenty-six he was a year older than Matthew Cutler, tall and athletic in build and possessed what James expected women would regard as striking looks in the form of dark eyes, a strong nose and jaw and black hair. He also evidently favoured dressing in the style made fashionable by Beau Brummell, but James saw no reason to hold that against him. For his first afternoon aboard the *Isla*, Keegan was wearing white trousers tapered at the ankles and disappearing into square-toed shoes, a smart linen shirt with a standing collar, a silk cravat tied in an intricate arrangement, a cutaway coat with a shawl collar and patterned waistcoat, and a rather tall top hat, which James suspected would end up in the sea if Mr Keegan wasn't vigilant. Costume aside, Gabriel Keegan seemed a positive sort, cheerfully introducing himself to the crew and offering to help carry luggage to the cabins as it was winched aboard.

James spent the next hour assisting the new passengers to settle into their cabins. The two single men seemed happy enough with their tiny quarters: each measured roughly six feet by five and was fitted with a single narrow bunk bed, a console on which to write that opened to reveal a mirror and wash basin, a chair, shelves and a porthole.

Mrs Seaton, on the other hand, was horrified, though the other two cabins were a little larger, declaring that she couldn't possibly be expected to live in such cramped quarters for up to four months. Matters weren't improved when Reverend Seaton announced, clearly without prior discussion with his wife, that he intended to appropriate one of the two for himself, as he required the extra space to meditate, write sermons and spread out his scriptures. At this, Mrs Seaton looked distinctly mutinous and the daughters didn't look much happier, so James retired and left them to it.

When he returned to request they attend the hospital for their medical examinations, necessary even though they were free passengers, he noted that the matter seemed to have been settled, and that Mrs Seaton and her girls had indeed settled into one cabin together while the reverend had magnanimously taken the smaller of the two available for himself. The girls, James noted, would be sleeping in officers' hammocks strung from the ceiling of their quarters — quite a good idea, actually, as, in his experience aboard ship, hammocks were more practical and comfortable than a bed.

The medical examinations revealed nothing unexpected or alarming. Reverend Octavius Seaton, aged thirty-nine, had the physical constitution of a man ten years older: he was overweight, had gout and a skin complaint in the order of psoriasis around the elbows, knees and groin area but was otherwise in reasonable health. He had, he told James chattily during the examination, high hopes of rising through the church's hierarchy, seeing himself perhaps as Samuel Marsden's right-hand man in the not-too-distant future, now that his reverence was getting on in years, even if that meant having to go somewhere Godforsaken like New Zealand for a little while, like poor Henry Williams had. He understood, of course, that his goals were of a magnitude that could not be achieved overnight, but in the meantime there were souls to be saved, good works to be done and plenty of acreage to be acquired in this wonderful new land of opportunity. Indeed, James said, and made a note to prepare two and half drachms of chrysophanic acid with ten drops of oil of bergamot in a simple ointment for Reverend Seaton to apply to his private parts.

Hester Seaton wasn't as scaly as her husband, but she was slightly fatter. On her, though, the flesh was marginally more appealing, lending her otherwise unremarkable features a sort of pillowy pink bloom, further enhanced by her abundant caramel brown hair, of which — again unlike a good missionary — she seemed very proud. She was thirty-three, she declared, and flushed and simpered when James asked whether there was any likelihood she might be expecting a confinement.

'Oh, no, my child-bearing years are well behind me,' she replied, giggling as though James had told a particularly clever joke.

James wondered why, if she was only thirty-three. One of the women he'd examined the other day who would deliver during the voyage was thirty-seven.

'Are there any physical matters you have concerns about?'

'No, I've always been blessed with good health.' A shadow passed across Mrs Seaton's face and she looked down at her chubby hands. 'Our first child died, when he was only five months old. George Edwin, we named him. He contracted whooping cough.'

'I'm very sorry to hear that, Mrs Seaton,' James said. He was, too, but it was a rare family that hadn't experienced the death of an infant, no matter its social rank.

He examined Mrs Seaton's eyes, ears and mouth, noting she was missing several back teeth and had evidence of gum disease, which wasn't at all uncommon, and palpated her limbs, belly and internal organs. Nothing was amiss, except for the extra weight she was carrying.

'You do seem to be in good health, Mrs Seaton, as you attest. I would suggest, however, that you take every opportunity to walk about the deck that presents itself.'

Hester Seaton took the hand James offered to assist her off the examination table. 'Why would that be, Mr Downey? Surely you are not suggesting that I need to be mindful of my figure?'

James couldn't tell if her question was posed in a jocular spirit or not. He suspected it wasn't. 'Not at all, Mrs Seaton. I'm advising all charges to exercise whenever possible, even those as hale as you clearly are. Enforced inertia can actually be very demanding on the constitution. Now, I assume you wish to chaperone your daughters during their examinations?'

Hester Seaton did. Both Eudora and Geneve were rudely healthy. Geneve had a slight cough, but it had come on only recently and Mrs Seaton thought it was nothing more than the result of a chill caught travelling in the coach down to London from their home town of Watford. James listened to Geneve's chest and agreed.

'If it worsens, or does not improve, tell me and we'll begin a course of treatment.'

Geneve had seen the jars where James kept his leeches, their currently pin-thin bodies pressed slimily against the glass, and her face paled slightly. 'Will it be leeches?' she asked almost in a whisper. 'I don't like leeches.'

'No, no, it will be an oral medicine and plasters, something of that sort,' he said hurriedly. 'Now, girls, I would like a moment alone again to speak with your mother.'

Mrs Seaton sat with her eyebrows raised in polite interest until her daughters had gone.

James decided she had probably seen enough of the world to appreciate a direct approach. 'Forgive me for saying so, Mrs Seaton, but I couldn't help noticing that Eudora has reached a stage in her physical development that suggests she is no longer a child.'

'*Physically* she has become a young woman, yes,' Mrs Seaton said warily. 'But she is still a child at heart.'

'Of course, and so she should be. But she is an attractive girl and so is her sister, and we — and a number of perhaps unprincipled sailors — are about to embark upon a long sea voyage. It pains me to say this, but I strongly recommend that you accompany them at all times.'

Hester Seaton's mouth puckered in distaste: she obviously knew to what he was referring.

'Confine them to the foredeck during the day, unless you are with them, and certainly do not allow them to leave your cabin at night.'

'Of course not!'

James sighed and wondered how best to couch what he wanted to convey without causing offence. 'It isn't just the crewmen, Mrs Seaton. Some of the prisoners may not take kindly to the sight of two smartly dressed young ladies promenading about. They can, on occasion, be … unpredictable.'

Hester Seaton brightened. 'Oh, I do understand, Mr Downey. I have studied the phenomenon of women in prison at some length, you know, and I have a copy of Mrs Fry's marvellous *Observations*. Have you read it?'

'Er, yes, I have.'

Mrs Seaton clasped her hands and raised her eyes to the ceiling. '"Punishment is not for revenge, but to lessen crime and reform the criminal." A wonderful quote of hers. I use it often. And I was *delighted* to discover that we were to sail with an entire *ship*load of female convicts because, you see, it has always been my ambition to work with poor wretches less fortunate than myself, and now it seems as though God has steered me directly onto my chosen path. "Oh Lord, may I be directed what to do and what to leave undone." Another quote from Mrs Fry — and such a very apt one, in my case!'

James was slightly nonplussed; in his view Eudora and Geneve's safety was a far weightier topic than their mother's philanthropic ambitions. But then Mrs Seaton — presumably — didn't know sailors, or indeed convicts, like he did.

'That's very commendable, Mrs Seaton, and I'm sure the prisoners will benefit from any contribution you might make to their welfare during the voyage. However, I do reiterate that your daughters' safety is paramount.' James had a sudden, excellent idea. 'Perhaps you could employ one of the women, one of the younger, better educated ones, as a companion for the girls?'

Hester Seaton looked at him, unable to disguise a faint expression of horror. 'One of the convicts, you mean? With my girls? In our cabin? Oh, no, I don't think so.' She stood in a rustle of skirts. 'Thank you, Mr Downey. Good day.'

Matthew Cutler and Gabriel Keegan were, as James had suspected they would be, fine physical specimens and in the best of health. Matthew, twenty-five years old, was bound for a position with the New South Wales Government Architect in Sydney, and very much, he told James, looking forward to it. Gabriel Keegan had secured a place with the Office of the Surveyor General, also in Sydney, and James gained the impression that he wasn't as pleased with the prospect of his new life in the colony as Matthew. He volunteered no explanation regarding the reasons for his emigration, however, and James didn't ask. Otherwise, James found him intelligent, good-humoured and engaging. Barring the possibility of unfortunate shipboard accidents, or perhaps severe seasickness, he expected to see neither man back in his hospital during the voyage.

By the time the convict women came up on deck for their evening exercise, the mess captains, who had been to the galley to collect supper, had breathlessly spread stories involving fine-looking gentlemen in silk toppers promenading the foredeck, and beautiful little princesses flitting about. There was, therefore, great curiosity and speculation regarding who the paying passengers were and what they were like. However, the foredeck's only occupant was Amos Furniss, the whites of his eyes shining in the growing gloom as he smoked his pipe, coiled ropes and winked at the women.

Rachel was deeply disappointed. 'You saw them, Sarah, didn't you? Were they really princesses?'

Sarah said, 'Of course they weren't. They were just ordinary girls, a couple of years younger than you.'

'What about the gentlemen in the silk toppers?'

Fed up already with the gossip, Sarah snapped, 'Who cares what their hats were made of, Rachel? They're just folk. And not very grand ones, either, if they can only get passage on a convict ship.'

Rachel looked hurt. 'I only want to know what they're like.'

'Why? You won't be talking to them. None of us will. You heard what the captain said. No fraternising.'

Friday, leaning against the ship's rail, drew on her pipe and puffed a cloud of smoke in Sarah's face. 'Don't be a bitch, Sarah. She's only having a little daydream.'

'Well, daydreaming's —' Sarah stopped. 'Did you hear that? A splash?' She turned sharply and peered down into the murky, scum-topped water of the Thames.

'A mermaid?' Rachel rushed to have a look.

They watched intently as choppy little waves slapped against the *Isla*'s shadowed hull twenty feet below. The stink of the fouled river rose to meet them, a broken barrel and other rubbish from the surrounding ships bobbed languidly past, and not far away a wherry with two people aboard rowed in a slow, wide circle, almost invisible in the descending darkness.

Harrie coughed on Friday's smoke. 'You must have —'

They all screamed as a white face burst up out of the water directly below them, arms stiff and outstretched, fingers grasping. Then, just as quickly, it was gone again.

'*Man overboard!*' Friday shouted. '*Oi! Man overboard!*'

A sudden crush as everyone on deck crowded to the rail to see, shoving and elbowing for the privilege, then the thud of running feet. First Mate Warren forced his way through.

'A face in the water, down there!' Friday exclaimed, one hand pointing, the other pressed over her thumping heart. 'Someone drowning!'

'A woman,' Sarah insisted. 'I saw her hair.'

Silas Warren's gaze shifted from where the face had emerged in the water to the previously circling wherry, now carrying three passengers and pulling swiftly away towards a point on the right bank beyond the dockyard. He swore, then barged his way back out of the crowd.

Harrie reached after him, clutching at his jacket. 'You have to help her, she's drowning!'

Warren shrugged her off and kept going.

'*You can't leave her!*' Harrie shrieked.

But Mr Warren was bellowing orders now: the ship's bell sounded and the deck suddenly swarmed with crew. Rattling and clanking, the quarterboat was lowered with a hard, flat splash and four men, descending the ropes like monkeys, dropped into it and snatched up the oars. Mr Warren, yelling from the rail, pointed vigorously and they set off, pulling hard, rowing alongside the *Isla*'s hull. Then they dug in the oars, slowed the boat and stared down into the black water. On deck, barely anyone moved, transfixed with horrible fascination on the scene below.

'Oh, she's drowned, she must have drowned,' Harrie said in a muffled voice, her hands over her mouth.

Finally, after what felt like an age, one of the crew reached out with a boat hook and snagged a barely discernible shape beneath the water. As it rose to the surface it transformed from a clump of dark rags into something possessing a head and limbs: the sailor settled his big hand on the pale throat, glanced up at Mr Warren and shook his head. A moan of shock rolled through the women.

The men in the boat dragged the dead woman aboard by her skirts. Her arms and legs flopped and her nether regions became exposed in the manoeuvre, prompting angry cries from the watching women.

It was too much for Captain Holland, already appalled by the first escape ever attempted on his watch. To have a prisoner drown was bad enough, but for another to actually slip over the side and abscond right beneath his very nose was unthinkable. Not only did it reflect on his prestige as a ship's master, but he would lose the fees the government was paying him to transport both women.

'*Get them all below!*' he barked at Mr Warren.

The *Isla* sailed the next morning, the third day of May, on the outgoing tide. Towed a short distance until the day's buffeting wind filled her unfurled sails, she tacked steadily downriver until Gravesend was nothing more than a smudge on the horizon behind her. The women, locked below on Captain Holland's orders, were bitter and morose, lamenting the loss of the only home most of them had known.

The night before gossip had spread through the prison deck like the Great Fire about Ruth Bowler and Mary Ann Howells, the women who had gone overboard. It had been Mary Ann who had drowned — her sheet-shrouded body had been taken off the *Isla* before their departure — but Ruth Bowler had clearly got away, and her triumph had given the women such a fillip, their cheers and singing reaching the captain's ears as he sat in his cabin and fumed. He'd ordered the quarterboat after the mysterious wherry and alerted the authorities at the dockyard, but of course it had been long gone, vanished among the river traffic if not already ashore, the escaped prisoner Ruth Bowler with it. She would be found eventually, he expected, and hopefully hanged this time for her sins, but what an infuriating occurrence — and on his last mission transporting convicts! They could stay locked below until the ship was in the middle of the North Atlantic ocean as far as he was concerned.

Equally irritated by the escape was Liz Parker, who'd had no inkling at all of Ruth Bowler and Mary Ann Howells' plans. They'd sworn allegiance to her, vowing to stand by her come what may, and running off like that just served to make her look stupid. They hadn't even been liked by the rest of the prisoners, Liz knew damn well they hadn't, and now Ruth was being touted as a heroine and Mary Ann a poor, tragic martyr. Well, the silly bitch couldn't swim — of course she'd drowned! And now she, Liz, was left with only three genuinely loyal souls in her crew. She would have to start recruiting again, bugger it, or she'd lose the balance of power and that whore Friday Woolfe would be lording it all over the prison deck. It'd be intolerable.

And two women down meant two women fewer to watch over the money she'd stolen from Woolfe's crew. It already wasn't easy organising the roster to ensure there was always someone on guard at the bunk: Woolfe and her girls were constantly watching and sniffing around. She hadn't made one of her crew dig around in that disgusting crapper just to have the dosh pinched back again.

Now, though, the women were quiet again as seasickness took hold. Around them the cocoon of the *Isla*'s hull creaked and squeaked as she tacked down the Thames; above them came thuds, bangs and shouts as the crew ran across the deck attending to sails and securing ropes.

Friday, who really had thought she might be spared because she hadn't felt even a flutter while the *Isla* had been bobbing at anchor, tried desperately to pretend she was feeling well, but when she began to yawn repeatedly, her mouth filling with spit, she knew she was in for a rough time. She'd opened the scuttlehole near their bunk and peered through it, hoping the sight of land would stabilise her roiling gut, but the giddying rise and fall of the distant riverbank only made her feel worse. She held on as long as she could, but finally blurted, 'Harrie! Bucket!'

Harrie lunged for a slops pail and whipped it over to Friday, who sat on the end of the bunk, feet on the floor, knees apart, bucket between them, and threw up what appeared to be several days' worth of food while Harrie held her hair out of the way.

'Phew.' Rachel fanned her own notably pale face. 'That smells of gin.'

Friday choked up another surge of vomit, letting go a fart at the same time. Coughing and giving a great, epiglottis-rattling sniff, she hoicked and spat into the bucket.

'Ever the lady,' Sarah remarked.

Harrie smoothed back Friday's hair. 'Better?'

'No.' Friday lay back on the bunk, then sat up again, looking wretched. 'God, it doesn't matter whether I lie down or sit, I feel foul.'

'Are you seasick or is it the gin horrors?' Sarah asked.

'Oh, who cares.'

Harrie placed her hand on Friday's sweating forehead. 'Shall I ask Mr Downey to give you something?'

Friday groaned and lay down again. 'No, just let me die.'

She wasn't alone in her suffering. At least a third of the women were prostrate on their bunks and the air smelt rank, the sharp stink of vomit enough to encourage those not seasick to part with the contents of their stomachs. James Downey had started visiting the prison deck every few hours to monitor the condition of his charges: so far no one was ill enough to be admitted to the hospital — and he hadn't expected that anyone would be, as the *Isla* had not even encountered open water yet — but that time would surely come.

Still, there was no real need for them to be locked below. During a heated exchange that could be heard by most of the crew, he'd quarrelled with Josiah Holland to let the women out, arguing that to keep them below for such a length of time was inhumane and that no one was likely to attempt escape now that the *Isla* was under full sail and approaching the Thames estuary. The captain, conceding to himself that it would perhaps be unreasonable to continue to pander to his own dented pride at the expense of the remainder of his human cargo, and mollified by the fact that they had made such good time downriver, relented and suggested to James that the hatch to the prison deck could now be unlocked. James, refraining from rolling his eyes, agreed it was an excellent idea and rushed off to do it himself before the captain changed his mind.

By the time the women came up on deck the sinking sun behind them had gilded the tips of the waves a dull gold and the final stretch of the Thames curved ahead before it widened into the estuary.

'Where are we?' Rachel said, gazing across the water, her hand above her eyes like an intrepid explorer. Friday burped loudly, slumped over the rail and was sick again.

'I don't know,' Harrie said, patting Friday's back. 'I've never been out of London.'

'I don't feel any better up here than I did below,' Rachel complained. 'Do you not feel ill? Lord, I do,' she added, and gave a sharp retch.

Harrie shook her head. 'No, I don't, sorry. Tuck your hair behind your ears, sweetie, just in case.'

Sarah took Rachel's arm and led her to the rail, where Rachel leant over and vomited convulsively. Holding on to Rachel's apron ties, Sarah said to Harrie, 'Don't say sorry just because you're not seasick. You're always saying sorry. Stop it. You've the least to apologise for out of all of us.'

Harrie opened her mouth, then shut it again.

Friday straightened and wiped her face on her apron.

'*Fri*day, that will smell of sick now,' Harrie scolded.

'Don't think it's going to matter soon.' In the dying light Friday's face, coated with a thin sheen of sweat despite the brisk breeze coming off the river, glimmered a ghostly white.

'Mr Downey says to drink lots of fluids if you're vomiting,' Harrie said. '*Not* alcohol,' she added hastily.

Sarah, who, like Harrie, did not feel unwell, said, 'I wonder what we're getting for supper?'

Friday threw up again.

During the night, the *Isla* sailed out into the Thames estuary and, by the time the sun rose the following day, was heading into the unforgiving North Sea. Of the one hundred and twenty-two convict women and children aboard, only eleven did not become seasick.

When James Downey came looking for Harrie, she was tending to Friday and Rachel, both prostrate in the bunk, horribly ill. Sarah, watching, sat very still at the long table, pale and sweaty, holding on to counteract the long, plunging roll of the ship, doing her best to pretend she wasn't finally feeling sick.

'How are they?' he asked, and ducked his head to peer in at them in the dim light.

Harrie felt embarrassed because the entire deck smelt eye-wateringly of sick and worse, and there were women everywhere in various states of undress. She knew they probably didn't care, especially while they felt so ill, but she wondered if Mr Downey might.

Rachel let out a pathetic little moan. 'Can you not give us something to make us feel better? Please?'

Friday simply covered her white, sweating face with her arm.

James shook his head regretfully. 'There is no cure for seasickness, I'm afraid. Drink as much water as you can manage. You'll find your sea legs soon.'

'Will they, sir?' Harrie whispered when he straightened up again.

'I expect so. Most people do. The first bout is always the worst.' James moved her a short distance down the aisle. 'I must say you look remarkably hale.'

His comment sounded to Harrie like an accusation and she felt the familiar heat born of guilt creep across her face.

'You're not feeling sick at all?'

Harrie shook her head.

'Well, that's good news, isn't it?' James said. 'Because I require someone to assist me in the hospital. I thought you might be rather suitable, especially as you're not currently indisposed.'

'No, thank you,' Harrie replied. 'I'd rather stay here and look after my friends.'

Realising what she'd said, or, more critically, to whom she'd said it, she clapped her hands over her mouth.

James frowned. 'I don't think you understand, Harriet. That wasn't an invitation. I'm telling you that you will be working for me in the hospital. I need someone with steady hands, a quiet disposition and her wits about her. I believe that is you. You can be of more assistance in the hospital helping with the infants and the seriously ill than you can here. Now, follow me please.'

Her face flaming, Harrie did. She followed James up the ladder and staggered across the waistdeck, where, wrestling with her skirts, she was buffeted and shoved about by the harsh, rain-seeded wind snapping the sails overhead, then down another hatch into the hospital. James pointed out that the prison and hospital were actually connected by a door in the bulkhead dividing them, to provide patient access on occasions when using the ladders was impractical, but kept locked by two hefty deadbolts on the hospital side. There were only two sets of keys: James held one of them; Captain Holland the other.

The hospital certainly smelt better than the prison deck, though the odour of vomit was still detectable. There was already someone there helping: a woman Harrie didn't know but had seen before often enough. She was holding a baby, patting it briskly as it mewled and spewed onto a strategically placed square of cloth draped over her shoulder.

'Do you two know each other?' James asked as he brushed rain off his coat.

'I know her,' the other woman said. 'It's Harrie Clarke, isn't it?'

Harrie nodded.

Caught off guard, James laughed. 'Harrie? Is that what they call you?'

Harrie felt herself reddening again. 'Yes, sir, sometimes.'

James silently debated the issue of protocol for a moment, then said, 'Actually, I'd rather you didn't call me "sir". "Mister" is fine, if you have to call me anything, all right?'

Harrie nodded yet again, feeling as though her head might be about to fall off. But she would nod all day for the next month if it made up for the terrible, rude, selfish thing she had said before. Mr Downey was right — he couldn't look after all the little children by himself. But, oh, were the others all right? Sarah said she wasn't sick, but she was and just wouldn't admit it; Harrie knew she'd soon be throwing up as violently as the others. And she had gone off and left them and they were family now, sisters, and you didn't just go off and leave family like that when they needed help. You did everything you possibly could for them. Everything.

Alerted by the woebegone expression on her normally pleasant face that Harrie wasn't very happy, James said, 'I apologise: that was uncalled for. How would you prefer to be addressed? As Harriet, or as Harrie?'

Harrie blinked, completely flustered by an apology from the sort of person who normally would never even think to say sorry to the likes of her. 'Um, oh, Harrie. Thank you.'

'Well, then, Harrie, this is Lil Foster.'

Lil nodded, her hand not missing a beat as she kept up a gentle rhythmic paddling on the baby's swaddled bottom. 'You're in

Friday Woolfe's crew. I saw you in Newgate. What are you on the boat for?'

'Shoplifting. Seven years,' Harrie said, embarrassed to be confessing her crime in front of Mr Downey, even though he knew about it, but accustomed by now to telling other women why she was being transported. For a strange, disjointed moment it felt as though Mr Downey were the one on the wrong side of the bars, not her and Lil.

'Fancy. You wouldn't think so to look at you.'

Harrie was getting quite sick of hearing that. Perhaps she should knock out her front teeth and get a few tattoos. 'And you?' She didn't really care what Lil Foster had done, but knew it was the convention to ask.

'Highway robbery, life.'

'Really?' Harrie was quite impressed. Lil didn't look the type, either. She looked ... motherly ... and to be in her early thirties. She didn't say it, however, because no doubt Lil was sick of hearing *that*. 'Highway robbery' usually conjured in the public imagination infamous Dick Turpin and Sixteen String Jack and the like, but it referred to theft of property from a traveller using any public road by one or more thieves on horseback. Lil's involvement could have been little more than waiting to carry the stolen goods to the pawn shop; she needn't have been the one brandishing the pistols and demanding, 'Stand and deliver!' Though you couldn't be sure of anything on God's green earth, Harrie was fast learning.

'They will survive, your friends,' James assured Harrie. 'Try not to worry about them. It is only seasickness and, as I said, it will pass. It's only the very young and those already physically indisposed who are really at risk. As you know I have advised that it is better managed above deck, where there is a view of the horizon. It helps to settle the stomach. But it seems that most prefer to languish below and I don't blame them. The weather is far from inviting. So we must wait until it eases. And when it does, the seasickness probably will, too. Until then, I'll need your help here in the hospital.'

James had brought in the sickest of the small children, three less than a year old and two more still in nappies, and two of the pregnant women who couldn't keep even water down. Harrie and Lil spent most of their time cleaning up sick and trying to get the patients to drink, because Mr Downey said it was very important, especially for the little ones because they dehydrated so rapidly.

Lil talked a lot but she worked hard as well and time passed quickly, and when Mr Downey told Harrie to have a break she went to check on Friday and Rachel and to pass on the surgeon's news that they would shortly be heading into the English Channel, where the seas would be likely to settle somewhat.

Sarah had forced herself to go on, wiping Friday's and Rachel's faces, giving them water, until finally she'd collapsed herself, dizzy, vomiting and really angry about succumbing. When Harrie found her slumped over the table, sick all over her skirt, she helped her out of her smelly clothes and dragged her into the bunk.

The seas did settle. Slightly. The ship changed direction with a great cracking and snapping of sails and a gentle tilt so that everything slid but didn't topple, then an hour or so later Harrie felt through the deck a different rhythm to the ocean and the *Isla* seemed to adjust her gait as she turned south to follow the coasts of Kent.

Eight

Those a little less sensitive to the rolling of the ship managed to throw off the worst effects of seasickness as the *Isla* picked up a fair nor-nor'-east wind and sailed past The Downs, Deal and Dover, then, still hugging the coast, Hastings, Eastbourne and Brighton. Captain Holland's intentions of managing his prisoners by employing a strict daily timetable, however, were in tatters, as half the women were still laid low. On the other hand, James Downey organised new rosters to facilitate the extra laundering of soiled bedding and clothing. As a result, the upper decks were daily festooned with drying blankets and items of clothing flapping stiffly in the wind, while mattresses were draped over everything, hampering Captain Holland's men while they worked. Resignedly, the captain held his tongue — it was always this way at the start of a voyage and in rough seas. You could expect little else from a ship packed to the gunwales with landlubbers.

They were not at ease, though, the convict women. They were distressed at being transported far from England, and the drowning of Mary Ann Howells had unsettled them even further. Her pale wraith had been seen floating just beneath the surface of the water on several occasions — and once even hovering some feet above it, level with the scuttleholes on the prison deck, imploring to be let in to rejoin her friends — and Matilda Bain had woken one night to the sound of her name being called by a thin, sorrowful voice beyond the *Isla*'s hull. Hysteria, Captain Holland muttered to James Downey, and James agreed, but a hysteria born of trepidation and despair, and so not entirely invalid.

On the seventh day of May, to the relief of most of those who sailed on her, the *Isla* dropped anchor at the Mother Bank off the Isle of Wight. There they harboured for five days while more provisions were brought on board and while they waited for the thirteen extra prisoners to arrive from Bristol gaol. Though it was not that the prisoners were late — it was because Captain Holland was early, having decided not to hang about at Woolwich.

Amos Furniss told Lil Foster, who had dark eyes and a proper, womanly figure, that the captain had only shoved off early from Woolwich merely because the winds had been favourable. He reasoned that if he shared privileged information with her, a lowly convict, she might feel beholden to him and let him take liberties. It was also another little strike in his private campaign against Josiah Holland, who had humiliated him once too often in front of the crew, and who'd appointed Silas bloody Warren first mate over Amos, even though Warren was younger and a less competent seaman.

Lil told Amos Furniss to bugger off. And, having not had the chance to say goodbye to her man and their children because of the captain's arbitrary decision to leave early, she passed on to everyone else Furniss's gossip. The mood below deck, therefore, was fairly volatile by the time the Bristol prisoners finally did arrive.

They were ferried by lighter over from Portsmouth and winched up one by one in the bosun's chair. The Newgate women, however, did not witness this as they had been sent below to clear the decks. Their humour had not been improved by the fact that Mr Downey had told them that, to make room for the thirteen extra prisoners, they could no longer spread out on the prison deck, some until now enjoying the luxury of only two to a bunk.

'I bet they're as rough as guts,' Friday said, cleaning under her toenails with one of her earrings. 'Bristol's a mean town.'

Harrie asked, 'Have you been there?'

Friday shook her head. 'It's a port city, though, isn't it? And I've known a lot of tars.'

'London's mean, too,' Sarah remarked. 'Can't see how Bristol can be any worse.'

'Different sort of mean,' Friday said, inspecting her feet. They looked like bleached prunes. Perhaps she'd go barefoot if the weather got warmer. She put her earring back in.

'Here they come,' Rachel said excitedly, as footsteps thumped overhead and a shadow blocked the hatchway.

One by one the women from Bristol descended the companion ladder backwards, bringing with them an assortment of bags, sacks, baskets and even several trunks. But when they reached the deck, instead of moving along the aisles, they waited, eyes darting about, taking in the Newgate contingent's silence and impassive stares. A sense of expectation swelled the air. No one moved; no one made a noise. Even the children were quiet.

'That's only twelve,' Rachel said in a whisper to Friday. 'There's supposed to be thirteen.'

But Friday was watching the ladder.

After what seemed suspiciously like a deliberately staged interval, a pair of smart, pale grey leather boots appeared on the top rung. As they stepped down, a heavy velvet skirt of dusky rose became visible, revealing a swish of petticoats as the wearer turned and deftly descended the ladder. Reaching the pool of sunlight at the bottom, she turned around again and paused, as though inviting everyone on the prison deck to take a good look at her.

She was tall, taller even than Friday, and very slender, the fine cut of her black grosgrain jacket emphasising her slim hips. Friday decided immediately she was either sick or liked being that thin:

she'd been in Bristol gaol but still possessed her finery, which meant she had money and could afford to eat if she wanted to.

Considered individually, the woman's facial features were a bit ordinary — a strong, crooked nose with a high bridge, curved lips and heavy-lidded, very dark eyes below plucked, arched brows. But combined, they somehow lent her a disconcerting sort of beauty. She wore kohl and lip stain, and her face was very white. Friday was putting her money on rice powder. Her hair, worn in heavy ringlets to her shoulders, gleamed like black jet, and on her head a squashy red velvet hat decorated with a white ostrich feather sat at a jaunty angle. A silk scarf was knotted around her throat and her fingers glittered with several large rings. She stared coolly back at the faces studying her, then, so suddenly that those near her jumped, she flicked open a black lace fan and flapped at the air in front of her face.

A child squeaked, 'Mam, who's that lady?' and was silenced by a muffled slap.

The Bristol women parted to let this last of their number through and the woman set off slowly down the aisle, hat in hand now to avoid crushing the feather against the low ceiling. Her gait already accommodating the roll of the ship, she looked left and right, peering into every berth and poking at mattresses with a long finger. Apparently transfixed, nobody stopped her, not even Liz Parker.

Bemused, Sarah said, 'What's she doing?' It came out quite loudly.

A Bristol prisoner cringed and touched a finger to her lips. 'Hush. She's deciding where she wants to sleep.'

Incredulous, Sarah exclaimed, 'What's wrong with one of the empty bunks?'

The girl flinched. 'Don't upset her! She'll go mad.'

Sarah and Friday exchanged a glance. Friday snorted. 'Who the hell does she think she is?'

The girl, noticeably pregnant and with something not quite right about her face, gave them a funny look. 'She doesn't think, she knows. That's Bella Jackson.'

'I've heard plenty about her,' Friday said, blowing a series of short, sharp smoke rings now that she was above deck, 'but I've never met her. Stupid thing to do, if you ask me.'

'What is?' Sarah could see Friday was annoyed.

'Putting her and Liz Parker on the same boat. Shit will fly.'

'But why?' Rachel asked. 'I've never even heard of Bella Jackson.'

'You wouldn't, shovelling cowshit in Guildford.' Rachel blinked, and Friday patted her hand. 'Sorry, love. That was mean. You know how Liz Fat-Arse Parker ran her own crooked little kingdom in Newgate and thinks she's going to keep on running it while we're at sea? Well, Bella Jackson ran a *real* kingdom before she was arrested, up in Birmingham. She was abbess of one of the busiest brothels, owned two or three more, not to mention a couple of dollyshops, and ran probably the biggest crew in the city. She had interests in gaming, broads, counterfeiting, all sorts of rackets. The watch have been after her for years. Very cunning article.'

'So what's she doing on a convict ship, then?' Sarah asked.

'I heard someone sold her up the river. I hadn't heard she'd be getting transported with us, though.'

'Perhaps it's a secret,' Rachel said, her eyes shining. 'Perhaps she's been sneaked on so no one can help her escape, like Ikey Solomon did.' Like most of England, she'd heard about the notorious criminal's daring escape from custody, aided by his father-in-law, on the way back from the Court of King's Bench, after which he'd apparently vanished into thin air.

Friday and Sarah looked at Rachel and Friday laughed. 'You know, you could be right about that.'

Rachel beamed.

'Is she from Birmingham originally?' Sarah said.

Friday shrugged. 'Nobody really knows. Apparently, she just sort of appeared there about ten years ago. Some say she hails from Bristol, some say Liverpool and others swear Cornwall.'

'You'd think it was Windsor Castle, the way she's carrying on,' Sarah said disparagingly.

Bella Jackson had commandeered two bunks, one above the other, her crew turfing out the original occupants. Within half an hour, a curtain had been erected right around the lower bunk, behind which Bella had disappeared, along with the trunks that belonged to her, without saying a word to anyone.

Two of the Bristol women had been allocated to join Friday, Rachel, Harrie and Sarah's mess, to make their numbers up to six. One was named Sally Minto, and the other, the pregnant girl, Janie Braine.

Janie appeared now, wearing her new prison outfit. The stiff apron stuck out over her belly, giving her the appearance of being eight months gone rather than the six she said she was.

She sat down on a barrel, knees apart, her face pale. 'Makes your tummy feel squiffy, doesn't it, the ship moving.'

'You wait until we set sail,' Rachel said.

Close up, in full daylight, they could all see what was wrong with Janie's face — she was blind in her left eye, which looked resolutely forwards, regardless of what the other eyeball did. And like Friday, she was tattooed — in Janie's case on the back of her right hand.

'Jane Braine: that's an unusual name,' Sarah said, the exaggerated tone of contemplation in her voice not quite masking the sarcasm.

'Jan*ie*,' Janie said. 'Not Jane. It does sound daft if you just say Jane.'

Rachel nodded at Janie's stomach. 'You'll miss your husband.'

'Only if I had one.'

'Oh,' Rachel said.

'You're not below attending to Queen Bella,' Friday remarked.

Janie made a face. 'It's a relief not to be. Where's that other girl, the nice one?'

'Harrie? She's working in the hospital,' Rachel told her.

Friday asked, 'Were you in Bristol Gaol with Bella Jackson?'

'Not for long. She was brought down from Birmingham, all the way in a coach, handcuffed to the door. Her and half a dozen girls. They had a week in Bristol with us, then we came down here.' Janie glanced furtively over her shoulder. 'I think she's a witch. I think she's cast a spell on the others. They'll do anything she tells them to do.' She shuddered. 'She just gives me the shits.'

Rachel's eyes were huge. 'Has Sally Minto been bewitched?' Aghast, she turned to Friday. 'What if we get a spell put on us?'

Friday patted her hand reassuringly. 'Then we'll cast one back. Is she one for the ladies?'

'Sally Minto?'

'No, Bella Jackson.'

Janie thought about it. 'Haven't noticed. Keeping it quiet if she is.' She glanced up at the foredeck. 'That toff up there's been gawping at you for ages, Rachel. He your fancy man?'

They all turned to look; there was indeed a man standing on the foredeck watching them. It was Mr Keegan, one of the paying gentlemen, and today he was togged out in a burgundy-coloured cutaway with a wide collar, a smart waistcoat, a starcher, fawn trousers and his usual top hat. The general opinion among the women was that lifting a leg to him as a potential source of income would not be a hardship. The fact that he was back aboard the *Isla* suggested they would shortly be setting sail: the paying passengers had all gone ashore when they'd dropped anchor on the Mother Bank a week earlier.

Mr Keegan waved, touched his hand to his hat brim, trotted athletically down the companion ladder and disappeared through the door that led to the passenger cabins.

'No, he is *not* my fancy man!' Rachel protested. 'I'm betrothed.'

'Fat lot of good that's going to do you, transported to New South Wales,' Janie said. She cocked a hand behind one large, pink ear. 'What's that I hear? Could it be the sound of a galloping knight in shining armour? Oh, no, it's just me guts rumbling.'

Friday tried not to, but she laughed.

On the verge of tears, Rachel shot back, 'You're a sarky cow, you are, Janie Braine. And *you're* no help either,' she added to Friday.

'I'm sorry, love,' Friday said.

Contrite, Janie said, 'Sorry, didn't mean to upset you. And you're a lovely-looking thing, I'll say that. Whoever he is, he's a mug if he *doesn't* follow you.' She gestured towards the cabins. 'You know, you could make yourself a bit of money on the way, start saving up to come back once you've done your time. Big money, too, with your looks.'

'Ew, that's revolting!' Rachel exclaimed. 'I couldn't have another man near me. Not after Lucas.'

But it did give her an idea. Several, in fact.

Becky Hoddle, reclining on the bunk, was suddenly alert. 'Watch out,' she said to Liz Parker, who was dozing, her bulky body sprawled across the mattress beside her.

Liz woke up with a start. 'What?'

'Here comes that little Winter girl from Woolfe's crew.'

Peering down the aisle, Liz muttered, 'What's she want?'

'Likely off to the bogs.'

But Rachel wasn't off to the bogs. Parking her small bum against the table she said, 'I've got a proposition for you, Liz Parker.'

'Ooh, sounds tempting.' Prepared to play along a little before humiliating her, Liz propped herself up on one meaty elbow. 'And what might that be?'

'I challenge you to a broads session. Your choice of game. The pot will be the money you stole from us. If I lose then we pay you double whatever's in the pot.'

Liz slowly sat up, her pendulous breasts shifting beneath her prison blouse. Now this *was* a proposition. Already her heart was beating faster.

Rachel crossed her arms. 'Think about it. You can't lose either way. If I win I take back what wasn't yours anyway. If you win, you double it. How much is left?'

'Thirty-one quid,' Becky blurted.

Liz glared at her.

Rachel whistled. 'Sixty-two pounds, Liz. You could come out of it with sixty-two pounds.' She drew the words out tantalisingly. 'A *fortune*.'

'Yous lot haven't got another thirty-one quid,' Liz said.

'You haven't got a clue what we've got.'

But it was already too late. Liz didn't care. It was happening — the blood skittering through her veins like a million busy ants, the sweaty palms, the growing sense of anticipation and excitement lifting the hair on her arms, a feeling better even than really good-quality gin. She could see herself now, holding hand after hand of winning cards, slapping them down one after the other, her elation building and building until the pot was hers. And it *would* be hers, because every game played brought her closer to that feeling of nirvana, that ultimate bright and burning thrill of victory.

'I'll do it,' she said.

'Liz —' Becky interrupted.

'Shut up. Five High, my deck. Best of three.'

Rachel shook her head. 'I'll play Five High, but not with your deck. Someone else's: a *clean* one.'

Liz shrugged, confident she could manipulate the game by other means if necessary. 'When?'

'In an hour?'

'Fine by me.'

When Rachel had gone, Becky warned, 'Don't forget she's a crack broadsman. No one'll play her any more.'

'Not as good as me, though. Why d'ya think she's never sat down across from me, ya fool? Too scared of losing, that's why.'

Becky didn't think so. Becky thought Rachel Winter was scared of Liz simply because she was such a foul old tarleather. Which meant it had taken real guts for the girl to challenge Liz, so Liz should be even more wary than usual. But she wasn't because broads, Liz's weakness, were involved, and the girl had known that. *Everyone* knew that. And only three games! A lot could go wrong in only three games.

On the other hand, perhaps it was time Liz Parker's reign of power came to an end. She was old and arrogant and she'd had her day. She was starting to make stupid decisions and now she was risking losing the money Becky had stuck her arm down that revolting bog in Newgate to retrieve. If someone knocked Liz off her pedestal, Becky wouldn't be sorry. In fact, for the right money, she could probably be persuaded to help.

Rachel walked back to the others on very wobbly legs. They were all staring at her.

'I've just challenged Liz Parker to a session of Five High. I'm going to win our money back.'

There was a long moment of shocked silence, then Harrie spoke. 'Perhaps you might have talked to us about that first, Rachel.'

'Why? You might have said no and I know I can win.'

'What happens if you lose?' Sarah interjected.

'Then we have to double the pot. Another thirty-one pounds.'

'We don't *have* thirty-one pounds!' Friday exclaimed, and flopped back on the bunk in despair. 'Bloody hell, we're buggered.'

Sarah scowled. 'Has that bitch spent nine quid of our money?'

'We're not buggered,' Rachel said. 'I'll win, don't worry.'

'What if she cheats?' Friday demanded. 'She always cheats.'

'She can't: everyone will be watching. And she's agreed we won't use her deck, or mine.'

Friday's face was full of misgiving. 'She'll have something up her sleeve.'

'We'll roll our sleeves up,' Rachel said, missing Friday's metaphor.

'Oh dear, Rachel, you really should have talked to us first,' Harrie said again.

Rachel shook her head. 'I can win. I can. Let me do it. I'm better at cards than she is. I've watched her play. And we'll never get our money back otherwise, will we? They're never going to leave it unguarded. The only time there's no one at their bunk, *we've* been made to go up on deck, too. And this way if I win — *when* I win — everyone will witness it and she'll *have* to give it to us. This is our only chance.'

It was, and they all knew it.

An hour later everything was ready. Thrilled at the prospect of witnessing a card duel between two very skilled players from opposing crews, everyone had crowded into the centre of the prison deck, standing hunched over on the benches, crammed into the aisles and squeezing themselves onto the bunks either side of the long table where Rachel and Liz sat.

Two grumbling women had been sent to stand guard at the hatch to warn of approaching crew and illegal candles had been lit and set on the table. Then there was disagreement about which deck of cards to use. Ten, belonging to various women, were placed on the table. Liz selected three, which Rachel examined and found to be marked. Rachel chose four, which Liz discarded because she didn't like the 'feel'. Of the three left, Liz insisted that two had been marked by Rachel, though they hadn't, and that the pattern on the back of the remaining deck was too distracting.

At that moment the throng near the table parted, jostling and swearing, and Bella Jackson appeared. There was no sign of her prison uniform — her costume was as fine as the one in which she'd embarked several days ago, except today her head was bare, bar a fan-shaped tortoiseshell comb holding back her ringlets.

She slid an octagonal rosewood box onto the table, its lid slightly curved and inlaid with brass. 'Open it,' she ordered.

Rachel did. Inside, lined with duck-egg blue velvet, were four card compartments and four smaller sections containing gaming counters.

'The cards have never been used,' Bella Jackson said. 'They are not marked.'

Rachel withdrew a deck and inspected it closely. They were beautifully illustrated and, no, they weren't marked. She handed them to Liz. After much squinting and holding the cards up to the candles, Liz nodded. They tossed a coin to determine who would deal first; Rachel won.

She shuffled, the cards moving so fast between her small hands they became a blur. She did a couple of show-off tricks to entertain the onlookers and settle her nerves, shuffled again, then dealt.

The first game was over fairly quickly. Every time Rachel threw down a card, Liz's hand hovered as she considered whether to pick it up or to choose from the unplayed cards. Her instinct must have been good because in short order she'd achieved Five High in spades, the second highest suit, and won. The crowd groaned.

Rachel looked up at Harrie, Sarah and Friday. Sweat beaded her upper lip and tendrils of hair stuck to her cheeks. She looked bewildered and a little frightened.

'My deal,' Liz crowed. She snatched up the cards and shuffled them backwards and forwards, tossing and flicking them around in an effort to outdo Rachel.

'Fucking get on with it, will you?' Friday snapped.

Liz smirked. 'What's the hurry? We got all day.'

She dealt two hands and contemplated hers with a furrowed brow. Deciding which one she didn't want, she threw it down and took a new one from the unplayed cards, then watched Rachel to see what she would do.

Rachel's mouth made a neat little cat's bum as she studied her cards. She moved two to the left of the spread and one to the right, then threw one down. Liz threw down a card, her hand came out, hovered, and she picked up an unplayed card.

Rachel threw down, picked up another unplayed card, Liz threw down and picked up Rachel's card.

'Stop!' Bella Jackson barked, making everyone jump. She pointed at Liz. 'This woman is cheating.'

Liz glared at her. 'I bloody are not! How dare ya?'

'You are. That girl up there in the bunk is signalling to you.'

Everyone turned to look. Louisa Coutts had flattened herself along the top bunk overlooking Rachel. She peered back, her eyes glittering in the candle and lamplight, then ducked her head.

'I saw her signalling,' Bella Jackson repeated impassively.

'Ya bloody liar!' Liz exploded.

'I think not.'

Their eyes locked for several long, poisonous seconds.

'Right!' Friday shouted. 'Everyone behind Rachel and Parker the Cheat move out of the way. Come on, clear out!'

'Why would she bother to do that?' Harrie asked Sarah. 'This is none of Bella Jackson's business. What's she got against Liz Parker?'

Sarah shrugged. 'Crew war? Who knows?'

There was much jostling and climbing about as folk reluctantly repositioned themselves and the game was restarted. Rachel won it, making the score one all.

Liz Parker's cockiness had evaporated by the beginning of the third game. Sweat trickled out of her lank hair, damp patches had appeared in her armpits and there was a particularly rank smell coming off her. Rachel dealt and they studied their cards.

They each discarded and picked up, discarded and picked up, attempting to determine by which cards were being thrown out what the other had in her hand and the suit being collected, which affected the value of the points. The pauses between each play grew longer and longer — and the onlookers increasingly enthralled.

The tension was unbearable. Harrie couldn't stand to watch any longer, but couldn't push her way out of the tightly packed crowd. Instead she kept her eyes on Friday, watching Liz Parker like a kestrel in case she cheated again. Sarah's gaze, though, was fixed on Rachel, willing her to win.

Harrie risked a quick, squinty peek at Rachel's face, sending her a blast of love and good luck. She glanced up and smiled, more relaxed and confident now.

Not long after that she lay her cards on the table. 'Five High, suit of diamonds. I win.'

The prison deck went mad. Friday screeched in elation and hauled Rachel off her bench and wrapped her in a huge bear hug, breaking off only to jerk up two fingers at Liz. Sarah and Harrie surrounded Rachel, enfolding her in their arms, and the four of them leapt up and down, jumping on people's toes, yelling and crowing in triumphant delight.

Liz Parker rose, spat on Bella Jackson's expensive playing cards, and shoved her way out of the throng.

The *Isla* hove to the next morning, sailing through the calm waters of Solent Strait between the Isle of Wight and the Hampshire coast, then out into the English Channel. As they passed the southern-most tip of Cornwall, Amos Furniss rather nastily let it be known among the women that Lizard Head would be their very last sight of England, and they all crowded the starboard rail for a final glimpse of their homeland's diminishing coastline.

Harrie and Rachel both wept bitterly; Sarah watched for a while then muttered, 'Shithole,' and went below again; but Friday remained silent. She would miss her friends, of course, especially Betsy, but there would be new opportunities in New South Wales. There always were new opportunities if you kept your eyes and ears open.

* * *

As the *Isla* sailed beyond sight of England, Rachel's beloved dog Shannon sat beneath his tree at the Winter family farm outside Guildford and howled loudly enough to disturb the dead in their graves.

Flora Winter, looking out of the window, said to her husband, 'For God's sake, Edgar, go and do something about that dog.'

Edgar, who had listened to his wife weeping almost constantly since they'd missed seeing the ship carrying their daughter set sail from Woolwich, and had wept nearly as much himself, put on his boots and trudged out into the yard.

Shannon turned his head to see who was coming, and patiently accepted Edgar's comforting scratch between his ears.

'Aye, you miss her, too, don't you, boy?'

Shannon couldn't answer, but he did. He missed his lovely mistress very much.

Out in the rougher open seas of the North Atlantic, seasickness recurred in those whose constitutions were slow to adapt and James Downey once more asked Harrie and Lil Foster to assist him in the hospital. Rachel and Sarah felt merely off-colour but Friday was brought low a second time and again announced she was to be left alone to die. Even Rachel's triumph and the return of their money (delivered by a sour Becky Hoddle while Liz Parker sulked threateningly from her crew's bunk) had lost the power to cheer her. The ship's exaggerated pitch and roll convinced her they were all about to perish shortly anyway and, though she tried, between vomiting and groaning, to make a joke of it, her friends could see she was terrified out of her wits.

Rachel thought back to all the times in Newgate Friday had stuck up for her — and even raised a fist for her — and wished she could do something to make her feel better. Then smelly old

Matilda Bain told her how she might cure at least one of Friday's maladies.

She waited until Harrie was at work and everyone not ill had gone up on deck, then slipped below again. Poor Friday was asleep, muttering and tossing, and Rachel took care not to wake her as she made her way towards the closed curtains surrounding Bella Jackson's makeshift compartment. Bella rarely left it, pleasing herself when she took her exercise, apparently not caring a jot about the captain's and Mr Downey's schedules.

Feeling very nervous about encroaching on Bella's private territory, Rachel took a deep, preparatory breath. But just then the ship gave a violent lurch and she lost her balance and fell through the curtains, sprawling across Bella's bunk.

Bella Jackson, lying on several pillows, reading a book by candlelight, gave a startled squawk and drew her legs up to her chest. 'God almighty, you clumsy little fool!'

Rachel scrambled to her feet. 'Sorry, I overbalanced.' Lord, she'd never get what she wanted now.

'Well, fall over somewhere else,' Bella cawed, her black eyes flashing. Her expression softened. She regarded Rachel thoughtfully, and put down her book. 'You're the broadswoman. Rachel Winter, isn't it? In the same crew as —'

'Friday and Harrie and Sarah, yes. And Janie and Sally, but you know them.' Rachel was chattering but she couldn't help it. She was gazing at Bella's lovely embroidered robe and all the nice things she had on the shelves around her bunk. And at her slippered feet; they were so pale. And she had no hair at all on her lower legs, or her forearms, for that matter. How fascinating.

Bella tucked her feet under her robe. 'Shouldn't you be up on deck with everyone else? Or are you feeling poorly?' The harsh tone had gone from her voice and she no longer reminded Rachel of an irate crow.

'No, I feel very well, thank you. I wanted to ... It was you I was hoping to speak to, Mrs Jackson.'

Bella gave a low, throaty laugh and patted the mattress. 'Sit down, Rachel, make yourself comfortable. And it's not missus — I'm a dried-up old spinster. Call me Bella. How can I help you?'

Rachel blinked: this wasn't what she'd expected at all. Gingerly she sat on the end of the bunk.

'Close the curtains, there's a good girl,' Bella said.

Rachel twitched the curtains shut.

'There we are, nice and cosy.' Bella reached for a small box on a shelf and offered it to Rachel. 'Turkish delight, my favourite. Would you like some?'

The delicate scent of rose drifted up into Rachel's nostrils and her mouth watered immediately. It had been a long time since she'd had a proper sweet. She selected the biggest piece, white confectioner's sugar coating her fingers, and bit into it, relishing the sensation of the firm, slightly squeaky jelly sliding over her teeth. 'It's really delicious,' she said.

Bella took a piece for herself and popped it into her wide mouth, the sugar leaving a white trace on her red-stained lips. Her tongue snaked out and licked it off.

Rachel had a horrible thought. She blurted, 'You're not ... I'm not ... I'm sorry, but I like men.'

Bella laughed and a puff of sugar blew out of the Turkish delight box. 'And I like Turkish delight. Don't worry, Rachel, you're safe with me.'

Rachel stifled her sigh of relief. 'Thank you for dobbing in Liz Parker the other day. I would have lost all three games if you hadn't.'

'My pleasure, Rachel. You're a very good player.' Bella gave an odd little smile. 'And I can't abide a cheat. Now, what did you want to speak to me about?'

'I have a friend who's terrified of being at sea. I heard that you might have —'

'Which friend? Harrie, Friday or Sarah?'

'I don't want to say.' Telling Bella would be too ... intimate, like breaking a trust. It didn't feel right.

'Go on, Rachel.' Bella reached out and touched Rachel's knee conspiratorially. 'You can tell me, surely?'

'Really, I just can't.'

Bella sat back. 'I understand. What did you hear?'

'Matilda Bain said you had some cauls for sale. To stop people from drowning?'

'Yes, though I've sold several already.'

Rachel's heart plummeted. 'Oh. Are there any left? I can pay.'

'There might be. For the right person. I would need to know who, though.'

Rachel pulled at a button on her jacket; the thread broke and the button came off. She put it in her pocket. 'It's for Friday.'

Slowly, Bella nodded. 'Friday Woolfe is very important to you, isn't she?'

Rachel said yes, unable for some reason to meet Bella's gaze. This, too, felt somehow like a betrayal and a tiny pang of doubt pricked her.

'Well, in that case, of course you may have one.'

'Really? Oh, thank you! How much will you want?'

Bella waved a slim, white hand. 'You can have it. I won't charge you.'

'But ... why not?'

'Because it must have taken a lot of courage for you to come and talk to me. And because a kindness deserves a kindness. And because I like you.'

'That *is* kind of you!' Rachel said, startled but delighted. 'Thank you *very* much.'

'You're more than welcome.'

Wrapping her silk robe tightly around her thin body, Bella unlocked one of the two trunks occupying part of the bunk.

Peeking surreptitiously over her shoulder, Rachel saw that the trunk was partitioned: one side contained a vast array of bottles and jars and packets and small boxes and bulging cloth bags, and the other held a collection of fashionable footwear and a large padlocked strongbox. From the latter, Bella took a folded sheet of heavy paper, locking both strongbox and trunk again immediately.

'Here you are,' she said, handing the paper to Rachel.

It was foolscap-sized and on it was a large brown splodge where a fine layer of skin, almost transparent in places, had been pressed and dried. Here and there bits had lifted and were flaking where the paper had been creased, and in the bottom left corner was something that looked like a flattened rat's tail. Rachel made a face and folded the paper again. It didn't look much but she knew its power.

'Would you like some more Turkish delight to take with you?' Bella asked, offering the box again. 'Here, help yourself.'

Rachel took several more pieces, eating one straight away. 'Thank you — and thank you for the caul. I know Friday will appreciate it,' she said through a mouthful of sticky, rose-flavoured sweet.

'You're welcome. How old did you say you are, Rachel?'

'I'm fifteen.'

'Well, you're a very pretty little thing. Close the curtains after you, won't you?'

Bella Jackson is really rather nice, Rachel reflected as she made her way back along the aisle, licking her fingers. Nothing like the nasty, calculating queen of vice everyone has been saying she is. Nothing at all.

That evening, before dinner, Rachel crawled onto the bunk beside Friday's prostrate body, prodded her alarmingly concave belly and said excitedly, 'Wake up, sleepyhead, I've got you a present.'

Harrie, having an hour off from her duties in the hospital, shared a mystified glance with Sarah. They lay down their cards expectantly.

Friday opened one bloodshot eye; Rachel handed her a folded square of paper.

'What is it?'

'Open it and see,' Rachel said, almost unable to contain herself.

Friday fumbled open the heavy paper. She stared uncomprehendingly for a long moment, then exclaimed, 'Rachel! Where did you get this?'

Sarah lurched off the bench, was launched sideways by a roll of the ship, righted herself, and squinted at the object in Friday's hand. 'What the hell is it?'

Harrie peered over her shoulder. 'I know what it is. It's a —'

'It's a caul!' Rachel interrupted, thrilled with herself. 'So now you don't need to worry about drowning and you can concentrate on not being sick instead!'

Trying valiantly to ignore her nausea, Friday heaved herself onto one elbow and tilted the paper to better catch the feeble light from the lamp. It was said that an infant born with a caul over its head would be forever safeguarded against drowning and that the possession of such a caul would give the bearer the same immunity. So they were harvested when the child was born, usually by the midwife who would carefully lay a sheet of paper or parchment over the infant's head and face and press the caul onto it. If done too roughly, the removal of the membrane could wound the child and leave scars, or the caul itself might tear. Some mothers kept the caul as an heirloom; others sold them. They were very popular with sailors. But who had sold this one to Rachel?

'Where did you get it?'

'Don't you like it?' Rachel sounded doubtful.

Friday looked at her friend and her heart sank. The delighted smile was fading. 'It's the best present anyone's ever given me, really it is. It doesn't matter what happens now: I know I'll be safe. Thank you.' She sat up and gave Rachel a peck on the cheek, holding her breath to avoid wafting the smell of vomit all over her. 'You're a real little sweetheart and I'm really grateful for it, I really am. But where did you get it, love?'

'I was given it.'

'By one of the sailors?' Harrie asked tersely. Friday could see by her worried expression she was wondering what Rachel might have traded for it.

'No, by Bella Jackson.'

Harrie let out a sigh of relief.

Friday turned back to Rachel, thoroughly nonplussed. 'Bella Jackson gave you a caul?'

Rachel nodded.

'She just walked up to you and gave it to you?'

'No, silly, I asked her for it. Matilda Bain said she had some for sale and I wanted to buy one from her but she said she didn't want any money. She was very kind to me.'

'That *was* kind of her,' Harrie said.

Friday lay back and rested her forearm across her eyes. She would give *anything* for this bloody seasickness to go away. God, what had Rachel done? It was just like her — scatty one minute, extraordinarily considerate the next. She might not have paid money, but the silly girl would pay a price for it sooner or later: it was the way the Bella Jacksons of the world worked. They relied on having people in their debt and ultimately they gave *nothing* away. As soon as she was back on her feet she was going to drag Bella Jackson out of that stupid compartment thing she was hiding in and punch the living daylights out of her. What did she think she was doing, taking advantage of someone as young and gulpy as Rachel? *Rachel* might have thought she was doing a lovely thing, but even if what was stuck on that paper truly was a caul from a human baby and not just some pig's afterbirth, it still wouldn't stop Friday sinking to the bottom of the ocean along with everyone else if the *Isla* was destined to founder. *Everyone* on the *Isla* would need one to stop that from happening. Oh *God*, when was this sickness going to go away?

'Friday?' Rachel said, looking hopefully down at her. 'Do you think you might feel a bit better now, knowing you can't drown?'

Friday took Rachel's hand and squeezed. 'Much better, sweetie, thank you. You're a proper little angel, you are.'

Rachel beamed and tucked the paper under Friday's pillow.

The ship's bell rang, signalling that supper was ready for the mess captains to collect.

'Will you be able to eat anything?' Harrie asked Friday.

Friday said no; if she tried she knew she'd only heave it up again. It was bad enough just having to smell it.

'Are you sure?' Harrie went on. 'There might be pudding with raisins. Not even a little bit of that?'

Friday wished Harrie would shut up. She knew she was only trying to help, and that Harrie was worried about her, but it was wearing her down. On the other hand, it was nice to be fussed over; she didn't want that to stop. Also, hurting Harrie's feelings would be really unkind, even if Harrie were being really naive about Bella Jackson's behaviour.

'Maybe in the morning, eh? I might be feeling better by then.'

'Well, if you're sure,' Harrie said doubtfully.

'Go on, or Sarah'll scoff the lot.'

While the others ate, Friday lay with the blanket over her face to block out the smell of pease pudding, thinking about Bella Jackson and getting angry again. So angry, in fact, she decided to do something about it tonight, seasickness be buggered.

She waited until everyone who could had gone up on deck after supper, then sat up, held her head while it stopped spinning, then shuffled on her backside to the edge of the bunk. She wasn't the only one still below; there were about thirty women and children still on the prison deck, and she hadn't seen Bella Jackson go up the ladder. But then Bella had barely been seen since she'd come aboard, except for her appearance at Rachel and Liz's card game. She didn't eat at the table and she didn't exercise up on deck. Was she sick, or just too arrogant to mix with everyone else? Well, it didn't matter either way — Friday was sorting out this Rachel business and that was that. She slid her feet into her boots and hauled herself upright, clutching the post at the end of the bunk as stars drifted across her vision.

Holding on to the table and various beams and pillars to steady herself, she made her way down the aisle, rolling with the ship, bumping her hips, knee, and, twice, her head. With each knock, her anger ratcheted up a notch. She was nauseated and horribly weak and her legs felt strangely watery. It was worse than the horrors — which was ridiculous, not to mention unfair, as she hadn't even had the fun of getting drunk. Nodding to two pale-faced women huddled in a bunk and stepping over a child sitting on the floor, she reached the curtained partition that was Bella Jackson's berth.

Friday rapped on the post, but competing against the creaks and low groans of the *Isla*'s timbers, her knuckles made no discernible sound. 'Open up, Bella Jackson, I want to talk to you.'

There was no response.

'Oi, open up!' Friday called again, louder this time.

Again nothing happened, so she whipped aside the curtain.

On the bunk, propped against a heap of pillows, her long legs crossed at the ankle, reclined Bella. The velvet skirt and jacket had been replaced by a long belted robe of pale green embroidered satin, worn over a white corset: Friday could see a shoulder strap peeking from beneath the robe, the edge of the corset's modest bodice, and the narrow waist the garment afforded the woman. The skin on Bella's décolletage was smooth and powdered; she wore an emerald silk scarf at her throat, and on her feet were satin slippers to match the robe. Several fat beeswax candles sat on a little shelf at the rear of the bunk, beside a hand mirror, a pair of silver tweezers and a slim enamelled case. Friday had seen the like before — it held cigarillos, the new, fashionable miniature cigars; her cullies sometimes smoked them. She might have known the bitch would smoke those rather than a pipe like everyone else.

Bella's face was as heavily painted as the day she'd embarked and her gleaming hair as beautifully curled, though the skin beneath her brows was swollen and reddened. On one side of the bunk — which she clearly wasn't sharing at all, never mind with three other women — were arrayed the two trunks the Bristol women had laboriously carted down the companion ladder. The air in the close compartment formed by the curtains was redolent not only of the prison deck, but of body odour, tobacco, honey from the candles, and a strong, heady perfume.

Friday registered all this in a single, stunned second, then let out a fierce bark of laughter. 'Christ, who the *hell* do you think you are?'

Bella Jackson, her white face unmoving, stared at her. 'Get out.'

'Get out yourself if you're not sick, you lazy slag.'

Bella leant forwards, grimacing slightly against the strictures of her corset, and wrenched the curtain from Friday's hand. 'I said *get out*!'

Friday snatched the curtain back and ripped it open even further. 'I don't think so. I want to talk to you. I want to know what you're doing giving crap like this to my friend.' She withdrew the paper from her blouse and flicked it at Bella's satin slippers.

Bella barely glanced at it. 'You can't prove it isn't genuine.'

'I don't care if it's genuine or not. I want to know what you're up to.'

'She was in the market for a particular item, for her *special friend*, and I provided it.'

She had a strange voice; melodious, low, deliberate and not unpleasant. A hint of West Country, but a touch of something else, too. Something made up, Friday thought uncharitably.

'Why didn't you charge her for it?' she demanded. 'Why did you just give it to her? She's gulpy; she hasn't even realised she owes you.' Twice over, she added silently. Her blood ran even colder as she remembered Bella's intercession during the card game. The abbess clearly wanted Rachel and Friday knew all too well how useful such a beautiful child-woman could be.

Bella shrugged. 'Not *everything* I do has to turn a profit. I felt like being generous. I felt like being *kind*. You really are doing me an injustice, you know.'

Friday snorted. 'That'll be the day.' A wave of gall for this clever, predatory, nasty, unnerving woman surged through Friday like shit through a flooded London drain. She was cut from the same flash cloth as Liz Parker but was far smarter and far more dangerous. For all her own resolve and bluster, there was nothing Friday could do to erase Rachel's debt.

Bella's eyes narrowed. 'I know all about you, Friday Woolfe. You just concentrate on getting your next drink and stay out of my way. There's room for just one boss on this ship, and that's me.'

Friday put her hands on the end of the bunk and leant in towards Bella, inhaling the unusually heady, slightly sickening notes of her perfume. Jasmine and violets, gone off in the bottle? 'You keep out of *my* way. And if you do anything to upset my friends, Rachel especially, I'll come after you, I swear it.'

She let the curtain fall and stomped back to her own berth, ignoring the startled looks on the faces she passed, heading straight for her stash of gin. Nothing calmed her nerves like a good, long slug of Blue Ruin. Halfway back, she realised with a sort of dull relief that, underneath the indignation and aggression and animosity racing through her body, she didn't feel seasick any more.

* * *

Three nights later, after the long, rolling waves had rocked Captain Holland and Mr Downey to sleep in their cabins and darkness had draped cloaks of privacy over the *Isla*'s little nooks and crannies, Amos Furniss unlocked the hatch to the prison deck and rapped on it three times. Moments later, a dozen or so shadowed figures emerged, dressed in their finery and smelling of cheap perfume, ready to ply their trade.

Nine

May 1829, North Atlantic Ocean

'Tell me, Captain Holland,' Mrs Seaton said as she helped herself to more preserved potatoes, 'is transporting a wholly female cargo of convicts the same as transporting a wholly male cargo of convicts?'

Josiah Holland didn't much like Hester Seaton — she had ideas above her station and she was fat but not in a particularly appealing way, *and* she was eating too many of the pickled potatoes, which at this rate wouldn't last the voyage — however she was doing a reasonable job of keeping at least some of the convict women occupied with her afternoon school, so he took care to be civil to her.

'No, Mrs Seaton, in all honesty I have to say that it is not. In my experience the two classes of cargo are quite different.'

'In what way?' Gabriel Keegan asked.

The captain shot him an unreadable look. 'Well, obviously, the females are females. They have different requirements from the male convicts, and behave in different ways.'

Keegan nodded. 'Which cargo do you prefer?'

'The males,' Captain Holland said shortly and went back to his dinner.

James Downey disliked these weekly midday meals in Captain Holland's great cabin, though it was hardly big enough to be described as 'great'. It was the captain's work area, and where he convened his meetings with his senior crew members, and once a week the table bearing his charts and other bits and pieces was cleared and set by the cook's boy with silver and some quite reasonable plate. James knew Josiah Holland didn't enjoy these occasions either, but the passengers expected them and, in fact, paid for them as part of their fee.

Keegan said to the minister's wife, 'How are you finding the prisoners, Mrs Seaton?'

Hester Seaton fussed with a tendril of hair that had slipped from beneath her best lace cap; sweat had stuck the curl to her cheek, giving her a girlish air that jibed with the grooves running from her nose to the corners of her mouth. 'They are somewhat trying, I must say, but of course I am working with souls who can neither read nor write and, being what they are, one can't expect them to be well versed in manners and other social graces. The Lord, however, provides one with an eternal source of patience, and one must be grateful that they are sitting still long enough to even begin to come to grips with the alphabet.'

'Well, you must be applauded, Mrs Seaton,' Keegan said. 'I've no doubt at all you're doing an absolutely sterling job.'

Hester Seaton blushed like a maiden. 'One tries.'

'Have you always been a teacher, Mrs Seaton?' Matthew Cutler asked, blotting his mouth with a napkin then, rather vulgarly, Mrs Seaton thought, his sweat-sheened forehead. Though it really was extremely hot in Captain Holland's great cabin, even with the little windows open.

'Oh, no, much of my time has been spent raising our daughters —'

'And what a marvellous job you've done of that, too,' Keegan interrupted.

Eudora and Geneve, sitting opposite, simpered as he beamed across the table at them.

'Thank you kindly. But when Mr Seaton was accepted for the New South Wales posting with the Church Missionary Society, I thought, well, why not bring some of my talents to bear and use them to spread the Lord's word among those far less fortunate than my daughters? I have a natural inclination for teaching, as you've observed, Mr Keegan, and the Lord knows there are plenty of lost souls in the colony. It has always been my ambition to pursue just such a vocation and now it seems as though God has steered me directly onto my chosen path.'

Hearing this speech a second time gave James an irrational and childish urge to laugh and he stared very hard at the salt dish.

'And the natives of New South Wales?' Matthew said. 'Will you be setting up schools for them also?'

Mrs Seaton looked nonplussed.

'I mean, you read in the papers occasionally about the mission stations for the Maoris in New Zealand, at settlements like Paihia and so on,' Matthew went on, 'but I've never come across much about missions in New South Wales. Why is that, I wonder? Is it that there are none? Or have I been reading the wrong papers?'

James looked at Matthew with admiration; a young man with a social conscience *and* the gumption to own up to it.

Clearly concerned that his wife was in danger of dominating the conversation, Reverend Seaton jumped in. 'Of course there are missions and by all accounts the natives are very grateful for our efforts! Perhaps you *have* been reading the wrong papers. And naturally if Reverend Marsden sees fit that I should expend my efforts in that direction, then I shall. Though I do have it on good authority that both races, the Aborigines and the Maoris, are doomed to die out completely within the next fifty years, so one wonders why the church goes to such lengths sometimes.'

'Because the Lord never turns a single soul away from the path of redemption,' Hester quickly reminded him.

Reverend Seaton looked as though he wouldn't mind whacking his wife on the head with the meat fork.

There was a bit of surreptitious elbowing between Eudora and Geneve and a snorted giggle, resulting in Eudora leaving the table to blow her nose. Both her parents glared at her as she returned.

Captain Holland stifled a sigh of annoyance. Changing the subject slightly, he said, 'We shall shortly be reaching the equator, Mrs Seaton. I hope you can devise a suitably demanding series of lessons for your pupils, as the doldrums tend to bring out the very worst in those who are not, as you have so aptly described them, well versed in manners and other social graces.'

So far, in his opinion, the prisoners had not behaved *too* abominably. They had been tiresome and there had been one or two incidents, but they had been managed. The doldrums, however, in his experience, tested even the most calm and measured of tempers, and the attendant becalming was usually when trouble really arose. Within the next few days, if the trades remained as they were, they would be approaching the smallest latitudes and, in between possible violent squalls that may or may not move them in the right direction, the wind would drop out of the sails, the sun would beat down on the deck like a great burning hammer and anything approaching civility among the convicts, and probably his paying passengers, would be discarded.

The always trying time would be worse on this voyage because this time he was being haunted. Not by a ghost but by thoughts of the big, loud, round-breasted, copper-haired girl they called Friday Woolfe. At first she had only come to him in his dreams, stepping into the tiny space that was his cabin, crossing silently to him and lowering herself onto his naked body, her breasts swaying with the movement of the ship, her long hair tickling his face, the hotness that was the core of her engulfing him until he awoke in a puddle of his own mess. But now he saw her when he was awake: on deck in chains stripped to the waist, her white back exposed and her breasts jutting, him behind her with the cat-o'-nine-tails; or naked in one of the ship's boats, her legs raised, smiling lasciviously, ready for him.

'Captain Holland?'

'I beg your pardon?' The captain mopped his gleaming face with a large green kerchief and stuffed it back in his pocket.

'I was saying,' Matthew said, 'how long can we expect to be in the doldrums?'

'It depends. Days at least; sometimes weeks. But that would be very unlucky. And unfortunate.'

'Is it true that a person can lose their wits while becalmed?' Mrs Seaton asked.

The captain looked at James. 'That's probably your field, Mr Downey.'

'Yes, that has been known to occur,' James replied cautiously. 'It can place considerable stress on the constitution. Though any such mania is seldom a permanent state of mind. If you are concerned, my professional advice would be to find ways to keep yourself occupied.'

'Oh, no, I'm not concerned for myself!' Mrs Seaton protested, mortified by the very suggestion that her constitution might be at risk of buckling. 'My daughters, however. Young minds are so much more vulnerable.'

And bodies, thought Gabriel Keegan, watching the way Eudora's small breasts rose and fell beneath her bodice. The minister's elder daughter looked really quite tempting — they both did, in fact. But although his preference was for flesh precisely that young and sweet, he doubted she could be induced to keep her mouth shut, which would only cause problems, especially on a ship this small on such a long voyage. No, it probably wouldn't be in his best interests to pursue that one. After all, he was only in exile now, en route for a dreary government job in a far-flung colony full of bizarre animals and wild black natives, because he'd misjudged a dalliance with a fifteen-year-old girl. It wasn't his fault the stupid, spoilt little cow had got herself pregnant and his father had had to call in endless favours. She must have been mad: why on earth would he, a handsome buck more than ten years her senior, want to tie himself down to a whelping bitch?

Since the seas had settled a couple of weeks earlier he'd managed a number of hurried grinds — the excitement heightened by the haste required — with an assortment of convict tarts on the foredeck; these had cost him but he didn't mind paying. He glanced at the captain. The old goat thought he had everything under control but had no idea Amos Furniss had turned whoremonger. Keegan suspected Furniss was in cahoots with the madam on the prison deck; it was he who let the whores out every night and raided the cargo for the Jamaica rum and French brandy some of the tarts preferred as part of their payment. When Furniss's watch ended, and before Silas Warren came up, the tarts would scamper back below, like the rats they were — everyone was happy.

He, Keegan, had seen the girl he really wanted, but unfortunately she wasn't one of those who came up at night. Her name, he'd been informed, was Rachel Winter, and she was very young, petite and exquisite looking. She was also constantly in the company of three other girls: a big redhead he wouldn't mind tumbling but certainly wouldn't trust with his purse; a smaller, dark girl who looked at him with more perspicacity than she had a right to and frankly gave him the shits; and another one who fussed about like a mother hen. With a few well-chosen words he knew he could put each of them individually in their place, but collectively they were proving to be a bit of a barrier. And since the stopover at Portsmouth, there'd been two more in the way — new messmates, he supposed — a sallow girl and an ugly pregnant one so close to dropping her bundle she looked as though she might burst any minute. He'd tried to attract the Winter girl's attention on deck — a bit tricky, as he couldn't walk among the women — but without success, as the others kept literally closing ranks. It was a problem, but one he was willing to spend time solving.

He liked a bit of sport.

Rachel's blouse was plastered against her back, and sweat trickled annoyingly down her scalp and sides, like the feet of busy little insects rushing to be somewhere. The heat seemed to have a physical body of its own, pressing against her skin and her eyeballs, and was giving her the most awful headache.

The weather had been sweltering for three days, with barely a breath of wind, the sails hanging flat and empty like an old woman's tits, and everyone was in filthy moods and moaning and complaining and fainting and generally being horrible. She lifted her skirt and flapped it, relishing the tiny breeze it stirred between her legs.

They were all up on deck, Mr Downey having expressly forbidden anyone to stay below. It was almost impossible to do so, even had anyone wanted to, as it was so hot down there. The wind sail over the hatch stopped working as soon as the breeze died away and it was like stepping down into a reeking, creaking furnace. It sounded to Rachel as though the *Isla* were groaning in pain, burning up in the relentless sun. The stink from the water closets was enough to make you pass out, even though they were still being cleaned three times a day with chloride of lime; Mr Downey had just told them they could pee in a bucket on deck behind the bathing screens and chuck it over the side. Not everyone wanted to but she would, happily.

They were sleeping on deck now, too. Amos Furniss was supposed to be mounting a guard to make sure the crew didn't get near them, but everyone — except Captain Holland, obviously, and probably Mr Downey — knew Amos Furniss was busy mounting Becky Hoddle and was taking a cut from what the working girls were making. Friday, Rachel knew, preferred to be paid half in money and half in drink and, as she seemed to get through quite a lot of customers each night, was building up her finances and contributing to the kitty while at the same time managing to stay constantly half mashed. Not that any of them had had to worry about money since the card game. But Friday had such a capacity for alcohol, it was only actually noticeable when she *wasn't* half mashed and went a bit morose. But at least she hadn't been seasick for ages, or said anything about drowning. Rachel was so pleased she'd given her the caul.

'Does it snow in New South Wales?' she asked, thinking longingly of cold winter days in Guildford.

'I don't know,' Sarah said, flapping at her sweating face with a fan made from a couple of Mrs Fry's religious tracts. 'I suppose it might, if there are mountains. But I'm not sure there are mountains.'

'There are,' Harrie said. There were only two patients in the hospital despite the heat, so she'd been given a day off.

Sarah looked at her. 'How do you know?'

'Mrs Fry said so. She said there are mountains to the west of Sydney Town. They might get snow.'

'Not in the summer, though, surely. I thought it was supposed to be hot in Australia.'

'Oh God, not as hot as this, I hope,' Friday said, blowing down the front of her blouse. 'I can't stand it.'

Even Bella Jackson had come up on deck. She sat in a tiny slice of shade afforded by the afterdeck, surrounded by her retinue. Unlike most of the women and the crew, who were barefoot due to the heat, unleashing the pervasive reek of unwashed feet, she wore black silk slippers, though no stockings. She had consented to half wear the prison uniform: the apron was nowhere to be seen and she had accessorised the dull skirt with a red bodice with intricate pin tucks and puffy three-quarter-length sleeves, a red and black-patterned scarf and gold pendant earrings. She also carried a parasol to ward off the sun, which garnered a lot of muttered sarcastic comments but looked rather glamorous to Rachel. She wished she had one to keep the sun off her face as her cheap prison-issue bonnet had already fallen apart.

Poor Janie Braine and the other expectant women were suffering the most. Janie's hands and feet had swollen alarmingly and so had her belly. So this morning she'd been to see Mr Downey, who had told her he thought she might be closer to giving birth than she thought she was. He'd suggested she was perhaps seven and a half to eight months along, which apparently made the father someone else, which had put Janie in quite a bad mood. But she'd cheered up when she realised she only had four to six more weeks left of weeing every hour, on the hour, if the baby was coming sooner than expected.

Liz Parker wasn't doing too well either, Rachel noticed. Not that she cared. Liz's round face was even redder than usual and she was lying on her back on the deck, a piece of wet muslin draped over her forehead, looking like a beached whale. Rachel had never seen a beached whale but she'd overheard Third Mate Meek telling another sailor that's what she reminded him of, and she liked the sound of the phrase.

She'd seen a whale in the sea, though — they all had, the previous day. It had been about half a mile away and it had 'breached', blown a lot of water out of its spout, disappeared for a few minutes then made an enormous splash with its huge tail. The crew had called it a 'right' whale and it had been a beautiful thing to behold. And they'd seen the most spectacular purple and pink and orange sunsets, and two days earlier a turtle, which Mr Meek said was lost and would no doubt die, swimming faster than the ship was moving, and schools of fish leaping out of the sea, and birds called boobies swooping down on them and snatching them up in their beaks. Rachel had asked were the birds lost, too, and Mr Meek, who was young and not really a mister and whom Rachel quite liked, told her they weren't and that they'd flown all the way from the Canary Islands and would probably fly back when they'd eaten their fill. But when Rachel had said why were they called boobies, then, and not canaries, he'd only laughed, until Mr Warren had given him a dirty look and he'd hurried off.

She liked the look of the two gentlemen, Mr Cutler and Mr Keegan, too, though neither was anything compared to Lucas. They were both very polite, lifting their hats, which they both still wore despite the heat and the fact they were in shirtsleeves now. They always stayed on the foredeck, though, only stepping off it to go down into their cabins. The minister and his wife spent a lot of time up there, too, especially now that it was so hot, though Mrs Seaton did come down to run the letters school in the afternoons. Rachel didn't attend because she could already read and write, so what was the point, but some of the girls who did go said she was a bossy old trout. She couldn't be that old because her daughters weren't very grown up — she just looked old. Rachel would have liked to talk to the daughters, but they never came down to the waistdeck, spending all their time on the foredeck twirling little silk parasols like Bella Jackson's, giggling with Mr Keegan, clothed in pretty, envy-making dresses with matching bonnets.

To look at, Mr Seaton was quite a frightening man with his bristling whiskers, boiled-ham skin and beady eyes, and at five o'clock every day he preached sermons listing the sins that littered the path of those who refused to find the Lord — stealing, cheating, fornicating and so forth. Everything in fact that the *Isla*'s convicts had been tried and transported for. But Rachel suspected she knew what sort of man Reverend Seaton really was. There had been, in her village, a preacher who had spouted the same sulphur-tinged messages of redemption. Despite this, not only had he been embezzling church funds, but he'd also managed to impregnate three of his flock. Rachel could see the same hot flicker of desire in the Reverend Seaton's eye as he cast it over his captive audience and wondered whether the rumour that he had made his wife and daughters share one tiny cabin so he could have the other to himself was true.

'That Keegan cove's having a good stare again,' Sarah said.

Friday turned to see. 'You don't like him, do you?'

'Well, do you?'

Rachel looked, too. 'What's wrong with him?' Sarah was always complaining about Mr Keegan standing on the foredeck looking around. What else was he supposed to do up there? 'I think he's quite nice. He's got lovely manners.'

'He's on the prowl.'

'Oh, he is not!' Rachel protested.

'How do you know he isn't? You don't even know him.'

'You're such a misery guts, Sarah, always looking for the worst in people.'

'And you're so naive,' Sarah replied. 'For God's sake, you're only fifteen years old. How can you be a good judge of character?'

'Well, you're only seventeen!' Rachel shot back.

'Yes, but I've lived on the streets a lot longer than you have. You haven't even *been* on the streets.'

'So? That doesn't mean I'm stupid.'

'I didn't say you were stupid; I said you're naive.'

'Oh, stop it, you two!' Harrie snapped. She'd been refereeing squabbles for the past three long, hot, sticky days and she was sick of it. 'If you can't say something nice, don't say anything at all.'

'Look,' Sarah said accusingly, 'now you've upset Ma.'

Rachel tried not to smile but couldn't help herself. She turned away, because she really didn't like arguing with Sarah. It was just that Sarah was so prickly: everything she, Rachel, did seemed to annoy her. And she honestly wasn't annoying on purpose, she really wasn't. But if Mr Keegan chose to look at her, she couldn't help that, could she? In fact, it was excellent, really, because it worked in perfectly with an idea she'd been mulling over for a while. She stood up.

'Where are you going?' Sarah asked quickly.

'To use the bucket,' Rachel replied, pointing to the canvas bathing cubicle.

'Oh.' When she was out of earshot, Sarah said, 'I'm worried about that Keegan. I don't like the way he's been ogling her. What do you think?'

Friday squinted up at the foredeck, but Keegan had gone. 'I don't like it either. I think he'd be on her like a stoat on a baby rabbit if he got the chance.'

Harrie, nowhere near as experienced in these things, asked, 'But how can you tell? He seems perfectly normal to me. What's he done?'

'Nothing, yet,' Friday replied. 'He's just got that look about him. I suppose when you've had as many cullies as I have, you get to pick it.'

Sarah nodded. 'Does he go with the women?'

Friday said yes. 'Not me, though. He slinks about with the others, trying to keep it quiet, but we all talk. And that worries me, him not approaching me. It's as if he doesn't want Rachel to know he uses whores.'

'Really?' Harrie said doubtfully. 'Are you sure? Surely no one would be that, what's the word? Calculating?'

Friday, hot, sweaty and short-tempered, turned on her. 'D'you know, Harrie, sometimes you're so busy looking for the good in people you can't see what shits they really are. It annoys me, it really does. You can't believe Keegan isn't a perfect gentleman and you think Bella Jackson's just a harmless madam. Well, she isn't. She's a cunning, devious bitch and she's dangerous.'

Shocked at the vitriol in Friday's voice, Harrie blinked at her.

'She is,' Friday went on, 'and now Rachel owes her a debt because of the card game and that stupid bloody caul. You've got *no* idea how these things work.'

Colour rose in Harrie's cheeks. 'Well, *you're* as bad as Sarah, always seeing the worst in people! You don't even know her! If she's that awful, what was she doing giving away the caul? I heard Maudie Robb paid nearly four pounds for hers! What's that if it isn't generosity? And why did she bother to point out that Liz Parker was cheating when she and Rachel were playing cards? What could she hope to gain out of that?'

Friday rolled her eyes so violently that for a second only the whites showed. 'Harrie, she's operating a shipboard brothel every night; and back home she ran a massive crew involved in thievery and counterfeiting and broads and all sorts!'

'All that last bit is hearsay. It's gossip. You shouldn't judge people on gossip. And you haven't answered my question about the cards.'

'For fuck's sake, Harrie, what's she doing here if it's *just gossip*?'

'Well, I'm here and I'm not a bad person.'

'No, but you're a bloody stubborn person! And dim! And she didn't accuse Liz Parker of cheating to help Rachel, she did it to undermine Liz — and me. She doesn't want competition; she wants to be top dog.'

'I'm *not* dim! All I'm saying is I haven't seen her do anything bad, but I have seen her do something kind.' Harrie raised her hand as Friday started to say something. 'No, I'm just trying not to be judgmental. If she does something I feel is wrong, then I'll change my mind.'

'And running a whorehouse isn't wrong?' Friday demanded.

Harrie's mouth set in a straight line. 'I'm not going to cast judgment on women as ordinary as me when they're only trying to make a living. And if I did that, I'd be judging you, too, wouldn't I? And I'd never judge you, Friday.'

Friday shook her head. 'God, you are *such* a saint, Harrie. It must really wear you out. And don't change the subject. Bella is the madam, not a whore, and *Bella's* taking half the money.'

'Not half, surely?'

'Oh, grow up, Harrie.' Friday rolled her eyes again.

Sarah said, 'I hope you do change your mind, Harrie. Bella *will* call in her debt and when she does, Rachel's going to need us. Friday's right, she's bloody trouble. And so's Keegan. Real trouble, judging by the way he's been leering at Rachel every chance he gets. I think we should keep a particularly close eye on her.'

Friday nodded. 'Me, too. I could be wrong about him, but I don't think so.'

'I don't think so, either,' Sarah said. After a moment she added, 'And if he lays a hand on her, I'll kill him.'

On the fourth windless day, just as many of the *Isla*'s passengers concluded they could no longer tolerate the dreadful heat or the unbearable tedium of barely moving across the flat, dull sea, several currents began to boil around the ship at once, causing her stern to sweep wide without warning, and much alarm on deck.

Immediately, the lookout, who had had the ill luck to be perched for hours on the top platform of the main mast, bellowed down, '*All hands on deck!*'

First Mate Silas Warren shouted back, '*Where away?*'

'*Black squall, from north-west!*' The lookout was already scrambling down.

Pandemonium, caused mainly by the women fighting to get below, briefly overwhelmed the deck, then the whistle commands came and the crew leapt to work readying the *Isla* for the wind and rain bearing down on her.

The squall came with terrible speed, a battalion of roiling charcoal and black clouds surrounded by a luminous halo racing across the water. The sea around the *Isla* bucked and heaved and she seemed at first sucked towards the squall, her masts tilted, everything loose on deck sliding to the starboard rail. Then the winds hit and blew out her sails with an ear-splitting crack and she was off, swooping around to the south-east with a great, hull-wrenching groan, skimming over the waves, the wind screaming through her rigging, canvas taut and proud. Sudden rain pounded the decks, sluicing away the salt-rimmed sweat stains of the previous four days, flattening discarded bonnets, drenching bedding, tearing laundry from the drying lines and flinging it overboard. At the wheel, Captain Holland forgot himself for a moment and let out a howl of pure joy.

Below, the women and children cowered in their bunks as the *Isla*'s hull squeaked and grated and boomed around them, held on and prayed they would not be drowned. The heat had been like slow death but this? This was pure, blind terror.

The squall blew itself out in an hour, but the *Isla* rode it all the way out of the doldrums, picking up a mild but steady wind from the west that took her across the equator and into the southern latitudes.

On the day she crossed the line, the fifth of June, the sailors held a ceremony to initiate young Walter Cobley and a new crewman named Babcock. The previous evening, two emissaries had appeared on deck during the exercise period with a summons for Walter and Babcock to appear before King Neptune the following day. The emissaries had been dressed as bears, wearing moth-eaten but genuine bearskins over their shoulders with the ferocious, yellow-fanged bear heads balanced atop their own, and had set most of the children, and not a few of the women, to screaming their heads off. There was a complaint, Captain Holland had had to be summoned, and explanations provided.

By the following morning, the women were all looking forward to it — the ceremony sounded like a right entertainment. After dinner, all were on deck waiting expectantly when a lurid spectacle appeared from beneath the afterdeck and lurched frighteningly into their midst, setting them all off again. But this time the shrieks were interspersed with giggles and only the children really cried. King Neptune was Mr Warren, wearing trousers rolled to the knee and nothing above the waist, showing off the anchor and dagger tattoos on his arms, fake hair made from unravelled rope dyed blue adorned with dried seaweed and a false blue beard that fell halfway down his muscular chest, and a golden papier-mâché crown accessorised with a trident. He was followed by his wife Queen Amphitrite — Mr Meek in a crown, lip and cheek rouge, someone's prison blouse open to the waist and a skirt raised to reveal his very shapely legs — and Davy Jones, played by Amos Furniss, who really did look horrid in a ragged black coat and trousers with his face and hands painted green and stuck all over with papier-mâché barnacles. The bears were there, too, and two characters introduced to the audience as 'the Barber' and 'the Doctor'.

The latter wasn't James Downey, however, who was standing on the afterdeck, watching with some misgiving. He had raised the matter of the ceremony with the captain the previous day, wondering whether it was a sensible idea to allow such an entertainment on a convict ship. His task after all was to keep his charges calm, not excite them by allowing them access to idiotic displays of barbarity. He'd never warmed to the more brutal customs exhibited by his naval fraternity. And there were quite a lot of those. It was the sea he enjoyed, not sailors.

But Josiah Holland had only said bluntly, 'I've always allowed it and nothing's gone awry.'

'But these are women,' James had argued. 'And children.'

'And so they were on my watches. Was it permitted on the female transports you've superintended in the past?'

'Well, yes.'

'Then I don't see a problem this time. The crew expect it. It's a rite of passage. And admit it, Mr Downey, those women won't be witnessing anything the likes of which they won't have seen before.'

And James had known he was right, but it had annoyed him all the same, especially as he'd also known that behind the captain's determined dismissal of his request had been an element of discomfort. Captain Holland had been leant on and James knew by whom: Josiah Holland was frightened of his second mate. Thanks to a guilty, confidential confession by Joel Meek, James was aware that Amos Furniss was a bully and unpopular among the crew, but that he nevertheless wielded considerable power over them. Furniss knew who owed money — a lot of it to him — who had been in trouble with the law and who had exactly which weakness. That power kept his position on the *Isla* relatively secure; if Holland dismissed him, he could probably induce the crew to follow. So if anyone really wanted the crossing the line ceremony, it was very likely Amos Furniss.

And here he was now, capering about with a horrible green face, scaring the children witless and thoroughly enjoying himself. As were the rest of the crew, James had to admit.

He gazed over the heads on the crowded waistdeck and noted Reverend and Mrs Seaton and their daughters standing on the foredeck viewing the proceedings, which surprised him as he hadn't thought they'd approve at all, the ceremony being somewhat pagan. But he supposed they were as bored as everyone else. Matthew Cutler and Gabriel Keegan were also watching, laughing uproariously at the goings on.

Cutler is a very decent young fellow, James thought, bright and personable and in all likelihood bound for a promising career with the office of the Government Architect. Keegan he wasn't so sure about. He was sharply intelligent, there was no doubt about that, and mannered and charming — Mrs Seaton and her daughters certainly thought so — but he seemed just a fraction insincere. James sometimes had the feeling when talking to Keegan that he wasn't really listening, as though he had far more interesting things to do and was only pretending to converse because he couldn't get off the ship and go and do them. But if that were the case, James couldn't really blame him: discounting the crew and prisoners, there were really only eight people Keegan *could* talk to, including James and the captain, and two of those were children. Perhaps he found his plans for the future more entertaining than his present company.

He also spotted Harrie Clarke and her friends. Harrie; it was an odd nickname for a young woman, but it did suit her. As he had initially suspected she might, she was proving extremely useful in the hospital — bright, capable and, above all, compassionate. She also seemed immune to seasickness: in fact she apparently possessed a stomach of cast iron, which was always useful in a sick room. Yesterday morning he'd admitted to the hospital a boy aged five complaining of severe stomach cramps, and at midday the child had vomited a worm easily three feet long. Lil Foster had gone rather pale, but Harrie Clarke had merely tutted and set about cleaning up, sweeping the feebly twitching creature into a bowl then despatching it overboard. Two hours later the poor boy had suffered a violent bout of diarrhoea, expelling even more worms, and Harrie hadn't batted an eye then, either. James wondered if she'd ever considered nursing as a vocation and made a mental note to ask her when he had an opportunity. At the very least he could provide her with a testimonial.

He was pleased to see that Harrie and her companions had accepted Janie Braine and Sally Minto, two of the Bristol prisoners, as messmates. He had worried that the Newgate four would not accept interlopers, but had they been allowed to remain a quartet there would no doubt have been complaints of favouritism, inevitably from Liz Parker, who, he'd noted, took every opportunity to protest about anything regarding Friday Woolfe.

Parker's position of authority, however, had lately been usurped by Bella Jackson, an intriguing, albeit alarming, character. He'd had little to do with her since she'd boarded at Portsmouth, except for her initial medical examination, which had been a strange enough experience, and rather hoped to avoid her for the remainder of the voyage. She had refused to be physically examined, but, when he'd informed her she had no choice in the matter, had grudgingly allowed him to peer into her ears, eyes and mouth, and listen to her heart and lungs with his stethoscope. She'd baulked violently, however, at his request to palpate her belly, liver and kidneys: she had been badly burnt across her entire torso in a fire several years earlier, she said, and the area even now was far too painful to touch. She certainly couldn't bear another set of eyes to witness the dreadful scars she bore. She was so thin James considered it unlikely she was hiding a pregnancy or any form of detectable internal scirrhi or benign tumour, so he had acquiesced to her wishes. Also, he was a little frightened of her. She spoke in a very abrasive manner, stared him straight in the eye, and, the whole time she was in his little examination cubicle, had given off such an aura of menace he'd been glad to see the back of her.

Liz Parker, he felt, was still to be considered a troublemaker, if only a mundane, irritating one in the order of a body louse, whereas Bella Jackson was something more akin to *rattus norvegicus* — vicious, extremely cunning, and deeply noxious. Where Friday Woolfe fell between the two, or even if she did, he wasn't sure, but of the three women he definitely knew with whom he would rather be marooned on a desert island, should that scenario ever eventuate. Of course, they would have to be marooned with an endless supply of gin as well, or his life would be even less worth living than Friday Woolfe's would be, given his professional knowledge of the behaviour of the alcohol-deprived drunk.

Gleeful shouts from the crew of 'Pollywogs! Slimy pollywogs!' drew his attention to a cleared area on the waistdeck near the main mast, where the new crewman Babcock and young Walter Cobley were being dragged towards a tub filled with what smelt, even from where James stood, suspiciously like the contents of the crew's urinal. Babcock appeared to be taking the proceedings in his stride but Walter, who was only ten years old, looked terrified.

First, a pile of refuse from the galley was upended on the deck and the two initiates forced to crawl through it on hands and knees, to raucous laughter and hoots of derision from the crew and the watching women — no doubt, James fancied, delighted to see someone other than themselves humiliated for a change. He noted that Amos Furniss appeared to be having a marvellous time cracking the cat-o'-nine-tails barely inches from their behinds. This was followed by 'the Doctor's' introduction of some sort of foul-looking liquid into the novices' mouths via an enormous glass pipette, which made Babcock cough and splutter and poor Walter vomit, followed by the application of the remainder of the liquid over their heads. Why the crew thought this was hilarious, James had no idea.

They were then paraded around the waistdeck, stripped to their trousers, until finally they were sat side by side on upturned buckets. 'The Barber' then got to work and shaved both their heads brutally, leaving nicks from which blood flowed freely, before they were dunked in the tub filled with their comrades' urine to the accompaniment of an almighty cheer, then presented to King Neptune and his queen, leaving behind the status of slimy pollywogs and becoming forever trusty shellbacks.

James shook his head and retired to his cabin.

They had been at open sea now for six weeks. They'd made very good time before the South East Trades, the doldrums were behind them, and the temperature had dropped somewhat. There was no need to call into either Rio de Janeiro or Cape Town, as the ship's water supply was holding up well — none of the barrels had spoilt or leaked. Captain Holland therefore set a course that would keep the island of Trindade, followed by that of Tristan da Cuhna, on the *Isla*'s starboard side before she rounded the southern tip of Africa and picked up the stiff westerlies of the southern latitudes, then sailed directly on to her destination.

Her passengers, both prisoners and free, had at last settled into a daily routine. It was generally agreed that the food, though limited in variety, was far better than that in the gaols; a number of prisoners were even gaining weight. Meals, depending on the whims of the *Isla*'s cook, were generally gruel in the morning with raisins or butter or sugar, dinners of beef or pork and biscuit and pease or plum pudding with bread, and suppers of pea soup or pudding with bread, made with the combined rations of each mess. Rations also included rice, suet, flour and tea, and water was issued every day. James Downey had begun doling out a daily ration of lime juice in Spanish red wine as soon as the *Isla* had sailed out of the Solent Strait: an ounce of lime juice to ward off scurvy, the Spanish red to encourage his charges to drink the lime.

The only really negative aspect of the meat-and-starches diet was the constipation, an outcome of which was frequent visits to Mr Downey's daily surgery for emetics. But one bonus resulting from unresponsive bowels was not having to make regular trips to the water closets. There were two, in a divided stall at one end of the prison deck, and they were noisome places even though they were emptied, scraped, sluiced and sprinkled with chloride of lime three times a day. The stench tainted the very timbers of the closets, which were perpetually damp and somehow greasy. Ultimately they were unavoidable, as slow or blocked bowels became uncomfortable after a while, then outright painful, so the inevitable could only be put off for so long.

To avoid using the water closets, some people had taken to surreptitiously shitting in buckets during the night, then emptying the contents down the privies in the morning. The smell then pervaded the prison deck, offence was taken and the matter reported to Mr Downey, who had outlawed the practice immediately for reasons of hygiene. But it had gone on, causing several bouts of slapping, hair-pulling and even fisticuffs when the culprits — Liz Parker and her crowd, of course — had been confronted.

Harrie was thinking about all this as she squatted over the seat of one of the water closets, one hand pressed to the wall for balance against the rolling of the ship, the other clutching her gathered skirts against her distended belly. She would love to crap in a nice clean bucket, but could never bring herself to do it even if it was allowed. She hadn't in Newgate, not in front of everyone, and wouldn't be able to here, either.

She grimaced as her thighs shook with the effort of supporting her weight; her bowel cramped sluggishly, and she let out a whimper as pain flared in her nether regions. This would teach her for not going to Mr Downey for an emetic, but she couldn't do that either. How could she? The embarrassment! Sweat popped out on her forehead, her bowel spasmed again and, finally, she did what she'd been needing to do for the previous six days.

Almost weeping from the relief, and resisting the urge to sit down, she retrieved a carefully hoarded square of fabric from her pocket and cleaned herself, ignoring the frayed tuft of rope and bucket of water on the floor. When she'd finished with it, she dropped the fabric down the hole, as Mr Downey had expressly forbidden the washing and reusing of such items, which included babies' clouts, bandages and menstrual rags.

Outside the stall she washed her hands with soap and water and dried them on her apron, feeling in a much better mood now but hoping the dull ache in her backside wasn't the start of piles, and thinking it was strange how something as ordinary as a successful visit to the privy could influence a person's entire outlook. It was curious, too, the way the existence of each and every woman had been reduced to the day-to-day activities aboard the *Isla*. It had, though. What they had known in London was behind them now, probably forever. All they knew about what might come next was their destination — Sydney in New South Wales — and that it was a penal colony, had a hot climate, and that they would be farmed out as servants for the length of their sentences. That wasn't enough information on which to base a future, so all they had was now, each day, aboard ship. To think any more broadly or ambitiously was too daunting and too hopeless a task.

Rachel still had plans, Harrie knew, of somehow saving up and going back to England to find Lucas Carew, if he didn't come to New South Wales for her first, but they hardly listened to her now when she started on about that. She was only hurting herself. But the day before, at supper, she'd come out with the strangest thing; she'd said what if they were the only people left in the entire world? What if they were sailing halfway around the globe and it was only them, on the *Isla*, still alive? It was true, occasionally it did feel like that, as they hadn't passed another ship in over a fortnight, but sometimes Harrie worried about Rachel. She could be perfectly sweet and bright and sunny one moment, then overcome with a really quite intense melancholy the next. The others passed it off as Rachel just being Rachel, but it frightened Harrie. She thought, if it kept on occurring, she might mention it to Mr Downey. He might know what to do about it.

Matthew Cutler sat at the small writing desk in his cabin, trying studiously to read the tiny print in his bible. It had been given to him as a farewell gift by his mother. She had written *To my dearest and most cherished youngest son, my little Matthew* inside the front cover, and she had wept while she'd done it and smudged the ink with her tears. Matthew felt guilty every time he opened it. Also, it was slightly embarrassing as he was twenty-five years old, not seven, but he loved her for it anyway. It must be quite a shock to have the last of your children grow up and leave you. But he'd vowed to write to her every week without fail — and he had, even though that meant she'd get lots of letters from him at once, then possibly none for ages, depending on how many ships they passed going the other way.

He sighed and closed the bible, defeated by the size of the print. He didn't normally read it just for fun, but was so bored he'd been driven to it. He wished he'd brought more books, and wondered if the surgeon had any worth reading. He doubted Gabriel Keegan did, as he didn't seem the bookish sort, and he thought it a safe bet that whatever Reverend Seaton might have in his cabin wouldn't be any more interesting than his bible.

He opened his little round cabin window and stared out at the undulating horizon for a few minutes, then turned his attention back to his desk, unscrewed the lid from his ink bottle, dipped his pen and began to write.

9th of June, 1829

My Dearest Mama,

I hope this letter finds you well. I am well myself. Nothing much has happened since the last time I wrote. Here aboard the Isla *the 'Slimy Polliwogs' seem to be adjusting well to life as 'Trusty Shellbacks'.*

The temperature is growing colder as we approach the southern latitudes and I suspect I will soon be grateful for the scarves you knitted so beautifully for me.

Yesterday we again saw whales, which was the highlight of an otherwise uneventful day. They are magnificent beasts, and are, I am convinced, the natural monarchs of the seas. They seem to swim so slowly and with so little effort, yet move with such awesome power and grace, one is left almost speechless observing them. They travel in packs, which is a good thing, as out here in all this ocean they must surely become lonely if they were to swim alone.

We continue to be served reasonable meals. What we lack in variety is compensated with quantity. Mr Downey has ensured that the ship has been well-victualled, though I am growing somewhat sick of pickled potatoes. Mrs Seaton is fond of them and requests the dish often. I miss fresh beef most of all. And I would kill for a pork or pigeon pie.

Matthew put down his pen and wondered about the next bit. His mother had been distinctly upset when he'd told her he would be travelling to New South Wales on a convict ship, even though the prisoners would all be women. Perhaps he ought to be careful what he wrote. On the other hand, she'd been on at him to find himself a wife since he'd turned twenty-one, so perhaps she would be pleased.

> *There is a young woman also travelling aboard the* Isla *to whom I have taken a fancy. Her name is Harriet Clarke. She has quite the sweetest face I have ever encountered, the most glorious, shiny brown hair, and a marvellous, caring nature. Unfortunately I rarely have the opportunity to speak with her as she is so closely chaperoned, but I hope to be rewarded with the privilege of a few more moments with her before the* Isla *reaches New South Wales.*

This last bit was pure obfuscation, of course, but his mother would have an absolute conniption if she knew her precious youngest son had his eye on a convict girl. He knew in his heart it was immense folly to even mention Harriet, but he couldn't help it — he had to say something to someone. He could just imagine his mother's questions: What does Harriet Clarke's father do? Who are her mother's people? How did they make their money? He added:

> *The prisoners really aren't what you might imagine. They work industriously all day from sun-up to sunset, cleaning, sewing, attending the school Mrs Seaton has established, and meeting for prayers. In the evening, after supper, they all gather on deck and play games and dance skilfully and have a very merry time of it.*

He didn't add that at least once a week the games and dancing came to an abrupt end due to fighting as the result of what appeared from the vantage point of the foredeck to be perceived encroachment over invisible lines delineating the different factions' deck spaces.

And what he'd written still didn't make the convict women look like a suitable cohort from which to draw a bride, not by a long shot and no matter how fancy their dance steps. He crossed out 'skilfully'.

And he hadn't actually spoken to Harriet Clarke at all. Captain Holland had made it very clear at the beginning of the voyage that, on his ship at least, fee-paying passengers would not be mixing with those travelling courtesy of the Crown and vice versa, but he, Matthew, had watched her every night when the women came up on deck. Of them all, she stood out as the most attractive and certainly the most appealing. She was the prettiest, the sweetest, and she possessed genuine integrity. Though, to be honest, how he knew that just by observing her from afar, he wasn't sure. He knew she assisted James Downey in the hospital, because he'd gone in there one day looking for him and had seen her, so he'd asked the surgeon her name, and why she was being transported. He was sure Mr Downey thought he was unhinged for wanting to know, but he'd been relieved to discover Harriet Clarke was only a thief, and not an axe murderer or something really heinous. That could be a little difficult to get past his mother.

Well, Mother, I will sign off now as it is almost five o'clock and Reverend Seaton will shortly be conducting the daily prayer service, which everyone aboard ship attends.

I will write again soon, and hope that in the coming days we will pass a ship that is homeward-bound, so that my letters may find their way to you.

Your Affectionate Son
Matthew

He blotted a smear, then set aside the letter to dry. He had a pile of letters to send now, and was beginning to find it difficult to manufacture things to write about. One day was blurring into the next, becoming as smudged as the words in his correspondence. He actually envied the women on the prison deck, with all their daily chores. Hard work, yes, but at least they had something to do. Gabriel Keegan somehow managed to sleep much of the day away; how, Matthew didn't know, not with all the banging and shouting going on from the crew. Perhaps he would ask the captain if he could be of assistance in some capacity. He'd sailed before — not on a ship as seagoing as this, of course, just yachting off the Devon coast when he was a youth — so he wasn't a complete novice.

Anything would be better than staring out of the window all day, waiting for Harriet Clarke to come out and dance.

Harrie could see that Mr Downey was writing his notes, so she tried not to disturb him as she descended the ladder into the hospital.

'Good morning, Harrie.'

Damn. 'Good morning, Mr Downey.'

'Sleep well?'

'Yes, thank you,' Harrie lied. No one had been sleeping particularly well on the prison deck since the *Isla* had set sail. It was too noisy, too smelly and airless, and too ... rolly.

'Have you spoken to Lil?'

'No, she went straight to her bunk.'

Mr Downey put away his writing things. 'I'm afraid we'll have to lance young Alfie Byatt's boil this morning after all.'

Harrie wrinkled her nose and moved to the cupboard where the surgical instruments were kept. 'Have you told him?'

'Yes, and he isn't very happy about it, are you lad?' Mr Downey said, crossing to Alfie's bed.

Alfie was six and had a colossal boil in the crease of his left buttock. His bottom lip quivering, he eyed the surgeon reproachfully before pulling the blanket up over his face.

'Where's his ma?' Harrie set out a tray containing a scalpel, a curette, a small trocar and squares of cut lint.

'She said she'd rather not watch.'

Harrie rolled her eyes. 'Well, that's helpful, isn't it?' she said to Alfie cheerfully, sliding the blanket off his head. 'Come on, love, turn over, there's a good boy.'

'Will it hurt?' Alfie asked tremulously.

'It will, but not for long, I promise. And you'll feel so much better afterwards.'

Beginning to cry, Alfie wriggled over onto his stomach. Harrie gently pulled down the ragged but freshly washed breeks he was wearing. He was so undernourished his backside was almost nonexistent, the boil a hard, shiny, headless mass whose angry redness spread from one side of his skinny buttock to the other. Holding her hand an inch above it, Harrie felt its poisonous heat. She winced and shared a worried glance with Mr Downey.

While he prepared his instruments, she took hold of Alfie's hands and said conversationally, 'Do you know, Alfie, I once had a boil on my bum the exact size and shape of an apple and damson pie?'

Alfie stopped crying.

'I was twelve at the time. It was terrible. I couldn't sit down for weeks. One day my ma had a look at it and do you know? It really was an apple and damson pie! Imagine that!'

'On ya bum?' Alfie said, amazed.

'Yes, and all the rats and mice in the house started scampering around after me trying to snatch a bite.'

Mr Downey smiled.

'Did ya give it them?'

'No, I did not!'

'How'd ya get rid of it then?' Alfie suddenly shrieked as Mr Downey poked the tip of a scalpel into the centre of the boil.

Harrie gripped his hands tighter as a great, foul stream of yellow-green pus poured from the wound, accompanied by the most revolting stink.

'I hung my bum out the window and let the blackbirds have it.'

Alfie was crying again but he still managed a giggle. 'That's never true.'

Mr Downey took a piece of lint in each hand and pressed on the boil, making Alfie scream again and forcing out more pus and a big, hard white core. The smell was almost unbearable.

'It is!' Harrie insisted. 'And the nits me and my brother and sisters used to get! They were so big we used to send them up the bakehouse to collect our loaf of a morning!'

'Our nits were bigger,' Alfie said, jerking as Mr Downey used the curette to scrape the last of the pus from the wound. 'We used to ride our nits round Hyde Park!' He giggled some more, delighted with his own wit.

'Is that so? Harrie said. 'Well, *ours* were so big the navy put masts on them and sailed them to China!'

Mr Downey burst out laughing.

Alfie lifted his head and strained to peer over his shoulder at his backside, forcing a thin trickle of watery blood from the wound. 'Sir, is it all out?'

'For the time being. Harrie, more lint please.'

James watched her as she returned to the supply cupboard, dropping the used lint into a bucket on the way. He liked that the way she did things was so neat and economical. She even moved tidily. She never wasted energy making a mess, so she seldom had to clean up after herself, though she never complained about cleaning up other people's messes, and God knew there were plenty of those.

He also liked the soft hint of down on her face, her small waist and the swell of her breasts beneath the hideous prison blouse, but he tried very hard not to think about those things. He would be mortified if she knew, or ever caught him looking at her. He would be mortified if anyone knew.

'Could a nit swim all the way to China, but?' Alfie mumbled, yawning.

'No, you'd really have to rely on the sails, I expect,' James said.

A poultice of carbolic acid was applied to Alfie's boil to help draw out any remaining poison, though the wound would have to be cleaned again tomorrow.

'Your family sounds very colourful,' James said after Alfie had fallen into the first pain-free sleep he'd had in over a week. 'Was that true, about the apple and damson pie?'

Harrie, tidying away the surgical instruments, gave him an amused look. 'Of course not. It was pear and cinnamon.'

Ten

Something was wrong with Bella Jackson; there was a horrendous, blood-curdling screeching coming from behind her curtain.

It was just after breakfast and as usual Bella had eaten hers in her little partitioned compartment. If she appeared at all during the day, it was rarely until later in the morning after all the chores had been done. Everyone had long given up complaining about her not pulling her weight as one of her girls always stepped in when her name appeared on the roster. After all, as Harrie repeatedly and patiently remarked at the conclusion of Friday's frequent tirades every time it happened, it didn't really matter who did the work, as long as it got done. Eventually even Friday came to see the arrangement as acceptable, declaring that Bella was such a slaggard she wouldn't do the job properly and they'd all suffer for it anyway.

The breakfast dishes had gone up, the table had been scrubbed, the women rostered to holystone the prison deck were standing by, and two crewmen were waiting to come through with the swinging stove to fumigate the space and sprinkle chloride of lime throughout. Everyone else was moving out, up to the tubs on deck to wash the breakfast dishes, or on to other rostered duties. It was noisy and chaotic, but Bella's shrieks froze everyone.

'What in God's name is she doing in there?' Friday peered along the prison deck, a heap of bedding in her arms.

Two of Bella's girls disappeared into her compartment; Bella let out a stream of invective at the top of her voice and they reappeared at great speed, flapping their hands, looking hugely panicked. A missile flew out of the compartment after them and shattered against a post, its contents splattering everywhere. One of the girls raced for the water closets, returning a moment later with a bucket; hefting it onto her shoulder, she rushed it into the compartment. Another splash could be heard and the screaming stopped abruptly.

There was a moment of silence.

Then Bella's voice barked: 'You fucking *whore*!'

'I hope that wasn't the arse-wiping bucket,' Friday said, and laughed so hard she dropped her armful of linen and had to sit down. Her loud hoots rolled down the prison deck and no doubt straight into the water-drenched ears of Bella Jackson.

Smirking, Sarah said, 'That's not very nice, Friday.'

'No, it isn't,' Harrie agreed. 'I wonder if she needs help?'

'So what if she does?' Friday replied. 'She's got her own flunkies.' She giggled again. 'She's got a worse mouth on her than I have. It was funny, though, wasn't it? Look, Janie's just about having kittens.'

They all looked at Janie, doubled over on the lower bunk, her face almost on her knees.

'No, it's not kittens,' she said, her voice strained.

Friday stopped laughing. 'Oh Christ, is it coming?'

Rachel's face lit up. 'Ooooh, the *baby*!'

'I'll get Mr Downey,' Rachel said quickly and disappeared.

'*Is* it coming?' Harrie asked, and felt her insides swoop in a rush of excitement and fright when Janie nodded. 'Are you sure?'

''Course I'm sure! It's me bloody third, I know what it feels like.'

Harrie opened her mouth then closed it again; Janie was barely older than she was herself. She felt slightly shocked, though she'd thought she was beyond shocking by now. 'What can I do?'

'Nothing yet, ta.' Janie rolled over onto her side. 'Have you done a birthing before?'

'Not really. I helped the midwife when my ma had my sisters and brother. But Lil Foster's done plenty.' A horrible suspicion crept over Harrie.

'So you have, then.'

'No! All I did was hold Ma's hand and help her push and then swaddle the babes. I wasn't even that grown up!'

'Well, I want you to do it,' Janie said flatly. 'You've got good little hands. Lil can help. I don't want some cove looking up me minge. It's women's business, birthing.'

Harrie felt suddenly bilious with nerves. She couldn't birth a baby; she was a sempstress with a knack for fancy needlework, not a midwife. 'But —'

'Don't argue,' Janie snapped. 'I've made up me mind. *Ow!*' She curled up again, in the grip of another spasm.

James Downey appeared. 'Have your waters broken?' he asked without preamble.

Janie nodded.

'How long have you been having the pains?'

'Since before sun-up.'

'Before *dawn*!' Harrie exclaimed. 'Why didn't you say something?'

Janie shrugged. 'Me last one took ten hours to turn up. What's the rush?' She grimaced again. 'Though this one might be coming a *bit* faster.'

'I'd like you to deliver in the hospital, Janie, if you don't mind,' Mr Downey said. 'It's up to you who you choose to attend you. I will be on hand if necessary.'

Harrie stared at James Downey with open admiration, then flushed as he caught her looking at him. How thoughtful and courteous! On the single occasion her ma had been able to afford a visit from a doctor, the ill-tempered bugger had accused her of being stupid and superstitious because she had tied blue beads in the little ones' hair to keep witches away, told her they all had bad coughs when she already knew that, offered no palliative, and then charged her a crown for the privilege. And here was the surgeon superintendent giving Janie a choice as to who she wanted to deliver her baby, including *himself*, for absolutely no fee at all!

'Harrie's doing the deed. She's already said so.'

Harrie cringed as Mr Downey said, 'I didn't realise you had midwifery skills, Harrie. That's marvellous. Why didn't you say so?'

'I —' Harrie began.

'Can't wait,' Janie finished for her, 'and neither can I. Help me get up them steps. I'm starting to feel like there's a watermelon stuck in me fanny.'

'Er, no, not the ladder. I'll open the connecting door,' James Downey said, and hurried off.

Janie gave birth to a healthy girl she named Rosie Isla Harriet Braine at twenty minutes past eleven that morning. Nothing went wrong and Harrie excelled herself, although her heart didn't stop pounding until well after the baby had been wiped down and swaddled and the afterbirth massaged out of Janie. Lil helped only minimally and James wasn't needed at all.

'See, I told you you'd be good at it,' Janie said as she sat up in the narrow hospital bed sipping noisily from a mug of black tea. It wasn't the bottle of stout all nursing mothers were allowed daily to enrich their milk, because hers hadn't come in yet, but it was better than nothing. The baby lay sleeping in a cradle nearby, because Mr Downey had said, for some strange reason, she wasn't to sleep in the bed with Janie, but she was settled and seemed content.

Harrie tucked in Janie's blanket. 'Janie?'

'Mmm?'

'Where are your other children?'

'The first one's with me ma now and the second one died.'

'Oh.' Harrie couldn't think of anything else to say. It was so awfully sad.

Lil Foster bustled over, looking intrigued. 'You'll never guess who's gone in to see Mr Downey.'

'Bella Jackson,' Janie said.

Lil looked deflated. 'Yes, actually. Anyway, I couldn't help overhearing —'

'With your great flappy ear against the curtain,' Janie added.

'You know,' Lil said, 'having a baby hasn't done anything to fix your smart mouth, Janie Braine.'

Janie took a last swig of her tea. 'No, it didn't last time, either.'

'She was asking for something to put on *burns*.'

Harrie and Janie looked at each other.

'Probably smoking those fancy little cigars of hers again,' Janie said.

'But you don't burn yourself that badly from *cigars*, do you?' Harrie said. 'And I didn't smell tobacco this morning, did you?'

'No. Maybe she was counting her piles of money and they caught fire. That'll teach her.'

'What piles of money?' Harrie asked.

'The money she gets from standing over them girls.' Janie laughed at the expression on Harrie's face. 'Honestly, Harrie, you're a right gulpy sometimes. She organises them — you didn't think she wasn't taking any blunt off them, did you? That's what a bawd does. How else would she make a living?'

'No, I knew. Friday said — I just didn't think it would be that much. You know, paper money.'

'Well, it probably isn't paper money. I just said that. It'd be coin.'

'But coin wouldn't burn.'

Janie sighed. 'Christ, Harrie, why do you always have to be such a pennant?'

'I think you mean pedant. And I thought she'd take just a small percentage of what they're earning. Friday says it's half. That's seems a lot.'

'It's more than that,' Lil said. 'My friend Josie says it's close to two-thirds. Bella must have a hell of a hold over them. Or be promising them the moon once we get to New South Wales.' She frowned. 'That prick Amos Furniss'll have something to do with it, I'd put money on it.'

Two-thirds seemed an enormous amount of money to give up. To Harrie it didn't seem fair at all, given what the women had to do to earn it. 'You're not saying Friday works for Bella, though?' Harrie thought this extremely unlikely, but she'd never actually asked Friday about her business arrangements.

Janie snorted. 'You know Friday better than that. What do you think?'

Lil said, 'Josie says Friday gets more cullies than any of them. She says it's a wonder she can sit down of a morning.' She and Janie tittered, but Harrie didn't. 'And Bella hates it.'

'Because Friday works on her own and Bella doesn't get any of the money?' Harrie asked.

'Partly. And because she's telling the girls they're being cheated. And now they're complaining to Bella and she wants revenge.'

She was late, which was irritating as he'd expressly requested in his note that she meet with him on time. He would give her another ten minutes, then go below. He'd had his evening's shag, his cock was ominously itchy and he wanted to get to his cabin to wash it. You couldn't be too careful with this calibre of whore.

He leant on the rail and stared down into the water as the *Isla* cut through a carpet of luminous plankton, the bow waves a startlingly bright iridescent blue. And suddenly she was there, smelling faintly of tobacco and ... jasmine perhaps?

'Good evening, Mr Keegan.'

He turned to face her. She was almost as tall as he was, but too thin for his liking, no meat on her at all. And far too old. She had a beaded black muslin shawl draped over her head and pulled across her mouth, as though she didn't want to be recognised. Stupid cow — everyone knew everyone on a ship this small.

'Mrs Jackson. Thank you for meeting with me.'

She inclined her head in acknowledgment. 'Miss Jackson. I am not a married woman. You wish to speak with me.'

It was a statement, not a question. She was very self-assured. Her rings looked expensive and she appeared to have applied the face paint she wore with a garden trowel, but you expected that from women who worked in her profession. In fact, her skin was deathly white and her eyes seemed nothing more than sooty smears, the pupils mere glints, or perhaps that was just the effect of the shadows and the moonlight.

'Yes, I do. I understand these women who come up on deck at night work for you.'

'Most of them do, yes.'

'I am interested in one girl in particular, although I've never seen her up here after dark. I had hoped you might be in a position to procure her services for me.'

Bella Jackson withdrew a silver case from the pocket of her jacket, opened it and offered him one of the new slender cigars. He declined and she put the case away. He was impressed: he'd expected a clay pipe.

'That will depend on the girl, Mr Keegan, not me.'

'I'm rather assuming it will depend on the money.'

'Perhaps. What is this girl's name?'

Keegan told her. 'Are you aware of her?'

Bella Jackson smiled. 'As it happens I am. And I have noted your interest previously. The foredeck offers a fortuitous vantage point.'

'It does.'

'It will cost you.'

'I'm sure it will. What's your price? More to the point, what's hers?'

'I don't know if she has one. That will be your business to negotiate. She is not to my knowledge a whore. My price, to deliver her to you, will be ten pounds.'

'Christ, that's steep.'

'For a girl who looks like that and is quite possibly a virgin? I don't think so, Mr Keegan. Of course, if you're not interested …' She turned to leave.

'Wait. Wait, yes, I am interested.'

'Then I will require payment now.'

Keegan shook his head as he dug out his purse — he might have known she'd demand the money up front. He withdrew a ten-pound note and gave it to her. She took it and slipped it away somewhere. As she did, her shawl caught on one of her rings and slid from her face, revealing a large scab on her right jaw from her ear to her chin. A burn? Some disgusting disease of the skin? Snatching at the shawl she hastily covered herself again.

'When do you want her?' she said.

Keegan felt his cock twitch. 'As soon as possible. And I want her in my cabin.'

'I'll see what I can do. I may have to deliver her under false pretences.'

'You mean, she won't know why she's coming to see me?'

'Possibly not.'

Keegan smiled to himself. 'Well, she'll soon find out, won't she?'

Giggling madly, Rachel whirled round and round, her hair flying and her prison skirt whirling out like a giant mushroom. All around her women clapped and danced to the sailors' fiddle, washboard, tin whistle and tub drum quartet, whooping it up and stamping their feet on the deck in time to the scratchy beat. Paired off in manless couples, they jigged and reeled energetically, sweating in the cooling evening air, or jumped about on their own, carried away by the music and the opportunity to sing lustily and shout.

Rachel was bursting for a wee, but like a barely pot-trained two-year-old, she didn't want to go below in case she missed something. But the more she danced the more she needed to empty her bladder, and very soon she was going to embarrass herself. Reluctantly, she made her way towards the prison deck hatch.

Sarah intercepted her. 'Where are you off to?'

'The bog. I'm *bursting*.'

'I'll come with you.'

'Oh, what for? I'll only be five minutes!'

Sarah glanced up at the foredeck. Keegan was there, yapping away with that other cove. That was all right; as long as she could see him, he couldn't be anywhere else. 'Well, mind you come straight back.'

'I will.'

Sarah turned back to Keegan too quickly to notice that someone else had followed Rachel down the ladder onto the prison deck.

As usual the light below was dim and, after being in the fresh air, the smell of body odour, bilge and the bogs enveloped Rachel unpleasantly. She hurried along the aisle to the water closets at the far end and shut herself into a cubicle, lifting her skirt and hovering above the seat with profound relief. When she'd finished she wiped herself with the hem of her skirt and barged out of the cubicle, eager to be back on deck before the music finished for the evening.

But someone was sitting at the table, just by the door that opened into the water closets.

'Good evening, Rachel,' Bella Jackson said in her low voice.

Rachel came to a rapid halt, her boots skidding on the smooth floorboards. Bella's face was in shadow; all Rachel could clearly see was the gleam of lamplight in her hair and her pale, long-fingered hands resting in her lap.

'You gave me a fright!'

'I didn't mean to. I saw you dancing up on deck. Very pretty. Charming, in fact.'

'Thank you.' Rachel's gaze searched the rest of the prison deck, trying not to make it obvious. Were she and Bella the only ones down here?

'Did your friend Friday like her gift?'

'Her gift?'

'The caul?'

'Oh! Yes, very much, thank you. She felt better as soon as I gave it to her.'

'Well, that's good news, isn't it?'

'Yes.'

'I'm always heartened to hear that a favour has worked out well.'

'Yes, it did. Thank you.' Rachel attempted to sidle past, but Bella put out a staying hand.

'And now I would like to ask a favour of you.'

Rachel began to feel uneasy. Perhaps she should have paid something for the caul after all.

Bella shifted slightly on the bench seat, allowing the lamp to illuminate her face. There was a big, scabby pink mark on it, below her right cheek. She smiled warmly. 'Tell me, Rachel, how would you like to make some money?'

'At night? Working for you?' Oh no, this was terrible. 'But I'm not a prostitute! I couldn't!'

'No, dear,' Bella said, patting her hand. 'I don't mean that. I've been approached by one of the paying passengers who is looking for someone trustworthy to launder his linen once a week. He's willing to pay very handsomely, I believe. I said I might know just the girl. Are you interested?'

'Laundry?' Rachel's heart was thumping so loudly at the thought of prostituting herself she could hardly hear her own voice. 'Which paying passenger?'

'The gentleman named Mr Keegan. Do you know the one I mean?'

'Yes.'

'Interested?'

Rachel nodded.

'Good. In that case he would like you to go to his cabin tomorrow night at eleven o'clock to discuss the terms of your employment.'

'Eleven at night? That's late.'

'It will have to be done in secret, Rachel. Remember that prisoners are forbidden to fraternise with the passengers. Have you forgotten?'

'No.' Rachel had.

'And a word of advice.' Bella leant forwards, though they were still alone on the prison deck. 'I strongly suggest you keep this from Friday and your other friends. They might become jealous if they realise you're earning such good money.'

'No, I don't think they'll mind. We're like sisters now, and all the money we make we share.'

'Really?' Bella frowned. 'Well, perhaps you'd like to save up and buy them something when you get the chance in Sydney, a token of your affection for them? I know what a generous little soul you are. You'd like to keep that secret, wouldn't you? Good girl,' she said as Rachel nodded in agreement.

Up on deck again Rachel began to realise what a stroke of good fortune she had just encountered. It was the most extraordinary thing because she'd been planning for weeks now to approach someone — either Mr Keegan, or Mr Cutler or even bossy Mrs Seaton if she had to — and offer to clean their cabins or take in their laundry. For money, of course, to go towards her Lucas fund, which she hadn't started yet, but she had better if she wanted to get back to England after she'd served her sentence. She couldn't play cards any more, not on the ship, as no one would play against her. And if Mr Keegan was actually offering laundry work, she wouldn't have to go begging for it. Though where she would find lemons and turpentine for washing silk she didn't know.

Bella Jackson was right, though, about keeping quiet about it. Not because of buying presents for everyone with the money, though that was a nice idea, but because Friday and Sarah disliked Mr Keegan so much. Rachel didn't know why as he seemed such a gentleman, and she really was quite a good judge of character.

Now she was lying in bed next to Harrie and Sarah, who were asleep, waiting for eleven o'clock to arrive so she could creep out and go to his cabin. Friday was already out, working, so she would have to be very careful not to bump into her anywhere up on deck. It was amazing, really, everything that went on on the ship at night. A real little hive of industry, Friday said it was. And all the while Captain Holland was snoring away in his cabin on the quarterdeck — and Mr Downey as well. Sarah said surely Mr Downey couldn't be that stupid, though she thought Captain Holland was, but Friday said the captain probably did know, but was turning a blind eye because he didn't want to upset his crew in case they mutinied, and Harrie reckoned Mr Downey took a sleeping draught at night, because he missed his wife, and slept like the dead.

Rachel had been feeling nervous about meeting Mr Keegan all day. Harrie asked her what was wrong and she'd lied and said nothing, and felt bad for it. She'd thought about passing the time by setting her hair in curls using pages out of Mrs Fry's bible, but her hair had grown too long for that and she wasn't cutting it for any reason. Lucas loved her hair and she'd vowed when she'd realised she probably wouldn't be seeing him again for a while — *really* realised, when the ship was leaving Portsmouth — not to cut it until they met again. Now, if she didn't tie it up, she sat on it and sometimes it made her eyes water. And she had nits, but she nearly always had nits.

The ship's bell tolled ten-thirty. Rachel carefully lifted off her blanket and sat up. She didn't have to worry about making a noise because the prison deck resonated with the usual sounds of over a hundred sleeping bodies, as well as the creaking and grinding of the ship, and neither did the odd bump matter, but Sarah and Harrie might wake if they got cold, so she made sure not to disturb their blankets.

In the sooty light of the permanently burning oil lamps, she wriggled stealthily to the edge of the bunk, put her bare feet on the floor and crouched, reaching for the sack containing her blouse and skirt. She wouldn't bother with her boots, even though it was cold enough to wear them on deck now.

Dressed, she crept the short distance along the aisle, looking left and right to make sure no one was awake and watching — because if even just one person saw her, *everyone* would know by morning she'd been up on deck — then climbed the ladder and pushed against the hatch. It was closed but not locked. It was extremely heavy and she had to really put her weight behind it, but finally she managed to open it and wriggle out without dropping it and making a horrendous crash.

The waistdeck was empty. She felt slightly disappointed. Not that she'd been expecting to see couples fucking all over it, but she thought she might have seen something at least mildly interesting. She padded silently across the boards, long accustomed by now to the roll of the ship beneath her feet, until she came to the narrow door that led to the cabins beneath the foredeck. Taking a last, quick look around to ensure she wasn't being observed, she grasped the door handle.

'You'll be sorry, girlie.'

Rachel almost wet herself. Stepping back and squinting into the darkness, she spotted him: revolting Amos Furniss, squatting on the foredeck where he wasn't supposed to be, hunched and crumpled like a gargoyle, back against the foremast, filthy black pipe in his mouth. She loathed him; everyone did.

'What did you say?'

'You and your fine, silky hair and your pretty eyes. You'll be sorry.' And he laughed.

'Oh, sod off.' Rachel pushed open the door.

At the bottom of a pair of steps the narrow corridor between the cabins was lit by a single swinging lantern. Four low doors led off the corridor, two on each side. One at the far end was slightly ajar so she headed that way. Rachel took a deep breath and knocked.

It opened almost immediately to reveal Gabriel Keegan, stooping slightly due to the low ceiling, but smiling widely and making a grand welcoming gesture with the hand that wasn't holding the door handle.

'My dear, you came! Come in, come in.'

Rachel stepped inside and looked around as he closed the door behind her. It was a tiny little cabin, much smaller than she'd imagined. Standing exactly in the middle she could just about touch every wall if she'd had a mind to.

'Please, make yourself comfortable,' Mr Keegan said.

She perched on the wooden chair in front of the little writing desk. Mr Keegan sat on the bed, a narrow, built-in cot with drawers beneath. There was nothing personal she could see, except for a trunk against one wall and Mr Keegan's hat on the desk. No pictures, no little knick-knacks, no nice things. But then this was a man's room, she reminded herself; her father and her brothers hadn't gone in for fripperies either and she hadn't had a chance to find out what Lucas had liked, as they'd shared so little time together. If it was *her* cabin, she would have made pretty cushions for the bed and the chair, a nice lace curtain with a satin sash to tie it back when the window was open, an embroidered runner for the desk and perhaps a rag rug for the floor. Those boards didn't look very inviting all bare like that.

She looked up to see Mr Keegan watching her. The window was closed and it was quite warm in here, despite the coolness of the night. He wasn't wearing a coat and several buttons on his shirt were open, showing a bit of chest hair. God, her mother would skin her alive if she could see her now.

'Bella Jackson said you have a laundry position available?' she said.

He smiled without showing his teeth. 'Is that what she called it? Yes, well. I assume you're not averse to the idea of making some money?'

'No, sir. I'm saving up, you see.'

'How does a half-sovereign a week sound?'

A whole half-sovereign? Just for laundering one man's shirts and stockings and bed linen? Rachel was astounded.

'Would you be wanting me to clean in here for that as well?'

'You can do whatever the hell you like, as long as you're available for me, and *exclusively* me, to fuck every night between ten o'clock and midnight. I might decide on some other girl's company, but you're still to make yourself available or you don't get paid, is that clear?'

Rachel felt as though she'd been punched in the face, and barely heard anything he said after the word 'fuck'. What a truly horrible mistake she'd made. What a rotten bastard!

She stood up. 'You bloody pig. How dare you?'

Keegan smirked, enjoying her shock and embarrassment, feeling himself stiffen. 'You're a whore — I thought you'd jump at the chance of a guaranteed income.' Though he knew she wasn't; if she was, she would be up on deck at night. But it was exciting seeing her humiliated.

'I'm *not*, and if I was, I wouldn't go with you anyway. The girls all laugh about you, you know.' She crooked her little finger and waggled it. 'John Thomas Junior.' It was an invention, but she knew it would rile him. And then, her rage and humiliation boiling over, she hoicked up a lump of phlegm and spat it at him.

The gob landed on the sleeve of his costly white linen shirt. He looked down at it for a moment, then back at her, and in the black depths of his narrowed eyes she saw what was going to happen to her. She lunged for the door.

Grabbing a fistful of her hair he jerked her backwards, cutting off her scream, and swung her around so she landed on her knees on the floor, her scalp burning. She scrambled towards the gap beneath the desk — perhaps he wouldn't be able to reach her under there — but he ripped her back by her hair again and picked her up, turned her over and dumped her on the bed, for a second knocking the breath out of her. She kicked out viciously and bit his hand, but he slapped her, knelt on her legs and punched her, hard, right in the middle of her face. She lay still then, shocked rigid, a high-pitched roaring noise filling her ears, stars bursting silently behind her eyes.

Keegan pressed his thin feather pillow down over her face. She couldn't see anything at all and the stink of him, of his skin and the pomade he used to dress his hair, filled her collapsed nostrils. Vaguely, as though yards away, she felt him fumbling around, then the heat of his freed cock against her hand.

She rallied and gave an enormous buck, almost unseating him, and flailed wildly with her arms, scratching his face, squealing as loudly as she dared but too frightened to inhale forcefully and really scream in case she sucked in the pillow casing and suffocated. Or drowned — her nose throbbed and there was blood trickling down the back of her throat and she couldn't swallow fast enough to get rid of it. Oh God, what if she drowned in her own blood?

She felt Keegan lift his weight off her and she thought for a heart-stopping second he might have changed his mind, that he wasn't going to do it after all, but then her skirt was pulled up and flipped over her head. She clamped her legs shut but felt his bony knee jam between hers, bearing down until her muscles gave way and he shoved his way between her thighs. He covered her completely, the top of her head under the pillow directly beneath his chest. She couldn't breathe at all now and began to struggle for her life, grunting and crying out in muffled terror.

It occurred to Keegan that he might actually kill her and he raised himself off her so she could breathe again, but planted his elbows on her arms so she couldn't hit out.

Grateful for the reprieve, Rachel lay still. His cock was too big and she was as dry as emery paper. It hurt badly. It was nothing like it had been with Lucas. Keegan tore her, and when he began to slide more easily she knew she was bleeding.

She let herself drift away, until it felt as though it were happening to someone else. She thought about Shannon. She remembered a rhyme about magpies she and her brothers used to chant until it drove their mother barmy.

One for sorrow
Two for mirth
Three for a wedding
Four for a birth
Five for silver
Six for gold
Seven for a secret
Not to be told
Eight for heaven
Nine for hell
And ten for the devil's own sel'!

She said it again now, over and over and over.

Keegan came to a vicious, thrusting climax that drove her into the mattress and rammed her head against the cabin wall, then rolled off her and lay panting. Rachel stayed motionless, too frightened to move.

After a minute or so he drew down her skirt, used it to wipe the blood and semen off himself, and removed the pillow from her face, frowning at the stain across it where her nose had bled.

Without looking at her, he said, 'You can go now.'

Rachel sat up, her head and face throbbing, a fresh line of blood trickling over her top lip. It tasted coppery and salty. She swiped it away with the back of her hand and gingerly swung her legs over the side of the bed. She felt as though she were suddenly eighty years old. Her back ached, her legs felt wrenched out of their sockets, everything between them stung and felt swollen and there was a deep ache in her lower belly.

As she shakily found her feet, a gush of something warm came out of her, and she prayed it was only his mess, not blood.

She staggered the few feet across the cabin to the door.

Matthew hadn't been able to sleep, and there had been a thumping noise going on and, about ten minutes earlier, a strangled sort of yelp that had sounded quite close. It had bothered him, so he'd climbed out of bed and pulled on his trousers and shirt.

Now, someone's cabin door was opening and closing. He went to his own, opened it a crack, and looked out.

Hester Seaton sat up in bed, her hair in curling rags under a lace bed cap, staring into the darkness, her daughters swaying in their hammocks gently above her. She, too, had heard worrying noises — a girl's cry?

Octavius would be snoring his head off next door, having spent himself, she reflected disgustedly, thinking about all that nubile flesh scampering about on the deck below him.

Really, it was hard enough trying to teach them to read and write: she couldn't be responsible for what happened to them if they chose to run about after dark. Truly, they were morally bankrupt and quite beyond redemption.

Deliberately, she lay down and jammed her chubby fingers in her ears.

* * *

In the corridor's dim light, Matthew saw what he at first thought was a pile of rags on the ground. Then he made out a small, white foot and realised it was a child.

The child pushed herself into a kneeling position and burst into tears.

'Are you all right?' he asked.

She looked up at him. She had long, pale blonde hair, strands of which, he saw to his horror, appeared to be stuck to her face with blood. His heart thudded even more wildly as he realised she was one of Harriet Clarke's friends.

'Oh God, are you all right?' he said again, bending down to help her to her feet. 'What's happened? Has there been an accident?'

But she shook her head and shoved him away, then sort of slumped to the ground again. So he picked her up and carried her to the door that led out to the waistdeck, struggled to open it, and stepped outside into the chilly darkness.

She thumped his chest weakly with a fist and muttered something.

'I'm sorry?'

She said it again and he only just realised her intent before it was too late. Quickly, he set her down in the shelter of the foredeck so she could crouch and vomit.

As he rested a steadying hand on her narrow back something struck him across the side of the head and sent him sprawling, his ear on fire. He lay stunned, face against the tar- and salt-smelling deck, then his head was hauled back by the hair, almost ripping off his other ear, and he was staring up at another of Harriet's friends, the big red-haired girl. The loud one.

'What the *fuck* have you done to her, you dirty little scourer?!'

She gave his head a sharp shake and he thought his hair might come out by the roots. He attempted to roll away, but her other hand tightened around his balls. Oh God. He could hear the little blonde girl coughing and spitting, then her wispy-sounding voice.

'Friday, no. He was helping me.'

The pressure on his crotch eased.

'What?'

'She's had an accident,' Matthew wheezed. 'She was in the corridor outside my cabin. On the ground.'

The vice-like grip on his hair abruptly let go as the one called Friday hissed, 'It was that *fucking* Keegan, wasn't it? Oh Jesus, Rachel, your *face*!' She abandoned him to crouch beside the smaller girl, draping a muscled arm around her.

The little one, Rachel, started crying again. 'He had some work for me. I thought the money could go towards my Lucas fund. It was supposed to be laundering.'

'But it wasn't?'

'No.'

'But he helped himself despite the "misunderstanding"?'

Rachel nodded.

And Matthew received the most awful, gut-plummeting shock: he was looking at a girl who had just been raped. A moment later he felt sick to his stomach, then a complete and utter fool for assuming over the past weeks that Gabriel Keegan was a decent fellow, for spending hours passing the time of day with him, for dining at the same table pretending they were all perfectly civilised people.

But he expected it was nothing compared to the way this girl Rachel felt.

'Who goes there?'

Matthew jumped: it was young Joel Meek, the third mate, doing his rounds on the early watch, his lantern held high.

'Sorry, sir, didn't mean to interrupt, like.' Meek sounded embarrassed.

'You're not,' Matthew said. 'In fact, I'd like to make a complaint. Please go and wake the captain. There's been —'

'*No!*' Wincing, Rachel struggled to her feet. 'No, please, don't.'

'No, don't,' Friday repeated quietly, but with such an undercurrent of menace in her voice that the hairs on Matthew's arms stirred. 'We'll deal with this our way.'

'There's been what?' Meek demanded, peering at them suspiciously.

Friday shook her head. 'Nothing. Forget the man said anything, or don't bother looking for me next time you're lonely.'

And Matthew received yet another shock. Obviously he was even more naive than he'd known. He wondered who else aboard the *Isla* knew. Clearly the crew were in on it, but surely not Captain Holland and Mr Downey? Feeling more than a little silly, he watched Meek struggle between loyalty to the master and desire for his favourite whore, then turn and walk off into the darkness.

He protested, 'But you can't let Keegan get —'

Friday turned on him. 'Look, what do you think the master's going to say when a convict girl complains of being raped in some cove's cabin in the middle of the night, eh?'

Matthew knew exactly what Captain Holland would say, whether he was aware of the after-dark prostitution or not and, for the shortest of seconds, to his mortification, he caught himself thinking the very same thing.

His face betrayed him and Friday saw it. Her lip curled in disgust. 'Ah, you're all the fucking same.' She slid her arm around Rachel's waist. 'Can you walk, love?'

Rachel nodded. 'I think so. But it hurts.'

'We'll get him, sweetie. Don't worry, he'll pay.'

Together they shuffled towards the hatch to the prison deck. Friday squatted, raised the hatch cover with impressive ease, and they disappeared down the ladder, leaving Matthew standing on deck in the wind and the dark, feeling like a thorough cad.

When Rachel awoke early the next morning she could barely move. Her whimpers woke Harrie, who let out an appalled squeak when she caught sight of her friend's swollen, blood-smeared face.

'Oh, Rachel, sweetheart, what happened? Did you fall in the night?' Harrie scuffled up onto her knees. 'Why didn't you wake me? Here, let me have a proper look.'

'Shush, them in the next bunk are still asleep,' Friday said tonelessly over her shoulder. 'And no, she didn't fall.'

Harrie's heart contracted as though dipped in ice water and all of a sudden she wanted to put her hands over her ears. She hadn't felt like doing that for ages, but now, just like that, she did.

She ran her fingers down Rachel's slender arms — badly bruised, she saw now — and gently closed them over the battered little hands. The nails were broken and rimmed with dried blood. And Harrie knew.

'Keegan got at her,' Friday confirmed.

Harrie began quietly to weep. She reached for Rachel, pulling her into her arms. Rachel flopped bonelessly and Harrie cradled her, rocking her slowly, stroking her tangled hair, wiping away the tears and bloodied snot with the corner of a blanket.

Sarah, lying on her back staring at the bottom of the bunk above, said bitterly, 'So what are we going to do about him?' She'd been awake for hours, woken by Friday then too angry to sleep.

'She needs to see Mr Downey,' Harrie said in a low voice over the top of Rachel's head, brushing away her own tears with the heel of her hand.

Friday said, 'No. She doesn't want to. And this is our business, just the four of us.'

'But what if he's hurt her?'

'He's bloody done that, all right. She could hardly walk last night.' Friday told Harrie how she had found Rachel. 'You can have a look, can't you?'

'But I don't know what to look for.'

'You birthed Janie's baby,' Sarah pointed out.

Janie's face appeared upside down over the end of the upper bunk. 'That's true, you did a grand job of that.'

Friday looked up crossly. 'Have you been listening to our private conversation?'

'I can't help it if the babe needs feeding at all hours.'

'What about Sally?'

'Dead to the world.'

'Well, shut up about it, all right?' Friday growled. 'This really is private. I mean it.'

'Fair enough,' Janie said. 'I knew that Keegan was a bloody queer gill. When you catch up with him, give him a good kicking from me, will you?'

In the end Rachel agreed to see James Downey, but only because she didn't want to encounter Gabriel Keegan and to stay below deck she needed the surgeon's permission. Harrie told James that Rachel had walked into a post in the night and banged her face and couldn't manage the ladder, so James, reluctantly and only because it was Harrie who had asked, unlocked the door in the bulkhead between the prison and the hospital.

He was expecting to examine someone who fancied a few days in bed, as many of the prisoners often did when they tired of their daily chores, so when Rachel Winter limped through the door from the prison deck, he was startled by her swollen nose and the purpling bruises beneath her eyes. He ushered her through to his cubicle and helped her to sit up on the examination table.

'Harrie said you walked into a post?'

Rachel nodded. James turned up the wick on the lamp hanging above the table to see better.

'Last night, this was?'

Rachel nodded again.

'You walked into it, or you *ran* into it?'

'I walked into it.' Her voice sounded very nasal, which wasn't at all surprising.

'Look up at the ceiling, please.'

James peered up Rachel's nose. Both nostrils were full of dried blood and mucus, and the septum cartilage was markedly crooked. He didn't want to touch it: it would only hurt her.

'It does appear to be broken, I'm afraid. However, I really am at a loss to understand how you did this simply by walking into a post.' It looked to him as though she had been punched directly in the face.

'I might have been running,' Rachel admitted.

James caught her eye and held it; there was a long moment of silence, but she didn't drop her gaze. He'd noted the limp of course, and there were also fresh bruises on her right wrist, not quite hidden by her sleeve, and several torn fingernails. He knew she was lying.

'How are your teeth? None have come loose?'

She shook her head.

He gave her another chance to tell him. 'Would you like me to attend to anything else? While you're here?'

'No. Thank you.'

James sat down. 'I can't do anything to fix a broken nose, Rachel. I can give you laudanum for the discomfort until the swelling and bruising go away.' One more opportunity. 'Are you sure there's nothing else?'

She hesitated, then said, 'I don't want to go up the ladder. I feel dizzy. But I can do my chores below, just for a few days.'

James winced, then made himself stop, aware she was watching him. He'd forgotten she wanted a sick note; this was even worse than he'd suspected. If someone had hit her and she didn't want to go up on deck, it was likely one of the crew. And if that were the case, there might have been more involved than just simple assault. Oh Christ. This had happened on one of the other transports he'd superintended and it had been an utter nightmare.

'Rachel, I know —'

She cut him off. 'I'd be very grateful for a note. And I'll take the medicine, thank you very much, sir.'

James looked at her. She was sitting up straight, her head was held high and her huge cornflower-blue eyes were bright with tears, but he didn't think they were tears of misery or pain. He could see anger in them, and a flash of pride, but nothing that spoke of weakness.

'You can come back about this, you know.'

She nodded and slid off the table, wincing as her feet hit the floor. He gave her lint with which to pack her nose should it bleed again and a small bottle of laudanum — telling her not to share it with anyone else — and let her back into the prison.

Eleven

Rachel stayed below for four days. Everyone was told she'd walked into something on the way back from the water closet, but rumours flew and some of them were almost the truth. The bruises on her face went from purple to green and her battered nether regions were tender for several days and stung when she peed, but the abrasions on her knees soon scabbed over.

Her physical wounds were healing, but she feared that her feelings of shame and humiliation, and her *anger*, might never go away. She could not stop thinking about what he had done to her, going over and over in her head what she might have done to stop him, what she *should* have done.

The others had interrogated her about what had happened, particularly Friday and Sarah, and she'd told them everything, except for the part that Bella Jackson had played. God, what a gulpy little child she had been, mistaking manipulation and nastiness and greed for kindness. But if she told them what Bella had done, Friday would be so angry and have a go at Bella and probably start a war and they had such a long way to go yet to New South Wales.

She couldn't settle. She knew she was driving the others to distraction with her bad temper and her questions about Keegan. Had they seen him? Was he on the foredeck? What was he doing? The thought of him was driving her insane. Then Harrie noticed she hadn't taken any of her laudanum, the taste of which she loathed, and made her, which she had to admit did help her to feel better — calmer and sort of removed from everything that was going on. But then the laudanum ran out, her bad temper returned, and at breakfast on the fifth day she announced that she wanted to go up on deck again.

'Why?' Sarah asked, wary of the belligerent tone in Rachel's voice.

'Why shouldn't I? I've just as much right to go up on deck as anyone else.'

'Not sure I like the sound of this,' Sarah said out of the side of her mouth to Friday, sitting beside her at the long table.

'Well, too bad,' Rachel said, overhearing. 'I feel like a bloody mole stuck down here.'

Harrie said cautiously, 'Sweetheart, do you remember you wanted to stay below for a little while? And you do seem to be, well, thinking about that man a lot.' She couldn't bring herself to say Keegan's name. She'd been so horribly, *horribly* wrong about him. 'I'm not sure it's good for you.'

Rachel banged her spoon into her gruel and pushed her bowl away. 'No, none of it's been very good for me, Harrie.'

The others stared at her, startled by the vitriol in her voice.

'I want to see him. You said you'd make him pay, Friday, and you *haven't*!'

Friday leant across the table. 'Be quiet, Rachel. Do you want everyone to know? The reason we haven't done anything is because we haven't seen hide nor hair of the prick. He's hiding. We haven't been lying to you, you know. *No* one's seen him.' She swivelled sharply to face Matilda Bain on her right. 'Having a good listen, are you?'

The old woman's whiskery mouth trembled with affront. 'Not my fault I've got ears.'

'Well, bugger off and dribble your food somewhere else.'

Matilda Bain whined, 'I'm entitled to sit and eat where —'

Friday gave Matilda a good shove: she went backwards off the bench, dirty, claw-toed feet in the air and her bowl of gruel all down her front.

Twenty feet farther down the table Liz Parker stood up and yelled, 'Oi! Don't you push that defenceless old woman!'

'*And you can fuck off as well!*' Friday bellowed and hurled a rock-hard ship's biscuit, delighted to have an excuse to let out some of the tension that had been building since she'd found Rachel on the deck five nights earlier. A lusty cheer arose from the breakfasting women.

What Keegan had done to Rachel had enraged her to the point that she literally had not known what to do with herself. At home, on the streets of London, she might have dealt with someone like Keegan by getting him drunk and beating him senseless, or perhaps have paid someone else to do it. What she wanted to do was kill him. If she did, she would without doubt be found out, thrown in the brig until they reached New South Wales, then tried and hanged. She'd never committed murder in her life, but Keegan's offence against Rachel was enough to make her start, and it would almost be worth it. By tricking her into visiting his cabin — and Friday wasn't convinced Rachel was telling the whole truth about how that had happened — he had separated her from those who cared and looked out for her, and that was just such an utterly deliberate, cruel and low thing to do.

But if she did kill him the whole sordid story would come out — that Matthew Cutler cove knew, after all — and quite aside from her own neck, she'd be risking Rachel's chances of making even a half-decent life for herself in New South Wales before she even arrived. She was already a convict girl: being tainted by a rape, never mind a murder, would ruin her beyond redemption. No, far better to keep the whole thing quiet.

Which was why they weren't going to report the attack to the captain. There was another reason, too: there wouldn't be any point. Because Rachel was a convict, Holland would assume she'd been whoring, and everyone knew it was impossible to rape a whore. Rachel would be punished and Keegan would simply get away with it. As well, it would put an end to any future business transactions after dark: Holland would have them well and truly locked in from sundown to sun-up, and the little enterprise Amos Furniss and Bella Jackson had going would be closed down. Bella, being the bitch she was, would no doubt take this out on Rachel, who would suffer even further for something that hadn't been of her making.

So, regardless of Friday's promises, big talk and threats, there wasn't a bloody thing she could do about Keegan, and it was enough to make her spit nails.

Bella Jackson's curtain whipped open, her painted face appeared, and she roared, '*Shut. Up!*'

Everyone fell silent, or as quiet as they could be. Liz Parker sat down.

Bella retreated. Friday gave the twitching curtain the finger, hating the way Bella had insidiously managed to assume control of the prison deck while hardly ever coming out of her little rat hole, but she was right. If they played up, Holland would order the hatch locked for the day.

'Shut up yourself, you bitch,' Rachel whispered, her eyes fixed on the table top.

Friday stared at her, every sense suddenly alert. 'What did you say?' What had happened to Rachel's high opinion of Bella?

Rachel wouldn't look at her.

'Rachel?' Friday prompted.

Matilda scrambled back onto the bench, grumbling to herself and scraping lumps of gruel off her blouse. 'This were clean on yesterday.'

'Oh, shut up,' Friday snapped. She felt uneasy and a bit sick. 'Rachel, why did you call Bella a bitch just then?'

But Rachel just shook her head and hid behind her hair.

Had Bella Jackson called in her debt?

Harrie pushed Rachel's bowl back at her. 'Finish your gruel. You need to keep up your strength.' She waited until Rachel half-heartedly began picking out the raisins and eating them. 'What will you do if we go up and you do see him?'

Rachel paused, a raisin halfway to her mouth. 'Nothing. What *can* I do?'

'You won't get upset?'

'No. I want to see him.'

Harrie exchanged a glance with Friday and Sarah.

'But *why*?' Sarah asked again.

Rachel sighed. 'I just want to show him I can look him in the face. I'm not afeared. That's all.'

And Friday, Sarah and Harrie, whose long roads to Newgate had all been very different, believed her.

The morning was grey, cold and blustery, though the swell only moderate. The *Isla* had just crossed the Tropic of Capricorn and in a week would be passing Cape Town, then sailing into the Southern Ocean and the strong southern westerlies of the latitudes known as the Roaring Forties, at their most aggressive from July to September.

About a third of the *Isla*'s complement of prisoners were on deck, washing dishes, hanging bedding to air and swabbing the boards, and perhaps half the crew. Mrs Seaton and her daughters were on the foredeck taking a brisk morning constitutional, as was Matthew Cutler, who was chatting to James Downey on the port side near the bow. For the first time in five days Gabriel Keegan was also on the foredeck, though Matthew was making a reasonably overt show of ignoring him.

When Keegan had failed to appear the morning after the incident with the girl Rachel, Matthew had fretted for hours, chastising himself for such uncharitable thoughts but wondering if she — and her friend Friday — had lied to him and in fact Keegan was lying in his cabin hurt or even dead. At midday he'd finally knocked on the door and hadn't known what to think when Keegan had called out, 'Who is it?'

He'd announced himself and gone in, his concerns turning quickly to anger then a deep repugnance as he'd observed Keegan lounging at his writing desk, stockinged feet on the bed, happily eating cheese and pickles from his private stock and drinking wine. There had been a long, angry scratch on his face.

He'd intended to leave immediately, but instead he'd blurted, 'There was trouble last night. I found a girl in the corridor, just outside — one of the prisoners. She said you'd attacked her.'

And Keegan had smirked and said, 'Absolutely *no* idea what you're talking about, old fellow,' and cut himself another wedge of cheese.

Matthew had had to stifle an overwhelming urge to strike him. 'She'd been ... compromised.'

'*Compromised?* A convict drap? Well, she's lying if she says it was me. Close the door on the way out, will you?'

Matthew hadn't spoken to him since. He had anguished over whether to report the matter to the captain, or even James Downey, but in the end he'd said nothing because he couldn't see that it would achieve anything positive: Rachel's friend Friday had been right.

But it was a small ship and James Downey had commented yesterday on a certain frostiness he'd noted between Matthew and Keegan: had they had some sort of falling out? Matthew, while not wishing to be rude, had said yes and left it at that, grateful that the surgeon had, too.

He hadn't seen Rachel up on deck since that night and he wondered if she was all right. Actually, he was fairly sure she probably wasn't. She'd looked in a terrible state. He'd thought about approaching Harriet Clarke, or even Friday, both of whom he had seen, but his nerve had failed him. Harriet didn't even know him; and Friday, well, he suspected he hadn't made a particularly favourable impression on her the last time they'd spoken.

He glanced over his shoulder at Keegan and saw that he'd crossed the foredeck to speak to Mrs Seaton, standing near the companion ladder that led down to the waistdeck. He hoped she had her daughters well and truly locked up at night.

'I'm sorry?' Matthew realised James Downey had said something.

'The weather. I think we've seen the last of the sunshine for a while. At this time of year and at these latitudes it can get really quite miserable and the seas rather rough,' James said. 'Still, almost everyone seems to have found their sea legs.'

'You'd expect so, though, wouldn't you?' Matthew remarked. 'We've been at sea for some time now.'

'Some people never do, you know. Sick the whole voyage.' James saw that something on the waistdeck had caught Matthew's eye and turned to follow his gaze. 'Ah. Excuse me, will you?'

Matthew took hold of his sleeve and pointed. 'Wait. That girl down there, the small one with fair hair?'

'Rachel Winter? Yes, I must have a quick word with her. Excuse me, Mr Cutler.'

Feeling horribly uneasy at the notion that whichever crewman had assaulted Rachel Winter might now be on deck watching her, James took a step forwards.

Beside him, Matthew impulsively decided he couldn't keep his awful secret any longer, not with Keegan leering and carrying on at Hester Seaton and her two young daughters less than fifteen feet away, and grabbed James's arm again.

'Mr Downey —'

But they were both too late.

Rachel was looking out for him even before she stepped off the ladder and onto the waistdeck. She saw him immediately, standing up on the foredeck, talking to the reverend's wife, his tall, top-hatted figure silhouetted against the sharp, white sky.

Deliberately, knowing that Friday, Sarah and Harrie were right behind her, she looked the other way and walked casually across the deck to a spot between the foredeck and the main mast. She was amazed that regardless of her furiously pounding heart and the hot, red rage boiling up in her, she could still appreciate the feel of the salty wind on her face after the days below, though it was stinging her poor nose a bit.

Should she do it?

She had nothing to lose. Keegan had taken everything. If Lucas had come for her a week ago, he would have been fetching a girl with a convict record, no money, some not very clever domestic skills, and a pretty face. It wasn't much, but the real gifts she'd been saving for him were her fidelity and her honour.

But they were gone now, thieved in a matter of minutes, nothing left of them but a dirty stain on Keegan's bed linen.

She raised her eyes to the foredeck just as Keegan gave a hearty laugh and settled his hand comfortably on Eudora Seaton's upper arm.

Yes. She would do it.

She turned and felt Sarah's hand on her wrist.

'What are you up to?' Sarah said suspiciously.

'Nothing.'

'Well, keep it that way.' Sarah, too, had spied Keegan, haw-hawing away with Mrs Seaton and her daughters. 'Really, Rachel, ignore him.'

'I will,' Rachel said. 'I promise.'

'Good girl.' Sarah let go of Rachel's wrist.

Rachel snatched up her skirts and made a break for it, sprinting for the ladder up to the foredeck. She was halfway up it before Sarah, her mouth open, started after her.

But Friday, ever watchful, was already there, only a few feet behind Rachel, until Amos Furniss appeared, hauled on her skirt and dragged her off the bottom rungs of the ladder.

'Convicts ent allowed on the foredeck,' he barked as he wrestled her to the ground.

Friday lashed out at him but it was too late — Rachel had already reached the foredeck.

She took two swift steps towards Keegan, who was facing the other way, and kicked him in the back of his knee. His leg buckled and he half turned, and she was delighted to see alarm flare in his eyes when he realised it was her. Reaching up she slapped his face as hard as she could.

Mrs Seaton let out a shriek and backed away, taking Geneve and Eudora with her.

'*That's for taking what wasn't yours!*' Rachel screamed, then punched Keegan in the stomach.

He barely registered the blow. 'Get away from me! I'm warning you.'

Rachel raised her hand to strike him again, but he reacted first. He planted his hands on her chest and pushed her hard, the force of it driving her backwards to the top of the companion ladder. She stepped back onto nothing and seemed, at least to the women watching in horror from the waistdeck, to take an age to fall through the air, her skirt and her long silver-white hair fluttering after her, before she finally hit the deck six feet below.

She lay very still, one arm outstretched, her skirt rumpled above her scabbed knees, lines of dark blood already collecting in the grooves of the deck boards beneath her head. The women gathering around her stared down at her in shocked silence, others pushing in close to see. Harrie let out a rising wail of despair.

Then James Downey was there, crouching over her, his fingers against her throat. Behind him Matthew hovered, his face as white as his shirt.

Harrie fell on her knees beside James. 'Is she dead? Oh, please, she isn't, is she?'

He seemed not to have heard, his gaze fixed on Rachel's still face.

Then he said, 'Wait. I think, yes, I can feel a pulse.' He glanced up and caught sight of Matthew. 'Help me, will you? I need to get her below.'

James lifted Rachel in his arms. On the deck where she had lain was a great puddle of dark ruby blood. The crowd gasped and murmured: surely a body couldn't lose that much of its life force and still be drawing breath? Rachel's head lolled against James's shoulder, her blood immediately staining the cloth of his blue jacket black. Harrie tore off her apron, wadded it and pressed it against the back of her skull. Between them Matthew and James carried Rachel very carefully down the ladder to the hospital, followed closely by Harrie, weeping openly.

Seconds later Josiah Holland came running, shrugging himself into his coat, fetched from his cabin by Walter Cobley.

'What's going on here?' he demanded, then stopped short as he noted the gore all over his deck.

Friday, a great rip in her skirt and her face scarlet with rage, pointed up at the foredeck and cried out, 'Attempted murder by that man there, Keegan! We all saw it!'

Holland lifted his gaze even as his heart sank. 'What?'

'He pushed Rachel down the ladder! He tried to kill her!'

Holland looked around for his crew and spied Amos Furniss. 'Is this true?'

'The gentleman did push a girl off the foredeck, aye,' Furniss said conversationally.

'What was she doing up there?' The captain looked bewildered. 'Prisoners aren't allowed on the foredeck. It's against regulations.'

'*Fuck* the regulations!' Friday screamed. 'He tried to kill her! Bloody well arrest him, you *buffoon*!'

Holland's face went a deep puce colour. 'Furniss! Take her down to the hold.'

While Friday was being bundled away to a chorus of loud booing from the crowd, Holland went up onto the foredeck. Mrs Seaton and her daughters were huddled against the starboard gunwale, their arms around each other. The girls were crying.

'Are you unharmed, madam?' he asked.

'We are well, thank you, Captain,' Hester Seaton replied. 'It was just rather a shock. She was quite unhinged! And then when she fell!' She retrieved a lace-trimmed kerchief from her reticule and dabbed at her eyes.

'Did you see what happened?'

Hester hesitated, then gave Eudora and Geneve the look they knew meant they were not to say a word. 'Not clearly, no. We were standing over here at the time.' It wouldn't do Octavius's plans for promotion any good if they were to be caught up in a scandal the minute they arrived in New South Wales. It was obvious now who the girl in the corridor the other night had been.

Josiah Holland had the distinct feeling he was being lied to. 'I suggest you retire to your cabin, Mrs Seaton. I may wish to speak to you and your daughters later, however.'

Gabriel Keegan was sitting on a coil of rope at the base of the bowsprit with his hat in his hands, the picture of dejection. He glanced up as Holland approached.

'Captain. I am as appalled as you, I really am. Obviously it was an extremely unfortunate accident. And as for her absurd allegations, I have no idea to what she was referring.'

Holland experienced a very unpleasant stab of anxiety. 'What allegations?'

Rachel's hair looked as though it had been dyed the colour of garnets.

She lay on the examination table on her side, breathing shallowly, one leg straight and the other bent so she wouldn't roll onto her face. James had carefully parted her hair over the wound and was now attempting to wash away the blood with damp lint.

'Won't the salt water be stinging it?' Harrie said.

Lil Foster patted Harrie's arm. 'I don't think she'll be feeling it, love.'

Harrie nodded, choked on another sob, and dropped the tin bowl she was holding in case Rachel vomited again.

Without looking up, James said, 'Harrie, I know this is upsetting, but if you can't manage your emotions a little more effectively, I'm going to have to send you away. This is most unlike you.'

'No! No, really, it's just ...' Harrie stopped babbling and picked up the bowl. 'I'm all right, really. Please let me stay.'

James sat up straight. 'I'll have to cut some of her hair.'

Harrie burst into fresh tears.

Ignoring her, James waved his hand. 'Pass me the scissors, Lil.'

He trimmed away the blood-sodden hair around the wound, swabbed it thoroughly with a weak solution of costic, and sutured it shut with catgut threaded through a curved, ivory-handled surgical needle. Twenty-one stitches running from the top of her head, across the back of her skull to the base of her left ear.

Deeply unconscious, Rachel didn't stir once. James had shouted in her face, slapped it lightly, lifted her eyelids and held the lamp close to her eyes — both pupils were markedly dilated, not just the right one this time — and tapped her knees and inner elbows with his plexor, all with no response. Yet she was still breathing, albeit shallowly. She had also vomited, and it had been very fortunate they had arranged her on her side or she could well have choked to death. It was clear the severe blow to her head had rendered her comatose, which was a grave state of affairs. He had seen only a handful of patients recover from coma, particularly those caused by blows to the head, and to his knowledge most of them had gone on to live lives fraught with problems both physical and mental. At this point, he didn't know whether Rachel Winter would recover at all, let alone to what extent.

He did, however, now know who had assaulted her five nights earlier — or he thought he did — and he was at least as disappointed with himself as he was with Gabriel Keegan. It was his responsibility to oversee the convicts' welfare and he'd let his inherent snobbery blind him to the possibility that it may have been a paying passenger who'd attacked Rachel Winter, not a crewman.

Gabriel Keegan should be tried in a court of law for what he had done — for both his attack on the girl today and for his initial assault on her. As soon as he had finished here, James was going to demand that Holland arrest the fellow and sling him in the brig for the rest of the voyage. It was absurd to think he should be allowed to wander at liberty about the ship. First, however, he would have to make very sure he had his facts straight. He finished winding a bandage around Rachel's head and tucked in the loose end.

'Harrie? Rachel's broken nose: she didn't injure herself walking into a post, did she?'

Harrie stood very still, staring down at the bowl in her hands, her ears slowly turning pink. James could see she was trying to decide whether or not to lie. It was very endearing, but at the moment not helpful.

'I need to know, Harrie, so please tell me the truth.'

'No, she didn't,' Harrie finally said. 'Someone hit her.'

As gently as he could, given how angry he felt, James said, 'It was Gabriel Keegan, wasn't it?'

A look of angry defiance flashed across Harrie's face at the mention of the man's name. 'Yes, it was. It damn well was.'

God, how was he going to ask this next bit? 'And during that episode, when her nose was injured, are you aware, Harrie, did Keegan perpetrate any other harm against her person?'

'Well, he bloody well raped her,' Lil said, banging the bandage box back on the shelf to demonstrate her disgust.

'Lil!' Harrie was aghast. 'How did you know?'

'Janie Braine.'

Even though he'd suspected it, James felt a wave of revulsion and dismay roll though him: Keegan would most definitely need to be locked up.

'But why didn't she report it?' he asked Harrie.

But Lil answered. 'Would you or the captain've believed her? Her word against a "gentleman's"?' She snorted rudely. 'Not likely.'

James knew he really should reprimand her for being cheeky, but he just didn't have the energy. Anyway, she was right.

'She was tricked, Mr Downey.' Very, very gently, Harrie stroked Rachel's cold, still cheek with the back of her fingers. 'She's only fifteen and not really the best judge of character. She's betrothed, to a soldier called Lucas Carew. A lieutenant. They ran off together but he had to leave her in London. She got into terrible trouble with her family for it. She was alone and she was tricked and she ended up in gaol. She's a good girl, really. She has this great plan. She's saving up and if he doesn't come to New South Wales to find her first, when she's served her sentence she's going back to England to find him.' Harrie looked up, tears rolling down her cheeks. 'That's a lot of "she's", isn't it?' She wiped her nose on her sleeve. 'Apparently Keegan offered her paid work, laundering or the like, but she's so naive. He just helped himself.'

James swallowed what felt like a burning coal and looked away. 'Was she ... did you ... was she hurt?' He waved a vague hand at Rachel's belly.

Harrie nodded. 'I did. She didn't want you to. No offence intended. There was ... blood. And bruising. I didn't know what else to look for.'

James felt himself reddening. Poor Harrie. Poor *him*. 'Er, yes. Well, these things can be very difficult to, well, yes.' Not that he was an expert, but he had encountered that previous case of forced sexual intercourse on a convict ship and one or two on emigrant transports. And, actually, several within His Majesty's Navy, now that he thought about it.

'Will she die, Mr Downey?'

James couldn't lie. 'I don't know, Harrie.'

Josiah Holland sat at the table in the great cabin, his arms crossed protectively over his painfully bloated belly. He was suffering a severe attack of indigestion, brought on, he was sure, by the day's unsavoury events and the distress of what he was being forced to listen to now, and wanted everyone to go away so he could dose himself with oil of peppermint and several of the charcoal wafers Downey had prepared for him. But they wouldn't leave, arguing and demanding for all the world as though they were in command of the ship, not him.

'Surely, Captain, it is clear what has to be done!' James Downey insisted, leaning forwards and slapping the surface of the table.

'Mr Downey, as I've already said —' Holland began, rubbing the bridge of his nose wearily.

'But he can't be allowed to just … go about his business!'

Holland breathed in deeply, which hurt his stomach, and sighed. 'Look, be rational about this, Mr Downey. What you have is a girl — a *convict* girl, who is being transported to the colonies for seven years for improbity — who says she was assaulted by a paying passenger. In his cabin. In the middle of the night.'

Downey almost launched himself out of his chair. 'No, *she* isn't saying it, because *she* can't! *She*'s lying in my hospital because Keegan pushed her off the foredeck and damn near killed her!'

Reverend Seaton, sitting opposite, said, 'I find your language offensive, sir.'

'So, who *is* saying it?' Holland asked, ignoring him.

'Her colleagues.'

'Colleagues,' sneered Amos Furniss, standing at the end of the table.

The reverend threw his hands in the air, the light reflecting off the large yellow stone in the ring he wore on his right hand. 'I find this entire situation preposterous. I interviewed Mr Keegan myself not an hour ago and he flatly denies any knowledge whatsoever of the female *felon* in question. In my opinion, the word of a gentleman should be more than enough to settle a simple dispute.'

Holland held his breath as Downey responded with admirable restraint. 'With all due respect, Reverend, this is considerably more than a simple dispute.'

He loosened his collar — it really was getting stuffy in here — and turned to Matthew Cutler to broach the matter that bothered him most of all. 'And you, Mr Cutler, are maintaining that there is a brothel being run aboard my ship at night?'

'Yes, I am,' Cutler replied.

Holland, to his dismay, actually tended to believe Cutler about this — after all, it wasn't as though there hadn't been precedents on previous transports, though not *his* ships — and one or two comments he'd inadvertently overheard from the crew now made sense. He noted, however, that Silas Warren, standing near the door, looked as perturbed as he felt himself.

'I even saw one of the women,' Cutler added. 'On deck, the night Rachel Winter was attacked.'

Furniss sniggered knowingly and Holland's gaze slid back to him. If there was any prostitution going on, he knew bloody well who would be at the bottom of it. He shifted in his seat, trying to ease the pain in his belly: he was in a very uncomfortable position, both physically and metaphorically.

If he accepted the story that the convict girl — what was her name, Winter? — had been assaulted, he would have to arrest Keegan. But if the crew had been merrily paying to have sex with some of the women for God knew how many weeks, they would have little feeling for a prisoner claiming she'd been raped. Their sympathies would more likely lie with Keegan, so who could be relied upon to guard him? None of their number could be spared anyway; he was running a tight ship as it was. Neither could Keegan be kept in irons or in the brig for the next twelve weeks, or however long it took them to reach Sydney. He, Holland, could well find *himself* up before the judge for that; Gabriel Keegan was just the sort of well-connected toff who could bring pressure to bear to see to it.

And there was the other matter, too, dreaded by all ships' masters. Furniss was a thug, which was why Holland hadn't promoted him to first mate, but he wielded a lot of power aboard the *Isla* and Holland knew it, though he certainly didn't like it. Should the crew take against their master because of a decision concerning Keegan, Furniss had the ability to push them that little bit further and Holland might find himself in the quarterboat, alone, in the middle of the icy Southern Ocean.

Holland sighed for roughly the fifth time. Furniss had said at the time that Keegan had shoved the girl, though Furniss would say anything if it suited his agenda, and God only knew what his agenda was regarding this affair. Deflecting attention from himself, probably. Hester Seaton was adamant about not seeing what had happened on the foredeck, though Holland couldn't understand how she hadn't: she and her daughters had evidently been standing right beside Keegan and the girl. James Downey and Cutler had been farther away, up near the head rail, and said it had *looked* like he'd pushed her, though he'd had his back to them, and that it was true she had attacked him first. They weren't prepared, however, to *swear* he'd shoved her off the foredeck deliberately, though clearly they strongly suspected he had — in an effort to stop her accusing him of rape, they were insisting. There was no doubt they had very much taken against him.

So what was he to do? Whatever decision he made he would be damned by one party or another. The *Isla*, however, was his ship; his sole objective was to sail her to Sydney and back to England again. And he could feel, even without looking, Furniss's malevolent stare burning into the side of his head like the sun through a magnifying glass, daring him to chance his luck.

Deeply aggravated by the position in which he now found himself, he sat up straighter in his chair and glared at the men assembled before him.

'Until the injured prisoner can speak for herself, Mr Keegan will remain at liberty.' He lifted his hand in warning as James Downey rose out of his seat yet again. 'No. *I* am in command of this ship, Mr Downey, and I will brook no argument. Mr Warren, please have Mr Trent change the lock on the prison hatch this afternoon, then bring *all* of the keys to me.' Stifling a painful, acid-laced burp, he added, 'Now, will you please all leave. I have work to do.'

Sitting alone minutes later, sagging with relief as the draught of bicarbonate of sodium in peppermint oil made its way down his tortured oesophagus, it occurred to him to wonder: if his crew had been buying sex from the prisoners, what had they been using for money? They probably had a little with them, but they didn't get paid until they arrived in Sydney. He must check the claret, port, brandy and whisky shipments in the hold.

Rachel had been in a coma for three days, suffering, Mr Downey said he suspected, from something called a cerebral haemorrhage. Harrie had washed most of the blood out of her hair, carefully avoiding the stitches, given her a sponge bath and put her into a clean shift. She lay now in one of the hospital beds, tucked up under several blankets: Mr Downey said it was important to keep her warm as she couldn't generate her own heat because she wasn't moving. She peed where she lay and every time she did Harrie changed everything all over again, giving the soiled things to Sarah and Friday to wash. It rained on the second day and nothing would dry and they soon ran out, but Janie and Sally Minto, and some of Sally's and Lil's friends, lent their things, and there was enough.

But today, and it was the middle of the afternoon now, Rachel hadn't peed once. Harrie and Lil had tried to make her drink, first a little broth and then just water, but it hadn't worked. The liquid had gone in but had either dribbled out the side of her mouth or she'd choked. So they'd stopped trying. She had coughed, though, and Mr Downey said that was a good sign.

But Harrie wasn't so sure about that; she wondered if it wasn't more of a natural sort of thing to do, to cough if you were choking. She was also starting to suspect that Mr Downey was just declaring things to be a good sign to make them feel better. If he was, it wasn't working.

They hadn't said it out loud, not even among themselves, but they thought she was going to die. Her face was as white as rice flour, except for her lips, which had gone a faint lilac colour, and her arms and legs seemed boneless. And her breath was awful, worse even than Newgate Gaol breath. She had talked, though. Yesterday afternoon she had mumbled 'magpies four a berth', and, late last night, something that had sounded like 'devil's own' something. Friday said she must be talking about Keegan, but it hadn't really sounded as though there'd been anything behind the words: her mouth was just saying random things.

Harrie fussed about straightening Rachel's blankets, then kissed her cold cheek and moved to the next bed to check on Evie Challis. Evie was enormously pregnant, due to give birth in three weeks or so, but had been 'showing' for the past week, and so prescribed bed rest. Evie was delighted, as she'd worked as a laundress right up until the day she'd given birth with her last two and felt as though she were being treated like a queen this time round, especially as someone else was looking after the next littlest one on the prison deck. Her elder child had been left behind in England as she was eight and too old to be allowed to be transported with her mother.

'All right, Evie?' Harrie asked.

'I think so.' Evie awkwardly manoeuvred herself onto her side like a cast cow. She began to cough, a dry rattle that had worsened during the voyage.

'I'll just check, will I?'

Evie flipped open the sheet and Harrie ducked her head and pulled back the folds of cheesecloth between Evie's legs. They were stained with blood, but not a lot of it. She would tell Mr Downey when he came in next, but she didn't think the bleeding was getting any heavier.

She popped the cloths back into place. 'Do you need anything?'

'Some oysters would be nice. Or winkles'd do. And mebbe a muffin or a crumpet? Toasted, mind.'

Harrie laughed. Poor Evie missed the food of London's street-sellers desperately. Perhaps her appetite would return to normal after her baby arrived.

'Evie Challis, you'd be completely round if you ate everything you fancied,' Lil said, then swore ripely as she dropped one of Mr Downey's leech jars.

Harrie rushed over to help her. 'Oh *no*, Lil, we're not supposed to touch those.'

'I was only giving it a wipe.'

'Quick, take the lids off the other two jars.'

Six or seven leeches were making a break for freedom, squirming their way blindly across the deck boards. Harrie snatched up a pair of tweezers, gingerly picked them up one by one from the wreckage and dropped them into the jars.

'Harrie?'

'Hold on, Evie,' Harrie said over her shoulder as she grappled with the last furiously writhing escapee.

'I never said that,' Evie said. 'She did.'

Harrie and Lil, crouched on the floor, skirts clamped tightly around their ankles, looked at each other, then slowly stood.

Rachel was sitting up, watching them. She licked her dry lips.

'Harrie, my head hurts.'

* * *

'Bella wants to talk to you.'

Harrie jumped. Concentrating on her sewing, she hadn't noticed anyone creeping up on her. It was Lucy whatever-her-name-was, one of Bella Jackson's girls.

'Me? She wants to talk to me?'

Lucy nodded.

Harrie hesitated. What on earth could Bella Jackson want with *her*? She didn't want to speak to Bella, especially not by herself. She had done them all a kindness by announcing Liz Parker's perfidy, but that didn't mean Harrie felt comfortable at the thought of being alone with her. Friday and Sarah had gone up on deck — perhaps she could wait for them to come back. It was annoying, too, as she'd been up with Rachel in the hospital half the night, and this was the first bit of time she'd had to herself since yesterday. She had made Janie's baby a gown from a piece of white lawn from Mrs Fry's scraps donation, and now that Rosie had been born she was embroidering a rose on the bodice. Over the past few weeks she'd amassed enough different-coloured thread to make up a really pretty pattern and she was hoping to finish it today.

'Now?'

'Yes, now.'

'About what?'

Lucy shrugged. 'I dunno, do I?'

Harrie sighed, put down her sewing and followed Lucy along the aisle to Bella's compartment. Lucy stuck her head behind the curtain for a moment, said something, then pulled it aside, revealing Bella sitting on the bunk.

'Good morning, Harrie,' Bella said pleasantly. She patted the blanket beside her. 'Please, do sit down.'

Harrie perched gingerly on the very end of the bunk. Bella was wearing a velvet turban and an embroidered satin robe, the value of which Harrie placed at roughly two years of the salary paid her by Mrs Lynch. The skin of her face was dusted quite heavily with rice powder and there was rouge on her cheeks and lips.

Bella said, 'I won't bite, you know.'

Harrie wasn't so sure about that. She waited in silence for Bella to get to the point.

'I'm told you're doing a sterling job in the hospital.'

Harrie blinked. She didn't know what she'd been expecting, but it hadn't been this.

'He must hold you in quite high regard.'

'Mr Downey, you mean?'

Bella nodded.

Harrie said, 'I suppose. Well, I'm not sure. He's happy for us to look after the patients when he's not there.'

'So he trusts you.'

'Well, he must do.'

'What else does he trust you with?'

For the first time, Harrie really noticed Bella's very pale skin, the exaggerated blackness of her eyes and the jutting collarbones beneath the scarf she wore at her throat. And, with a dismayed little jolt, she realised that Bella Jackson quite possibly had an intemperance of some sort. For the poppy, perhaps?

'Oh, no, I'm sorry, I can't get you anything from the hospital. If you need … something, you'll have to see Mr Downey yourself.'

Bella laughed. Harrie noticed she had several teeth missing from her upper jaw at the back. 'Oh dearie me no, I'm not asking you to *procure* for me, Harrie.'

'Well, what *do* you want?' Harrie said. This was starting to get annoying.

'I want to borrow something.'

Harrie stared at her. 'Borrow what?'

'The use of a key.'

'What key?' Harrie bit her lip: she was sounding like a parrot.

All traces of conviviality disappeared from Bella's face. 'The key to the door between the hospital and the prison.'

'But ... what for?'

'Thanks to the trouble your little friend has caused, there is now a new lock on the prison hatch, my girls can't get out at night and my business is suffering.' Bella's voice became harsh. 'You and your witless crew owe me a debt. You make sure that door is open every night so my business can continue and I'll consider the debt paid.'

Friday whipped aside the curtain, almost giving Harrie a heart attack. 'And if she doesn't?'

Bella also jumped. She hissed a curse, her fists clenched. 'Then I promise you, you'll be watching your backs for the rest of your lives.'

Friday smiled coldly. 'There're four of us, Bella: we can do that. Who'll be watching yours? Let's go, Harrie, there's a terrible smell in here. Could it be, yes, it is, it's the stink of ... betrayal. I need some fresh air.'

'You're cutting off your freckle-beshatted nose to spite your face, Woolfe,' Bella spat after them. 'You can't work either!'

'No, but I don't really care.'

'You'll pay for this!'

Friday whirled around, her face contorted with fury. 'And if you've done what I think you've done, you'll fucking pay as well.'

Bella smirked, suddenly in control again. 'I'm afraid I've *no* idea what you're talking about.'

'You're a dead woman, Bella Jackson, if I can prove it. And I will.'

Reaching for her cigarillo case, Bella shrugged. 'Go on, then. Except your little friend is in the hospital, isn't she? With half her brains missing? I've heard she can barely even remember her name.'

Harrie, her face growing redder by the second as realisation dawned, exploded. 'What an utter bloody bitch you've turned out to be! And to think I actually defended you!'

Bella struck a match and held it to her cigarillo. 'That'll teach you.'

Twelve

July 1829, Southern Ocean

Sarah ducked, but the next missile — Rachel's boot — hit her square in the back, causing her to spill her tea all over the table.

'Ow! Rachel, that hurt! Friday, do something!'

Friday swivelled around on the bench, stepped over it, reached into the bunk and dragged Rachel, screaming and thrashing, out by her bare ankles. By the time she was all the way out, Rachel's skirt was up around her ears as she swore the air blue and hit out wildly at Friday. Friday picked her up and sat on the edge of the bunk, holding Rachel on her lap so firmly she could barely move while Harrie got out the bottle of laudanum.

'*No!*' Rachel shrieked. '*No, I don't want to go to sleep!*'

Harrie blinked back tears as she poured a spoonful. 'It's for your own good, sweetie.'

'*I don't want it!*' Rachel kicked out and sent the spoon flying.

Someone retrieved it from beneath the table and Harrie tried again. Everyone was watching now; this was the third time in three weeks that Rachel had erupted in a fit of temper.

Sarah left the table to stand behind Rachel and hold her head back, careful not to touch her scalp where the scar was still tender and some of her hair was only about an inch long. She gripped a longer strand and gently pinched Rachel's nose closed. She hated doing this, but it had come to be her job; Friday was the only one of them strong enough to actually hold on to Rachel while she was having one of her fits and Harrie was so soft-hearted towards her she could barely poke the spoon into her mouth.

The laudanum went in, but was spat out again immediately.

Harrie sighed. 'Oh, Rachel, please, do be a good girl and swallow it.'

'*No! No! No!*'

Sarah sighed as well and exchanged a glance with Friday. They both thought it was pointless babying Rachel when she was like this because it didn't get them anywhere, but Harrie always did it.

'Try again, Harrie,' Sarah said. 'Come on, hurry up.'

'I am hurrying.'

The next spoonful went in and Sarah clamped her hand over Rachel's mouth so she couldn't spit it out. There were a lot of angry 'Mmmmm!' noises then she finally swallowed and Sarah managed to get her hand away without getting bitten. It was a huge relief. Rachel would go to sleep in about fifteen minutes and hopefully stay that way for four or five hours, and an even bigger crisis would be avoided.

The first time she'd had a fit like this had been a fortnight after her injury. She had complained of a bad headache and the fit had come on an hour or so after that. They were accustomed to Rachel's bad moods of course, she'd had them since they'd first met her in Newgate, but these tantrums were on a different scale altogether and involved screaming, breaking and throwing things, hitting, and swearing that impressed even Friday. When asked later Rachel said she couldn't remember much at all except that her head had really hurt, as though it was caught in a vice and was being relentlessly squeezed.

During her first fit, Rachel had gone up on deck and caused such a fuss the captain had ordered her put in solitary, and when the tantrum had receded she'd been utterly terrified. After that Harrie had taken her to see Mr Downey, who had prescribed laudanum to sedate her should she have another episode of mania, as he termed it. He understood that putting her in solitary would only make her worse, and the laudanum was to make sure she didn't end up there again. She'd had two more fits since then. But it was very odd because between the fits, Rachel was her ordinary self. Well, as ordinary as she could be given what had happened to her over the past five weeks.

Sarah stepped out of the way as Friday sat Rachel on the bench facing the bunk, keeping a good grip on her. She was reaching the maudlin stage now: her face was crumpling but there were no tears yet. She kicked viciously at a post, barking her bare toes against the hard wood, so Friday flicked out a leg and tucked her little feet behind her own, keeping them out of harm's way.

'Show's over, ladies,' Sarah announced to the fascinated audience and went back to her mug of tea, even though most of it was all over the table. She took the lid off the teapot and swirled the contents around inside, pretending she didn't care that their business was being aired for the entire prison deck to observe and gossip about. There was some tea left so she poured it into her mug, relishing the strong, bitter smell. The daily tea allowance was the single redeeming feature of life aboard this stinking ship — it was more than she'd ever been able to afford in London. She sighed and said to Harrie, 'I think we need to talk to your Mr Downey. I think she's getting worse. She can't keep doing this and neither can we.'

'I know.' Harrie straightened the things on the table that had been knocked around by Rachel's flying boots. 'I'm worried sick.'

'You're always worried sick,' Sarah said, but she didn't say it to be unkind. Harrie was the one who looked after them, and they let her — it felt as though it were her job. They were a family and she was the mother. Friday looked *out* for them, which was quite a different thing, and she, Sarah, did the ducking and diving, getting them whatever they needed to make their lives less unpleasant.

Harrie's embroidery cottons, for example — for weeks Sarah had been trading and buying different-coloured threads from the other women, mostly gleaned originally from the bags Mrs Fry had gifted them. And last week she had managed to approach Silas Warren and trade a good clay pipe, stolen from Louisa Coutts, one of Liz Parker's crew, for a new set of prison slops for Rachel, as she had all but destroyed hers during her last fit. Sarah knew she didn't have Friday's outgoing and undeniably mesmerising character, and she certainly couldn't calm and soothe the way Harrie could, but if there was a deal to be done, above board or not, she was the one to do it.

Rachel was nodding, the effects of the energy-sapping tantrum and the laudanum conspiring, as hoped, to send her to sleep. But she was fighting it. She stood up.

Friday pulled her back down. 'Sit down, Rachel, there's a good girl.'

'Don't talk to me like a *child*,' Rachel grumped. She rubbed her eyes and yawned, then cupped the back of her head where the raw scar lay. 'Fuck me, I've *such* a sore head.' She turned sideways, rested her forearms on the table and let her head sink onto them.

Friday waited five minutes until she was sure she was asleep, scooped her up, lay her on the bunk and pulled a blanket over her.

'God almighty,' she said as she joined the others at the table. 'We can't keep shoving that shite into her, you know. We'll be turning her into an inebriate.'

Harrie nodded. 'Sarah thinks we should go and talk to Mr Downey.'

'You already did,' Friday said, frowning into the empty teapot. 'And all he did was give her that bloody medicine.'

'Only so she wouldn't run amok and end up in the brig.'

Friday made a face that made her top teeth stick out and her chin recede. '"Run amok". That sounds like one of your Mr Downey's toffey sayings.'

'Will you stop calling him "my Mr Downey"?' Harrie snapped. 'You're just angry with him because he wouldn't prescribe you medicinal rum for your "problem".'

Sarah laughed, then so did Friday. 'That's true. I am. Doesn't make him a good doctor.'

'Well, I think he is,' Harrie said. 'And so does Sarah. Don't you?'

'I didn't say that,' Sarah replied. 'But I can't say he's a bad one either. And we have to do something.'

They all looked at each other.

'Yes,' Friday said eventually. 'Yes, we do.'

Liz Parker had watched the shenanigans at the table with the Winter girl along with everyone else and thought, good job. That would teach the little bint for thinking she could beat Liz Parker at broads and get away with it. Now all she had to do was get revenge on Bella Jackson for dobbing her in for cheating and the score would be settled. Except for the money of course, but she might have to wait until they got to that women's gaol in Sydney before she stole that back again. Waiting was all right — the Woolfe bitch and her motley lot couldn't spend it on the ship.

What annoyed her most about Bella Jackson was she'd admired her when she first came aboard. She was a cool customer and had a reputation to match. They were very similar in a lot of ways, her and Bella Jackson — both canny and sharp, both notorious. She'd even been thinking of inviting the woman to join her crew. Not as an equal of course, but maybe as her lieutenant. But then Jackson had ruined that idea by making a fool of her and now she was honour-bound to retaliate.

The trouble was, Bella Jackson so rarely came out of her compartment it was proving very difficult to get in there to steal anything or find something suitable for blackmail purposes. God knew Becky and Beth and Louisa had been trying for weeks. It was just so bloody tricky to do anything on the sly on this piddly little boat.

This afternoon, though, the prison deck was almost empty. Woolfe and her crew had apparently gone off to see that molly surgeon and nearly everyone else was up on deck making the most of the sun. Not that it was that warm any more. In fact, it was getting bloody cold. And Jackson had gone up, too: she'd been standing at the bottom of the ladder just after dinner, wearing a mantle with a fur collar. Bloody fashion plate. Well, she'd gone somewhere and there weren't that many choices, were there? So here at last was the perfect chance to turn over her things.

Liz heaved herself off the bunk, noticing not for the first time she'd lost a bit of weight since the *Isla* had set sail. It was the atrocious food they were getting. No pies, no muffins or hot cross buns dripping with butter, no tasty saveloys or oysters, no fresh raspberries swimming in cream. Some days when she stood up she felt distinctly light-headed! She'd eaten better in bloody Newgate.

She made her way around the end of the table, not bothering to keep quiet as it was always noisier down here than a blacksmith's foundry, and started up the other side towards Jackson's compartment. Actually, there *were* a few women still below, sleeping, and a handful of kids. She'd better keep an eye on her things — light-fingered, the lot of them.

She stood before the curtain concealing Bella Jackson's bunk and thought about what best to take. Her clothes? That would hurt: she loved her clothes. Money? Or should she look for something incriminating she could threaten to take to the captain? The possibilities were endless.

She glanced around to make sure no one was watching then twitched open the curtain. And just about died: Bella Jackson *hadn't* gone up on deck.

A heavy crystal tumbler flew straight at Liz's face. She reared back, dropping the curtain, but not quickly enough. The tumbler struck her temple and then the table, shattering into countless diamonds twinkling in the lamplight.

She hurried away, her heart pounding madly, wiping a trickle of blood from her eye, but she was smirking. She'd just seen *exactly* what she needed.

'Got ya,' she whispered.

James sat in his cubicle writing up his notes from the morning's surgery. He had been busy, the women as always making the most of having access to free medical consultations, some with real complaints, others with maladies fabricated with an eye to getting them excused from chores for a day or two.

It had been the usual procession of complaints concerning mostly costiveness or flux, lumbago, worm fit, oedema, bules, colic, various forms of corruption, cephalalgia, foul tongue, nostalgia and anxiety of mind. The digestive problems stemmed from the low-fibre shipboard diet. He normally treated the problem with a purgative such as calomel, and recommended extra oatmeal and exercise. Constipation was, unfortunately, a fact of life for everyone on long sea voyages. On the other hand, conditions on the prison deck were generally unsanitary, despite strict measures concerning hygiene, and this, coupled with the prisoners' own less than ideal sanitary habits, quite frequently resulted in stomach ailments such as diarrhoea. This he treated with an emetic followed by a purgative, which was usually successful. If not, he admitted the patient to the hospital for further treatment. Children and infants with diarrhoea he admitted immediately as they were more susceptible to complications than adults.

Cephalalgia, or headaches, lumbago and foul tongue tended to clear up along with bowel problems, and the other complaints were also often related to poor diet and hygiene, but nostalgia and anxiety were maladies for which he really had no effective remedy. They were disorders of the mind and, he sometimes suspected, of the character; and if his patients felt badly about the fact that they were being sent sixteen thousand miles across the seas from their homes and loved ones for years on end if not forever, he couldn't blame them. To those he suspected of malingering he prescribed chalk and peppermint tablets, no matter what they claimed was wrong with them, allowed no time off, and told them to come back in a week if their symptoms had not abated.

He had also seen Janie Braine's infant Rosie that morning, and was pleased to see she was doing very well, as was Janie herself. Very robust girl, Janie Braine, despite her wall eye, and quite bright. She would make someone a good domestic when she arrived in New South Wales, if she could manage to keep her mouth buttoned. He hoped she would be permitted to take the child with her, though he doubted that would be the case; either both would remain in the Female Factory for some time or Rosie would be sent to the Orphan School. Evie Challis had delivered late a week ago and her infant was also doing reasonably well, though Evie herself was not. She had developed some form of childbed fever: she had a very high fever and a foul-smelling discharge from her womb. Her baby, a boy and not yet named, was presently in the care of Janie, who had generously offered to wet-nurse him. Which reminded him, he would have to arrange with Reverend Seaton to get the child baptised, something Evie had spoken about before she had fallen ill.

He blotted the last line of his entry and stared at it, willing the ink to dry so he could close his journal.

'Excuse me, Mr Downey?'

James recognised Harrie's voice and his heart lifted, as it always did whenever he encountered her sweet face and pretty, untidy hair. He rose from his chair and pulled back the curtain that afforded his cubicle privacy. But his mood deflated again when he saw she was accompanied by big, noisy Friday Woolfe and the other girl, Sarah Morgan, whose intense, knowing gaze always put him on edge. He suspected they didn't much care for him. Well, he *knew*

Friday Woolfe didn't. They were no doubt suspicious of him. He had discovered it paid to tread very carefully when it came to the close and convoluted relationships these women developed.

He thought Harrie looked nervous. 'Harrie. Good morning. Isn't this your day off?'

'Yes, it is. We'd like to talk to you about Rachel, please.'

'Ah, a professional visit.' That explained the presence of her companions. 'By all means, come in.'

He stepped aside and the girls filed in. There were only two chairs; Harrie took one and her friends perched on the examination table.

He sat on his chair beside the writing desk and crossed his legs. 'How can I help you?'

Harrie moved her seat with a scrape so she wouldn't have to crane her neck to see the others. No one said anything. The *Isla* creaked and groaned, noises so familiar now no one even heard them any more, and the curtains swayed gently against the ship's steady roll. Beyond the cubicle in the hospital Evie Challis cried out and Lil Foster's voice murmured in response. The corruption of the womb resulting from Evie's childbed fever was so foul he had instructed Lil to roll back the cover on the ventilation hatch and burn some aromatic pastilles.

'We don't think you're doing enough for Rachel,' Sarah Morgan finally said with characteristic bluntness.

'Sarah!' Harrie exclaimed.

'Knocking her out with laudanum might keep her out of the brig,' Sarah went on, 'but will it fix her? I'm not a doctor, but I can't see how it can. She seems to be getting worse, if anything. What's actually wrong with her? Or don't you know?'

Her sleek, dark head was up and she was staring at him, daring him to reprimand her for being so forthright and for challenging him.

So he did. 'Perhaps you have forgotten that you are a prisoner and I am an officer of the Crown. Please award me appropriate respect.' He stared at Sarah until she looked away. 'With regard to your questions, at this point in Rachel's progress, no, I don't know specifically what is wrong with her. Medical science concerning the brain is not precise. It is a matter of finding a treatment that best manages her symptoms.'

Harrie looked startled and, he had to admit, a little disappointed. 'But you must know. You're the surgeon.'

'I'm a doctor, Harrie, yes, but I'm not a specialist when it comes to matters concerning brain injuries. Rachel struck her head very badly —'

'Keegan shoved Rachel six bloody feet onto the deck,' Friday interrupted, spitting out every word with individual emphasis.

'Yes,' James said, ignoring the bad language, 'which caused a very severe concussion, from which she was lucky to recover at all. These episodes, I'm sure, are directly related to that.' He hesitated. *Was* he sure? He recalled the permanently dilated pupil of Rachel's right eye, which she said had been that way for as long as she could remember. Had she mentioned having headaches or fits of any kind in the past? He didn't think so.

Sarah rolled her eyes. 'Yes, but what's actually *wrong* with her? And will it get worse?'

She didn't ask the obvious question, though, and James was glad.

'Without the benefit of a consultation with a specialist, I am presuming that a portion of her brain has been damaged, causing these fluctuating changes in behaviour. It could be that there is some swelling of the brain, applying internal pressure, which would certainly be cause for her headaches, or perhaps a sliver of skull has travelled into the brain itself.'

There was silence at that.

James continued, unable to stop himself from adding a little gloss to the prognosis, from offering a measure of hope. 'Will it get worse? We will have to wait and see. As I said, I'm not an expert in these matters. But in my experience, most patients would have died after such a horrific injury. However, Rachel did not, so I don't know what to tell you. I did once see a case where the patient recovered from a dreadful head injury — in fact he lived the rest of his life with the shaft of a whaling spear embedded in his skull — with no ill effects whatsoever, but that would be the exception to the rule. And Rachel could prove to be another exception. When we reach New South Wales, ideally she should be seen by a physician better qualified than I am to give a prognosis.'

'Well, that's not going to happen, is it?' Friday said.

James saw the distress etched on the handsome planes of the freckled face. He wanted to offer his sympathies, for Rachel and for their collective predicament as her unofficial guardians, but expected they probably would be rebuffed.

'It's unlikely,' he agreed.

'So, what else *can* you do for her?' Sarah asked.

'I can certainly make her comfortable. More laudanum for the headaches, of course, soporifics to help her sleep.'

Friday sighed and pushed her hair back off her face. 'Christ, who's going to look after her when we get to Sydney? We'll all be assigned, won't we?'

Sarah glared at her. 'You're making it sound as though she'll be an invalid.'

'Well, she will,' Friday snapped. 'Won't she?' she demanded of James.

'There's no need to regard her as such at present, but if she continues to deteriorate, I'm afraid she could be. She certainly won't be considered fit for assignment as a servant, not even in her current state. There is, however, a hospital at the Female Factory at Parramatta, where you will all go when you first arrive.'

'The thing is,' Harrie said in a very small voice, 'it might not just be her.'

They all looked at her.

Harrie flushed. 'Last month she didn't get her, well, you know, and I thought nothing of it because she said she isn't always regular, then she missed again this week. And now I'm wondering ...'

Sarah, an appalled expression on her face, counted off on her fingers. 'Not Lucas then, she'd be out here if it was him. Shit. Are you sure?'

James watched the exchange with growing dismay.

'No, I'm not,' Harrie said. 'She might just have missed because of the shock of everything. You know how it is sometimes.'

'But if she is,' Friday said, her brow furrowed as she worked it out, 'and it's *his*, she'd only be, what, nearly six weeks? She'll have to get rid of it.'

Harrie gasped.

'What's the matter?' Sarah said. 'There's still time.' She shot a look at James.

He stared stiffly ahead, refusing to acknowledge he'd heard what she'd said.

'*No!*' Harrie exclaimed, her face a picture of despair. 'It's a *child*!'

'It is not, it's a hideous mistake,' Friday said matter-of-factly. 'Be reasonable, Harrie.'

James couldn't keep silent any longer. 'Excuse me, please. Has anyone talked to Rachel about this? Surely she must know what's going on with her own body. She may not be ... in a predicament at all. Harrie, have you actually asked her directly?'

'No, I just noticed she didn't need any new cloths. I didn't like to, just in case —'

'She *is* knapped,' Sarah finished angrily. 'For God's sake, Harrie. Pretending it isn't happening won't make it go away.'

'But what if she isn't?' Harrie protested. 'Mentioning it would just bring it all back again.'

Friday frowned. 'Would it? Everything to do with Keegan seems to have fallen right out of her head. The rape, him pushing her off the deck, everything.' And any part Bella might have played as well, so now Friday would never be able to prove it. 'Is that possible, forgetting like that?' she asked James.

'Quite possible. A head injury of such magnitude can have a catastrophic effect on memory. You know,' James ventured, 'it might have been a good idea if you *had* raised the matter of pregnancy with her, Harrie.'

Sarah turned on him. 'You keep out of this. It's got nothing to do with you. And don't criticise Harrie, she's doing her best. She *always* does her best.'

James stared at her coolly. 'May I remind you *again* that you are speaking to an officer of the Crown. Rachel Winter is one of my patients. She has a grave medical condition and this latest development may have a serious bearing on her welfare. May I *also* remind you that *you* approached *me* for advice. Please do me the courtesy of at least listening to it.'

There was an awkward silence, shattered after several seconds by a hoot of laughter from Friday.

'That's telling you, Sarah!'

Sarah continued to glare at him.

Then Harrie did what James had observed she did far too often — she apologised. 'I'm sorry, Mr Downey, we didn't mean to be rude.'

Indulging in a somewhat childish game and refusing to drop his gaze first, he looked at Sarah properly and saw not just anger in her eyes but pain and a great deal of frustration. It occurred to him she must also be capable of considerable compassion, to attract friends the calibre of Harrie, and yes, even boisterous Friday Woolfe and fey little Rachel. He decided to take a risk.

'I understand that Rachel's state of health, and now this new potential complication, are very worrying, Sarah, but what is really upsetting you?'

Sarah regarded him for so long he thought she wasn't going to answer. She looked down, picked at her thumbnail, then said at last, 'It's that bloody Keegan. You know what he did, don't you? What he *really* did?'

James was aware he was suddenly on trial. 'I know that he beat and sexually violated Rachel Winter, then caused her grievous harm by, I strongly suspect, deliberately pushing her off the foredeck.'

'So you do believe she was raped?'

'I do.'

Sarah's eyes flashed with outrage. 'So *why* is he being allowed to get away with it? Rape is a capital offence.'

The short answer to that, James thought, is Josiah Holland doesn't want his crew to mutiny. 'I can't answer that, I'm sorry.'

'Can't or won't?' Sarah demanded.

'Can't, because it isn't my decision. Or jurisdiction. Captain Holland is master of this ship, not me.'

'Sounds like a pile of shite to me.'

'I'm sure it does,' James said. 'But Gabriel Keegan isn't exactly walking free. Have you seen him up on deck lately? He has voluntarily spent the last six weeks in his cabin.'

The girls looked at each other. Keegan had indeed become a pariah, shunned most notably by Matthew Cutler though also by the Seatons, who the surgeon suspected of distancing themselves out of fear for their own reputations. James knew Keegan was sitting in his quarters, drinking himself senseless, seeing only James himself, who visited dutifully once a week, and the deeply unpleasant Amos Furniss, with whom Keegan seemed to have struck up a friendship. Keegan no longer attended the weekly dinners in the great cabin, rarely mixed with the crew and had only appeared on the foredeck once since the day he had pushed Rachel Winter. He might as well be locked in solitary for all the difference it would make to his life aboard the *Isla*. All the while he continued to profess his innocence in the matter of the rape and the assault. James, however, had stopped listening to him, sickened by the man's selfish arrogance.

Sarah snorted. 'So? And then what? We'll get to New South Wales and he'll just step off the ship and walk away!'

'Not necessarily. I will be submitting my report to the appropriate authorities.'

'Will Captain Holland?' Harrie asked.

'That will be up to him,' James replied.

But he doubted it. And he doubted the British government would act upon anything he put in his report concerning an assault on a convict woman by a civilian, especially a civilian whose father had such illustrious connections as did Gabriel Keegan's. He would, however, try.

'In the meantime,' he added, 'I really do suggest you talk to Rachel about her condition as soon as possible.'

But Rachel didn't want to talk about it. It was a secret and she wasn't going to share it. At least, not yet.

It was a lot colder now they were sailing through the Southern Ocean. She wore her boots every day, with lovely stockings Harrie had knitted from some of Mrs Fry's wool. They were made up of different colours and a bit scratchy, but that didn't matter because they were nice and warm and went right up over her knees and Harrie had made them for her especially.

Her head hurt a lot these days. It had been sore on and off before her accident, but, Lord, it was a lot sorer now. It was a funny thing but she couldn't really remember the accident, or what had come before or after it, not for quite a while in either direction. The last thing she could remember clearly was dancing on the deck at dusk, and then one day she woke up in the hospital with the most enormous headache and a line of prickly stitches across her skull. But when she tried to think about the bit in the middle, all she got was a nothingness, as though that part of her life were a page in a book with a big hole burnt in it. If she thought about it hard enough she could even see the scorch marks around the edges, but perhaps she was imagining those.

After she'd woken up Harrie had asked her over and over about what she could remember and she'd answered nothing, which had been the truth. Why *was* she in the hospital? And Harrie had said she'd had a bad fall and split her head open. But when she was well enough to go back to the prison deck — and that had taken nearly two weeks because she'd been quite barmy there for a while and couldn't even hold her own spoon — Liz Parker had come up to her and called her Gabriel Keegan's whore. And Friday *and* Sarah this time had given the mean old cow a real beating and there had nearly been a riot by the time Liz's girls had got involved.

And then Harrie had sat her down and held her hands and told her she might not realise it but Gabriel Keegan had done something really nasty to her, and told her what. Harrie had been crying but she, Rachel, had just been confused. She didn't remember anything at all happening like Harrie said Keegan had done — and if it really had happened, she was pretty sure it would have stuck in her mind. So as far as she was concerned, it hadn't. And that was that. Forever. Lucas would understand about her falling off the foredeck, but he'd be very upset by anything else.

The others — Friday, Sarah and Harrie — were treating her as though she were poorly. She didn't know why. Yes, she had the fits, and once they'd passed she could only very vaguely recall anything about them, but she wasn't what she would call ill. She knew it wasn't very pleasant for them, because they told her what a roaring little witch she'd been, but it wasn't really her fault. Was it? It felt as though something bad took possession of her body so that there was only a tiny bit of her real self left — not enough to tell the bad thing to go away. And then she would sleep for a while and the bad thing *would* go away and she would be all right again. But she wasn't poorly. Except for the headaches.

They always started at the back of her head, *not* where her scar was but on the right, halfway up her skull, just above the knobbly bit. First would come a pinprick, not even of pain, just a little shaft of sensation telling her a headache was coming. Then, within the hour, it would flare into a burning mass and burrow into her brain with teeth of shattered glass and claws of fire, gouging out a hollow where it would settle and throb like a new heart for more than a day and a night. Sometimes the pain would get so bad she would take a needle and push it into the meaty pad at the base of her thumb, just to cause herself more hurt to distract herself from her sore head. Now, though, she could have Mr Downey's special medicine whenever she wanted it and what a difference it made! The headaches hadn't gone away, but now she could sleep through them. It was a blessing.

It meant she felt more rested and less worried about being a drain on poor Harrie and the others, and she could do her chores again, which she really quite liked, except for cleaning the water closets. Though Mr Downey said she wasn't allowed to go near the ship's rails. Under any circumstances.

She liked being up on deck, wrapped in her jacket and snug in her boots, though the wind did make her ears sing and the cold went straight though her. Yesterday there had been whales again, great gleaming beasts with backs the colour of thunderclouds, and darting porpoises, and a high, wheeling albatross that made the sailors curse. She liked the porpoises, in particular the way they seemed to laugh up at her when they leapt out of the waves, as if to say, we know your secret, yes we do.

She was expecting Lucas's baby. It was only very tiny, nestled there all warm inside her tummy, but she knew. She'd missed two courses now and felt squiffy in the mornings though she hadn't actually spewed up, and her bubbies were sore, and she knew. Lucas was going to be so pleased with her and she could just see the smile of happiness on his beautiful, handsome face. He said he wanted lots of babies, boys and girls. It might even be born by the time he came for her, and together they would go back to England, a perfect little family, and start again.

Harrie *was* going on at her, though. And Friday and Sarah. Asking her if she'd been on the rag yet, did she feel sick, on and on as though her expecting a baby was something to worry about. But it wasn't. Janie had a baby. She had two, in fact, now poor Evie had died. And other girls on the ship not much older than fifteen had babies. Why couldn't she have one? She was betrothed to Lucas, after all. It was silly. She *would* tell them, but not until … it was too late.

It was very cold, though, and she knew she'd got thinner while she'd been in the hospital. Her hip bones stuck out now and Sarah said she looked as scrawny as when they first came on board the *Isla*. She was worried that if it got any colder she wouldn't be able to keep the growing baby inside her warm enough. It was even cold down on the prison deck, despite them all being jammed in there at night. It was the temperature of the sea around the ship's hull, according to Mr Meek, but anyone could have worked that out. They saw icebergs nearly every day now, towering mountains off in the distance to starboard, glittering green and white in the harsh sunlight. The crew said only one eighth of an iceberg could be seen above water, but she didn't know if she believed them. It was all very strange and beautiful.

But it was still bloody cold. She had Harrie's stockings now, and was wearing the new set of slops Sarah had found for her over the patched and repaired skirt and blouse she'd wrecked during one of her fits, but still she shivered, especially during the day. At night it wasn't so bad, tucked up snugly in the bunk between the others, but during the day and up on deck she felt the cold in her bones. Harrie had sewn a lining of duck into her jacket, and that helped, but she did wonder if she would ever be warm again. They were saying New South Wales had a balmy, sunny climate, and Captain Holland said yesterday at muster he thought they would reach port in seven weeks, so that wasn't much longer to wait, she supposed. Seven weeks. She would be thirteen weeks gone by then and perhaps a month after that she could expect to feel the baby quicken inside her.

And when that happened she could write to Lucas every day and tell him all about what their baby was doing.

Captain Holland lowered his spyglass. Not that he needed it; the columns of charcoal-hued storm clouds roiling on the western horizon were so ominous there could be only one course of action. Already there was a hard following sea and spume flickering across the deck, and above his head the mizen sails cracked like whips.

'*All hands!*' he bellowed as he collapsed the spyglass. '*Trice up and trim sails, we'll outrun her!*' He gestured at the prisoners milling about staring up at the strange, yellowing sky and ordered Silas Warren, 'Get them below and lock the hatch.'

'Is that wise, sir?' Silas ventured.

Holland barked, 'They can't stay up here!'

Silas grabbed at his hat before the wind snatched it away and extended an arm towards the mass of black cloud to the west. 'No, sir, I meant running.'

'No choice, Mr Warren. Now snap to it.'

Silas Warren passed the order to Joel Meek, who swung down the companion ladder to the waistdeck and herded the women, beginning to panic now at the looming storm and sudden flurry of activity from the crew, down into the gloom of the prison deck. Struggling to suppress his own fear, he closed the hatch after them, neglecting to slide the bolt home.

Friday, a balloon of terror swelling in her chest, threw herself onto the bunk and blurted, 'Bloody hell, did you see those storm clouds? I've a terrible feeling, a terrible, *terrible* feeling.' Her voice, already shrill, went up a notch, competing with wails of alarm from the other prisoners. 'We'll be trapped in here if the ship goes down and we'll not get out and we'll go down with it and we'll drown and —'

Sarah slapped her.

'Ow!' Friday's hand went to her cheek. 'What was that for?'

'You're panicking.'

Harrie sat on the edge of the bunk beside her. 'Take lots of slow, deep breaths. In and out, that's right.'

Friday tried hard, but still a little scream welled up and squeaked out. 'Fuck it, where's my pipe?' She dug around in her things until she found it, furiously tamped in tobacco wheedled from Joel Meek and lit it, her face and shoulders relaxing visibly as she sucked in the smoke.

Around her, other women followed her lead and took the opportunity to break the rules and smoke below deck. What did it matter, if they were all bound for watery graves? The shouting and babble died away as smoke began to fill the long cabin and the women hunkered down to ride out the storm. Those with children drew them close. Janie Braine abandoned the top bunk and squeezed in below with Harrie, Rachel, Sarah and Friday, jammed against the hull with her two infants wrapped in a blanket and tucked in her arms. Sally Minto, not keen on being flung about in the top bunk by herself, climbed down and squashed in with four of her friends in another bunk. The temperature, already low, dropped even further.

They hunched in the semi-darkness, oil lamps swinging wildly as the *Isla* heaved, rolled and groaned over the rising seas, listening to the wind howl ever more furiously across the deck above and waiting in terror for the storm to overtake them.

And finally it did. With an ear-shattering boom the rain came, crashing onto the upper deck with a noise like a hundred thousand drummer boys, and pouring though the cracks between the planks and into the prison. Soon not a square inch nor a body was dry and the floor of the deck lay knee-deep in water, even though it was spilling on through into the hold below. The women, utterly powerless, lifted what they could and held on tight and prayed.

Hours or perhaps only minutes later, the *Isla*'s timbers groaned even more hideously as the seas rose higher still. Those not firmly wedged in place tumbled about in peril. Harrie watched in horror as two women and a child rolled off a top bunk onto the floor and were washed towards the stern along with the water as the deck tilted at an angle of almost forty degrees. They came to a jarring halt as one of the women lodged against the base of the companion ladder, skirts rucked around her waist, her lower leg bent at a horrid angle. Grimacing in agony, she clawed at the edge of a bunk and hauled herself onto it.

Friday, her eyes screwed shut and her own long legs jammed against a post at the end of the bunk to keep everyone in, cried out in terrified anger, 'Lord have mercy, for God's *sake*! *Fuck!*'

The ship pitched the other way and the child in the water reversed direction, screaming his head off. Harrie reached out, scooped him up and dumped him between herself and Rachel. He was hysterical, his face a mass of scrapes and snot. She put her arm around him and held him tight against her.

It went on and on, the ship pitching and rolling at angles far too steep to allow anyone to move deliberately. The noise remained cacophonous: a steady, high-pitched shriek from the wind tearing across the deck and through the rigging, the constant roar of pounding rain, and the relentless smashing of the mountainous waves against the *Isla*'s hull.

Friday yelled something.

'*What?*' Sarah shouted.

'*What if they're all dead?*' Friday pointed upwards.

Harrie thought it was the single most cheerless thing she'd ever heard anyone say.

Shouts and shrieks came from farther along the prison deck. Harrie couldn't see what was happening and didn't want to. She took hold of Rachel's hand, pulled the boy closer and closed her eyes.

More time passed. Gradually, the seas became calmer and the rain eased off. The storm was passing. There was no way of telling what time it was, or even whether it was day or night.

Eventually Friday, unable to bear being below deck any longer and bathed in sharp-smelling sweat, every inch of her body aching from nervous tension, declared, 'I'm going up.'

'You can't,' Sarah said. 'They locked the hatch.'

'Then I'll bang on it 'til they *un*lock it. I can't *stand* it down here!'

She stepped off the bunk into more than a foot of sloshing water, though the level seemed to be going down, but it must still be raining as water was dripping steadily through the upper deck. Or was it sea water? She stuck out her tongue. Salt.

'Wait for me.' Rachel scrambled after her, clinging onto the table as the ship continued to roll.

They climbed the ladder with difficulty, slipping on the icy rungs, and hammered on the hatch, shouting to be let out until Friday pushed hard against it and realised it wasn't actually locked. She managed to raise it several inches, the wind grabbed it and flipped it open and they scrambled up on deck, where a vicious gust almost knocked them off their feet.

Behind them there was a mad rush as relief at not having drowned galvanised the women and they poured up out of the prison onto the waistdeck. Where, like Friday and Rachel, they stopped, open-mouthed.

'*Get back below!*' Captain Holland shouted from the afterdeck where he had been battling with the wheel for almost six hours. He was drenched, utterly exhausted, frozen to the bone and in a filthy temper. And he was frightened. '*God's blood, Mr Warren, get them below!*'

But the women ignored him. Stormclouds the colour of tin plate lay so low there was no distinction between sky and ocean; they were adrift in a great, lightning-slashed dome of greyness and water. And no more than a thousand yards to port rode a decrepit-looking vessel, her mouldering stern gallery looming as she gathered way, gun ports visible along two crumbling decks, wisps of low cloud drifting through remnants of torn and ragged sails hanging limply from her towering masts. She seemed to hover for a moment, the waves breaking through gaping black holes in her hull, and then she was gone, dissolving into the rain and spume.

A shriek came, then more, before the sound was torn away by the wind.

'*I said get them below!*' Holland bellowed until his voice cracked.

So back down the women went again, the crew easing their own fear, and their anger at being pulled from their posts, by shoving them hard and delivering the odd sly kick.

Waiting at the bottom of the ladder for the aisle to clear, Friday said to Sarah, 'Did you see it?'

'See what?'

'That ... whatever it was. You must have.'

'It was the *Flying Dutchman*.' Rachel's eyes sparkled with excitement. 'The ghost ship! Matilda was talking about it the other day. She says the crew are doomed to sail the high seas for eternity.'

Sarah snorted and took a splashing step along the flooded aisle as someone pushed into her from behind.

'*I* saw it,' Rachel insisted. 'Matilda says the phantom crew sail around looking for folk to deliver letters addressed to loved ones long dead, and if you accept one you'll have terrible misfortune until the day you die.'

'Let's hope Matilda was offered one,' Sarah said.

Rachel looked at her, then giggled.

'I don't believe you didn't see anything,' Friday said, clutching at a bunk post as the ship rolled steeply.

Sarah shrugged. 'I don't believe ghosts exist.'

Friday turned to Harrie. 'You saw it, though, didn't you?'

'I saw something.' Harrie shuddered. 'It made the hairs on my arms stand up. Do you really not think ghosts are real?' she asked Sarah.

'No, I don't,' Sarah said, and turned on the girl behind her. 'Will you stop pushing me!'

'Well, move along then, my feet are getting cold,' the girl complained.

Sarah stood on her tip-toes to see what might be causing the hold-up. She couldn't. 'Friday, why aren't we moving?'

Friday didn't need to stand on tip-toe. She peered over the heads of the women waiting to get back to their bunks. As always the light was dim and the air still hazy with pipe smoke and the usual greasy emissions from the oil lamps; all she could see was a knot of figures around one of the lower bunks towards the end of the deck.

Less than a minute later they heard: Liz Parker was dead.

Thirteen

August 1829, Southern Ocean

15th of August, 1829

My Dearest Emily,

It has been several weeks since I have found time to put pen to paper, though you will not notice that of course, receiving these letters in a single large bundle as you will.

It has been a somewhat eventful few weeks, the highlight of which was perhaps the dreadful storm we encountered on the last day of July. I have been extremely busy tending to patients with various sprained and broken limbs since then. The storm itself was harrowing enough, but at its passing it was discovered that one of the prisoners had died. This, as I have recounted to you on several occasions, is not an unexpected occurrence during severe weather events at sea. Folk fall or are struck by unsecured items, crew are swept overboard, but the demise of this woman has left a distinctly unpleasant taste in my mouth. Her name was Liz Parker and, without wishing to speak ill of the dead, she really was rather an unsavoury character.

Most of the prisoners had been up on deck watching the tail end of the storm and when they returned below she was found wedged against the hull at the rear of a berth, apparently dead from asphyxiation. I did not perform a post-mortem, but I did carry out a thorough external examination of the corpse.

James put down his pen, wondering how much he should tell his wife. He didn't want to upset her. He *could* have done a post-mortem on Liz Parker but there had been no need for one; it was obvious from the blue tinge around her mouth that she had suffocated and, frankly, given her size, she could easily have been cast face down on the mattress and fatally jammed against the hull during the panic and crush of the storm. It was a cause of death he would have been happy to enter onto the certificate had he not also observed the pair of livid, thumb-shaped bruises on her throat and the grossly ruptured blood vessels in her eyeballs.

I will spare you the unpleasant details, my dear; suffice to say I did find unsettling evidence suggesting she may have been throttled.

Naturally I reported the matter to Captain Holland, together with my supposition that no one of slight stature would possess the strength to choke the life from a neck as bullish as that of the deceased. However, no men were on the prison deck at the time — all were above deck battling the storm.

We are now facing a quandary. Not unsurprisingly, no one has confessed to killing Liz Parker, and no one has helpfully accused another of killing her, so do we hold the entire contingent of prisoners responsible? The captain favours recording her death in the manifest as 'accidental', but Captain Holland, as I have already complained to you, has proved himself to be a somewhat weak character. In fact, he refuses to launch an investigation for fear of stirring up the women when we are so near the end of our journey. The matter, however, falls under his jurisdiction, therefore I must let it rest at this moment, though I most certainly will be providing a full report to Governor Darling when we reach Sydney Town.

Of much lesser importance, but still worthy of note, is another incident that occurred in the dying moments of the storm mentioned above. I did not witness the 'event' myself as I was tending a crewman with a fractured forearm in the hospital, but evidently a number of folk on deck saw a vision of the Flying Dutchman. *I attribute this to mass hysteria brought on by the excitement of the storm coupled with the extraordinary atmospheric conditions we were experiencing at the time. Needless to say, a significant number of the crew swear they saw the mirage too — no sailor worth his salt would admit to not having seen it.*

The captain says, all things being well, we will reach port at the end of the first week of September and I for one will be greatly relieved when this voyage comes to an end. The death of the Parker woman coupled with the incident concerning the young girl I recounted in my previous letters have conspired to make this the most unpleasant posting I have endured.

I have talked of this before, my dear, but I think the time has come for me to consider retiring from the navy and seeking a position ashore. You will, I know, be delighted with this notion. As I am still a relatively young man there is plenty of time for me to establish myself in private practice. I am assuming you are still agreeable to the possibility of emigrating to Australia? I am convinced the warmer climate there will far better suit your delicate constitution than the rains and heavy winters of England.

In anticipation, I will make tentative inquiries about private positions while I await my ship back to England.

I miss you and, as always, look forward to the day I am again by your side.

Yours with love,
James

Friday had had a complete and utter gutful. Being stuck on this stinking, rat-ridden boat in the middle of the ocean was sending her mad, she was desperate for a decent drink and would give her left arm for a jug of gin, Rachel was still refusing to say whether she was pregnant or not, and everyone was suspicious and jittery as a result of Liz Parker's death.

She knew vindictive fingers were being pointed at her, because she was big and strong and everyone knew she'd hated the bitch, but she hadn't done it — she'd been first up on deck and everyone had witnessed that. But it certainly served Parker right for being such a nasty piece of work. Friday had seen the corpse, though, when they'd carted it up, and it hadn't been a pretty sight. Parker's ugly mug had been dark purple, the tongue sticking out and the eyes bulging like a frog's.

The gabble and accusations had started straight away, naturally, and were still buzzing round the prison deck and making everyone look twice at who they sat next to, but no one was any closer to finding out who'd topped her. Not that anyone seemed to be trying very hard — and not that it mattered: she'd been a mean, trouble-making old tarleather. She wouldn't be missed and her girls had already settled in with other messes, while a core of tough nuts, namely Becky Hoddle, Louisa Coutts and Beth Greenhill, had shifted their allegiance to Bella Jackson.

But Friday knew prisons, and Parramatta Female Factory was a prison by another name if what she'd heard back in Newgate was true, and there'd be another Liz Parker there without a doubt.

There always was. There was one on the *Isla*, in fact, and a much smarter, nastier and more predatory version than old Liz Parker to boot. So bugger Liz, may she rot in hell: there were much more important things to worry about than her.

Rachel's fits were getting worse and there was something new now — she wouldn't stop talking about the ghost ship they'd seen. Or thought they had; Friday still wasn't sure what it was. She'd shrieked her head off along with the rest of them, but to be honest her poor nerves had been stretched so tight after the storm she would have screamed at almost nothing and perhaps she had. What they'd seen may have been little more than the 'phenomenon' the captain had described at muster on the day following the storm — a dense patch of low-lying cloud strangely illuminated by receding lightning — and the way he'd said it had implied they were all fools to imagine they'd encountered anything else. She'd noticed he'd given his crew a good hard look when he'd said it, too. But ghosts were a fact of life, whether Captain Holland — or Sarah — liked it or not.

However Rachel was still going on about it, in between pitching her fits, which seemed to be getting worse every time she had one. Friday was at her wits' end about how to help her, and feeling more and more frustrated because it was her job to sort it out. *She* was the boss of her little family, which was how she thought of them now. No one else had ever cared about her the way Harrie, Sarah and Rachel did, not even her gin-sodden mother. What would Megsie Woolfe have done about Rachel? Left her to fend for herself, probably, which was all she'd done for Friday.

If Rachel carried on like this much longer people would think she was a lunatic, especially when they got to New South Wales. Were there lunatic asylums in Sydney? Was that where she would end up? And if she *was* pregnant, God — Friday couldn't think of a worse pickle. It was Keegan's fault and no doubt that evil cow Bella's as well, and every time she thought about Keegan lounging in his comfortable cabin calmly waiting to walk off the ship and into his new, free life, her fists clenched and she felt her blood pounding in her head. It was eating a hole in her — Rachel's crumbling health, the failure to make Keegan pay, being stuck on this ship — all of it.

And there were still *weeks* to go before they reached New South Wales.

Hester Seaton was *thoroughly* sick of attempting to teach slow-witted and, frankly, wilfully idle convict women to read and write. She had tried her utmost and there still remained a good proportion who could not even string together enough letters to form their own names. Really, she did wonder whether some were only attending her school for letters to avoid daily chores or to fill in time. And they were paying even less attention now that there were glimpses of land to be had from time to time, and other signs that they were finally, after all these months at sea, nearing their destination.

Of course — she had to be truthful — a handful were doing remarkably well and she must assume that those who had chosen not to attend at all could already read and write, and there were a surprising number of those. But really, the novelty of bringing the gift of education to the underprivileged was wearing off and she had in fact tired of it some time earlier. A temporary effect relating to the confines of shipboard life, no doubt. Also, the atmosphere had been somewhat tense since the unfortunate incident involving Gabriel Keegan. Once her feet were back on terra firma and any taint of scandal left behind on the *Isla* and her daughters as far away from Mr Keegan as possible, she would feel differently, she was sure.

Thank the Lord that in just over two and a half weeks, if Captain Holland's calculations were correct, they would be dropping anchor in Sydney Cove.

* * *

Harrie took off her apron and dropped it into the laundry hamper, grateful she didn't have to wash it herself; one of the children had been sick on it and the vomit had been a hideous yellow colour and eye-wateringly smelly. Her shift was over and she was very tired. As she crossed the floor Mr Downey came out of his cubicle.

'Harrie, I have something for you.' He held out a letter folded and sealed with wax.

Nonplussed, she looked at it but didn't take it. 'What is it?'

'It's a recommendation.'

'Oh. What for?'

'I thought it might help you obtain a suitable assignment. I don't make a practice of this, but you really are very good with children, and in the hospital in general.' He flushed slightly. 'I thought it might help you.'

Harrie, blushing herself, took the letter and ducked her head. 'Thank you very much, Mr Downey. I'm very grateful.'

'Yes, well.' He cleared his throat, embarrassed. 'I'm aware that female convicts aren't always assigned to positions that make the most of their vocational strengths. It would be a shame if you couldn't use yours.'

Harrie thought so, too. She really wanted an assignment where she could sew and embroider and generally use her needlework skills.

'Well,' Mr Downey said again. 'I'll take this opportunity to wish you the very best of luck now, Harrie, as things will become quite hectic in the next two weeks before we go into harbour. I've enjoyed having you as my assistant. I hope things go well for you. I've often wondered …'

Harrie waited, but he didn't finish, and looked even more embarrassed.

'Anyway,' he said, 'good luck. I've also noted where I'll be lodging for the month before my ship sails, which is the King Hotel on King Street. If you need help, that is. I mean, if Rachel should require assistance, you'll know where to send word and I'll see what I can do.'

'Thank you, sir. That's very kind of you.'

As she crossed the waistdeck she tucked the letter down her blouse, out of sight. It had been a very thoughtful and generous thing for him to do, but she wasn't sure she wanted a testimonial from him. It would give her an advantage over Friday and Sarah and Rachel when it came time for them to be assigned, and she didn't want that. She wanted them to stay together. Which was silly, she knew, because from what they'd heard it was very unlikely they *would* be assigned together, but still, it felt wrong. If she used it, or even thought about using it, it would feel like a betrayal. Mr Downey wouldn't even think about a thing like that.

Not that it looked like Rachel would be assigned. Oh, she still had her good days, but there were certainly bad days, too. What happened to girls who weren't fit enough to be sent out? If her condition worsened, she might even be confined to the Factory hospital, which, Harrie was sure, would be nowhere near as clean or orderly as Mr Downey's. And why would the silly girl not admit to being pregnant? Harrie was sure now she was. Sometimes she felt like taking Rachel by the ears and giving her head a thoroughly good rattle just to wake her up.

Friday, too, was in a foul mood, and she wouldn't talk to anyone either. Well, she would, but not about what was upsetting her. Harrie knew she was worried about Rachel and suspected she felt responsible, though God knew why; what had happened hadn't been Friday's fault. And Harrie knew from their time in Newgate that when Friday was out of sorts she drank heavily, except her means of obtaining alcohol on the *Isla* had been cut off, except for a tiny ration Harrie thought she might be scrounging from Joel Meek, which wasn't enough, not for Friday. Harrie really wasn't looking forward to what might happen when they finally arrived at

Sydney Town, because if Friday could get her hands on drink there, she most certainly would.

Sarah wasn't much better. She never really said much anyway and was saying even less these days. She was very patient with Rachel, surprisingly so, and Harrie had caught her crying once when she'd thought no one was looking, after Rachel had had a particularly ugly fit. But then Harrie had watched her when they'd buried Liz Parker — well, dropped her body over the side of the ship — and her face had been as hard as rocks and wearing an expression, she'd realised later with shock, close to triumph. And she'd wondered, guiltily, whether Sarah had done it, had killed her. And Sarah must have read her mind, in that way she had, because the next day she'd said, 'You think *I* did it, don't you?'

And Harrie, who'd known exactly what Sarah was talking about, had gone red and said, 'Did what?'

'Topped Liz Parker.'

'No I don't!'

And Sarah had laughed. 'I was up on deck with you, remember?'

But not straight away you weren't, Harrie had recalled disloyally.

Then Sarah had said, 'It wasn't me, Harrie. I certainly felt like it, she was such a bitch to Rachel. She was a bitch to everyone. But it wasn't me. You know me better than that.'

Harrie did, and felt bad for even only half thinking it.

Sarah had given her one of those rare, real-Sarah smiles that not many people saw. 'It's all right, Harrie, I'm not offended. And if I had done it, it would have been for Rachel. You know that.'

And, strangely, the more Harrie thought about it, the more acceptable that notion seemed. Which frightened her badly, so she'd pushed the thought to the very back of her mind.

Except it kept popping back out.

* * *

Gabriel Keegan peered out of the small window of his cabin at the distant shoreline. It was miles away, the dark line of land shrouded in low cloud. According to Holland, they were less than two weeks out of port, which was fortunate as he'd polished off his personal supply of cheese and wine and was sick to death of taking his meals in his cabin, not to mention his own company. Downey had made it clear he wasn't welcome either in the great cabin or on the foredeck, thanks to that sanctimonious prick Cutler and the self-righteous Seatons. But he only left his cabin at night now anyway.

He'd made that decision himself though, never mind Downey. A few days after the little blonde tart had attacked him he'd been on the foredeck when some slag on the waistdeck had hurled something at him. The missile had been a turd.

Bloody slit-arsed bitches.

Josiah Holland carefully rolled up his blueback charts, slid them into a leather map case and hung it on its hook. He'd left two charts out on the table, their curling corners held down by glass paperweights, as he'd need them for navigating into Sydney Cove, but the remainder he wouldn't require again until the return voyage in six weeks' time. Once they'd dropped anchor, the convicts had been disembarked and the — slightly depleted — cargo unloaded, he would pay the crew then write up his report. He had also decided to inform Amos Furniss he wouldn't be required on the homeward journey. And now that the threat of mutiny had passed, if he coerced other crew members to resign, then so be it: there were plenty of sailors in Sydney willing to work. He'd just about had enough of the man's insolence. He would severely dock his pay, too, to compensate for the missing rum and brandy from the hold.

This voyage had been a nightmare. Thank God it was almost over.

* * *

Sarah knew they would be split up after they left the Parramatta Female Factory, but while they were there, they'd be all right. She'd heard talk of the Factory in London and, though by all accounts it wasn't a pleasant place, as in any prison there were ways in which life as an inmate could be made better. She'd also gathered that the assignment system itself could be worked to advantage if you kept your wits about you, which was something she understood well. But she wouldn't know what that would entail until they actually arrived, and sitting around on this ship waiting for that was stretching her nerves almost to tearing point — and there was still another whole week to go.

Once they left the Factory they'd need money — they might well have spent their kitty by then. Who knew what they'd have to pay for inside? And it didn't look as though Rachel would be playing broads for a while, if she ever did again. Their assignments as servants wouldn't earn them anything, so that meant reverting to the skills that got them transported in the first place. Harrie would make a hopeless criminal, so she was out as far as that went. But Friday, Sarah knew, would be on her back at the first opportunity as it was the quickest way to pay for gin. She could make a *lot* of money and was happy to share it, and Sarah had plenty of schemes of her own.

The money would go first to care for Rachel. Sarah didn't know what form that care would take, but she didn't need to yet. Harrie would be provided for next, as she couldn't make her own money while virtually enslaved to someone else. She deserved an allowance — she was the loving heart that held them all together. (There, she'd said the word that always gave her such trouble: love. Thought it, at least.) And if Rachel *were* pregnant, there would be a child to support as well, because soon it would be too late to do anything about it. It would come and it would not be Keegan's child, just Rachel's.

It could all be done with careful scheming, a bit of hard graft, and money, because money fixed most problems. And in Australia there would be no flash man like Tom Ratcliffe to take it all away from her, or to beat the hell out of her or tell her she was ugly and unwanted.

She wasn't unwanted here. Or unloved. She had Harrie and Friday and Rachel.

Matthew Cutler sat at the desk in his cabin writing what would be the last of his shipboard letters home to his mother in England. Some weeks it had been a colossal strain coming up with something interesting to tell her, but lately, over the past month, there had been plenty to write about.

There had been the terrible storm, though he'd played that down so he wouldn't worry her; the sighting of the *Flying Dutchman*, which he'd described at length as she was very interested in matters concerning the spirit world; the mysterious death of the convict woman; and the increase in flora and fauna as the *Isla* neared the southern coasts of Australia.

There had also been the ongoing tension concerning Gabriel Keegan, who had shut himself in his cabin, to the relief, Matthew was aware, of almost everyone. He saw the girl Rachel Winter on the waistdeck from time to time and was gratified to see that, remarkably, she seemed to have recovered from her awful injuries, though James Downey had hinted she wasn't as hale as she looked. She appeared even more of a waif with her trailing, silver-white hair and stick-like wrists, but then Matthew supposed that travails of the nature she had endured would certainly sap a person of her strength. He definitely hadn't mentioned to his mother anything about that particular affair; she would have found it all extremely distasteful. He had himself and couldn't wait to see the back of Gabriel Keegan.

Because of it, he'd never summoned the courage to speak to Harriet Clarke and now he supposed he never would. He might have if Keegan hadn't sullied the waters by committing his brutal assaults, but since then the line between the prisoners and the passengers had been as impassable as a brick wall, crossed only by Mrs Seaton and her school for letters. He'd lost his opportunity, and he'd lost his convict girl.

He took up his pen again:

We expect to be dropping anchor in Sydney Cove in five or six days and I must say I am very much looking forward to my new life. My first task will be to post these letters to you, and what a large bundle they will make. My second task will be to report to the offices of the Government Architect — and I do not mind admitting, Mother, that I am somewhat nervous about the prospect — and my third will be to find suitable accommodation. Though, on second thoughts, perhaps after I have located the post office I will visit the nearest public house that will sell me a good meal consisting of fresh vegetables and beef. We are coming to the end of our better edible provisions and if I have to eat one more tooth-cracking, stomach-bloating ship's biscuit I shall mutiny. We have even run short of lime juice, though not wine, though it is not very good wine that remains, being a very rough Spanish red.

But the sun is shining, despite a cooler temperature than I had expected, and my spirits are high, and I will be stepping onto Australian soil with a glad and expectant heart.

Matthew nibbled the end of his pen. Should he also add that he was very much looking forward to not having to listen to any more of the Reverend Seaton's interminable sermons, or the sound of his snoring through the cabin walls every night? No, perhaps not.

I will write as soon as I have found myself rooms. Until then I remain,

Your Affectionate Son,
Matthew

7 September 1829, Port Jackson

The girls were on deck with everyone else watching Port Jackson open up before them. Last night barely anyone had slept, such had been the level of excitement as the *Isla* had sailed the last few nautical miles through the Tasman Sea up the coast of New South Wales, and this morning everyone had been out of their bunks well before the ship's bell had rung, ready to come up on deck. More than a few had taken the time to pretty themselves: for those who used it, rouge had been applied to cheeks and lips, bright scarves retrieved and the mould wiped off, and silk flowers and ribbons threaded into prison bonnets. Many women wore their own clothes beneath their prisons slops, the cheap Navy Board garments now in varying and immodest states of disrepair. They had passed through the towering cliffs of Sydney Heads after breakfast and the women had hurried through their chores to be free to watch the scenery and other ships pass by on the final leg of their journey into Sydney Cove, where they would drop anchor later in the morning.

To the English and Irish women aboard the *Isla*, the landscape appeared utterly foreign.

For a start the rocks that rimmed the vast harbour were coloured a startling peach to orange to grey, and stood or lay in great slabs that dropped right into the sea. The trees, too, were disconcertingly strange. They ranged from scrubby clumps of acacia and paperbark and banksia, low and dense and hugging the earth, to fan-crowned cabbage-tree palms, to eerie, soaring stands of blackbutt and red gum with slender white trunks like the bones of a hand. Absent entirely were the majestic trees of England, the elms and oaks and beeches. But Port Jackson was breathtaking, the sea eating into the craggy shoreline and reaching fingers far inland, forming tiny islands and endless sandy bays and coves and peninsulas and headlands, making patterns like the gaps in an intricate piece of filet lace. Nothing like the Thames, which drilled into the side of England and simply kept going until it was absorbed.

At first the landscape seemed to be empty, but soon a patchwork of fields and a handful of tiny buildings near the shore became visible. And the farther the *Isla* sailed into the long harbour, the crew shouting to one another and tacking furiously as the wind changed direction, the more evidence of civilisation was revealed. Then, rounding a headland and encountering the bristling masts of dozens of schooners and cutters, brigs and barques, whalers and even warships, the women realised they had reached Sydney Cove.

To their right lay a scrubby headland that dipped then rose again to a hill on which squatted Fort Phillip. Behind it, inland, were various prominent buildings including a vast windmill. On the horizon were half a dozen more windmills and perhaps three or four church steeples. Buildings several storeys high, solidly built of pale stone, dotted the low hills that ringed the harbour — from this perspective appearing as though placed at random by a child playing with miniatures. Where the hills ran down to the sea the clusters of buildings grew more dense, in places seeming to grow out of the rocks themselves, and stores small and great lined the shore where several wharves extended into the water.

On the deep cove's left was another headland, on the tip of which sat the rather mediaeval tower of Fort Macquarie, and behind that lay a vast expanse of park land. Overall the impression was one of open space. To the women on the *Isla* there appeared to be none of the cramped, overhanging garrets and rookeries of London, no smoke and soot-blackened lanes, no festering cesspits brimming with shit and the corpses of cats and dogs. On the sea air there was, however, the unmistakable taint of a slaughterhouse somewhere not too far distant.

'It looks pretty enough,' Sarah remarked, gesturing at the shore.

'It isn't home, though, is it?' Harrie said, her voice cracking. Home was where her mother and brother and sisters were, and that wasn't here in this strange, bright new land.

'But is this where the Female Factory is?' Friday said.

Amos Furniss, eavesdropping as he secured a rope, laughed unpleasantly. 'Hell no. That's miles upriver, and what a shithole it is, too. Nothing but preachers and bloody farms. And cows. Like *you* lot.' He spat and walked away.

'Arsehole,' Friday muttered.

'Don't listen to him,' Harrie said, anxious to avoid a last-minute scene in spite of her unhappiness. 'We're nearly there.'

'We are, aren't we?' Rachel said brightly. 'And guess what? I've got such good news.'

Harrie, Friday and Sarah stared at her with sudden frightened expectation, each knowing already what she was about to say, but still hoping it would be something else.

Rachel clapped her hands delightedly. 'I'm having a baby!'

Part Three

Parramatta Girls

Fourteen

September 1829, Parramatta Female Factory

The great anchor chain descended through the bow with a deafening rattle as First Mate Warren bellowed orders. The women, jammed onto the waistdeck with their ratty possessions heaped around them, waited expectantly. Bella Jackson stood beside her two trunks wearing a full skirt of oxblood velvet, a beautifully fitted jacket in emerald taffeta, a very fancy bonnet with a black ostrich feather and her grey kid boots; her prison slops were nowhere to be seen. Her waist was *tiny*.

Friday, Harrie and Sarah stood in silence, feeling unsettled and vaguely sick, even though they weren't particularly surprised by Rachel's news. Harrie held Rachel's hand. Rachel was crying, upset that they weren't as thrilled by her announcement as she'd expected.

Mr Warren strode about, waving his arms and clearing a path between the door beneath the foredeck and the gap in the ship's rail where the bosun's chair had been rigged. There was already a great pile of luggage on the crowded deck, presumably belonging to the paying passengers, brought up from the hold this morning and in the process of being lowered into the wherry waiting below.

The Seatons themselves then emerged from the cabins, Mrs Seaton wearing a bonnet even fancier than Bella's, followed by Matthew Cutler. Hester Seaton waved regally as she shepherded her daughters towards the bosun's chair. One by one they descended into the wherry, until only Mr Cutler remained.

The women watched restlessly, muttering among themselves, and Captain Holland and James Downey, standing on the afterdeck, watched the women. They had discussed the matter several days earlier and decided there was no easy way of doing this. Perhaps if the *Isla* had come in to harbour at night something could have been arranged, but she hadn't and, frankly, Josiah Holland hadn't felt inclined to make much effort.

At last, Gabriel Keegan appeared.

The convict women fell silent, the only sounds the creaking of the *Isla*'s timbers, the sea washing against her hull and the cry of sea birds overhead.

His arrogant gaze swept over them as he walked across the deck towards the ship's rail.

Someone made a loud pig noise.

'Oh Friday, don't,' Harrie whispered.

It was picked up and the women launched a barrage of grunting, jabbering, snorting animal sounds, the pitch and volume rising until the alarmed crew clapped their hands over their ears.

'Pig!' a voice shouted.

'*Pig! Pig! Pig!*'

Matthew Cutler glanced over his shoulder as Keegan approached.

'Hurry up!' Keegan urged.

Matthew fiddled about with the sling on the bosun's chair. 'I seem to have the ropes tangled. Won't be a moment.'

Keegan bared his teeth as behind him the taunts continued. Finally Matthew slid the seat beneath his backside and was launched into the air.

'*Rapist!*' someone shrieked.

'Dirty *bastard*!'

A pottery bowl flew through the air and hit Gabriel Keegan on the back.

'Are you going to do anything?' James Downey asked the captain.

Josiah Holland examined his fingernails for a moment. 'No point, really. He'll be off in a minute.'

'That's true,' James said.

The bosun's chair returned and Keegan threw himself into it, at last descending into the wherry below. Before he was even seated the watermen pulled away from the *Isla* in a wide arc and set out for the shore, passing the line of four lighters waiting to collect the latest shipment of convict women to arrive in New South Wales.

A crowd awaited them on shore — a number of women, but mainly men with a hankering for a wife or simply come to inspect the plumage on the most recent cageful of His Majesty's canaries. Some of the convict girls played up to them, and Friday was one of the worst, swishing her skirts about, showing her legs all the way up to her thighs and yelling out ribald comments. She was angry about Rachel, and this was the only way she had of letting it out. Sarah sulked and was aggressive. Walking on solid ground after so many months at sea was surprisingly difficult and the women staggered about as though in their cups. A man in the crowd shouted at them, 'Drunken whores!' and Sarah lunged out of the line into which they'd been herded and spat at him before a guard knocked her down and dragged her back. The crowd cheered, thoroughly entertained, then roared even more loudly when Friday swore the air blue then bared her backside at the guard.

Harrie slipped a comforting arm around Sarah's shoulder, but Sarah shrugged her off. Blinking back tears, Harrie looked around for Rachel, trudging along behind them, dragging her sack of possessions, still crying quietly, lost in her own muddled little world.

Unable to stop it, Harrie burst into tears herself. This was absolutely awful. It seemed that they were as despised here as they had been in London, never mind that Sydney Town was filled with folk who had been convicts themselves, the mean buggers. And no matter how cheerful they'd tried to be on the *Isla* about their prospects in New South Wales, they were now thousands of miles from family and home and on the eve of a minimum seven-year sentence of what amounted to slave labour. It couldn't get much worse.

A hand slipped into hers; Rachel's.

Harrie squeezed and held on.

They stayed only one night in Sydney Town, under lock and key in a shed on the waterfront, where they were mustered and had their papers checked by a man who announced himself as Mr William Tuckwell, superintendent of the Female Factory at Parramatta. The next morning they set out for the Factory, a journey of around fifteen miles up the Parramatta River, in six boats rowed by two dozen burly watermen. Their military escort distributed themselves two to each vessel, Mr Tuckwell riding in the lead boat. On the first leg, Harrie had sat only inches from a waterman, his face red and sweaty, his knees banging against hers as he'd rowed, and he'd not looked directly at her once.

They had stopped so the watermen could be relieved, and now the river was narrowing, its banks lined with mangroves whose roots reached down into the water. It was warm and muggy on the waterway and hordes of voracious mosquitoes were out in force, giving rise to energetic swatting and swearing.

At times, between the grumbling and slapping and the steady dip of oars into the river, could be heard the harsh cries of a familiar bird.

'That's a raven!' Friday exclaimed, a note of pleasure in her voice. 'Fancy having English birds here.'

''Tis not. Them's crows,' Matilda Bain argued.

Friday shook her head. 'Ravens.'

'Crows.'

'*You're* a bloody old crow.'

Harrie held her breath, worried Friday would lose her temper. 'It doesn't matter, does it? They're both English.'

'No, these ones are native to Australia,' the young soldier sitting in the stern said. 'Nearly the same as the English ones, but bigger. And it's a raven. Ravens go "aarr, aarr, aarrrrrrrrrrrr"; crows go "ark, ark, ark".'

Everyone turned to stare at him. He went pink, adjusted his cap and looked away.

He proved useful again later when an unearthly cackle rang out across the river and made them all jump and look around wildly, advising that it was a bird called a kookaburra, even though Matilda pronounced it to be the sound of the devil himself laughing at them as they were rowed towards their doom. This time Friday pinched her until she squawked.

Rachel, who was getting a headache, slumped with her head in Harrie's lap and her legs across Sarah's.

Finally, when they were convinced their backsides couldn't tolerate the wooden seats any longer, the watermen veered towards the right bank and landed the boats. The women, stiff from sitting so long with their knees bent, disembarked with their possessions and trudged in a long ragged line towards a high, pale stone wall, their military escort marching beside them, Mr Tuckwell leading the way. Fearing that she might have a fit in the boat, Harrie had lightly dosed Rachel with laudanum: now she was dozy and Friday carried her on her back, Sarah following with an armful of sacks and bags.

Skirting the moat beyond the base of the wall, which was easily fifteen or sixteen feet high, they plodded along in the wall's lengthening shadow until they came to tall wooden gates set into an archway. The gates were flanked by towering pillars of sandstone — and they were closed.

'It's a prison,' someone remarked, with an almost comical note of disappointment in her voice.

There was a bit of weary laughter at that. What else had they expected?

Friday said in Sarah's ear, 'Give me the kitty. And a bit of cloth, a kerchief or something.'

A wicket was set into the left-hand gate: Mr Tuckwell rapped on it and it creaked open. A short exchange occurred with an unseen person, then it closed again.

They all waited.

'Jesus, hurry up,' Friday said loudly as she crouched and slid Rachel off onto the ground, where she slumped, her head nodding. 'Me bladder's bursting!' She walked off a short distance, turned her back, lifted her skirts and squatted. The soldiers stared.

Discomposed, Mr Tuckwell shouted at Friday, 'Hey, you, no! Wait until you're inside!'

A moment later the big gates swung ponderously open, grinding across the dirt and gravel beneath them.

Bella Jackson, her girls struggling with her trunks, shoved her way to the front of the line. Harrie and Sarah picked up Rachel between them, leaving Friday to carry everything else. The soldiers closed in and herded the women inside.

Behind them, the gates shut with an echoing bang.

They found themselves packed into a small outer yard; ahead of them rose another lower wall and a second set of gates. One of the children started to cry, which set them all off. But not a single mother slapped or reprimanded; the day had been long and everyone was tired, thirsty and hungry.

A porter — or port*ress*, as she was a woman — opened the gates. Through they went, leaving their military escort behind, into yet another yard, this one reasonably spacious and well-kept. Directly in front of them rose a wide, three-storey building with windows along each floor, divided exactly in the middle by a blunt, full-height transept more likely to be found in a church, and, rather incongruously given the unwelcoming appearance of its unadorned, sandstone facade, an elegant cupola on the roof and a clock set under the eaves of its entrance. The yard was enclosed by buildings on three sides, including the three-storey structure, and by the wall and gates through which they had just entered.

In the centre, facing them, stood a woman. She looked middle-aged, was solid but neatly built and wore a white ruffled bonnet and a black dress that gave off a slight sheen in the late afternoon sun. For a long moment she observed them in silence, her face unsmiling, hands clasped loosely at her waist.

'She looks a dour piece of work,' Sarah said out of the side of her mouth.

Friday stifled a snort of laughter.

The woman's head turned and her hooded eyes narrowed. 'Is that girl ill?' she demanded, pointing a short-nailed finger at Rachel.

Harrie, struggling to support Rachel, felt a squirt of panic. 'No, ma'am, just sleepy.'

There was a ripple of laughter and the woman clapped her hands sharply. 'Quiet! My name is Mrs Gordon and I am matron of Parramatta Female Factory. This will be your home until you are sent on assignment. For some of you that will occur almost immediately, which I certainly hope will be the case as at present there are four hundred and eighty-nine women and seventy-two children here, not including yourselves.' She paused to take a breath. 'The Factory operates a class system. All inmates eligible for assignment are drawn from first class, and first class only. Second-class inmates are on probation and third-class inmates are those confined to the penitentiary for crimes committed while on assignment.' She paused again and deliberately swept the faces before her with a stern gaze. 'My task is to ensure every adult inmate is eventually assigned. Until that occurs, all inmates fit for work will undertake industrious employment while at the Factory. Shortly you will bathe, undergo inspection, and be allocated quarters. I understand you were issued slops when you boarded your transport at Woolwich. You will only be issued with replacement slops if those which you currently possess are unserviceable.'

From somewhere in the middle of the shuffling, rag-tag group came the unmistakable sound of fabric being torn. Someone tittered and soon it had spread until everyone was giggling and laughing.

Mrs Gordon clapped her hands again. 'Quiet! *Quiet!* Let it be known now that I will *not tolerate* insubordination or wilful disobedience.' She waited stonily until the giggling had died down. 'The Female Factory fulfils many roles. It is a labour exchange, a manufactory, a lying-in facility, a nursery, a hospital, a penitentiary, and I have even heard it referred to as a refuge and an asylum, but above all it is an institution for convicts and *that is what you are*. This entire colony was originally established as a gaol. It will serve you well never to forget that.'

'As if we could,' Friday muttered.

Mrs Gordon turned on her heel and walked off, her full black skirts swishing, crossing the courtyard and entering the three-storey building.

'So what do we do now?' Sarah said grumpily.

'Well, I can't muck about,' Janie Braine said behind her. 'I have to feed these babies. Me tits are bursting. Here, hold Rosie, will you?'

Sarah took Janie's baby while Janie opened her blouse and put William, Evie Challis's orphaned infant, to her breast. He suckled half-heartedly, his delicate eyelids closing, long lashes brushing his cheeks, mouth working weakly.

'Poor little tyke,' Janie said, gazing down at him. 'He's so sickly compared to Rosie.'

'Will you keep him?' Sarah asked.

Janie nodded and looked up, her bung eye staring blindly. 'As long as I can. Well, he's got no one else, has he?'

'What about Evie's little girl? Who's got her?'

'One of Evie's mates. I'd like to take her, too, so as not to split them up. But we'll see.'

Friday appeared at Sarah's elbow, waggling her fingers at Rosie and pulling the baby's bare toes to make her smile. 'Come on, we're moving.' She nodded at three women wearing keys at their waists. 'Turnkeys.'

The women herded the unwieldy group towards the three-storey building. The entrance door was quite narrow and they had to go through one at a time. Once inside the foyer, bigger than expected and with a soaring ceiling, the turnkeys directed everyone through yet another door on the far side and out into a third walled yard. Small clusters of inmates stood about, watching the newcomers. They wore the same clothes as the turnkeys, though many were barefoot.

'So they're lags, the turnkeys,' Friday remarked to Sarah.

Sarah's expression was ambivalent. 'Good and bad. Easier to bribe, harder to fool.'

There were also curious female faces peering through windows in the buildings at the end and on the right side of the yard, though the wall of the building on the left side was windowless and blank.

Mrs Gordon was waiting for them in the far corner, beside a flight of stone steps apparently descending into the ground.

She clapped her hands once again, then indicated a doorway in the wall to her right. 'On my say so, line up and move in an orderly manner through the workshop to the storeroom to receive your new slops. I remind you again, take *only* what you require. Return here with your new items, remove *all* your clothing, children included, and in groups of twenty at a time descend to the baths and wash your personages and hair thoroughly. You can be assured that there are no males in this area of the Factory to observe you. Leave all your possessions including your old clothing here in the yard, take only your new slops down to the baths with you. Your personal, non-regulation clothing will be stored until you are assigned. The wearing of non-regulation clothing at the Factory is *not* permitted.' She gestured to a woman standing beside her. 'This is Mrs Dick, one of my two assistant matrons. She and the monitresses will assist with the inspection. Now, please make a line.'

There was the usual shuffling and milling about that accompanies the formation of a queue, then the first women moved into the building Mrs Gordon referred to as a workshop. Harrie, Friday, Sarah and Rachel followed. In each wall of the workshop was a doorway — the entire Female Factory seemed to comprise a maze of walls and doorways — but the line snaked to the right into a storeroom whose wooden shelves held piles of folded clothing, the slops Mrs Gordon seemed so anxious should not be distributed willy-nilly. Two women behind a counter were getting into a muddle handing out the various items that made up the Factory uniform.

'We don't usually get such a large intake all at once, you know,' one grumbled loudly as she pushed a pile of clothes across the counter. 'And don't come complaining if it doesn't all fit. I can't be held to blame for the sizing.'

By the time the girls left the storeroom their arms were full. Like everyone else they had sworn that the slops they'd been issued at Woolwich were falling apart, which was more or less true, so in effect they now had new wardrobes, if not very stylish ones. Outside in the yard Friday dropped her armful of garments on the ground and stood looking down at them.

It was more clothing than some of the women had ever owned, but the quality was poor. To wear on weekdays they'd received one drab serge over-petticoat, one drab serge jacket, one apron of factory-made linen and two calico caps. For Sunday best there were a blue gurrah over-petticoat, an under-petticoat of factory flannel, one white calico apron, two shifts, a long dress with a muslin frill, a red calico jacket, one pair of grey stockings, a pair of shoes, two checked cotton handkerchiefs, a straw bonnet, a white cap, and a bag in which to hold everything.

'A lot of clobber, isn't it?' Friday observed. 'Not exactly the height of fashion, though, eh. Can't see me pulling many cullies in that lot. And how are we supposed to wear all that just on Sundays?'

'I think we're supposed to try to keep the best bits for Sunday and wear the rest during the week,' Harrie suggested. 'And you'll be someone's servant soon. You won't have any customers.'

Sarah rolled her eyes at Harrie's naivety. 'Did you normally wear the latest fashions when you were working?'

'No.' Friday sat on the ground to try on her ugly new shoes. 'These are too small.'

'Then stop complaining.'

'They might fit Janie, though,' Friday said. 'The soles are out of hers.'

They did, which was fortunate, as only the first three dozen women received new shoes before the store ran out of footwear.

There was no sign of Mrs Gordon now; Mrs Dick gave the order for the first group of women to go down to the baths. There was some initial grumbling and reluctance but they stripped and, carrying their slops, descended the steps, the late afternoon breeze raising goose bumps on pale skin scarred from prison sores and other mishaps, and here and there birthmarks and tattoos. Before the head of the last woman had disappeared below ground the monitresses — who behaved exactly like the turnkeys at Newgate — began to go quickly and efficiently through the women's possessions and discarded clothing, raising shouts of protest from those still waiting. It soon became clear that money was the prize, as any discovered was swiftly deposited in a large leather pouch.

Harrie, looking on anxiously, whispered, 'Friday, where's our money?'

'It's safe, don't you worry. Oi!' Friday shouted to one of the turnkeys. 'What do you think you're doing?'

'Mind your own business,' came the reply.

'Like hell I will. I'll wager that ends up in the matron's pockets,' Friday said loud enough for Mrs Dick to hear.

The turnkey shook her head but didn't look up from her task. 'Benevolent Society, to help the destitute.'

Friday let out a yelp of laughter. 'We *are* the bloody destitute!'

The corners of the girl's mouth twitched, but she refused to be distracted.

Friday glanced at Bella Jackson, standing still as stone watching the proceedings, her two trunks nearby, new prison clothes piled on top. She wondered how much chink Bella had stashed away but suspected it must be a lot, and felt a surge of satisfaction at the thought of what she would lose if she hadn't been smart enough to take precautions regarding the inevitable search. Though no doubt she had; she was mean but she was far from stupid. As she watched, Bella retrieved a tiny pot of rouge from a pocket, dabbed a little on her lips, then walked across the hard-packed dirt of the yard in her smart boots towards Mrs Dick. A short conversation ensued and Bella's trunks were searched immediately, revealing to a fascinated audience her finery and other luxury items such as lengths of gorgeous dress fabric no one had seen before, and several beautifully beaded reticules and shawls. No money was found, either in her luggage or on her person, after which Bella sat down on a trunk and opened her parasol.

Friday's mouth fell open. Was Bella not going to be made to bathe? She must have bribed the assistant matron, which no doubt was the reason for opening her trunks. The cow must have stuffed her dosh up her fanny, too, though Friday didn't know how anyone could fit in much more than she'd done, which she was finding most uncomfortable.

The turnkeys went back to going through the sad little piles of possessions, and the first group of women emerged from the baths dressed in their new slops, the fabric clinging to them damply. The next lot stripped and went down, Friday, Harrie, Sarah and Rachel among them.

The baths, filled with cold silted water from the river, were in a dank, gloomy subterranean room lit by smoking oil lamps. Rachel, groggy from the laudanum, squeaked as she stepped in, but when Harrie began to splash water over her she revived rather quickly. The girls used the lumps of cracked, hard soap lying about to wash themselves and their hair; it didn't lather well but it was certainly more satisfactory than washing in salt water. Even so the experience of bathing underground in the half-dark was thoroughly unpleasant and they got out quickly, dressed and hurried back up the steps, vowing not to go down there again. There was a trough in the yard — surely that would do for washing in future.

They emerged into the sunlight to see Harrie's basket being rifled, and two of the half-dozen bottles of laudanum intended for Rachel being passed to Mrs Dick.

'*Stop!*' Sarah shouted. 'That's medicine. You can't take that.'

'Medicine for whom?' Mrs Dick said, her eyes narrowing suspiciously. 'Whose basket is this?'

'It's my basket and that's mine too so give it back,' Harrie said, snatching a bottle out of Mrs Dick's hand.

'How dare you?' Mrs Dick said and slapped Harrie's face.

The bottle slipped from Harrie's hand and smashed on the ground.

Rachel fell on her knees next to the puddle rapidly soaking into the dirt. 'It's *my* medicine!' she wailed. 'For my headaches and I *have* to have it and you've just wasted a whole bottle, you fucking old *cow*!'

Looming over Rachel, Mrs Dick raised her hand again but Friday grabbed her wrist and said in her ear, 'Touch her and I'll beat you black and blue. And I swear, nothing you can do to me will be worse than what I'll do to you.'

Fear flickering across her face, Mrs Dick slowly lowered her hand. Stepping away from Rachel she wrenched the cork from the bottle she still held and sniffed. 'Opium. We don't tolerate drug or alcohol intemperance here.'

'No,' Harrie protested, 'it was prescribed for her by the ship's surgeon. She has to have it.'

Mrs Dick clicked her fingers at the turnkeys. 'Confiscate it.'

They did.

Rachel burst into tears.

When everyone had bathed, changed into their new prison clothes and been relieved of any money or contraband, they were herded back into the foyer of the three-storey building. On either side of the foyer, which had two stairwells, were ground-floor dining rooms, above which the dormitories occupied the first and second floors. From the foyer they ascended the stairs on the left side to the west wing, their feet clattering on the wooden risers until they reached the first floor. The first half of the group, including Harrie, Rachel, Friday and Sarah, were directed through a doorway into a long room while the rest — including Bella Jackson, thank God — continued up to the floor above.

The first dormitory was already occupied by approximately forty women, who stared with expressions ranging from apathy to belligerence, and perhaps a dozen small children. Some of the women were sewing, others were dozing; all were wearing various incarnations of the Factory uniform, though many were barefoot. They all sat or lay on the bare wooden floor. Piled against the only windowless wall were rows of thin mattresses, rolled up with a folded blanket on top of each. Many of the windows in the other three walls were missing their glazing, and there were no drapes or shutters.

Friday turned to a turnkey. 'It's full. It's already crowded.'

'So it is,' the woman replied.

'Well, what about upstairs?'

'That's full, too. You're to get a mattress from Mr Gordon at the store in the front yard, if there are any, and bed down here.'

Friday dumped her stuff on the floor and walked across to a window. It faced north-west and from it she could see the yard they'd just come from with its enclosing perimeter of workshops, empty of inmates now, and to the right of that another large yard where laundry hung to dry together with rows of something fluttering from frames that might be raw wool. In the 'L' formed by the two yards lay a high-walled compound she assumed was the penitentiary, containing a compact two-storey building and various outhouses. If she hung out of the window as far she could and craned her neck to the left she could see yet another yard, this one dotted with small, stand-alone buildings, and knew instinctively that these were isolation cells. Behind that, but still within the prison walls, was an area strewn with rocks and rubble. Hard labour.

Beyond was the river itself and on its far banks a grand house with neat, manicured gardens leading down to the waterway. What a lovely view for the occupants, she thought. She crossed the room and looked down onto the yard they had first entered and at the big gates that had banged shut behind them with such finality.

She sighed heavily. Parramatta Female Factory was smaller than Newgate, and didn't smell as rank, and instead of a great bustling city beyond its walls there were trees and farmland, but it was, as had already been remarked, without doubt a prison.

That evening, after supper, Sarah appeared with a young woman in tow and sat her down on one of the two narrow and miserably lumpy mattresses shared by Harrie, Rachel, Friday and herself — all Mr Gordon, the storekeeper, said could be spared because of the current overcrowding.

'This is Nancy Crouch,' Sarah said. 'She'll tell us what's what in here, the dodges and what have you.' She looked at Friday. 'For a shilling. I've already paid it.'

Friday nodded; it was a worthwhile investment.

'Did yous come with a crew?' Nancy Crouch asked. She was quite an attractive girl with wavy black hair pushed behind her ears, brown eyes, all her teeth and quite a good complexion. The skin on her neck below her left ear was marred by the tail of a thick, purple scar, which she hadn't bothered to conceal with a scarf, though other women were wearing them despite the rules about the uniform.

'No, just the four of us,' Sarah said.

'Small crew.' Nancy nearly but not quite sneered.

'It's *not* a crew. And it works fine for us,' Friday said defensively.

'What about the abbess upstairs?'

'Who?'

'The mot who come in with all the flash clobber?'

'Bella Jackson?' Friday shook her head. 'Nothing to do with us. How did you know she's a madam?'

''Cos she's recruitin' already.'

'Really?' Harrie was shocked. 'But she'll be sent on assignment like the rest of us. Won't she?'

Nancy Crouch snorted and laughed at the same time, blowing out a ribbon of snot that landed on Harrie and Rachel's blanket. She rubbed it in with the heel of her hand. 'Got a lot to learn, haven't yous?'

Friday said sharply, 'Yes, that's why we just paid you a shilling. So, when you're ready.'

'Well, what do yous want to know?'

'Everything.'

Nancy puffed out her cheeks. 'Well, rations are doled out daily and the cooks are lags like us but they're paid a bob a day. It's a privilege to have a job as a cook, or a midwife or a turnkey or a washerwoman or the like, but you have to get in Matron's good books for that.'

'How do you do that?' Sarah asked.

'Behave and keep your gob shut, for a start. Or you buy your way in.'

'Garnish?'

'That'll work with the turnkeys all right. They say higher up bribery'll get you a long way. Haven't tried it meself.'

'Already seen it,' Friday remarked.

Nancy pointed towards the ceiling, eyebrows raised.

Friday nodded.

'Thought so,' Nancy said. 'She looks like she could afford it.'

'Is the food nice?' Rachel asked.

Nancy stared at her. 'Is the *food* nice? You're a gawney one, aren't you?'

Irritation flashed across Rachel's face. 'I'm not gawney. Don't call me that.'

Harrie silently cheered, buoyed to see a return of the old Rachel spirit, but Nancy only laughed, and not very pleasantly. 'Well, what a stupid question.'

But no one laughed with her and, though the expressions on the faces looking back at her barely altered, she sensed a sudden element of frostiness radiating from the newcomers and shuffled back slightly off the mattress and onto the bare wooden floor.

'It's all right, when there's enough,' she said, her voice brazen to disguise her uneasiness. 'Breakfast is wheaten bread, and tea with sugar and a drop of milk. Dinner is soup made with meat, greens and potatoes, and bread. And supper is more bread and tea.'

No one said anything — they'd all existed on more meagre rations in Newgate, and at home if it came to that, except perhaps for Rachel.

Sarah asked, 'And this "industrious employment" the matron was talking about? What's that?'

'We all have to work here, except for the properly sick ones. First class spin the flax and wool and make slops for the Factory and for the lads at Hyde Park —'

'That's where the male convicts go, isn't it, Hyde Park Barracks?' Harrie interrupted, changing position on the mean mattress; her bum was going numb.

"Tis, some of them. Second and third class do the weaving. Parramatta cloth it's called, 'cos it's made here. We sell some, too.

Second and third class pick oakum as well. We don't do that. It's a rotten bloody job. We get paid if we make more than our daily quota, but you don't get it all 'til you leave.'

'I heard third class has to break rocks,' Friday said, giving Nancy a sceptical look.

'Depends what you're in for, what *crime* yous have done. In second class you get paid for going over quota as well, but third gets nothing. In summer we start work at six and go for ten hours with two breaks, and in winter we start at eight and go for eight hours with one break, 'cos it gets dark earlier. In our "leisure hours" there's a school for reading what's run by the Ladies' Committee, and straw-plaitin' lessons.'

Friday and Sarah looked at each other and sniggered.

Nancy shrugged. 'Not my idea. What else? Mornin' and evenin' prayers in the dining rooms every day, Papists on one side and Proddies on the other, Sunday services, weekly bath, mornin' inspections for nits and the like.'

Sarah scratched her head reflexively. 'And the flash mob? Who's the boss woman?'

Raising her eyebrows slyly, Nancy said, 'Yous are in luck at the moment. There isn't one.'

'Really?' Friday wasn't sure whether to believe this. 'Why not?'

'It were a terrible thing,' Nancy replied without a shred of regret. 'Edie Dansey, her name were. God, she were a hard woman. Take the pennies off a dead man's eyes. Been in second class forever. Had a shockin' accident in the baths and drowned. Only a few weeks ago, it were.'

Friday looked thoughtful. 'And there's no one taken her place?'

'There's a few of her crew staking a claim, but they're not up to it. Don't have the balls. So no, no one's taken her place. At least not until you lot arrived. Her upstairs, I mean.'

Friday glared at Nancy.

Nancy stared back. 'Or you. It's between her and you, isn't it?'

'Maybe.'

'Well, if you want Edie's crew you'd better get in quick or her upstairs'll grab them.'

Friday said nothing; she had no intention of poaching dead Edie Dansey's girls, but she certainly wasn't discussing anything of that nature with someone like Nancy Crouch.

'Doesn't matter anyway,' Nancy said. 'You don't need a crew, this whole place runs on a series of rackets. You'll find out.' She scratched her armpit vigorously, then her groin. 'Any more questions?'

Thinking of Rachel, Harrie asked, 'What's the hospital like?'

'Crowded, not enough beds, but the doctor comes every day. Useless bugger. And I hope none of yous is knapped, 'cos the midwife isn't a proper paid one.'

Nancy caught the quick, shared glance among the four girls and pounced. 'Which one of yous is it? On the ship, eh? Well, at least someone made a bit of pocket money.'

Very frostily, Harrie asked, 'The babies, the ones that come from England and those born here, they stay in the Factory with their mothers?'

''Til they turn four, then they're sent to the orphan school.'

Harrie immediately thought of Evie Challis's daughter, already five, and her heart sank. And all the other children over the age of three who had travelled on the *Isla* with their mothers. What had been the point?

'Where is it? The orphan school?' Rachel asked, her voice uneasy.

'Down river. Not far.'

'But who the hell stays here for four years?' Friday said.

'Mothers with kids under four do. But if they really want to get out, their kid might die.' Nancy winced slightly. 'There's a lot of that.'

Horrified, Harrie gaped at her. She swallowed. 'But the children who do go to the orphan school, the mother gets them back?'

'Usually not 'til she gets her ticket of leave. Most employers won't have a servant with kids hanging off her apron strings.'

'So what happens to them?' Rachel asked. 'The little children?'

'They stay in the orphan school,' Nancy replied.

Sarah demanded, 'Do they ever see their mothers?'

'Sometimes. I suppose so. I dunno. I haven't got any kids, have I? Yous'll have to ask someone who has. Look, I got to be somewhere else now.'

'Just a minute, please,' Harrie said. 'Can we send letters out?'

Nancy nodded.

'Visitors?'

'On Sundays, approved by Mrs G.'

Friday's final question was predictable. 'Drink and tobacco?'

'If yous can pay, there's ways.' Nancy couldn't resist a question of her own. 'So come on, tell me, which one of yous is expectin'?'

The response was a stony silence.

Rachel, wide awake now that it was night and she should be asleep, got up from the mattress and crossed the floor to stand by a window. The September night was cool, but not cold. The air was different here, much clearer than it had been in London, and the stars were so very beautiful, the sort of thing a princess who lived in the sky might wear in her crown.

She had glimpsed something earlier in the evening, just after dusk, something even more beautiful than the stars, a dark shape that had glided on the silky air only a few feet from the window. She had run to see and minutes later more and more had sailed past, just a few at first then dozens and dozens, coming from the direction of the river, silent and graceful, the sharp black curves of their arms silhouetted against the bruised sky, their little sweet faces lifted to the rising moon.

She'd come back to the window often just in case there were more, even though Sarah said they were probably the same as in

England and only came out at dusk. But Rachel wasn't convinced she was right. And she couldn't sleep anyway.

She heard a noise behind her, and knew it was Harrie.

'I can hear them, Harrie,' she whispered. 'I can hear them crying.'

Harrie rubbed her eyes. 'Who, sweetie?'

It was her turn this time — Friday had got up an hour ago. They were terrified Rachel would have one of her fits; without any laudanum, there would be nothing to stop it escalating into a full-blown episode that would see her in the hospital, if not the penitentiary.

'The girls.'

'What girls?'

'The girls who've died here.'

Fifteen

James Downey sat in the dining room of the King Hotel and sniffed the milk that had arrived in a small jug with his pot of tea; it smelt off so he pushed it aside. He preferred milk in his tea but was so accustomed at sea to going without that drinking it black was no hardship. He poured himself a cup, added sugar and stirred while contemplating the correspondence lying beside the remains of his breakfast. One letter he knew was from his wife Emily, but the handwriting on the second he didn't recognise at all. And what an odd letter it was: instead of the usual pages folded and sealed with wax, this was a packet fashioned from what appeared to be a checked cotton handkerchief. On one side was attached, presumably sewn but with stitches so tiny he couldn't detect them, a square of white fabric, and it was on this that his address had been written in ink, in a very tidy hand.

He put it aside and opened the letter from Emily, the third he'd received from her since he'd departed England. The first two had been carried on a clipper whose voyage to Sydney had evidently been faster than the *Isla*'s, and had, to his delight, been waiting for him when he'd arrived. This letter, dated the 29th of May, had arrived on another yesterday evening. Knowing Emily, he would receive many more before he set sail for home in a month or so.

He sipped as he read, turning the pages sideways to follow her handwriting where she had written down the paper as well as across. She thought she was saving money by doing this, but really all she was doing was hastening the arrival of the day when he would be forced to wear spectacles.

She was keeping busy, she said, preparing the garden for summer and helping her sister Beatrice with her four children. Beatrice's children, all under the age of six, were quite a little troupe of tearaways, James privately thought, but he and Emily hadn't managed to have any of their own yet and Emily absolutely adored children, even Beatrice's, so she might as well get in some practice before theirs came along. He did wish she wouldn't potter about in the garden, though — they had a man who came in to do that. Picking flowers for the parlour and the bedrooms was fine, but Emily insisted on actually digging holes with her trowel and planting things. Her mother was well, the weather was still a little unpredictable but improving, and there was a suspicion that Tara, Emily's foxhound, had gone on one of her illicit evening jaunts and come home 'in a certain condition' again. She loved him and missed him very much. Emily, that was, not Tara.

James sighed and refilled his cup. After Tara's previous litter Emily had cried for a week when he'd given them away. He'd had to. He owned a very nice house on the city side of Kensington, left to him by his mother and father along with a modest inheritance, but it was quite small, too small anyway to accommodate seven scampering puppies skidding on carpets, chewing furniture and piddling everywhere.

He felt a twinge of disappointment and loneliness at the knowledge that Emily wouldn't yet have received any of his letters, as he'd only posted them three days earlier — his first opportunity. Perhaps he should have passed them to one of the *Flying Dutchman*'s doomed phantoms.

Folding Emily's letter, he slipped it into the inside pocket of his coat, picked up the cotton packet and turned it over several times. Obviously, the sender had not wanted anyone else to read the message contained within. He carefully slit one side with his penknife and removed a sheet of paper, looking immediately for the signature. Harriet Clarke. Well.

9th of September, 1829

Dear Mr Downey Sir,

I hope you are finding your accommodations at the King Hotel comfortable. We are managing to settle here at the Parramatta Female Factory, and hoping to be assigned soon.

I also very much hope that you are not offended by me writing to you, but I cannot think of anyone else who might be willing to assist us.

Our possessions were searched on the day we arrived, and the medicines you prescribed for Rachel Winter were taken from her. We are very much afraid that without them she will suffer a fit, the consequences of which will cause her physical harm and result in her being punished and consigned to the Second Class, beyond our reach and our ability to care for her. Please believe that I am not exaggerating this.

You will think I am very rude, for which I apologise sincerely, but we would be very grateful if you could see your way to visiting Rachel at the Factory, if you have the time, and perhaps also speaking to someone in authority here. Visiting days are Sundays. We can pay you for your services. Please do not mention that we have written to you, as there may be repercussions.

Thank you very much in anticipation.

Your humble servant,
Harriet Clarke

Her handwriting was as tidy as she was. James imagined poor Harrie must have died a thousand deaths plucking up the courage to actually write the letter. He was delighted to hear from her, but shocked to learn that legitimate medications had been confiscated from a Female Factory inmate. He wondered who currently held the position of Factory surgeon and fervently hoped it wasn't still the man who had presided in 1826 when a convict by the name of Mary Ann Hamilton had died from starvation. This after being handcuffed and tied to the floor as punishment for mashing and eating the bones in her ration and picking and eating weeds. The surgeon at the time had attended the Factory so infrequently he hadn't even known of the woman's death until the coroner's inquest. But that was prior to Governor Darling instigating his reforms and James had heard that things had improved somewhat since then.

He slid Harrie's letter behind Emily's and sat staring into his empty tea cup, thinking. He was at fault; he should have provided Rachel — or better still, Harrie — a letter explaining that the laudanum was essential to his patient's wellbeing. Ex-patient now, however.

The first-class yard had trapped the noonday heat and the women, in particular the newcomers unaccustomed to the occasional sweltering days that accompanied an Australian spring, were crowded into any sliver of shade they could find.

Harrie and Sarah watched as Friday walked towards them, her wild copper hair ablaze in the sun. Rachel sat with her back pressed against the wall, hands shading her eyes.

Friday sat down. 'I've been in the bog talking to a girl called Katie about this assignment business. She said it's almost all domestic service.'

Fanning her face with the brim of her Factory bonnet, Sarah said, 'Did you ask her how it works?'

'Apparently if someone wants a servant they apply to old Tuckwell. The application gets matched with Gordon's list of eligible inmates — that's us from first class. The employer has to pay a bond, but if he or she doesn't collect us within fourteen days they miss out and we come available again.'

'What happens to the bond?' Harrie asked.

'Dunno. Goes in someone's pocket, I suppose.'

Sarah said, 'And what if you don't like your assignment?'

'Well, this Katie says there's things you can do, but it's more usual the assignees don't like us.'

'Why wouldn't they?' Harrie demanded, offended on principle.

'Oh, because we get drunk, we're shiftless, we're idle, we won't do as we're told, and we're rude and immoral.'

Harrie said, 'Speak for yourself.'

'I'm just saying what she said.'

'So what can you do if you don't like it?' Sarah asked.

'Plenty of things,' Friday replied. 'Be annoying or useless, or misbehave, but without doing anything criminal or you could end up in the penitentiary. Shagging the master is a popular one, apparently.'

Sarah frowned. 'But what's the point?'

'The point is your master or mistress will be so fed up they'll send you back here. And then you can get reassigned somewhere else. Or stay here for years if you play your cards right.'

'Christ,' Sarah said. 'Why would you want to stay here?'

'Because it would be better than wherever you were before.'

They all considered the high stone walls and dirt yards and hollow-eyed, shoeless women for a moment. Better?

'And playing up to get sent back really works?' Sarah swatted at a fly buzzing around her face.

'So Katie says. As long as the authorities don't catch on.'

Harrie looked doubtful. 'Isn't there a punishment for being returned? Girls would be doing it all the time, otherwise.'

Friday frowned. 'I didn't ask about that.'

'Well, next time you're on the throne for hours chatting away,' Sarah suggested sarcastically, 'perhaps you should.'

Rachel burst out, 'I don't want to have to sleep with my master!'

It occurred to Harrie that Rachel might not have realised she possibly wouldn't be assigned at all. She took her hand. 'Sweetie, try not to worry about it, please.'

'I'll kill myself before I do that.'

'You won't have to, love, really, you won't.'

'What's that noise? I don't like it,' Rachel complained. 'It's hurting my head.'

The noise, whatever it was, *was* extremely irritating — a sort of high-pitched trilling.

Sarah said, 'What do we actually get when we're assigned? Did you ask that?'

'Food, board and clothing. Katie's already been assigned once. She's a whore by trade. She's hoping her next assignment will give her a bit of time off at night. She says she's sick of having no money.'

Harrie looked confused, rather than shocked. 'Convict girls can't do that, can they?'

'Well, *I'll* have to,' Friday said bluntly. 'I don't do any other sort of work. I'll run out of dosh if I don't.'

'Is it against the law here?' Sarah asked.

Friday shook her head. 'Only operating a brothel. But Katie says convict girls caught whoring go straight to the penitentiary.'

'Oh, Friday,' Harrie said anxiously.

'Oh, Harrie,' Friday teased. 'Don't fret. I'll be all right. Katie says there's a place in Sydney Town called the Rocks where everyone goes. A bit rough but plenty of business with tars and the like. I'll go there.'

'If you can,' Sarah said. 'From what I'm hearing some girls get hardly any time off at all.'

'Do you know what *I* heard?' Harrie said suddenly. 'I heard that men come here, to the Factory, to choose a wife.'

Friday and Sarah stared at her. Even Rachel stopped rubbing the back of her head and raised her eyes.

'As though they were at Billingsgate or something?' Sarah said, incredulous.

Harrie nodded. 'All the women who want a husband line up and the man drops his handkerchief in front of the one he likes the look of and if she picks it up they get married.'

'Not his trousers?' Friday said, and hooted with laughter.

'No, I think just the hanky.'

Sarah snorted in disgust. 'God, why would you agree to that?'

'Well, I suppose if you got a nice one you'd have more freedom than if you were assigned,' Harrie replied. 'Wouldn't you? And someone to look after you?'

Friday rolled her eyes. 'Don't be daft. More likely some bastard after a free fuck and someone to scrub the shite stains out of his kecks. It's whoring without the bother of having to stand on the street.'

Letting out a moan of distress, Rachel whimpered, 'Harrie, can you make that noise stop? It's *really* hurting.'

Harrie looked around but couldn't see the source. The sound seemed to be coming from everywhere.

Rachel stood up, stumbled forwards a few steps then squatted, jammed her hands over her ears and squealed, 'Make it stop, Harrie, make it *stop*!'

'What the hell is it?' Sarah rose and turned in a full circle, peering all around the yard.

The sound was extremely high-pitched, a sort of feverish rattling and ringing as though an army of miniature blacksmiths was banging away with a thousand tiny hammers. The *Isla* women were all staring about now, too, confused and startled, children grasping at their skirts. Even Bella, standing in the shade of a workshop wall, looked disconcerted.

Friday waved to attract Nancy Crouch's attention. Nancy, sitting on the ground smoking a pipe, returned the wave but didn't get up.

Friday went over. 'What the hell is that bloody noise?'

'Cicada,' Nancy replied. 'A bit early, though. You're in my sun.'

Friday stepped aside. 'A what?'

'A cicada. Like a grasshopper, only bigger.'

'Just *one*? God almighty.' Friday looked up, down and around. 'Where is it? I'm going to kill it.'

'Do your best: the buggers are really hard to spot.'

'Well, it's sending us bloody barmy.'

'Well, yous'd better get used to it, 'cos they do it all summer.' Nancy glanced across at Rachel, crouched on the ground, rocking and moaning. 'And it's not as if *she* wasn't gawney to start with, is it?'

Friday felt a surge of anger, but forced herself to walk away. There was no sense in starting a fight with Nancy Crouch while they might still need her.

'It's an insect,' she said, looking down at Harrie, who'd slipped a comforting arm around Rachel. 'Like a grasshopper.'

'For God's sake,' Sarah said in disgust. This country was revolting. The weather might be warmer but the light was too sharp and the sun fierce and the seasons were completely the wrong way round, the trees were the most miserable specimens she had ever seen, and the wildlife — such as she'd experienced so far — was hideous. Strange birds shrieked and cackled, frogs from the river kept them awake at night with their throbbing, droning racket, there were enough bats overhead of an evening to blot out the moon, and the insects! The night before last, she had unrolled the mattress she and Friday shared, spread the blanket, sat down, and from underneath had skittered the hugest, most loathsome fat grey spider imaginable. She had almost shat herself, and had quite badly twisted her knee scrabbling out of the way. And now this!

'Her headache's getting worse,' Harrie said. Rachel had woken up with it this morning. 'This terrible noise isn't helping.'

'Ah, shite.' Friday swept her hair back off her face. 'What are we going to do?'

'Take her to the hospital,' Sarah suggested. 'The doctor might give her some laudanum.'

Friday frowned. 'Nancy said he was useless.'

'He still might give her some laudanum.' Sarah asked Harrie, 'You've not heard anything from your Mr Downey?'

Harrie shook her head, unable to meet Sarah's eye. Writing to James Downey had been a long shot, she'd known that, but he *had* offered his help, and she really thought he might at least have sent a note back, even if only to say he couldn't come to the Factory himself but suggesting what they might do. But there had been nothing, and her imaginings regarding what he must have thought when he'd read her letter were humiliating. A convict girl sending someone like him a note asking for help — it was outrageous when you thought about it. If only she *had* thought about it — properly — before she'd sent it. She felt horribly embarrassed and, under that, deeply disappointed.

'Typical,' Sarah said.

Rachel let out a howl that sounded uncannily like a dog's. It was eerie and disturbing and everyone turned to stare.

'Right, come on.' Sarah pulled her up off the ground. 'We'll try the hospital.'

But the pain in Rachel's head had grown so monstrous that everything else had burnt away. All she knew now was a primal rage and a desperate need to feel nothing at all. She tried to bite Sarah's hand, but Sarah dodged her and took a firmer grasp on her arm. Harrie gripped her opposite wrist and together they made for the entrance to the dormitory building, on the other side of which lay the hospital. Friday followed, glaring at anyone nosy enough to follow the little procession, which was almost everyone.

Mrs Dick stormed out of the dormitory building to meet them. 'Where do you think you're going?' She whipped a watch out of her pocket and tapped it hard enough to break it. 'Work starts in two minutes.'

'To the hospital. She's sick,' Sarah said, nodding at Rachel slumped between them, panting, her head bowed with pain.

'Can she not speak for herself?'

'No, actually, she can't.' Fear and worry made Harrie bold. 'She has a blinding headache.'

'Well, you haven't, have you? And neither have you, or you,' Mrs Dick added, pointing at Sarah and Friday. 'So get to work. She can make her own way to the hospital. I assume she still has control of her legs?'

Rachel slowly raised her head and said in a querulous voice, 'Mrs Dick?'

'What?' Mrs Dick put her watch away. 'Quickly, I'm busy.'

'Why don't you fuck yourself, you dried-up old minge.'

Mrs Dick gaped at her.

'And I *do* have control of my legs.' Before Harrie or Sarah could stop her, Rachel wriggled out their grasp, stepped forwards and kicked Mrs Dick on the shin as hard as she could.

And then she was off. She shot into the dormitory building and a moment later glass shattered as a teapot crashed against one of the few unbroken windows of the second-class dining room.

A great cheer of approval rose from the women in the yard and Mrs Dick, bent double over her throbbing leg, scrabbled for her whistle and blew on it until her face turned scarlet. But Friday, Sarah and Harrie barely heard as they tore after Rachel.

They clattered into the foyer just in time to see Rachel disappear up the stairs, her skirt hoisted so she could run faster. They thundered up after her into the first-floor second-class dormitory, where she dashed across the floor and came to a halt beside a broken window in the far corner.

'*Stop!*' Sarah bellowed, to Friday and Harrie as much as Rachel. 'She'll do something stupid!'

She did. She raised her right leg, kicked out the wooden mullions in the bottom half of the sash, then leant out so far it seemed certain she would fall, cutting her right arm on the shards of glass that remained in the frame. Friday launched herself across the room and tackled her, knocking her away from the window and onto the floor.

Rachel screamed like an animal, kicking out at Friday, scratching and spitting and swearing and punching, and managed to wrench herself out of her grasp, leaving half of her poorly constructed Factory jacket in Friday's hands.

Sarah threw herself onto Rachel, but Rachel, with extraordinary strength, shoved her off, dashed past Harrie, knocking her over, and raced out of the room, drops of blood spattering the floor behind her. A second later there were raised voices, then echoing shouts, then nothing at all.

Friday, Sarah and Harrie staggered towards the doorway, Friday wiping her bloodied nose on her sleeve.

On the landing outside the dormitory door was more blood, but no sign of Rachel. Terrified of what they might see, they leant over the balustrade.

Below, in the foyer, stood Mrs Dick, Mr Tuckwell, several turnkeys and others in a circle. On the floor, face down, her hair fanned out like a silver nimbus, and so very, very still, lay Rachel.

Being Church of England, Harrie stood on the Protestant side of the first-class dining room for the Sunday service, eyes closed, hands tightly clasped in prayer. Friday was a Catholic though she hadn't been to church since she was seven, but it was a wet day and rain was coming in on the Catholics' side so she'd joined the Proddies. Sarah thought it all a load of rubbish but attendance was compulsory so she loitered near the back, gazing out of the window at the wet yard while the chaplain droned on.

As the women jostled out of the dining room at the end of the service, a turnkey tapped Sarah on the shoulder.

'Are you Harriet Clarke?'

'No. Why?'

'I am,' Harrie said.

The turnkey said, 'You're to go to Matron's office right now.'

Harrie's heart thudded wildly: it would be about yesterday, she was sure. It had been her fault. She should have taken better care of Rachel and she hadn't. Tears welled in her eyes, already sore and puffy from weeping, and she blinked hard. Perhaps it was the constabulary come to arrest her.

She took a deep breath and stepped out into the rain, dodging puddles as she crossed the yard to Matron's office next to her apartments.

She ducked into the porch, knocked on the door and stood waiting nervously next to a sodden cape hanging on a hook. When Mrs Dick opened the office door, Harrie's gaze flicked past her to the other occupants — Mrs Gordon and James Downey.

Her shock at seeing him was followed immediately by a wave of relief that left her feeling quite light-headed, coupled with a disturbing lurch of her heart. Seeing his honest, open face again felt a little bit like coming home, and the feeling gave her a jolt of alarm. He was soaking wet from the waist down, the fabric of his trousers clinging disconcertingly to his muscled thighs, and his hat and gloves, resting on a side table, were dripping onto the floor. The golden hairs on the backs of his hands were standing up in the room's chill air, and there was a small leaf or something stuck to the side of his face. She wanted to wipe it away for him. How inappropriate of her. The thought made her blush.

'Come in, Harriet,' Mrs Gordon said.

Mr Downey stood. 'Good morning, Harrie. I'm very sorry to hear about Rachel.'

Harrie stepped inside and, finding no vacant chairs, stood near the door.

'Have my seat, though it's probably wet,' Mr Downey offered.

Mrs Gordon frowned, Harrie noted. The expression on Mrs Dick's face was a busy combination of disbelief, annoyance and deep disapproval.

'Thank you.' Harrie sat. The chair *was* wet and she felt her bum growing damp through her skirt immediately.

'I dropped by on the off-chance that I might observe Rachel's progress,' Mr Downey said to Harrie.

She breathed an invisible sigh of relief, grateful he wasn't going to let on she had written to him.

'As my hospital assistant aboard the *Isla*, you will recall I was experimenting with a new therapy regarding management of her brain injury. Mrs Gordon is of course aware of her fall on the voyage out, which is recorded in the ship's muster.'

Harrie nodded like the village idiot. She was aware that the only thing entered onto the ship's muster, or manifest, was that Rachel had had a bad fall — nothing about the rape or Keegan pushing her off the foredeck. All of *that* Mr Downey had decided to include only in his report to Governor Darling, for fear of tainting not just Rachel's chances of finding a satisfactory assignment, if in fact she was fit enough, but those of all the convict women transported on the *Isla*.

'So I am extremely sorry to hear of yesterday's tragic incident,' Mr Downey went on, his face grim. 'Mrs Gordon has informed me of the Factory policy regarding contraband and Mrs Dick has recounted her version of the laudanum being confiscated, and what occurred yesterday. But I'd like to hear your version of events, Harrie.'

'Version?' Mrs Dick snapped. 'There are no *versions*. There is only the truth and I have already told you that.'

'I accept that, Mrs Dick,' Mr Downey said. 'But I understand that Harrie and her friends were in the dormitory with Rachel before the accident?'

Mrs Dick nodded reluctantly.

'Then I would like to hear what happened there. And also how Harrie perceived the confiscation of the medicines.'

So Harrie told him, resisting the urge to embroider her account of Mrs Dick meanly taking Rachel's laudanum without a thought regarding the outcome. And she didn't need to embellish what had happened yesterday; it had been horrific and the image was seared into her memory forever.

Mr Downey listened with his hands behind his back. The leaf on his cheek finally fell off.

'So despite the fact that you were told that Rachel Winter had been prescribed the laudanum by me and that it was essential to her welfare, you confiscated it anyway?' he said to Mrs Dick in a deceptively conversational tone.

'Yes. I did.'

'May I ask why?'

'I thought she was lying. I thought they all were. I suspected they'd stolen it. If you care to recall, sir, most of these women are inmates of the Factory for lying in some form or another. And if they weren't lying, I thought they would trade or sell it. Neither practice is permitted at this institution.'

Harrie kept her eyes on the floor; trading, selling and smuggling of contraband went on every day, and not just among inmates. Mrs Dick should know, having apparently feathered her own nest considerably.

Mr Downey said, 'You were wrong, Mrs Dick, and your mistake resulted in yesterday's tragedy. I believe you did Rachel Winter a grave injustice by depriving her of her medicines and, as surgeon superintendent of this shipment of convict women, I will be including my comments on this affair in my report to Governor Darling.'

Mrs Dick opened her mouth, then shut it again. Harrie felt deeply gratified at the expression of guilty trepidation that settled across her pinched features.

* * *

Mr Downey introduced himself; Sidney Sharpe, the Factory surgeon, shook his hand. He was older than Mr Downey, and shorter and fatter, and Harrie hoped he was equally proficient as a doctor.

'What is your interest in this patient?' Mr Sharpe asked, his tone clearly indicating that the real question was, *What are you doing in my hospital?*

'I prescribed her the laudanum after her initial injury.'

'Ah. Yes.' Mr Sharpe inclined his head towards Harrie. 'I've been informed of the history.'

'If she'd been allowed to keep it,' Mr Downey said tersely, 'this might never have occurred. I happened to drop by this morning to enquire regarding her progress.' He frowned slightly. 'Pardon me for asking, but how long have you been surgeon to the Factory?'

'Just over twelve months.' Mr Sharpe looked at Mr Downey shrewdly. 'So no, I *wasn't* in attendance during that business with Mary Ann Hamilton.'

Harrie noted that Mr Downey had gone pink and wondered why.

Mr Sharpe started walking. 'I wasn't here when she was brought in. Your ex-patient, I mean. I don't live on the premises. I attend from one to three every afternoon, unless there is some sort of emergency. I was summoned yesterday morning just after nine o'clock. The patient has a gash to the ventral aspect of the right forearm, not too serious but requiring sutures, and a closed fracture of the right radius and ulna near the wrist. I'm astounded there are no other injuries, given the distance she fell. It is her mental state that concerns me, however. She is obviously deeply disturbed.'

He also explained that Rachel had been given a bed to herself, not because the hospital wasn't crowded but because he had thought it very unwise to put another patient in with her. When brought in she had been foul-mouthed, noisy and, despite her injuries, violent.

He stopped at a metal bedstead topped with a thin mattress. On it lay Rachel, apparently asleep. Her right arm was splinted and bandaged from above the elbow to the tips of her fingers. Blood had leaked through the bandage onto the mattress. Her left arm and ankles were manacled to the bed, and a rope had been passed around her chest and beneath the bed frame so she couldn't sit up. A strong smell of urine suggested she had peed where she lay.

Mr Sharpe said, 'We considered a straightjacket but decided against it because of her arm.'

At the word 'straightjacket' Harrie bit her lip. She reached over the bed-end and gently stroked Rachel's bare white foot.

'She was manic when she came in. She had to be sedated and I have recommended she be kept in that state for the time being. There will also be some pain in the wrist, of course,' Mr Sharpe added.

Harrie had not been allowed to stay with Rachel after she had been brought to the hospital so there was a question she *had* to ask.

'Sir, has there been, has anything else happened with ... with her body?'

Mr Sharpe looked at her sternly from beneath bushy brows. 'What do you mean, with her body?'

Harrie sent an agonised glance towards Mr Downey.

'Perhaps the question Harrie is attempting to ask is has the patient showed signs of suffering a miscarriage? I believe she may have been with child?' He raised his eyebrows at Harrie for confirmation.

Harrie nodded miserably.

'Not to my knowledge, she hasn't,' Mr Sharpe said. 'I'll check with the nurse. If she is expecting I'd be damned surprised if a fall like that doesn't dislodge the foetus.' He stood for several seconds, deep in thought. 'However, if she remains pregnant, it presents the Board of Management with a quandary.'

Mr Downey said, 'In what way, Mr Sharpe?'

'Well, I was going to recommend transferring her to Liverpool Asylum.'

'*No!*' It was out of Harrie's mouth before she could stop herself. She didn't know what or where Liverpool Asylum was, but something about the way Mr Sharpe had phrased the words sounded horribly ominous.

'I *beg* your pardon!' Mr Sharpe was quick to reprimand her lapse.

Mr Downey said, 'Liverpool is nowhere as grim as Bethlem, Harrie.'

'But it *is* a mad house?'

'It's an *asylum*,' Mr Sharpe said, 'and, given the patient's erratic and violent behaviour, she should be transferred there.' He sighed, but not as though he were angry, Harrie thought, more as though he considered Rachel's awful confluence of physical and mental conditions to be just another sad fact of life. 'But she won't be now, not while she requires medical care and not if she's pregnant. They don't have the facilities for lying-in. And if she stays here she won't be eligible for assignment, which will be reflected in the Board's financial returns to the colonial government.' He shrugged. 'Perhaps when her arm mends she can make straw bonnets.'

Harrie felt her hopes soar. 'So she'll have to stay at the Factory?' Along with all the other women who seemed to have managed to make a home there. She wondered how *that* was reflected in the Board's financial returns.

'Only if she remains pregnant. Providing she *is*,' Mr Sharpe said somewhat suspiciously. 'I see no evidence of that. How far along is she, did you say?'

'Thirteen weeks. Fourteen, perhaps.'

'How can you be so sure?'

'I looked after her when she had her … courses …'

Mr Sharpe moved around to the side of the bed, pushed up the sleeves of his coat, bent and palpated Rachel's abdomen with extended fingers. She didn't stir at all.

'Yes, definitely expecting,' he confirmed less than a minute later. 'I would say approximately three months, perhaps a little more. I'll have the nurse watch for spontaneous abortion.'

'In the meantime, the laudanum?' Mr Downey prompted.

'For the head injury? Yes, I suppose we should reinstate it. What dose were you prescribing, Mr Downey?'

'Six drachms in the first instance when her cephalalgia begins, and another four to six should the first dose not be effective and an episode seems imminent.'

'An episode being one of these fits, as demonstrated yesterday?'

Mr Downey nodded.

'And who administers the doses?'

'Harrie does.'

'Are you her guardian? A family member?' Mr Sharpe asked Harrie.

'I'm her sister,' Harrie replied immediately.

Because she was. Her, Sarah and Friday. They all were.

Rachel was asleep, but she wasn't. She was full of medicine again, and that was nice, but her mind was far away. She thought there might be people somewhere nearby, but she didn't know who, and it didn't matter.

Her arm hurt, but the pain felt a long way away, too.

She remembered flying, as clearly as though it had happened only a moment ago. Perhaps it had.

It had been wonderful. Her arms had lifted up from her sides and her feet had left the ground and over the balustrade she had gone, soaring and swooping and diving. And then it had ended, just like that, in blackness.

And no matter how hard she tried, she hadn't been able to make it happen again.

But, oh, she wanted to.

* * *

Harrie, Friday and Sarah sat on the ground in the middle of the first-class yard the following afternoon after the midday meal, far enough away from everyone else to not be overheard. Still, they lowered their voices whenever others passed too closely — and quite a few did, curious to know what the friends of 'the gawney girl' were talking about.

Harrie was still very upset, unable to get the image of Rachel bound into a straightjacket out of her mind.

'But she wasn't, though, love, was she?' Friday said. 'So don't keep on about it. You're only torturing yourself.'

'I know, but Mr Sharpe thought she was disturbed enough to need one,' Harrie insisted.

Sarah, ever pragmatic, said, 'Well, she is.'

'And Mr Downey said whatever's wrong with her head will probably only get worse, remember? And it *has*.' Harrie was almost in tears again.

'No,' Sarah said firmly, aware that Harrie was winding herself into a tizzy, 'he said we'll have to wait and see.'

'Who will look after her when we've gone?' Harrie went on. 'She'll be all alone and frightened. And what about when she gets bigger? She could … she could kill herself *and* the baby.'

Friday tamped tobacco into her pipe, to hell with the Factory rules. 'What about Janie?'

'Janie *can't*.' Harrie was losing her temper now. 'She's got two babies of her own. She can't go running around after Rachel all the time. And it wouldn't be fair to ask it of her.'

'Won't they keep her in the hospital?' Sarah asked.

Harrie shook her head. 'They've two to a bed and mattresses on the floor as it is. As soon as she's settled down she'll be back here with us. It's a horrible place anyway.'

'What did you tell her family?'

'Just that she can't write herself because she's broken her arm and that apart from that she's doing well. But surely they'll be wondering why they've *never* had a letter in her own hand? I certainly can't tell them what's really happened, can I?'

Friday breathed jets of smoke out though her nostrils like a small, fiery-haired dragon. 'I've been thinking. One of us will have to come back. Or not go out on assignment at all.'

Sarah looked at her. 'Get a job here, you mean?'

'Yes!' Harrie almost leapt to her feet in excitement. 'Me! I could work in the hospital! I've got a recommendation from Mr Downey to say I'm good at it. He gave it to me on the ship.'

'Did he?' Sarah said. 'You didn't tell us that.'

Friday looked thoughtful. 'We'd need money to grease a few palms, but we've got enough.'

'We have now,' Sarah said, 'but from what I hear we'd have to keep on greasing. One bung isn't going to be enough. And what about when the baby comes? Rachel will need decent food for her milk and what have you. You've seen how hard it is in here for mothers and babies. We'll need good money coming in to afford that.'

'So? We'll just have to go out and make some,' Friday declared.

Sarah looked at her. 'Well, at the moment, you're sitting on the fastest way to do that.'

Friday shrugged. 'Fine with me.'

'Good. Then this is what we'll do. You'll stay here, Harrie, and look after her. Friday, you and I will make as much money as we can get our hands on. I'll do what I can but it might take me a while to get up to speed.'

'What do you mean?' Harrie asked suspiciously. 'How are you going to make money?'

Sarah winked and tapped the side of her nose.

'Oh, *Sarah*! In fact, *both* of you!' Harrie shook her head in complete frustration, her excitement at staying behind to look after Rachel ebbing at the thought of the trouble they could get themselves into. 'You're both ... *really* bloody well irresponsible, do you know that? You'll get caught and end up in the penitentiary, and how will that help Rachel? You might even be sent to Norfolk Island or ... or *hanged*!'

'Well, have you got a better idea?' Sarah said.

'No.'

'Because we'll never save enough money while we're on assignment.'

'I know that!'

'So can I finish what I was saying, then? We use the money to care for Rachel and the baby when it comes, for as long as we need to. And as soon as we can get them out of here, we will. We can apply to be their legal guardians or something.'

'We won't be allowed,' Harrie said. 'Not convicts.'

'I don't know. I haven't looked into it. Let me finish. When you become a sought-after dressmaker, Harrie, you can help with the money then. For now, we'll just have to find it the best way we know how. Any way, because we need it. Are we agreed on that? All of it? Is it a pact?'

Friday said yes immediately and, a moment later, so did Harrie.

Harrie stood nervously before Mrs Gordon's desk, waiting for her to finish writing. Finally she did, slotting her pen into its holder and rolling a blotter over the page.

She looked up. 'Yes?'

Harrie's mouth suddenly felt completely bereft of spit. She cleared her throat, making a noise like one of the raucous birds that woke everyone at the crack of dawn. She'd had to wait three days for this appointment and now she was here she was terrified.

'Thank you for seeing me, Mrs Gordon,' she began croakily. 'It's about my friend Rachel Winter. She's very poorly.'

'I am aware of that.'

'You might recall that on the ship out I was assistant to the surgeon superintendent, Mr Downey. He gave me a letter of recommendation because I was so good at it.' Harrie spoke as quickly as her dry mouth would allow in case Mrs Gordon cut her off. She reached inside her jacket for the letter. 'I was hoping that I could stay here and care for Rachel. I can also —'

But Mrs Gordon did cut her off. 'I'm sorry, Harriet. I do understand your concerns for your friend, but you've just been assigned. To …' she consulted a ledger on her desk '… a Mr and Mrs Overton in Sydney Town. You'll be leaving in approximately a week's time. There has also been interest expressed in your associate Sarah Morgan.'

The disappointment was so crushing Harrie felt as though a barrow of bricks had been dumped on her chest. She could barely breathe and her eyes welled with hot tears. 'And Friday?'

'Friday Woolfe has not yet been assigned.'

Hope flared in Harrie's heart. 'Could Friday stay?'

Mrs Gordon frowned. 'Certainly not. That girl is a troublemaker and we have enough trouble here as it is.'

Sixteen

Sarah sat in the first-class dining room, tight-lipped, legs crossed, one foot swinging agitatedly. There were bars on the ground-floor windows of the dormitory building and it felt like being in Newgate again, but at least the sky and the late afternoon sun were visible through these ones.

She and the three women waiting with her had been put forward by Mrs Gordon for a specific assigned position, but apparently the employer wanted to interview them before he made his decision. There was a bet on in the dormitory that he was looking for a wife, and if he was, he could stick it up his arse as far as Sarah was concerned. She'd rather break rocks in third class for a year.

Mrs Gordon strode in, the nails in the heels of her shoes ringing on the paved floor. She was accompanied by a man dressed head to toe in black except for a white shirt with an unfashionably short collar, whose tread in his polished black boots was silent. Sarah and the other women stood, as they had been told to do.

'This is Mr Green,' Mrs Gordon said. 'Line up, please.'

Sarah shuffled into the short line, gaze directed at the floor, aware her face was as sour as a lemon and not caring.

Mr Green spoke. 'Good afternoon. I have requested an interview as I am looking for a specific set of capabilities.'

His voice wasn't deep and it wasn't high. It was just a voice, an

English one with a hint of an accent Sarah recognised. She thought he might be somewhere in his late twenties — certainly older than her anyway. He was perhaps five feet six inches tall, slender, wore his tar-black hair long and tied back, which was a bit old-fashioned of him, and had dark, contemplative eyes and pale skin, as though he spent too much time indoors. He was quite attractive really, but she still wasn't marrying him. For the first time in ages, though, she felt conscious of the scar on her face, which annoyed her. This wouldn't do.

He extended his arms like some sort of illusionist. 'What are these on my hands?'

Fingers, Sarah thought.

Two of the girls said 'rings', and the third answered, 'A sapphire and pearl ring, one with a red stone, and a monkey ring set with a diamond?'

It suddenly occurred to Sarah that he was quite possibly a jeweller and she was instantly plunged into the most appalling emotional turmoil. It had never even entered her mind that while serving her sentence in New South Wales she might return to the craft she loved. But what about Rachel? She couldn't abandon her just because some cove had waved a couple of rings in her face. But if he chose her and she refused to go with him, she would be relegated to second class. It could be months before she was eligible for assignment again, time she could have used outside the Factory walls making money.

Of course, she wasn't *just* a jeweller, she was a thief, too. A very good one.

She asked, 'May I have a closer look, sir?'

Mr Green slid off all three rings and passed them to her. Mrs Gordon made a move as though to prevent such a foolhardy action, as if she thought Sarah would somehow make the rings disappear — swallow them, perhaps? — but he raised his hand in a blocking motion.

Sarah turned the rings over and inspected them closely. 'These two are eighteen-carat gold, though this one I think is twenty-two. The one with the engraving on the shank is a cabochon garnet, foiled with a closed back, and it looks like quite an old mount. Thirty or forty years, perhaps? *This* one is a rose-cut sapphire surrounded by seed pearls and it's raised on prongs so it's a recent piece.' She glanced up at Mr Green; smiling slightly, he appeared to be enjoying himself.

One of the girls swore disappointedly under her breath.

'And the monkey ring?' Mr Green asked.

'A genuine diamond, but the ring's ugly.'

'You don't think it's just good paste?'

Sarah squinted. 'Good paste wouldn't have a slight flaw in it, see here, down near the culet? You must have skinny fingers: these are ladies' rings. Except for the monkey ring, that would be for a man's little finger. No self-respecting lady would wear that.'

Mr Green burrowed in his jacket pocket. 'What do make of this, then?'

On his palm sat a bracelet of black-lacquered metal, its links of flowers and leaves as intricate as any fine lacework, and just as ethereal.

'Berlin iron,' Sarah said immediately. She'd seen lots of it in London. It was very popular as mourning jewellery. 'Quite possibly Horovice.'

'Manufactured in …?'

'Bohemia.'

Mr Green's smile widened and he turned to the matron. 'This one will do very well, thank you, Mrs Gordon.'

'Just a minute,' Sarah said, handing back the rings. 'Tell me what the job is first.'

'Sarah Morgan!' Mrs Gordon exclaimed. 'You will accept this assignment regardless of what your duties might be!'

'I require someone to assist me with my jewellery business and, it seems, by the greatest good fortune, I have found that person,' Mr Green said. 'Also my wife needs domestic help. We have not yet been blessed with children, so there will be no nursery duties involved.'

Sarah felt immensely relieved: at least he wouldn't be getting any ideas about marriage applications. There was still the matter of unwanted sexual advances — she'd heard plenty of stories about that sort of thing during the ten days they'd been at the Factory — but she was confident she could deal with that if or when she had to. He wasn't a particularly big man, nowhere near as solid and muscled as Tom Ratcliffe had been.

Mrs Gordon nodded in approval. Sarah had been gifted with a plum position.

'When will you collect her, Mr Green? You will recall that you forfeit your bond if she doesn't leave the Factory within fourteen days.'

'I had planned on taking her back with me today. Now, in fact.'

'No!' At the thought of not even saying goodbye to the others all the blood seemed to drain from Sarah's head and she thought for a second she might faint. 'No, please, I can't just go. I have friends here.'

She stared at Mr Green, silently imploring him to exhibit some compassion; to her profound relief she saw it in his eyes and in the way his expression softened just a fraction.

'Very well. I will be back at nine tomorrow morning. Will that suit you, Mrs Gordon?'

'Yes. I'll ensure she is ready,' Mrs Gordon replied, though her tone implied she considered his generosity to be thoroughly unnecessary.

And it was, from his perspective, Sarah thought, and felt grateful, though she would never admit as much to her new employer.

Leaving Friday, Harrie and especially Rachel had been a terrible wrench, but Sarah knew it wouldn't be forever. Rachel was out of the hospital now and Mr Downey had made sure Harrie had plenty of laudanum to give her whenever she needed it. Despite Sarah's opinion of him he had turned out to be quite a decent cove after all, though she still wasn't sure she trusted him totally.

Rachel's arm remained splinted and would stay that way for some weeks. Harrie would be leaving the Factory soon, but Friday hadn't been assigned yet, and Rachel would be all right until she was. She had already established both the contacts to smuggle in the contraband to ease harsh Factory life — proper soap, towelling, extra food, decent boots, a pile liniment for Rachel's poor bum — and the tough reputation to discourage other inmates from stealing it all. She also had the patience to stand at the dormitory window for several hours every evening with Rachel while she watched for the bats with which she'd become utterly obsessed. Janie Braine was also on hand to help, when she wasn't tending to her two infants.

And when Friday did go, well, there was a plan in place to manage that — provided Harrie could pull it off. Sarah thought she could, and would, because Rachel's welfare was at stake, though what was required went so against Harrie's nature that it would be great fun to be a fly on the wall in Harrie's employers' house just to watch it all unravel. As long as she didn't overdo it. And when it did unravel, Harrie would be on her way back to the Factory.

It all seemed rather random: if you misbehaved on assignment and were sent back to the Factory, often you were put into second class on probation and would have to earn your way back to first class — unless you'd done something criminal, of course; then you went into the third-class penitentiary. But not always; some women returned from assignment went straight into first class again. Perhaps it depended on what your ex-employer had to say about you when you were sent back. But if you were expecting, or had children under the age of four, or were ill — in other words clearly not suitable for assignment — you were also categorised as first class, the group from which those eligible for assignment were drawn! Sarah suspected the classification system might have more to do with the moral judgments of those who managed the Factory, and perhaps appeasing guilty consciences, than anything else.

Now, she sat in Mr Green's gig, as far across the seat from him as possible so she wouldn't have to touch him. She'd said not a single word for the last half-hour and neither had he. The gig was in a slight state of disrepair and the leather seat torn, with bits of horse hair poking through the hole. Sarah pulled on a piece and a large tuft came out. Alarmed, she glanced at Mr Green.

He smiled wryly. 'Don't pull too much out; the whole thing might collapse.'

Sarah felt too silly to say anything then, but a few minutes later asked, 'Where are we going?'

He looked at her, his expression of belated realisation almost comical. 'I do apologise. I haven't said, have I? Sydney Town. My wife, Esther, and I live in George Street. Our house is above our shop, opposite the military barracks.' He gave the reins a flick. 'I'm impressed with your knowledge. Whom were you apprenticed to? It was in London, I assume? You must have come quite close to completing your apprenticeship.'

'I did complete it. Then I lost my job.'

Mr Green nodded gravely. 'You stole from your employer.'

'No, the jeweller's son and I had a disagreement. I was let go. I've been pursuing other opportunities since then.'

'Such as picking pockets?'

'Yes, that's right.' Well, if he was going to state it outright like that, so was she.

'I was transported myself,' Mr Green said. 'For receiving. But that was a while ago now. I have a conditional pardon. My wife is also an emancipist. And my name isn't actually "Green", it's "Greenstein" — Adam Eli Nathaniel Greenstein.'

Sarah gave an inward sigh. Another bloody smouse.

'You may call me Adam as we are to work together,' Mr Green went on, 'but preferably not within earshot of Esther. There is a slight age difference between us and I'm afraid she's viewed every servant we've had as some sort of threat to her position as mistress of the house.'

Sarah immediately imagined Esther Green as wrinkled and balding with half her teeth missing. She must have amassed some wealth, for Adam Green to have married her: with his looks he could have had his pick. It could pose a problem, having a jealous wife watching every little move she made.

She was silent for some time, unwilling, as always, to make friendly overtures. However, she couldn't resist asking, 'Were they all jewellers, your previous servants?' Not that that was likely.

'No, that would have been too good to be true. Though here *we* are, two qualified jewellers, both transported for our crimes. But one had been employed in a jeweller's salon. And that other girl I saw yesterday had a vague idea of what she was looking at.'

'Worked for a fence, probably. Or in a pawnshop.'

'Possibly.'

They felt silent again and little else was said for the remainder of the trip into Sydney Town, except when Adam pointed out the odd landmark of note. He seemed almost as reticent and as unwilling to encourage familiarity as Sarah, which suited her.

They'd crossed the Parramatta River by punt soon after they'd begun their journey then lost sight of it, but now, hours later, wide stretches of water were again visible to her left. Part of the great inlet, she suspected, that formed the tidal river's mouth.

'That's Ultimo House,' Adam said, pointing to a moderately grand two-storey house off in the distance. 'It belongs to John Harris and was designed by Francis Greenway, the same architect who designed the Female Factory. He was also a convict.'

Uninterested, Sarah didn't respond.

A little farther on, as they approached the town proper, he pointed out a steam mill on the harbour's edge, apparently owned by someone named John Dickson. Sarah barely gave the brick buildings and tall puffing chimney a glance; she'd seen enough industrial buildings in England to last a lifetime.

The streets were busier than she'd expected, bustling with people and animals — dogs apparently running wild, pigs, geese and chickens, and goats, the latter in particular. They were everywhere. It hadn't really occurred to her that New South Wales wasn't *just* a penal colony, that folk were emigrating here of their own free will and that those who had been transported and served their sentences were now living lives as free citizens. She'd been too busy worrying about Rachel and Harrie and Friday to take the time to properly consider opportunities that might be available. This was a real town. Just look at the traffic. There were plenty travelling on foot, but, more interestingly, there were just as many on horseback and riding in fancy carriages — and that meant there was money here. If you knew how to get your hands on it.

Adam pointed out a large bare plot on the corner of Bathurst and George streets where, he said, a cathedral would soon be built, and the graveyard next to it, then Park and Market streets bordering a covered marketplace, and King Street, all neatly bisecting George Street, which ran north down to Sydney Cove.

'Why are you telling me all this?' she asked.

'Because I'll need you to run errands for me. That quite grand building on the right is the police office and that, of course, is the military barracks.'

The barracks was massive, plonked right in the middle of what appeared to be Sydney's prime commercial precinct and surrounded by a stone wall ten feet high with only a single gate that Sarah could see. It looked as ugly and forbidding as the Factory. At the base of the wall, on the ground, sat a group of black-skinned people.

'Who are they?'

'Aborigines. Australian natives.'

Sarah thought they must be really hot, sitting there in the sun. 'Where do you stable your horse?' she asked, considering the potential need for a quick getaway in the midst of such a prominent military and police presence.

Adam brought the horse to a halt. 'I don't. I hired it. And the gig. We've arrived.'

Relieved, Sarah climbed stiffly down from the gig, her back and bum aching from bouncing and jerking around for hours on end. The road in from Parramatta had been paved with gravel and stone and was somewhat potholed.

She stretched, retrieved her bag of Factory slops and bits and pieces from the gig and, while Adam fussed about securing the horse, had a good look at the little shopfront whose door opened straight onto the street.

The door was painted a deep slate grey and mounted with a heavy nickel-plated knocker in the shape of a bat with wings outstretched, which immediately reminded Sarah of Rachel's obsession with the horrible things. What an odd thing to have at the entrance to a jeweller's salon. It seemed an omen of some sort, not that Sarah believed in such things. The door stood to the left of a bowed mullioned window that was perhaps ten feet wide and six feet high. Its lower sill sat three feet above the ground. The cornices over the door and window were narrow to allow light into the shop, and across the fascia were the words 'Adam Green Fine Jewellery' in gold lettering, which matched the sign swinging above the shop door. The pilasters flanking the shopfront were also painted dark grey, but the mullions, the sill and stall riser below the window, and the door trim, were all finished in a very soft grey. The effect was very stylish and the equal of anything to be seen on Bond or Regent streets.

'I'll introduce you to Esther then I'll have to return the horse and gig to the stables,' Adam said.

Sarah wondered how long he'd been watching her. She picked up her bag and followed him into the shop.

The interior was small, no more than fourteen feet by twelve. Glass-fronted wooden cabinets lined two walls and, at the rear of the shop, behind a counter, stood a woman.

She was taller than Sarah, and slim but shapely beneath her well-cut china-blue dress. The front of her honey-coloured hair was parted in the middle with the sides falling in small ringlets over her ears, while the back was pulled into an elegant bun on top of her head. Her nose was small and slightly tilted and she had a very pretty mouth and wide brown eyes framed by thick lashes. She looked Sarah up and down with a long, appraising stare.

'Sarah,' Adam said, 'this is my wife, Mrs Esther Green.'

Harrie started crying the moment she left the Factory on the morning of the 29th of September. Her new employer, Henry Overton, tried to ignore it but they had a long trip ahead of them and by the time they'd reached Homebush, where he liked to have the occasional flutter at the racetrack, he was ready to tell her to start walking back to Parramatta and bugger his bond.

'For God's sake, girl, will you stop that wailing?'

Harrie glanced at him from beneath the brim of her Sunday bonnet. He had wavy brown hair going grey at the temples, side whiskers, a large red nose and tired-looking eyes. His frockcoat didn't fit him very well and he wore an odd, rough-woven fibre hat to keep the sun off his face.

'Come on,' he said tetchily, 'what's the matter with you?' He gave the horse's reins a flick and they surged forwards, the boxes of fruit and vegetables he'd purchased in Parramatta sliding back against the cart's tailgate.

Her throat was sore from forcing out sobs and she'd run out of tears ages ago and had had to keep her head turned away so he wouldn't notice and now her neck hurt. But she really did feel dreadfully upset. Her heart ached and every time she thought about what could happen to Rachel once Friday also left the Factory her stomach roiled with dread. Janie would be there for her, of course, but Janie, for all her kind and practical attributes, wasn't Friday. And Friday would almost certainly go soon; she was fit and strong, eligible for assignment, and Mrs Gordon thought she was trouble and wanted her out.

Even Bella Jackson had gone. It had been the strangest thing. First a woman had come to visit her on the Wednesday of two weeks earlier, even though inmates were only allowed visitors on Sundays. The woman had arrived driving her own phaeton and wearing smart clothes and the most enormous leghorn hat. *Everyone* at the Factory knew about it because the portress had told one of the nurses in the hospital, and she had told everyone else. Bella Jackson, true to form, had not said a word about her visitor, but the following Tuesday morning she was at the front gate in all her finery waiting with her trunks — this again according to the portress — and an older gentleman, *quite* an older gentleman, had arrived and driven off with her in his fancy rig. The story had gone round that Mrs Gordon had brokered a marriage — nasty, foul-mouthed, devious Bella Jackson *married*? — but if that was so, who had been the woman in the leghorn hat?

But even if Bella Jackson had managed to hook a husband, she was still a convict working out her sentence and assigned to a master, though one, if the union was successful, who could potentially offer her a life similar to that of a free married woman while she did. She could share in her husband's business affairs if he permitted her, be mistress of her own home, and raise a family — though the general consensus was that she was more likely to eat a child than raise one. But she would have to work for it. If the marriage failed before she'd obtained her ticket of leave — which, if you behaved, you could apply for after four years if your sentence was seven, or after six years if you were doing fourteen as was

Bella, or eight years if you were a lifer — she would be back in the Factory awaiting reassignment to the same dreary, laborious servants' positions as everyone else.

With a ticket of leave, however, she could work as a private individual or start her own business — clearly she was very capable of that — and also be 'off the stores', meaning that the colonial government was no longer responsible for supporting her. She would have to pay a fee for the ticket, but that wouldn't be a problem for Bella, and she would still be a convict in legal terms and have to attend regular musters and not be permitted to move to another district without permission. But from what Harrie had heard in the Factory, she imagined there would be plenty to pique Bella's business interests in Sydney, especially around the rough Rocks area. And after a certain amount of time she could then apply for a conditional pardon, a remission of her original sentence, though she would not be able to leave New South Wales, and then ultimately an absolute pardon, meaning she could finally return to England. All providing she kept out of trouble, of course. And no doubt she would, as Bella seemed adept at getting other people to do her dirty work for her.

It seemed so unfair to Harrie. Bella was such an unpleasant and obviously corrupt character and she'd swanned out of the Factory to a life of comfort and relative freedom in a matter of days. Friday had been absolutely spitting.

'I said, cat got your tongue?'

Harrie realised Mr Overton was frowning at her. 'I'm sorry, Mr Overland, what was the question?'

'Over*ton*. Not Overland, Over*ton*. And I said, what's wrong with you? You've been bawling like a calf since we left the Factory.'

Harrie put as much of a sad little wobble in her voice as she could manage. 'I miss my friends.'

Mr Overton rolled his eyes. 'We're only just out the gates this morning! I asked for a girl with a sound constitution, a good mind and no fear of hard work, not a homesick little halfwit!'

'I'm sorry, Mr Overland. I'm trying, I really I am.'

'It's Over*ton*, for God's sake!'

Harrie looked away, terrified she might smile. She didn't think it was just her annoying him, though; he'd been out of sorts when he'd arrived to collect her from the Factory. Perhaps he'd been short-changed when he bought his onions, potatoes and carrots. He was a grocer, selling fresh produce and dry goods in Sydney. He was married and had several children and her job was to help with the little ones and the domestic work while Mrs Overton assisted in the shop.

In a long letter she'd sent off the other day, Harrie had also told her mother and Robbie, Sophie and Anna that the Overtons were well-off and lived in a lovely big house on a hill overlooking Sydney Harbour with gardens full of flowers and fruit trees and a pond with goldfish, and that she was very lucky to be working for such a generous and well-respected family. She'd made it up but her mother would never know that. It would set her mind at rest, though, and so would the money she'd included in the letter to cover the enormous cost of receiving it.

They rode in silence for some time and, with every jolt and bounce of the cart, Harrie became more aware she needed to pee.

Mr Overton said, 'You were transported for shoplifting, is that right?'

'Yes, sir.'

'And what was it you pinched?'

'A bolt of cloth, sir.'

'Well, I'm warning you, if I catch you stealing anything from my shop, *or* my home, I'll have you up in front of the magistrate so fast your feet won't touch the ground, understand?' Mr Overton said, looking at her sharply.

'Yes, sir.' As if I'd want to steal your poxy carrots or green potatoes.

Eventually they came to a hotel. Mr Overton pulled off the Parramatta Road, climbed down off the cart and went inside, leaving Harrie sitting by herself. She wondered, just for the very briefest of seconds, if she grabbed the reins and took off, how far she'd get. But she really did have to get down if she wasn't to embarrass herself, so she slid off the seat and walked around the side of the hotel looking for somewhere private to squat.

There were four or five big wooden barrels stacked against the wall and if she kept her head down and her bum in, and no one walked around the building from the opposite direction or looked out of the window from above, she should be safe. She hoisted her skirt, crouched and let go. Honestly, it went on forever, the wee making a widening lake in the dirt between her boots, but finally tapered off to a few last dribbles and stopped. She shook herself and straightened, and that's when she heard it: a tiny squeak so piteous her heartstrings twanged like a fiddle's.

She turned around, searching for the source. It came again, a reedy little mewing, but still she couldn't see where it was coming from. And then, finally, on her hands and knees, she did.

Wedged between two barrels, right at the back against the wall of the hotel, its eyes glittering in the shadows, was a very small kitten.

'There you are,' Harrie whispered. 'I've been looking everywhere for you.'

The kitten opened its mouth but this time nothing came out.

Harrie reached into the gap, her palm grazing the egg-shell fragility of its skull beneath silky fur, pinched its scruff between her thumb and index finger and carefully pulled it out. It hung shivering from her hand, bright blue eyes blinking in the sunlight, back paws curled against its tummy, front paws extended like little starfish.

It was black and white, but quite possibly the oddest kitten Harrie had ever seen, with a face divided exactly down the middle by black fur on one side and white on the other. But it was very fluffy, which, in Harrie's opinion, more than made up for its unfortunate colouring. It surely couldn't be more than three or four weeks old and weighed almost nothing.

'Aren't you the sweetest little thing?'

It squeaked again, revealing a pale pink tongue and the beginnings of miniature teeth.

'You must be hungry. Are you?'

No response. It certainly wasn't very warm. Harrie cupped its quivering little body in her hand and had another good look around the barrels in case there were more, but couldn't see any. Obviously she couldn't leave it here to starve or be eaten by ... whatever ate defenceless kittens in this part of the world.

She slipped it down the front of her blouse so that it settled just above the waistband of her skirt and hurried back to the cart. Rachel would love it.

As Mr Overton drove the cart down George Street, still reeking of the whisky he'd imbibed earlier, Harrie saw Sarah outside a shop, cleaning the windows. Her heart almost leapt out of her chest and she shouted out her friend's name at the top of her voice, almost deafening Mr Overton, who clapped his hand over his ear.

Sarah heard, turned and waved wildly as the cart rattled past.

Harrie grinned hugely and waved back.

'At least something's put a smile on your face,' Mr Overton grumbled.

Harrie was still smiling when they turned left off George Street into Charlotte Place past what Mr Overton informed Harrie was St Philip's Church — which had what Harrie thought was a strangely ugly fat round tower on the end of it — and had to stop temporarily to allow a group of shabbily dressed men to cross the dirt and gravel-strewn street, their leg-irons clanking as they shuffled along in single file.

'Convict work gang,' Mr Overton observed morosely. 'That was me fifteen years ago.' Then he brightened. 'Not now, though. Self-made man, I am.'

He flicked the reins and they drove uphill then turned right into a street named Cumberland. The street headed north towards the Battery at Dawes Point, around which the women from the *Isla* had been rowed from Sydney Cove on their way up the Parramatta River, but Harrie had no sense of direction and no idea where she was now (and hadn't then, either). She would have to walk these streets half a dozen times before she found her bearings.

Mr Overton was a shopkeeper, so she wasn't surprised when the cart slowed outside a store. The street itself was pleasant enough, a mix of cottages and shops on the side of a hill overlooking the harbour — a street where tradespeople lived and worked, she thought. And perhaps even wealthier types, as farther along, towards the northernmost end of Cumberland Street, she spied the chimneys of grander houses, though on the hill below, in the narrow lanes and alleys, roofs crowded together and backyards were mean and dank, and the stink of cesspits and slaughterhouse rose up on the sea breeze.

The little whitewashed cottages on Cumberland Street, however, had verandahs and occupied plots with enough room for trees and gardens; one even had birds in a cage near the front door, a pair of pink and grey cockatoos. Harrie had seen them in the trees outside the Factory and heard their dreadful screeching racket, too.

Mr Overton didn't stop outside the shop, however, but turned the horse down an alleyway at the side of the store, arriving in a fenced and roughly cobbled yard littered with dog turds and crowded with wooden crates and barrels and pallets. A boy of around eight, about to hurl a stick for a squat white bulldog, froze when he saw the cart.

Mr Overton glowered. 'Toby! I thought I told you to work in the shop today!'

Toby dropped his stick; the dog grabbed it and raced off with it. 'I am in the shop!'

'Doesn't look like it.'

'I'm having my tea. Merry's behind the counter.'

Harrie looked around. On one side of the yard a single stable sat adjacent to a shed whose door was fitted with a solid, dully gleaming padlock. In the opposite corner was wedged a chicken coop, though the chickens were roaming freely, annoying a tethered goat munching its way through a pile of hay and the remains of a cabbage. Between the stable and the coop lay a cesspit, its ill-fitting lid doing little to curb the stench rising from it.

She slid down from the cart, careful not to wake the sleeping kitten nestled against her midriff. Rescuing it had seemed such a marvellous idea at the time, but she was fairly sure convict servants weren't allowed to keep pets. *And* it had done a wee — she could smell it.

'Get your things, Harriet, and follow me,' Mr Overton said.

Harrie hoisted her Factory-issue bag over her shoulder and followed him through a back door into a tiny vestibule with just enough room for a wall of shelves loaded with packets and paper bags and jars, and a narrow staircase. From upstairs came the sound of a child wailing. Peeking through the door that led into the shop, Harrie saw a girl of about ten or eleven behind the counter serving a customer.

The wailing grew louder as Harrie ascended the stairs behind Mr Overton, praying fervently the kitten wouldn't wake up, Toby thumping up behind them. At the top there was no landing: the stairs simply arrived in the middle of the Overtons' parlour. A large, harassed-looking woman with dark brown hair escaping from a house cap sat in an armchair rocking an infant perhaps a year old. The baby wore a white cotton gown and a broderie anglaise bonnet, though the bonnet had slipped sideways to reveal an extraordinary shock of black hair. Its face was bright red from bawling.

On a sofa opposite perched a little girl embroidering a handkerchief, her tongue sticking out like a tiny round of boiled ham, and on the floor sat a toddler making a high-pitched, slightly frenzied humming noise as he played with a spinning top he couldn't make spin. The moment he saw his father, he pushed himself to his feet and lurched towards him, anchoring himself to Mr Overton's trouser leg.

Throwing his hat on a side table, Mr Overton announced, 'Susannah, this is Harriet Clarke. Harriet, this is my wife, Mrs Overton. Harriet, you've met Toby, this is Lydia, six, and Bart, two, and baby Johanna. Merry, my ten-year-old, is downstairs in the shop.'

Harriet felt a pang of sadness. The children looked nice — they reminded her of Robbie, Sophie and Anna.

Susannah Overton heaved herself out of the armchair and passed the baby to Lydia. Susannah's stays, Harrie saw, were strained to their limits and her chest was quite remarkable, though that was understandable if she was still nursing. Her wrist bones were very fine, however, which suggested she was not naturally a heavy woman. Perhaps having five children in a row had taken their toll — though where Harrie had come from that usually wore a woman's body to the bone, not the opposite — or maybe it was being married to a successful grocer that had filled her out.

'You're later than I was expecting,' Mrs Overton said somewhat crossly.

'Waylaid,' Mr Overton said, as though the single word explained everything.

'Bushrangers?' Toby asked eagerly.

'Business,' his father replied.

Mrs Overton moved closer to Harrie and looked her up and down. 'Well, dear, at least you look healthy. The last one we had coughed all hours of the day and night and spent half her time in bed.' She wrinkled her nose and stepped back. 'What *is* that smell? It reminds me of ... cats. I *really* can't tolerate cats.'

Seventeen

1 October 1829, Sydney Town

Over the past fortnight, Sarah had discovered three things.

The first was that Adam Green didn't own the shop or the rooms above it where he and Esther lived, but paid a significant amount of money every six months to lease the property, shops on George Street being considered prime real estate. He'd taken out the lease in 1825 for a period of ten years, with an option to renew at the end of 1835, and there were heavy financial penalties if he broke the agreement. Sarah knew this because one night she crept down the stairs from her tiny room at the top of the house, picked the lock on the drawer in Adam's desk and went through his papers. He banked with the Bank of New South Wales and had two accounts, one for savings and one for the business. According to correspondence from the bank, the business account had sufficient in it to serve as working capital as far as she could tell, but the savings account went up and down alarmingly. This, she suspected, was probably due to Esther's spending habits, about which Adam and his wife fought frequently.

This was the second thing she had discovered — Adam and Esther's marriage didn't appear to be a very happy one. They argued often, though never when they thought Sarah could hear them, though she usually did, and the atmosphere in the small house was often frosty. Esther was fond of raising her voice, and Adam wasn't, so Sarah had to strain to hear his side of the disagreements, which always followed a similar theme: she wanted him to make more money and he wanted her to spend less.

The third thing was that Esther Green didn't like her — that had been plain from the day she had arrived. Far from being the old bag Sarah had imagined, Esther was very attractive — infinitely more alluring than Sarah believed herself to be — so why she'd taken against her, and so immediately, Sarah didn't know. It was possible she just didn't like the idea of another woman in her house, but as Esther refused to do laundry, sweep floors, wash pots or dishes, make beds, clean fire grates, empty chamber pots, sew, dust, polish, scrub or do anything else that resembled housework, it was clear she had desperate need of one. Surprisingly she did cook, and rather well. She also enjoyed reading; fiction was her favourite, especially books by lady writers such as Jane Austen and Fanny Burney. She was intelligent, that was obvious, and Sarah wondered why she didn't help Adam by doing the accounts for the business.

She also shopped, mostly, it seemed, for things for the house. In fact, she went out shopping so often Sarah suspected her relentless spending might be some form of attack on her husband. Their home was already very nicely furnished. Her sofas and chairs were upholstered in heavy jacquard brocade; she had rugs in almost every room and on the stairs; the drapes were good-quality velvet and lace; the lamps were great ornate things that were a bugger to clean; there were mirrors and paintings and little tables and bits and pieces everywhere; and her kitchen held every tool a cook could possibly want. And in the last two weeks she had still come home with more! Really, it was as though she were possessed with the need to buy and buy and buy. No wonder she and Adam fought about it.

It didn't make her happy, however, all the spending. She was a very bad-tempered piece of work, Esther Green. Tempted on occasion to ask Adam why, Sarah decided in the end her moderate level of interest didn't warrant summoning the nerve. It was their business, not hers. Whatever the reason, when Esther was home she went out of her way to test Sarah's tolerance and patience. She watched her constantly, presumably to prevent her from stuffing stolen property up her skirt, and checked that chores had been completed to her high standards, but Sarah ploughed through the housework quickly and efficiently, ensuring Esther could never legitimately complain about anything. Then she waited for Adam to call her into the shop or his workroom, which only irritated Esther even further, which she demonstrated by appearing unannounced at irregular intervals for no apparent reason. Sarah wondered if Adam had at some point been sprung dallying with a servant, leaving Esther perpetually mistrustful and on edge. But really, why should she expect *her* husband to be any different from any other woman's?

At the end of each day, Sarah was exhausted and utterly relieved to trudge up to her room and collapse on the iron bedstead, bleary-eyed and sore. After her forced inactivity in gaol and the limited exertion during the voyage on the *Isla*, working from dawn until nine at night was physically gruelling, but already she could feel muscles firming and her strength returning. It hurt, but in a way that felt good, helping her focus her thoughts when she was awake. And when she wasn't she slept without dreaming, which was a blessing.

6 October 1829, Parramatta Female Factory

Rachel looked guileless. 'I took it off to go to the privies and now it's gone.'

Friday sighed; Rachel had lost her sling again. It was good muslin and someone would have pinched it. This was the third one misplaced, but she didn't blame her. It was hard enough keeping your balance over those disgusting pits as it was, without having to wipe your arse with one arm hoisted up to your neck.

'Never mind, we'll get you another one,' Janie said, a baby balanced on each hip.

Rosie was doing remarkably well, especially given how many other infants weren't, at the Factory. But poor Willie was failing, even though Janie had plenty of milk for him. He'd never really thrived; he frequently spewed up his milk and cried far more than Rosie did. He didn't like the light either, screamed at loud noises, and was often feverish. Mr Sharpe suspected tuberculous meningitis, but he hadn't needed to tell Janie that — she'd seen it plenty of times in England. Consumption of the brain killed babies and small children all the time. It was usually passed to them in the womb by their mothers, and Janie was sure Evie Challis had had galloping consumption, though she'd always denied it. Evie's daughter had gone as well. Too old to remain at the Factory, she'd been removed to the Female Orphan School a few miles downriver. Janie had been devastated, but there was nothing to be done about it.

'I want *Friday* to get me another one,' Rachel said.

A wave of guilt churned through Friday's gut. It felt awful, stirring up pain she'd thought long buried. 'I can't, love. I'm leaving, remember? I've been assigned.'

'I know, but can't you stay just one more day?'

'I'm really sorry, love. But Janie'll look after you.'

Janie gave Rachel one of her radiant if crooked smiles. 'You can help me with the babies. It'll be good practice.'

'And don't forget,' Friday said, 'Harrie'll be back soon.'

'When?'

'As soon as she can.' Though God only knew when that might be. Friday certainly didn't. How long *did* it take to annoy your employers to the point that they sent you back to the Factory, without actually crossing a line that might land you in real trouble?

Rachel met her gaze and held it. Today, she knew exactly what was what. 'She has to be careful, doesn't she?'

Friday took her hand. 'Yes, she does. But she will be, don't worry.'

'And will you and Sarah come and see me?'

'Of course we will.'

They hugged fiercely, but as Friday turned to go, Rachel grabbed her sleeve.

'Friday?'

'What love?'

'I'm never going to leave here, am I?'

Friday stood outside the gates of the Factory, smoking her pipe and still feeling upset and distracted, aware that the portress was watching her through the slot in the wicket. She turned and gave her the finger then looked up at the gathering, pewter-edged clouds, hoping it wasn't going to rain. Her new employer apparently owned a hotel on the Rocks and would probably collect her in some shitty old cart normally used for hauling kegs and hogsheads, which meant she would get soaked on the long ride into Sydney Town.

If the cove turned up at all: she'd been standing here for an hour.

God, she hoped Rachel and Janie would be all right. She thought they probably would be; Janie wasn't anywhere near as gormless as she looked. She was tough and capable and would look after Rachel as best she could. In any case, the biggest source of trouble they might have faced, as far as Friday could foresee, had already left the Factory. Bloody Bella Jackson — what a cunning cow! How the *hell* had she managed that? She'd barely been in the bloody place long enough to open those bloody trunks of hers. And instead of being delighted to see the back of her, Friday had felt angry and *bitterly* disappointed. Because it wasn't finished between them, not by a long shot. Still, Sydney wasn't a big town. Her chance would come and she knew how to wait.

At last, she heard the distinct sound of hooves approaching along the gravel road and tapped the tobacco embers out of her pipe. Though what came to a halt before the gates was not a shitty old cart, but a landau with its hoods up, drawn by a handsome four-in-hand. The body of the vehicle was lacquered a deep, gleaming maroon colour and had no identifying insignia on the door, and the single window space was covered by a gauze shade. A coachman sat high on his seat at the front, staring impassively ahead.

As Friday stood gaping, the door swung open and a voice from within commanded, 'Come on, hurry up and get in. It's going to rain soon.'

A female voice.

Friday placed her foot on the step, climbed up into the landau and sat down without being invited, the interior being too low-ceilinged for her to remain standing. She pushed her bag beneath the seat.

The woman sitting opposite had clearly been beautiful in her youth and, though she was still handsome now, time had done its best to rob her of her looks. Lines nested around faded green eyes and ran from her nose to her mouth, accentuating slight jowls that would only droop even more in coming years. She was a little overweight, which helped to plump out cheeks that might otherwise have sagged and gave her a bosom a younger woman might envy. Her hair was henna-ed chestnut brown and she wore a touch of rose-tinted balm on her lips and cheeks and an old-fashioned beauty spot on the left side of her top lip. Unless it was a real mole — Friday didn't want to look too closely.

For a woman whose husband owned a pub, her clothes were very smart, as smart as her mode of transport. It was a warm day, despite the threat of rain, so she wore no cape, but her dress was of quality polished cotton — not that Friday really knew what she was talking about when it came to dress fabrics, Harrie was the one for that — in a vibrant orange-red colour, with the fitted waist and puffy sleeves that had been the rage with the nobby women in London. The ribbon and silk flowers on her straw hat matched perfectly.

Friday pulled off her horrible Factory bonnet and scratched her head, her curls springing out in all directions. 'I thought I'd be working for a bloke. Gordon said I'd be going to a Mr B Hislop.'

'Well, you're not,' the woman said, 'you've been assigned to me, Elizabeth Hislop. Mr Hislop is my husband and he's away at sea much of the time.'

The carriage rocked slightly and the coachman's face appeared at the window. He was a good-looking cove, Friday noted, and perhaps a potential source of profit? She winked and was encouraged by his smirk.

Mrs Hislop seemed not to notice. 'Back to town, thanks, Jack.'

Jack disappeared and a moment later the landau moved off in a wide arc, gravel crunching under the wheels.

Mrs Hislop reached into a large reticule on the seat beside her and took out two oranges, offering one to Friday. 'Tell me about yourself, Friday. I like to know a bit about the girls who come to work for me. Your name, for instance. It's quite unusual.'

Friday stared at the orange in delight; she hadn't had one in ages. In fact, the last one she'd eaten she'd pinched off a stall at Covent Garden market. Carefully, she bit into the skin to start the peeling process.

'No, dear,' Mrs Hislop remarked benignly, 'we don't peel oranges like that. Not in my house, anyway. Use this.'

She passed across a small utensil with a mother-of-pearl handle concealing a short blade, which looked to Friday suspiciously like a fancy flick knife. She opened it and had the peel off her orange in about five seconds.

'Friday is short for Frideswide, as in Saint,' she began, juice running down her chin. 'Ma was a Catholic and always praying to this saint and that saint. And when I came along I suppose she thought Frideswide was as good a name as any. St Frideswide was a beautiful rich virgin who lived over a thousand years ago and built a church in Oxford and took the veil and did miracles, or something.'

'And you've no children of your own?'

'No.'

'Husband?'

Friday shook her head and broke off another segment of orange.

Mrs Hislop dabbed at her mouth with a linen handkerchief. 'The documentation Mrs Gordon provided stated you were sentenced for robbing a man of his watch and walking stick. Is that correct?'

'It is.'

'I know as well as you do that the word "robbing" means you stole those things from his person, so do you mind if I ask what you and he were doing at the time?'

'Well, it's not hard to work out, is it?' Friday looked ruefully at her last three orange segments. Should she eat them now or save them for later? 'I'm a prostitute, right? The plan was to loosen him up, get his kecks off, then grab the swag and run.' She laughed. 'But he was nervous and such a weedy little cove. He drank too much and passed out and we helped ourselves.'

'Mmm.' Mrs Hislop finished her orange, blotted her mouth again and replenished her lip balm. 'I own a hotel in town, down on the Rocks, the Siren's Arms. You may have heard of it?'

Friday shook her head.

'No, of course not, you've only just arrived. We do meals, accommodation and the like. I have quite a large staff as we get very busy of an evening and there are the rooms to look after, too. So I'm often taking on domestic servants, and of course I need bar staff, and there are always a few lads to help out with the heavier work, the kegs and what have you.'

'Is it grand then, your hotel?' Friday asked.

'I'll be frank, dear: no, it isn't, but there are far worse on the Rocks, I can assure you of that. We cater to a lot of sailors, but all sorts come in regularly and some of them are quite particular. I've come to know many of them well and I make a point of trying to provide them with something a little out of the ordinary.'

Friday decided to eat the last of her orange after all, studying Mrs Hislop's face while she did. Mrs Hislop watched her back.

'What will my duties be?' Friday asked.

'I'll start you as a chambermaid. Changing linen in the guest rooms, sweeping floors, dusting, perhaps helping in the laundry. Can you cook?'

'I'm not famous for it.'

'Oh well.'

'And after that?'

Mrs Hislop raised her eyebrows. 'And after that what?'

'I think you're running a bawdyhouse, Mrs H. You've just about said as much. I don't want to muck about sweeping floors, I want to make real money doing what I'm good at.'

The landau slowed and came to a halt. Mrs Hislop lifted the gauze shade and peered out of the window.

'Only the toll gate. Jack will take care of it. You don't mind if I keep the shades down? This southern sun is so harsh on the skin.' She settled back in her seat. 'Well, you certainly have the looks for it and I'm not saying you wouldn't be an asset in my house. Though you could do with a bit of bicarbonate of soda on those tobacco stains on your bottom teeth. The prostitution laws are the same as in England, but you do realise that because of your convict status, if you're caught you'll be charged, and if you're convicted you'll do time in third class back in the Factory? Good. Never let it be said I encourage the girls assigned to me to prostitute themselves. That decision is always theirs to make.'

'But I won't be nabbed, will I? If the laws are the same it's only illegal to operate a house, and I'd be working in yours and you haven't been nabbed. Or have you?'

'Not in New South Wales, I haven't.'

'There you go. And you're not encouraging me. Whoring is my job. I'm good at it.'

'Do you enjoy it?' Mrs Hislop asked. 'No man wants to pay for a sour-faced girl, no matter how buxom she is.'

'I enjoy making money.' Friday wasn't about to admit that frequently she utterly loathed the men she had sex with. 'That *always* makes me smile.'

Mrs Hislop rummaged about in her reticule again, this time extracting a bunch of grapes. 'I'd expect you to sign a contract. Our current fees are five pounds for full, that's per hour, the same for Greek, four pounds for thighs only, three pounds each for hand or mouth, a full night is eight pounds, anything else is negotiable and up to you. I don't cater to men titillated by children — all my girls are seventeen and over. The split is forty–sixty in your favour, bed and board included for assignees naturally, two whole days off a week and, if your performance isn't up to the high standards I require, you really will be sweeping floors and working in the laundry. Also I've heard a rumour lately about yet another new house starting up. There's always the risk that some of my girls will imagine the grass will be greener somewhere else. It won't be, because my terms are very generous, but I'm insisting they all sign contracts. If they want to leave they'll have to give a month's notice to give me time to find suitable replacements.'

Friday thought that was reasonable. 'Are there a lot of brothels in Sydney?'

Mrs Hislop ate a grape. 'At least twenty I know of, most of them around the Rocks, which is quite a number for a town of only fifteen thousand. And I'm not sure how many streetwalkers. It's all the sailors. I don't know anything about this new madam, but you might. Apparently she came over with your lot. Got herself married in about twenty minutes flat. Shand, her married name is. Stella Shand.'

Friday stared at Mrs Hislop. 'You don't mean *Bella*?!'

'Bella, that was it. Grape?'

* * *

James Downey trotted downstairs to the King Hotel's pokey front desk to ask if any mail for him had been delivered. He was leaving for England in a week, and he'd not had a letter from Emily lately. He was expecting quite a pile, as a ship had arrived from England the previous day.

The clerk handed over two letters tied together with a piece of ribbon and a quick scan revealed neither were from Emily, which was disappointing. James sat down in a slightly grubby wingback chair and opened the first, from Emily's sister Beatrice.

8th of June, 1829

My Dearest, Dearest James,

    I am so terribly, terribly sorry but I have dreadful news. Our darling Emily has been taken from us. On the first day of June she cut her hand whilst gardening, contracted a rampant and consuming fever and passed away less than a week later on the 6th.

James must have cried out because suddenly the clerk was hovering, asking if he could be of assistance.

James looked up at him blankly. His ears were ringing, he could no longer feel the chair beneath him, and it took a few seconds for the man's words to register.

'No. Thank you, no.'

The clerk waited a moment longer, regarding James anxiously, then retreated to his desk.

His heart thudding massively, and not really comprehending the words on the pale cream paper, he read on.

Victor did all he could, and called in other physicians he thought could be of assistance, but to no avail. She went so quickly, James, but at the end she was tranquil, and we were all at her side. Your name was the last word to pass her lips.

We laid her to rest at St Mary Abbots this morning. Upwards of three hundred mourners attended. She was so loved, James, but you of all people know that.

You must be strong, dear. We are all utterly devastated but you will be heartbroken beyond words and I would give anything for you to be here with us as you read of this terrible news so that we may provide even a little comfort. All we can do is send you our love and prayers and wish you a speedy journey home.

Our Heartfelt Love,
Beatrice, Charles and the children

Feeling oddly detached, as though he were watching someone who looked a lot like himself opening the morning post, he slit open the second letter; it was from his good friend Victor Handley, a surgeon with whom he'd served at sea. Victor had been invalided from the navy after badly breaking his leg, and was also a confidante of Emily.

8th of June, 1829

My Dear James,

I sincerely hope you've read Beatrice's letter first. If not, please put this letter down and do so right away.

I'm so very sorry about Emily. I just do not know what to say to you that might help, except that, for the most part, she did not suffer unduly. It was the most ghastly and unexpected shock for us so I can not imagine what you must be feeling now.

She nicked the base of her thumb in the garden and by the end of the day it had developed into a whitlow and she felt quite ill. She sent for me and I thought at first it might just be a type of diary fever, or perhaps heat sickness as she had such a high body temperature, then maybe even

sudor anglicus *because of the sweating. But by the third
day it was clear the problem was septicaemia. I called in
Hugh Rathbone and Theo Manning but the disease was
too far advanced and she just went. She was not in pain,
James, I swear. She just slipped away.*

*At Beatrice's suggestion I am staying at your house, to
keep an eye on Tara and everything else until you return
home. Also, I have been kicked out of my club again.*

*You are going to have to keep your chin up, James, but
I know you — you are far tougher than you think you are. I
suggest you work on the way home. Find some sort of bug
to study or something. Whatever you do, do not brood. I
hesitate to say do not grieve, as you must do that, but do
not* brood.

*She was a wonderful girl, and you were lucky to have her
as long as you did. Try to hold on to that.*

*Your Very Good Friend,
Victor*

James let Victor's letter fall to his lap. The pain in his chest was monstrous and coupled with it was a great surge of guilt. For months now he hadn't been able to remember the sound of Emily's voice. He could recall her face, and her hair, and her mannerisms, but not her voice. Instead, in its place, was Harriet Clarke's, entertaining him with stories of antics below deck on the *Isla*, and silly recollections of her family in London and, amusingly, her awful employer Mrs Lynch, steadily but surely buffing the sharpness off his own loneliness over the long weeks and months at sea, brightening his days.

In his heart he had not been entirely true to Emily, and he knew it. Was this horrible grinding guilt the price he now had to pay?

* * *

Sick to death of cleaning, Sarah leant on the counter flicking the feather duster listlessly across the smooth wooden surface. When the bell over the shop door chimed she opened her mouth to call for Adam, but shut it again when she recognised the customer.

'Good morning, Mr Downey. How are you?' Though she wasn't sure she wanted an honest answer, because he looked like shite.

His face was distinctly pasty and it appeared he hadn't brushed his hair in days; in fact he looked ten years older than when she'd last seen him, little more than a month earlier.

Mr Downey stared at her as though he couldn't quite place her. Sarah wondered if he'd been on the jar.

'It's Sarah Morgan, from the *Isla*. Rachel Winter's friend.'

'Ah, yes, of course it is.' He glanced around the store. 'So this is where you've ended up?'

Sarah waited for the inevitable comment regarding the wisdom of letting a convicted felon loose in a jeweller's shop, but it wasn't forthcoming. She watched Mr Downey's face. He seemed to be struggling with something momentous; she could almost see the internal mechanisms of his head whirling about.

'That's right, Harrie said you'd trained as a jeweller,' he said finally.

Was that it? God, what was wrong with the man?

'What can I do for you, sir?' She wasn't supposed to be serving in the shop yet — Esther had put her foot down about that, insisting Sarah couldn't be trusted alone behind the counter — but this was only Mr Downey.

'My wife passed away,' he blurted. 'In June. I only just received the news.'

'I'm very sorry to hear that, Mr Downey.' And actually, she was. Fancy, all that time on the *Isla* when he was running around trying to fix everyone else, his own wife was dying and he hadn't known. 'Please accept my condolences.' No wonder he looked such a shambles.

'Thank you.' He gestured vaguely at a display cabinet. 'What can you show me?'

Sarah fetched the keys from their hiding place in the secret drawer she'd recently discovered, opened the cabinet and brought out a tray of rings.

'These are gentlemen's styles, ready made. A nice solid engraved gold shank, and a quality faceted rock crystal and just the plain gold bezel.' She turned the ring to show him the underside. 'See, you open the back and put in a lock of your beloved's hair, or a portrait if you prefer, then snap it shut.'

'I don't have a lock of her hair. Or a portrait.'

Sarah showed him some styles that didn't require the incorporation of a personal artefact, but he shook his head.

'Perhaps you could try another jeweller,' Sarah suggested. It wouldn't do Adam Green any favours, but this was Mr Downey and he had been very kind to Rachel.

'Really, I can't be bothered. I only came in here because it's just around the corner from my hotel. Could you not make something?'

Sarah thought about it. 'Do you want stones?'

'Not particularly. Just something elegant and dignified. Like … my wife.'

'And her name?'

'Emily.'

Thank God, Sarah thought — names like Ermintrude and Winifred are such a bugger to squeeze onto a ring.

She reached beneath the counter for a pencil and a scrap of paper and began quickly to sketch. Adam appeared in the doorway between the workroom and the shop, but Sarah barely noticed him.

A minute later she said, 'Something along these lines, perhaps? A flat band in twenty-two-carat gold, with black enamel running around the middle here, except for Emily's name set in gold on one side, and this pattern of forget-me-not flowers, engraved to make them stand out better, on the other. You could wear whichever side up you felt like at the time — her name or the flowers.'

Mr Downey gazed at the sketch for so long Sarah convinced herself he didn't care for it. Then he nodded. 'I think Emily would have liked that. How long would it take to make?'

Sarah glanced at Adam: eyes twinkling, he gave her a grin of such open admiration and encouragement that for a second she felt the floor shift beneath her feet.

'We could have it finished by Friday,' he said.

'And your fee?' James Downey asked.

Adam named what Sarah thought was a very reasonable price, and he and Mr Downey shook hands before Adam disappeared back into the workroom, still smiling to himself.

'You have a talent, Sarah,' Mr Downey said as she measured his finger to ensure a correct fit. 'Thank you.'

As he was about to depart, Sarah, buoyed by Adam's approval and awash with generosity, said, 'Sir, if you don't mind me saying, well, your clothes.'

Mr Downey looked down at himself. 'What about them?'

He looked as though he'd slept in them for a week and there were stains on his waistcoat and mud on his trousers, but that wasn't what Sarah meant. 'Should you be in mourning costume, sir?'

Mr Downey sighed, and the sound was laden with such misery and loneliness she felt genuinely sorry for him. It was a pity she wasn't Harrie — she would have known what to say to make him feel better.

'Yes,' he said. 'I suppose I'd better find a tailor.'

Eighteen

Friday was annoyed and frustrated because Elizabeth Hislop really had started her off sweeping floors at the Siren's Arms — and wiping the long tables in the bar and stripping beds and replacing oil in the lamps and other deathly dull jobs.

She soon discovered that all Mrs Hislop's convict girls started off doing domestic work, including servicing the accommodation rooms upstairs, where a handful of the girls from the brothel boarded. After a month of careful observation Mrs Hislop knew who was likely to be receptive to the idea of working in the brothel, either as a domestic or an actual prostitute, and who would be best left to dust and polish in the hotel. However, a girl had left the brothel a few days before Friday had been collected from the Factory, and Mrs Hislop had been very taken with Friday's looks and character, so, fairly confident of the nature of the girl she was dealing with, she'd been happy to discuss the matter openly then and there.

'It's only for a week,' Mrs Hislop said when Friday complained. 'I want you to get the feel of the Rocks. I want you to look around and see what kind of customer we cater to.'

'What's to see? There's sailors, there's the odd toff and there's the respectable family men in the middle. I did them all in London. How different can they be here?'

'It's called, it's called ...' Mrs Hislop made a face. 'Bugger, there's a word for it and I can't think of it. Look, are you bored?'

'Stiff. And I need the money.'

'You're not in debt *already*?'

Friday shook her head. 'A sick friend, in the Factory. Me and my mates, we're paying her way. You know how things work out there.'

Mrs Hislop regarded her. 'Well, if you're really champing at the bit I'll start you on Friday. When was the last time you worked?'

'On the town? The ship, but that all got shut down mid-voyage so not for about four months.'

'And you don't have the pox or the clap? Crabs?'

'The first two, not as far as I know. I've got crabs.'

Mrs Hislop waved her hand airily. 'Bit of per chloride of mercury and chloride of ammonium on the bush will fix that. Stings, though. I have a doctor check my girls regularly. If you're sick and looking rough, you're not to work until you're right again. My customers pay for healthy, attractive girls and I wouldn't offer them anything less. I run a class establishment. The bicarbonate of soda worked a treat on your teeth.'

'Came up nice and white, didn't they?'

Mrs Hislop opened the watch dangling from the crowded silver chatelaine around her solid waist. 'I've got time. Come on, I'll take you over there now.'

Lucky Sarah isn't here, Friday thought — she'd have that whole thing off you in two seconds flat and you wouldn't even notice until you went to look at the time again.

She followed Mrs Hislop out to the yard behind the hotel, waggling her fingers at Jimmy Johnson, only twelve years old and already a convict. He was rubbing down a customer's horse before he led it into the stables, where he also slept, and gave her a cheeky grin.

Mrs Hislop crossed the yard, dodging piles of horseshit buzzing with flies, and stopped at a tall gate in the wooden fence that formed one boundary. Unlocking it with a key from her chatelaine she ushered Friday through and locked the gate again behind them. The cobbled alleyway beyond it was so narrow Mrs Hislop's skirts brushed both sides of the high brick walls, and at the far end it turned sharply and opened onto another yard, this one much smaller and clearly belonging to someone's house.

The Siren's Arms was on Harrington Street near Argyle Street and, while it was very obviously a pub with its big entrance doors and sign displaying a naked woman with long, ridiculously luxuriant hair sitting on a rock, presumably luring sailors to their deaths with her singing, this house was a tidy sandstone affair with multiple chimneys and sparkling windows, the latter prettily draped against prying eyes. From the street the two businesses appeared wholly unconnected but customers with a key to the gate at the hotel end of the alleyway could enter the house with the utmost discretion.

Inside the house the furnishings were not excessively luxurious or ostentatious, but they did create an atmosphere that was very comfortable and inviting. Downstairs were a large parlour where the girls gathered, a smaller room for customers who preferred a higher degree of anonymity, Mrs Hislop's office, and a small kitchen accessible from the back porch. Upstairs were the eight individual rooms where the girls worked, remodelled apparently from the house's four original bedrooms, and a large cupboard used for linen storage. Each room contained a brass bed made up with good linen, an armchair, a bedside cupboard with a jug and bowl, and a dressing chest on which sat an inexpensive carriage clock.

'What do you think?' Mrs Hislop asked, back downstairs again.

'Looks very nice, but I have to say I don't know my arse from my elbow when it comes to whorehouses. I'm one for the streets myself. Have been for years.'

'Why is that?' Mrs Hislop sounded genuinely interested.

Friday met her gaze and held it. 'I have my reasons.'

'I'm sure you have. I won't pry. But it is safer working in a house. *My* house, at least.'

'I can take care of myself.'

'Yes, well, no doubt you can, but I think, in your current situation, you're far better off working for me. If you're nabbed on the streets you'll be —'

'Straight back to the Factory. I know. Where is everyone today? The girls, I mean.'

'It's their day off. We never work on Mondays, and I give every girl one other day off each week. You need your breaks.' Mrs Hislop opened the front door and they stepped out into Argyle Street.

As they walked around to the Siren's Arms, only three doors along on Harrington Street, Friday said, 'I'd like to find out where my friends are.'

'Do you have addresses?'

'Only names. Sarah went to some cove called Adam Green, a jeweller here in town somewhere. And Harrie went to someone called Overton, a grocer.'

'Harry? That's a funny name for a girl.'

'Harri*et*.'

'Oh. Well, I don't know of Adam Green, but most of your jewellers will be up around George and Pitt streets. There's plenty of them. And if you mean Henry Overton, I've known him for years. He's in Cumberland Street, just up Argyle Street here: it's the first cross street but you turn left.'

Friday's heart leapt. 'Really?' She pointed excitedly. 'Just up here?'

Mrs Hislop nodded. 'In fact, I'm getting a bit low on my special tea. It's called souchong.' She handed Friday some coins. 'Henry knows which one I like, anyway. And tell him Bette sends her love, but only if his wife isn't listening.'

Friday was off up the street almost before she'd finished speaking. Mrs Hislop watched her go, shaking her head. But she was smiling; she knew what it was like to be separated from your friends after all that time in gaol and then on the ship out. She'd experienced it herself almost seventeen years earlier. Of course, things had been rather different then, though she herself hadn't changed much over the intervening years. She was older, fatter and definitely richer, but she liked to think she could still remember how it was to be a lass.

Almost trotting as she rounded the corner from Argyle into Cumberland Street, and puffing because of the hill, Friday barrelled straight into someone.

'I beg your pardon,' the man said, stooping to retrieve his hat. Then, when he looked at her properly, recognition sparked in his eyes and he took a precautionary step back.

'You're that cove,' she said.

'Yes. You had a go at me, that night on the ship.'

Friday recalled belting him rather viciously across the head and felt her cheeks turn very slightly pink. 'Well, I thought it was you that had hurt her. Sorry. What was your name again?' She'd forgotten it.

'Cutler. Matthew Cutler.' He offered his hand and, after a second's hesitation, Friday shook it.

'I didn't think your sort lived on the Rocks.'

'I'm boarding with a family on Princes Street. It's quite smart actually.' He said this with an exaggerated plum in his mouth, which made Friday laugh. 'Er, the other girl with you, the pretty one, Harriet Clarke. You don't happen to know where she is, do you?'

Friday thought about it for a moment. 'Write down where you live and I'll ask her if she wants you to know, how's that? If she does, she can write to you.'

He hesitated.

'Don't worry, we won't come and do your house over.'

'I wasn't thinking that.' Mr Cutler looked offended. 'I was thinking I don't have anything to write on. No cards or anything. You'll have to remember it instead.' He recited the address and Friday did her best to commit it to memory. 'And the little blonde girl, how's she getting on?'

Friday scowled. 'She's still out at the Female Factory. She can't work.'

'Because of ... what Keegan did?'

'Yes. Also ...' She held her hand out in front of her belly.

A barely disguised expression of revulsion passed across Matthew Cutler's face.

'Don't you dare blame her!' Friday warned.

'Oh God, I don't!'

'Good. Do you see him at all?' She made the question sound casual.

'Occasionally. Around here now and then, and my office isn't far from his.'

'Do you talk to him?'

'Never.' The word was almost spat out.

'Does he go in the pubs?'

'Around here he does, and no doubt the brothels.' Mr Cutler's face reddened, probably recalling what Friday did for a living.

'No doubt,' she agreed. 'Nice talking to you, Mr Cutler.'

'And you, Miss Woolfe. It's Friday, isn't it?'

'Yes.'

'Don't forget to mention me to Miss Clarke, will you?'

'I won't.'

She waited until he'd crossed the street and turned a corner before she hurried off along Cumberland Street. Fancy that. Did Harrie have a suitor? Had she even noticed on the ship? Probably not — Harrie was so modest and unsure of herself she thought she was invisible. Mind you, lately she'd come out of her shell a fair bit. The more Rachel needed their help, the stronger Harrie seemed to become, which was good for everyone, really, Harrie included.

Outside Overton's grocery she stopped and peered in through the windows. Harrie wasn't in the shop, but she wouldn't be if she was supposed to be looking after the family's kids. She entered, stepping over a white bulldog lying in the doorway, and approached the counter, where a girl of about ten was tipping boiled sweets into a tall glass jar.

'May I help you?' she asked, a dozen of the sweets clattering across the counter. She swept them up with her hands and dumped them in the jar.

'Hello, love,' Friday said. 'I'm after some tea. It's called ...' But it was no good, the name had fallen out of her head.

The girl recited, 'We've got gunpowder, hyson, bing, imperial, congou, pekoe, bohea, souchong —'

'That's it, that last one.'

'How much would you like?'

Friday stared at her. 'I don't know, love. It's an errand, for Mrs Elizabeth Hislop.'

'It's all right, I know what she gets.' The girl came out from behind the counter and crossed to a row of tea chests. She scooped out a measure of loose tea, weighed it on a scale, decanted the leaves onto a sheet of newspaper, rolled it deftly into a sausage and twisted both ends.

Friday gave her the money. 'I'm also looking for a girl called Harrie Clarke. Is she here?'

The girl retreated behind the counter, deposited the money in the cash drawer, stuck her head through a doorway and bellowed, '*Da!*'

They waited, Friday and the girl looking at each other. The girl smiled; Friday decided she was pretty. Presently, her father arrived huffing and puffing, carrying a huge bag of flour. He lowered it to the floor and wiped his hands on his apron.

'Da, this lady's looking for Harrie Clarke.'

'Oh, aye?' Mr Overton said. 'And why would that be?'

Friday gazed at him through her eyelashes and ever so slightly shifted her weight to one hip. 'She's a friend. I heard she was working here and I'd very much like to see her, sir, if it isn't too much trouble. Just for a few minutes. Oh, and Bette sends her love.'

Mr Overton looked uncomfortable. He glanced quickly at his daughter, then nodded his assent. 'Not long, mind. She's busy — breaking something, no doubt.' He pointed at the ceiling. 'Just go up.'

That sounded promising. As Friday went up the stairs she heard the girl say, 'Da, who's Bette?'

The Overtons' parlour looked as though a whirlwind had gone through it. Children's toys littered the floor; a mountain of clean laundry waiting to be ironed and folded had avalanched from a chair; some sort of food was squashed into the pale carpet in the middle of the room; a box of old kitchen implements had been upended and strewn about; and an empty vase lay in a pool of water beside the sofa, a trail of bedraggled carnations leading from it into the next room. A little girl sat in a chair calmly turning the pages of a picture book, while a toddler lay on the floor, simultaneously picking his nose and eating a biscuit.

Friday smiled to herself. The little girl looked up.

'Hello, love, is Harrie here?'

The girl nodded.

'Harrie, it's me!' Friday called.

She appeared a moment later, carrying a baby with a red face.

'Friday!' She looked both shocked and delighted. 'What are you doing here?'

'I've come to see you, haven't I?' Friday thought Harrie, who was wearing a boring light grey dress and a silly house cap, looked healthy but a bit flustered.

She passed the baby to the girl on the sofa. 'Lydia, hold Johanna for a moment, please.'

'She stinks.'

'I know, I'm about to change her.'

Lydia took Johanna, propped her up beside her and went back to her book, a hand over her nose and mouth.

Harrie gave Friday a fierce hug and stepped back. 'How did you find me?'

'It turns out my boss knows your boss. I'm just around the corner in Harrington Street at the Siren's Arms.' She held up the packet of tea. 'I'm on an errand.'

Harrie picked up Bart and put him on a chair. 'And you're treated well there?'

'It's been all right so far.' Friday gestured at the chaos in the parlour. 'This looks a right mess. Things are going well then?'

Harrie lowered her voice and turned away from Lydia. 'Very. Mrs Overton thinks I'm completely useless. She calls me clumsy and dull and says I couldn't think for myself if my life depended on it. I'm a disgrace in the kitchen, too. I manage to burn something every day.'

'So how long, do you think?'

'A fortnight? Perhaps even sooner. The children are sweet, but Mrs Overton can't cope with them. I'll miss them.'

'All we have to do now is find out where Sarah is.'

Harrie's face lit up. 'But I know where she is! We passed her the day I arrived, cleaning windows on George Street.'

'Did you stop?'

'I couldn't, could I? And I haven't been allowed any leave since I got here.'

'Christ, Harrie, you're entitled to *some* time off.'

'I know.'

'Well, demand it. Kick up a fuss. Can you remember where the shop is?'

'Opposite the military barracks.'

Shouldn't be too hard to find, Friday thought. 'I bumped into someone just before, Matthew Cutler. You know, the other passenger on the ship, the one I belted?'

'The one who tried to help Rachel?'

Friday nodded. 'He asked me if I knew where you were.'

'Me?' Harrie looked startled.

'I said I did, but if you wanted him to know, you'd get in touch with him.'

'Why would I do that?'

'I don't know. Anyway, he gave me his address.' Friday gave Harrie a sly wink. 'If you want it.'

'Well, I don't. I'm too busy.' A sneaky look crept across Harrie's face. 'Unless he wants a kitten.'

Friday laughed when Harrie told her how she'd found the orphan, smuggled it in and made it a little sand box, which she kept hidden under her bed and cleaned out three times a day to minimise the smell. She'd tried feeding it cow's milk pinched from the table but that had given it the shits, so now it was taking goat's milk, which seemed to better agree with its digestive system.

'Rachel will just love it, though,' Friday said. 'You do have some good ideas, Harrie. It'll be good company for her, and keep the rats away.' She frowned. 'Unless she kills it while she's having one of her fits.'

'*Fri*day, what a horrible thought. Actually, if Mrs Overton found the kitten, she might send me back for that, mightn't she? She hates cats. I could accidentally let it out.'

'Wait 'til we've seen Sarah.' Friday wrinkled her nose. 'Christ, that kid really does stink.'

Lydia had moved, leaving Johanna on the sofa by herself. Harrie laid the baby on her back, lifted her gown and removed her napkin, setting it to one side. Expertly she wiped Johanna's bottom, put on a fresh nappy and set her on the floor to crawl around.

Mrs Overton chose that moment to appear, bleary-eyed, her face creased from her daily nap. 'I thought I heard voices. Harriet, who is this?'

'I hope I didn't wake you, Mrs Overton,' Harrie said. 'This is my friend Friday.'

Friday waved. 'Hello, Mrs Overton.'

'Harriet, who gave you permission to receive visitors?'

'It's all right, Mrs O, your husband sent me up,' Friday explained brightly. 'And I'm just leaving. See you on your next afternoon off, Harrie, all right? Send me a note, let me know when it is.'

Harrie reached for the soggy and full napkin, gathered the corners together, and headed for the stairs. Unfortunately the nappy fell open, depositing a large and squashy turd on the carpet.

Bart, who had remained remarkably quiet for the preceding fifteen minutes, let out a screech of glee, crying, 'Jobbies, Mama! Jobbies!'

His shriek was almost drowned out by Mrs Overton's. '*Harriet*, for God's *sake*, it's on the *floor*!'

Harrie flapped her hands ineffectually and turned in a circle before picking up the turd with a lace doily snatched from a side table.

'Bye, Mrs O! Nice meeting you!' Friday, her hands firmly over her mouth, could barely get down the stairs and out of the shop fast enough.

16 October 1829

Friday had seen him walking down Argyle Street twice now: once when she'd been sitting in the parlour idly looking out through the drapes, and again when she'd opened the window to air her upstairs room after a customer had departed. Both times her heart had almost leapt out of her chest. His profile and swagger had been unmistakable and the sight of him had sent a bolt of rage right through her. Another afternoon she'd seen Amos Furniss go past. She'd moved out of sight when he'd looked up and didn't think he'd seen her, but it had been an unpleasant shock; she'd assumed he had gone back to England on the *Isla*. What was he doing still in Sydney Town?

Since then she'd made a point of watching for Keegan, worried he would come into the brothel and that she might have to service him. He wouldn't know who she was; she doubted he'd recognise anyone from the *Isla*, barring perhaps Rachel. Even the thought of lifting her leg to him made her want to vomit. Also, it might be useful to find out where he lived.

When he actually did come in, at first she didn't know whether to hide or attack him with a kitchen knife.

She did neither. She was coming down the stairs when she saw him standing in the hallway, hat in hand, talking to Mrs H. Her heart thumping, she backed up and sat down on a step to listen.

'I'm looking for something a little special,' he said, 'and I'm hoping it's a service your establishment might offer.'

'And what might that be, Mr Coroglen?' Mrs Hislop replied.

You lily-livered bastard, Friday thought. What's wrong with your real name?

'I'm interested in girls,' Keegan said.

'I have girls here. Very beautiful girls.'

'I mean young girls.'

'How young?'

'Twelve,' Keegan said. 'Eleven. The younger the better.'

There was a long silence before Mrs Hislop replied brusquely, 'Then I'm afraid you're in the wrong house, Mr Coroglen. I don't cater to men of your tastes. Good day.'

She crossed the floor and held the front door open for him. The very public front door, Friday noticed, stifling a snort. Keegan set his hat back on his head and left.

This evening she had a feeling in her bones Keegan would come sauntering down Argyle Street again.

She glanced at the carriage clock on the dressing chest, wishing the man grunting away on top of her, Mr Leech, would hurry up and finish. Mr Leech was fifty-five years old, half bald, and had bad teeth and a pizzle like a pair of peanuts still in their shell. Also, his wife apparently didn't believe in intimate relations except for the purposes of procreation. His children, he'd told Friday, were aged thirty and thirty-two.

Friday moaned realistically, sped up her hip action and dug her fingers into Mr Leech's skinny rump. He obliged by increasing his own thrusting, politely taking his weight on his bony elbows, his shiny pate level with her chin. The bed began to squeak and Friday made a mental note to mention it to Mrs Hislop; perhaps Jack the coachman, who also did odd jobs and worked behind the bar, could come and have a look at it. And while he was at it he could tighten the latch on the bedside cupboard — that was a bit loose, too.

At last Mr Leech came to a shuddering halt, collapsing with his face buried between her breasts. Tempted to flick him off and leap off the bed, Friday lay with gritted teeth, patting his back. It took him several minutes to recover enough to roll off her and sit up. Friday checked the clock again; he had eight minutes left.

'That was wonderful, my dear,' he said, still out of breath. 'You really are the loveliest specimen of womanhood I've ever had the pleasure of knowing intimately.'

Yes, yes, Friday thought, get your kecks on and piss off. 'Thank you, Mr Leech. You're a very fine figure of a man yourself.'

He laughed gaily. 'Surely you jest, my dear.'

I certainly do. Friday watched as he staggered around trying to get his feet into his trousers, then took ages fiddling with the laces in his shoes. The moment he said goodbye, leaving an extra sovereign for her on the dressing chest, she dashed to the window, just in time to see Keegan appear at the intersection of Harrington and Argyle streets, whistling and swinging his cane. He hesitated, as though considering which route to take, then turned down Argyle.

Friday threw on her robe over her fancy satin corset, snatched the sovereign from the dressing chest, burst out of her room and pounded down the stairs. At the bottom she turned left and headed out the back door and across the yard past the privy and the drying line to the alleyway. Running as fast as she could, breasts bouncing painfully and bare feet slipping on the mossy cobbles, she barged past Mr Leech, almost knocking him over.

Then she realised she didn't have a key to the gate.

'Quick, Mr Leech, the key!'

Thrilled beyond words at the sight of Friday's wild hair, bare legs, exposed crotch and heaving bosom, Mr Leech thrust his key at her.

She opened the gate, flipped the key back at him, tightened her robe around her waist and ran across the yard to the stables.

'Jimmy? Jimmy! Where are you?'

The boy appeared, startled. 'What is it, what's wrong?'

She showed him the sovereign. 'Want to earn yourself a quid?'

Jimmy's eyes lit up.

'All you have to do,' Friday explained, 'is follow a cove. I want to know where he lives. Can you do that?'

Jimmy, who had been transported for picking pockets, nodded confidently.

'Good. Keep out of sight, though, eh.'

She described Keegan and said he would probably be on George Street by now. Jimmy nodded again and took off.

Toby was larking about with his spindle and ball outside the shop when Harrie returned from collecting Mrs Overton's new shoes from the bootmaker. He was supposed to be sorting through the fruit boxes for fruit that had gone over, but as usual was skiving off.

'You're in trouble,' he said as Harrie passed him, and flicked the spindle so the ball on its piece of string flew at her.

'That will make a change, won't it?' Harrie said brightly. Most children she liked, but Toby she could take or leave. He was a surprisingly shiftless boy, given the inherently decent character of his father.

She traipsed up the stairs to find Henry and Susannah Overton sitting in the parlour, clearly awaiting her return. The other children were nowhere to be seen. A covered wicker basket sat on the floor at the end of the sofa, emitting plaintive little squeaks. Oh dear, Harrie thought, they've been in my room.

'Here are your new shoes, Mrs Overton.' She placed the parcel on the armchair.

Mrs Overton pointed to the wicker basket. 'Would you care to explain the meaning of this?'

Harrie bent down and opened the lid. 'It's a kitten.'

'I jolly well *know* it's a kitten, Harriet. There's cat mess all over the ground outside your bedroom window. I discovered the wretched creature hiding in your bed, *under* your bedclothes.'

Harrie wondered who had tipped her off, though only Toby would have done it to deliberately cause trouble.

'And that's not all,' Susannah Overton went on. 'You went out the other night, didn't you? And don't deny it. One of the children saw you coming home.'

'Yes, ma'am,' Harrie admitted. It was true. She'd crept out on Monday and gone to meet up with Friday and Sarah.

'It wasn't your evening off; you know that.'

Harrie nodded and made an effort to look contrite. It wasn't difficult: her half-day off was on Sundays, and the Overtons could barely spare her that, between the shop and the children. She'd felt quite guilty.

Henry Overton said, 'You were with that red-haired girl from the Siren, weren't you? I knew she was trouble the moment I set eyes on her.'

This was the confrontation Harrie had been angling for since she'd arrived, so she pushed it as far as she dared.

'No, sir, I was out with my man.'

'Your *man*!' Mrs Overton looked aghast. She turned to her husband. 'Henry, this really is the last straw!'

Part Four

On the Wing

Nineteen

January 1830, Parramatta Female Factory

James Downey rode through the outer gates, dismounted and passed the reins to the porter. This worthy was one of the few males working within the Factory walls, though only William Tuckwell, Sidney Sharpe and Mrs Gordon's husband regularly passed through into the Factory proper.

'See that he gets water, will you?'

The porter nodded; the day was suffocatingly hot and the doctor's horse dripping with sweat, a dirty cream lather rimming both girth and bridle straps.

James crossed to the inner gates and waited as the portress opened one side for him. 'Mrs Dick said to tell you Rachel Winter's in the hospital again.'

James thanked her. That wasn't good news, but neither was it unexpected. Rachel was well into her third trimester of pregnancy and, though the confinement had progressed with surprisingly few problems, the heat must surely be taxing on any expectant woman, never mind someone who suffered the magnitude of headache she did.

Since October, he had ridden out to Parramatta once a month on a Sunday to visit her, even though she was Mr Sharpe's patient, not his, and to talk to Harrie about her progress. He was more than happy to do it. He was also happy to work as many hours as he was offered at the surgery in Pitt Street where he'd recently taken a position. Well, perhaps not happy, as Emily's death still weighed very heavily on his mind — willing was probably a more appropriate word. He found the work filled his days and sometimes even his evenings, keeping at bay the loneliness he at times feared would overwhelm him.

To be truthful, he went out to Parramatta to visit Harrie as much as he did Rachel. Harrie had been so kind after Emily had died, which had only made his feelings of guilt worse. Some weeks after he'd received Victor's and Beatrice's letters she had appeared at his hotel on a Sunday afternoon to tell him she was very sorry to hear of his bereavement. She'd handed him a posy of flowers, which to his embarrassment had brought tears to his eyes, then burst into tears herself, apologised, said she didn't like to see people she cared for in pain, apologised again and left.

He'd resigned from the navy in October, having decided to stay on in New South Wales as he and Emily had planned. There was no real reason to return to England now — he would only be reminded of what he'd lost. He'd written to Beatrice explaining his decision, and to Emily's mother and father, and to Victor, whom he'd asked to stay on at the house in Kensington indefinitely. Someone had to look after Tara. He hoped they would all understand his decision, even if they couldn't entirely forgive him for staying away.

He removed his hat and gloves, used the gloves to mop the sweat from his brow, and entered the hospital.

Rachel was in a bed near an open window, though there was no breeze to speak of. Harrie sat next to her, wiping her face with a wet rag.

'Good afternoon, Harrie.'

'Hello, Mr Downey.' Harrie dipped the rag into a bowl of murky-looking water, wrung it out and draped it across Rachel's forehead.

He gazed down at the patient. Her belly looked huge because she herself was so tiny. In actual fact, according to Mr Sharpe, the foetus was a normal size. The rest of Rachel was very thin, her arms and legs almost spindly, her face pale and her closed eyelids a transparent, smudged blue. Her breasts, however, had enlarged, getting ready to feed her baby, due in nine or ten weeks.

'Asleep or sedated?'

'Sedated,' Harrie replied. 'Another headache. Mr Sharpe wanted her in the hospital because of the heat. He says her pulse is too fast. He fears a burst blood vessel in the brain.'

James nodded; it was a possibility.

Harrie, he knew, had been returned to the Factory at the end of October for failing to perform as a domestic servant in a satisfactory manner, though he found that hard to believe. Harrie, with her thorough and capable work habits and constant willingness to please? He had asked her what had gone wrong but she'd eluded his questions with a guile he hadn't previously suspected of her and he had not broached the subject since. Whatever had happened was clearly, she felt, none of his business.

Since then she had been working in the Factory hospital as a nurse, a position she had managed to secure with his previously written recommendation supported by a private word from him with Mrs Gordon. It wasn't until December that it occurred to him that Harrie's failure to perform on assignment and her subsequent desire to work in the hospital — where Rachel Winter was a frequent patient — might be connected. It gave him new insight into Harrie Clarke's character, though he couldn't fault her for her apparent duplicity as she had been motivated by loyalty. It had also amused him, and he appreciated that, as very little had lately.

He moved to the head of the bed and gently lifted each of Rachel's eyelids. Her left pupil appeared normal, perhaps a little large but that would be the effects of the laudanum, but the right was fully dilated to the extent that only the narrowest rim of blue was visible around it, and the sclera was shot with red. The eye had been in the same condition the month before. He let the eyelid close again.

'It looks awful, doesn't it?' Harrie said.

'I don't expect it's painful, however. You were in Newgate Gaol together, weren't you?'

'That's where we met, the four of us.'

'That eye, the pupil, can you recall if it was enlarged then?'

Harrie dipped the rag again and reapplied it. 'Nothing like it is now.'

'But you noticed a difference?'

'I think so. A little. I can't really remember, I'm sorry.'

A woman cried out for a nurse and Harrie went to her. James watched as the patient vomited, partly into a bowl but mostly on herself and her mattress. Harrie began to clean her down.

The hospital was full beyond capacity, a result of accommodating the overflow from Parramatta Hospital and sometimes even farther afield, further reducing the minimal level of care provided.

Other than women lying-in, the patients suffered from a range of maladies, most commonly dysenteria, anasarca, ulcers, opthalmia, abscesses, debilitas, syphilis, febris, and psora, as well as broken bones and wounds from accidents and fighting. The nurses were all Factory inmates and neither was the midwife salaried — only Sidney Sharpe had advanced medical qualifications. The hospital environment was not sanitary, and in weather conditions such as those of January 1830, the stink of suppurating wounds, vomit and faeces was nauseating and the flies that accompanied it a constant, droning pest.

James carried a second stool over to Rachel's bed, sat down and lifted her delicate wrist, noting that the bones had mended as well as could be expected, and took her pulse. It *was* somewhat rapid.

Harrie washed her hands and came back.

'Does she still believe the baby is her lover's?' James asked.

'Yes, she does. And she still thinks he's coming to get her.'

'Even when she's lucid?'

'Yes. And I don't think there's any point telling her otherwise any more, do you? It just upsets her. She's got it fixed in her head and nothing will shift it.'

'And she's never remembered anything of what really happened?'

Harrie looked down at Rachel. She straightened the hem of her shift. 'Sometimes I do wonder, but if she has she's never said.'

'It isn't unusual for a particularly unpleasant experience to be permanently erased from the mind. And her head injury has no doubt contributed to her memory loss as well.'

Harrie said, 'You've a loose button. Would you like me to sew it back on for you?'

James glanced down and saw that a button was indeed dangling precariously from his coat. 'Please, if you don't mind. Thank you.' He removed his coat — mourning black, like the rest of his costume — and gave it to her.

From her apron pocket she took a long bone reel with three different coloured cottons on it, opened a compartment at one end and extracted a needle, threaded it with black cotton, and very deftly reattached the button, biting off the thread when she'd finished. James tried not to stare at her teeth, which were small and even and not discoloured at all, or at her smooth, full lips. She pulled on the button to test her handiwork for strength, then handed the coat back.

'Thank you, Harrie. I appreciate that.'

'You're welcome, Mr Downey.'

'I ran into someone from the *Isla* the other day. Matthew Cutler. You might recall he was a paying passenger. Pleasant young fellow. Asked me if I knew where you could be found. I'm not sure why he thought I would know.'

'Yes,' Harrie said. 'Friday spoke to him not long ago, in the street on the Rocks.'

'Perhaps you have an admirer.' James said it in jest, though actually he didn't find the notion particularly amusing. And possibly neither did Harrie, because she looked embarrassed. 'How are Friday and Sarah faring these days?'

'Sarah's still at the jeweller's. I'm not sure she and Mr Green's wife get on very well, but, well, you know yourself what Sarah can be like. Mr Green seems to be happy with her. And Friday is fitting in nicely at the Siren's Arms.'

'She's a domestic servant there, isn't she?'

An expression James couldn't quite fathom flickered across Harrie's face. 'Yes. They do accommodation and meals. She and Sarah come out to visit Rachel when they can, which isn't often because the round trip by coach takes all day and neither of them gets much time off. Friday's been out more often than Sarah has.'

'Yes, it must be difficult. When Rachel's time comes, would you like me to be on hand, or are you happy for Mary Ann Neale to manage the delivery?'

Harrie smoothed Rachel's hair back from her damp forehead. 'Well, I suppose it depends on what state she's in. Mary Ann has delivered dozens and dozens of babies, and if Rachel's lying-in is straightforward she should be able to manage, shouldn't she?'

'I expect so. Mr Sharpe tells me she's a very competent midwife.'

'Shall we discuss it next time? She'll only have six weeks to go by then.'

James stood and collected his hat and gloves. 'Yes, we shall. And perhaps you could also consult Mr Sharpe for his opinion?'

Harrie regarded him with embarrassment, then giggled. 'I'm not her doctor, am I? I keep forgetting.'

James allowed himself a smile, finding unexpected joy in this new, less formal relationship — it could almost be called a friendship now, though in his most private moments he was prepared to admit he yearned for more. She was changing: her confidence was growing and she seemed more at ease, more settled. He liked it.

* * *

Rachel was in the sky far beyond the pain in her head, the delicate membranes of her wings catching the wind and suspending her high above the Factory, her precious cargo nestled within her fur-covered belly. She delighted in the way that one twitch of her wrists tilted her wings this way and that to take advantage of the breeze, her tidy little ears open to every sound.

Far below lay the Factory grounds, stark and ugly. The main buildings formed a long rectangular compound, the penitentiary end abutting the river. Surrounding them were the yards, and beyond the solid outer walls clustered the houses and gardens of Parramatta township.

But for now no wall was high enough to keep her captive. She circled and circled, riding lazily on the breeze, free of pain and fear, content to wait until she knew she would have to return.

February 1830, Sydney Town

Friday called for Sarah at two o'clock sharp, the bell over the door chiming as she entered the shop. Sarah gave a low whistle.

'Well, don't you look the well-to-do tart?'

Friday did a twirl, the skirts of her new, hydrangea-blue muslin dress fanning out prettily. The sleeves were full above the elbow but fitted to the wrist, and the waist was snug, the bodice ending in a point. The neckline was wide and low — Sarah noted Friday had declined to wear the lace pelerine collar that would usually accompany such a daring cut — and her hat was a startling confection trimmed with feathers and copious loops of ribbon.

'Pretty, isn't it? I thought I'd treat myself.'

'The colour suits you.' Sarah felt positively dowdy in the plain, sage-coloured dress Esther Green had purchased for her to wear as a uniform, but then she'd never been one for flaunting her charms. You had to actually possess them to flaunt them. She put on her small straw hat, not bothering to check the angle.

'Adam, I'm off out now!'

Adam Green appeared, his eyebrows lifting slightly as he caught sight of Friday's ensemble.

'Good afternoon, Miss Woolfe.'

'Mr Green,' Friday replied silkily.

'Don't be too long, Sarah,' Adam said as he lifted the hatch in the counter for her. 'Esther will be back by four o'clock.'

'I won't.'

Outside on George Street, Friday teased, '"Adam", is it? Sounds cosy.'

'Oh, don't be an arse,' Sarah snapped.

'He fancies you.'

'He does not.'

'He bloody does.'

'You're full of shite, Friday Woolfe. Now, where shall we go? I've only got two hours. And I need to see Skelton.'

'Skelton? That sounds promising. Tea shop, I thought.'

Skelton's pawnshop was on Upper Pitt Street, tucked between a tailor and a gun maker. They'd almost arrived when Friday noticed they were being followed by half a dozen filthy, undernourished dogs.

'Don't turn round, but there's a pack of dogs behind us.'

As Sarah looked two darted past, faced them and growled.

'Don't look them in the eye, they'll attack,' Friday warned.

Sarah dug in her shopping basket and pulled out a heavy wooden cosh about eighteen inches long.

'Bloody hell, where did you get that?'

'Bought it.' Sarah slipped her hand through the wrist strap and swung it at the nearest dog's head, shouting wildly.

The dog retreated a few steps then stood its ground, barking. The others, growling menacingly, moved closer.

The door of the pawnshop opened and Mr Skelton emerged carrying a fowling piece, which he fired at the dogs. They scattered in all directions, yelping and howling, then ran off, peppered with shot.

'Damned wild dogs,' he said. 'If it's not them it's the damned feral goats eating everything in sight. Come in, ladies.'

The shop was crammed with used goods including furniture, carpets, flatware, pots and pans, tools, clothing and linen. Cabinets displayed fancy pipes, watches and jewellery. Mr Skelton propped his gun in a corner and returned to the carriage clock he was disembowelling on the counter.

'What can I do for you today, Mrs Dunn?'

'I have some items that may interest you, Mr Skelton,' Sarah replied. 'Unfortunately, my personal financial situation has not improved since we last spoke and to my regret I find myself having to part with even more of my collection.' She retrieved a velvet bag from her basket and emptied the contents onto the shop counter — a pair of gold drop earrings, a small peridot and a matched pair of even smaller almandine garnets. 'I never had the stones set,' she said. 'I meant to, but there was never the money, and now that I'm widowed there never will be.'

She held Mr Skelton's gaze, aware that he knew she was lying. But that was the way this game was played, and they were both practised at it.

He held the earrings up to the light streaming through the shop window, then examined them through a jeweller's loupe. 'Well crafted,' he remarked, then produced a grubby handkerchief, spat on it and rubbed at one briskly, checking for black marks.

'Twenty-two carat,' Sarah said. 'It's not pinchbeck.'

Satisfied, Mr Skelton nodded. He had a close look at the stones. 'Nice cuts. I can offer you five pounds the lot.'

'I was hoping for a little more.'

'I'm afraid that's the best I can do at the moment, Mrs Dunn.'

Sarah made a show of deliberating. 'Then I'll take it, thank you, Mr Skelton.'

He placed the jewels in a metal box, popped it beneath the counter, opened his cash drawer and handed Sarah the money. 'Come and see me next time you find yourself having to pawn more of your collection, Mrs Dunn. I'm sure we can continue to do business.'

'Perhaps, Mr Skelton. Good day.'

Outside the shop Friday said, 'I bloody hope you know what you're doing there, Sarah. Can you trust him? That wasn't a good price.'

'I haven't got much choice, have I? It's not as though I can go round interviewing every fence in Sydney.' Sarah smirked. 'Anyway, it was pinchbeck. With just a touch of lacquer.'

Friday laughed. 'And Adam hasn't noticed anything's missing?'

'I'm still working for him, aren't I?'

'How are you managing it?'

'Very carefully. Come on, let's have that cup of tea.'

The five pounds would go in the bag carefully hidden under the floorboards in Sarah's room, together with the usual tenner Friday put aside from her own earnings each week. An account at one of the town's banks might have been more secure, but only men had the authority to open one.

Since the beginning of November the amount in the bag — the 'Rachel fund' — had grown to an extremely pleasing figure, though some of the money earmarked for her had gone straight to Harrie at the Factory. Privately Sarah felt guilty because she contributed so little but, short of robbing Adam Green even blinder, there wasn't much else she could do for now. She could pick the odd pocket while she was out, but she had neither the time nor the crew to operate the sort of lucrative caper in which she'd been involved in London. To her surprise — shock, in fact — she felt rather uncomfortable stealing from Adam, given that he was being decent to her, but if she didn't, she couldn't contribute anything to Rachel at all, and she'd feel even worse for abandoning her. Their charge wasn't really abandoned, of course, she had Harrie, but Sarah had made a promise to look after her, and she couldn't renege just because she'd expected to loathe her master and didn't. Now she felt guilty about that as well. God, she despised guilt — it was such a pointless waste of thought and effort.

They chose a tea shop on the corner of George and Hunter streets, sat down at a table near the window and ordered a pot of tea and a plate of sandwiches and cakes.

'Who'd have thought we'd be playing ladies like this?' Friday said, looking around and almost taking Sarah's eye out with a peacock feather.

'I'm not playing anything,' Sarah said. 'I'm a servant and you're a tart.'

'A very well-paid tart, though. Much better money here than in London, even though I'm handing nearly half of it over to Mrs H.'

'Why's that, do you think? The money?'

'Not enough women here. Mrs H says there's three blokes to every girl. The beauty of supply and demand, she calls it.'

'You must be busy.'

'Flat out.' Friday snorted at her own wit. 'Except when they want it some other way. My minge is on fire come the end of the night, I can assure you.'

A pair of middle-aged women at the next table stared at Friday, cake forks suspended between mouth and plate, faces frozen in shock.

Sarah said, 'That came out a bit loud.'

'Anyway,' Friday said, 'you're not a servant. You're a jeweller.'

The tea and cakes arrived. Sarah poured. 'All right then, a jeweller who scrubs floors, empties chamber pots and polishes furniture. That bloody Esther: I could quite easily throttle her. Every time I think I've finished she finds something else for me to do, anything to stop me being in the workroom with Adam.'

'She probably thinks you're lifting your leg for him.'

'I know she does.'

Friday reached for a jam tart. 'Are you?'

'Really!' First one woman stood, then the other. Leaving their afternoon teas unfinished, they swept from the shop.

'No, I'm not. What I said earlier, though, about Adam not noticing, I can't just keep stealing bits and pieces. He will notice soon and then I'll be buggered. And what I'm taking isn't even worth much, especially by the time it gets to Skelton. A fence will never give you the full price of what a piece is worth. If I could get my hands on some good paste I could replace some of the better stones Adam has, then fence the genuine ones.'

Friday eyed her shrewdly. 'But you don't really want to do that.'

Sarah felt her face grow warm, as though she'd just been caught telling an enormous lie. 'How do you know I don't?'

'Because you like him, don't you?'

'I do not!'

'And *I* say you don't want to because if you're caught you'd get another seven years for it. It isn't worth it because you don't need to. I'm already making piles of money.'

Sarah was silent for a while, scraping the jam out of the middle of a tart with her fork. Finally she said, 'I *could* always pick a few pockets on my day off, I suppose. Just to keep my hand in.'

Friday shrieked with laughter at Sarah's pun.

They finished their tea and paid. Outside, a very smart curricle, lacquered midnight blue with a raised black hood and pulled by a matched black pair, went past. The driver wore livery and carried a long whip, while the face of his passenger was almost hidden beneath a large hat. The shape of her nose was very familiar, however, and when she turned her head towards them, Harrie and Friday both recognised her.

She looked away quickly, but it was clear she had also recognised them.

* * *

'I saw Bella Jackson this afternoon,' Friday said to Elizabeth Hislop. The shock of it was still making her heart thump.

'I'd like to see Bella Jackson or Shand or whatever her bloody name is myself,' Mrs Hislop said as she viciously jabbed a knife into the hinge end of an oyster and prised it open. 'The cheek of the woman!' She tipped the oyster into her mouth, tossed the empty shell out of her office window and reached for yet another from the huge bowl on her desk. The oysters came from Sydney Cove and were fresh this morning. 'Fancy one?'

'No thanks.' Friday hated them. 'Why?'

'I thought you might have a taste for them.'

'No, why do you want to see Bella Jackson?'

'To give her a piece of my mind, that's why. I wouldn't be bothered if she was hiring out a handful of scabby whores from some rat-infested hovel, but she's set up in direct competition with me. She's leased a house in Princes Street — *Princes Street*, for Christ's sake! — and tricked it out with velvet wall hangings and fancy carpets and chaise longues and God knows what else, and the next thing you know she'll have my clientele sidling through her back door, thinking her girls are better than mine!'

'Are they?'

'Her girls? How would I know? I haven't seen them. I doubt it. My house has had a reputation for the best girls on the Rocks for years, and that's because I do have the best girls. Unless she's suddenly conjured a dozen exotic beauties out of thin air, which I can't see, myself.'

'But you know what men are like. They'll have to try it out.'

Mrs Hislop nodded in weary resignation, because she did know what men were like.

'And she'll undercut you,' Friday added.

Mrs Hislop looked alarmed. 'Will she? Like that, is she?'

'Hard as a box of nails and cunning as a shithouse rat.'

'Crossed swords already, have you?'

'Crossed swords? I'll kill the bitch if I ever get the chance. I don't understand though, Mrs H, how she can set up a bawdyhouse when she's just got off a convict ship. Isn't she supposed to be assigned like the rest of us?'

Mrs Hislop selected another oyster, thought better of it, and dropped it back in the bowl with a clatter. 'She *is* assigned — to her husband. Clarence Shand is fifty-six years old, an importer and exporter with warehouses and lumber yards on Sussex Street and Phillip Street and down on the waterfront, and filthy rich. Well, by Australian standards. A bit shady, and a bit of a bastard by most accounts. His wife of some years died twelve months ago.'

'So Bella *is* his servant?'

'Hold on, let me finish. A man who marries a woman still serving her sentence becomes responsible for her, so she comes off the stores, which is one reason marriage is encouraged here. But she's still a bonded convict, so no, she can't run a business. Marriage to Clarence Shand, however, means Bella can quietly dabble in whatever venture takes her fancy under his protection, because their marriage itself was a business deal. It was brokered by a woman who arranges these sorts of things for the wealthy. Very discreet and charges a hell of a fee. I expect it's quite a suitable set-up for old Clarence. He gets what he wants, and Bella gets what she wants.'

'How do you know all this?'

Mrs Hislop tapped the side of her nose. 'I've lived on the Rocks for nearly eighteen years now, love. I've got all sorts of people owe me favours. And a few I owe, too. There's not much goes on here I don't know or can't find out about.'

'So what *does* Shand want?' Why anyone would choose to marry Bella Jackson was a complete mystery. It would be like taking an adder to your bed.

'A woman who scrubs up reasonably well and keeps her mouth shut.'

'About what?' And then Friday realised. Honestly, she was so dim sometimes. 'He's a mandrake, isn't he?'

Mrs Hislop nodded. 'And it's much easier to be one of those with a loving wife on your arm.'

Friday snorted. 'He won't get much loving out of Bella Jackson.'

'Luckily he won't want it.' They laughed. 'But will she?'

'Doubt it. She'll be too busy counting her money and scheming to expand her criminal empire.'

'Is she really that flash?'

'She really is. If I were you I'd watch my back. If I were *Clarence* I'd watch my back.'

'Mmm. Perhaps I won't go round to Princes Street and throw bricks through her windows then. You should watch your back, too, Friday, if you've already had run-ins with her. You really don't like her, do you?'

'Like I said, I'm just waiting for my chance.'

Mrs Hislop gave Friday a worried glance. 'Really? You'd swing for it, you know. Even if she is as rum as you say.'

'Be worth it.'

'Will you tell me why?'

It might be a relief to tell someone older and wiser about Keegan's crimes against Rachel, and how Bella very likely orchestrated them, and for a second Friday considered confiding the whole story to her. But only for a second. 'One day I will. But not now. I'm sorry.'

'Does it involve your friend? The one still in the Factory?'

Friday nodded.

'Well, I'll not pry,' Elizabeth Hislop said. 'God knows we've all got secrets. I have to tell you, though, love, I can't allow you to bring trouble into my house. Do you understand?'

'Yes, Mrs Hislop,' Friday said. 'I do. Very well.' And she did.

* * *

February 1830, Parramatta Female Factory

Janie sat on the floor in the hospital, Willie in her lap. His skin was pale and clammy and his blind eyes half open, eyelids fluttering fitfully. He was naked except for his clout, the rapid rhythm of his tiny heart visible in his sunken belly.

Harrie set a cloth and a fresh bowl of water on the floor. Willie's head lolled in her direction, then his arms flew out, fists clenched and his spine arched as he was taken in another fit. Janie slipped one hand beneath his buttocks and the other behind his neck, supporting his rigid little body until the spasm passed.

She looked at Harrie helplessly, tears welling. 'I know it's a terrible thing to say, but if I could put an end to his misery and get away with it, I would. It's so cruel, Harrie.'

'It can't be long now, Janie, surely. Mr Sharpe doesn't think so.'

'Mr Sharpe doesn't know his arse from his elbow. I've seen babies like this go on for weeks and weeks until they starve to death. And so have you, so don't deny it.'

It was true: Harrie had. If a convulsion didn't kill him, Willie could die from lack of food. He was taking very little nourishment from Janie now; his bowels had stopped; he was barely conscious much of the time; he was blind; and he seemed in constant pain. She dipped the cloth into the water and gave it to Janie.

'And he still can't keep the tincture of opium down?'

'I've even tried mixing it with some of me milk in a spoon, but he just spews it everywhere.'

'Keep trying, Janie.' Harrie turned to go; she had to check on Rachel. 'It will help him, even just a little bit.'

Janie nodded, kissed the top of Willie's head then rubbed her cheek gently along the side of his face. 'I will. I'll not give up, Harrie. I'll do anything to make him feel better.'

Outside Harrie walked through the dormitory building and out into the first-class yard. Rachel was sitting on a blanket in the shade of a wall, Janie's baby Rosie in a basket beside her. The heat and humidity were stifling and Rachel had taken off her blouse and shift, revealing breasts patterned with delicate blue veins and tipped with large brown nipples. Her belly was huge. She'd drawn up her skirt around her thighs and the kitten, now approaching six months, whom Rachel adored and had named Angus, lay between her legs asleep on his back, paws in the air.

'Rachel, sweetie, put your blouse back on.'

'It's too hot.'

'I know, but you'll get mosquito bites and then whitlows.'

Rachel gathered her hair — falling well past her bottom now — in one hand at the base of her neck, twisted it into a bun and stuck a filigree tortoiseshell comb through it. The comb had been a gift from Friday and, while Rachel loved receiving presents, Harrie and Janie had a hell of a time stopping other inmates from pinching them.

Angus rolled over, expecting a tickle. Harrie obliged. 'Has Rosie been asleep the whole time?'

'Mostly.' Rachel slipped her blouse back on, her fingers fumbling with the buttons. 'She woke up once and had a little grizzle and I sniffed her nappy but it's clean.'

'Do you want some help?'

Rachel's shoulders slumped and she nodded. Over the past month she had begun losing the strength in her left arm, which was odd, given that she'd broken her right wrist.

Harrie fastened her buttons for her. She and Janie had no concerns about leaving Rosie in Rachel's care — not when Rachel was feeling well, anyway. And she had been feeling really rather good lately. She'd had a nasty headache a week earlier and needed her laudanum, but there had been no fits for over a month now. It seemed that the closer she came to her lying-in, the more settled she became. Perhaps her body, small as it was anyway and now wasted from her long illness, had only enough strength for one task at a time and had chosen to concentrate on bearing a child. Or perhaps she was simply getting better, her poor head finally healing. Harrie fervently hoped so anyway.

She checked Rosie, who was fast asleep, her pink, sweaty face pressed against the side of the wicker basket. Harrie moved the round head slightly, and waved away the flies that continually lit on the child; they rose for a second, hovered, then landed again. The hundreds — thousands, probably — of flies that crawled and buzzed over everything at the Factory were disgusting and could drive a person to distraction, but she knew there would be just as many in Sydney Town, except perhaps when a stiff breeze blew in off the harbour. In the end she gave up, sat down, lifted Rosie out of the basket and cradled her.

Rachel picked up Angus and lay him across her belly, where he flopped bonelessly, staring up at her with adoring eyes long ago turned gold.

'Harrie?'

'Mmm?' Harrie looked closely at Rosie's neck; she had a very faint spotty rash in the folds of her skin. Perhaps it was only from the heat but she would ask Mr Sharpe about it just in case. Scarlet fever started with a rash.

'That man, Gabriel Keegan,' Rachel said. Her tone of voice was both questioning and thoughtful, though she didn't look up from Angus, continuing to stroke his dusty fur over and over.

Harrie sat very still, startled and uneasy: she'd been sure Rachel had lost all recollection of Keegan and what he'd done to her. 'Yes,' she said noncommittally.

'He hurt me, didn't he?'

Harrie felt sick. Should she lie, or should she tell Rachel the truth and upset her all over again, just when she seemed to be settling, getting ready for her baby? And what could she say about *that*, about whose child she was carrying?

She laid Rosie back in her basket, and took a deep breath. 'Have you remembered something?'

'I don't know. It's like when you see something when there's lightning at night. Just ... flashes of things. Pictures. He did this, didn't he?' Rachel touched the back of her head where the long scar lay.

'Oh sweetie, yes, he did.'

Frowning, Rachel said, 'And you told me a long time ago he raped me, didn't you?'

Harrie couldn't speak; she felt awful. She swallowed and nodded.

Rachel ran her fingers down the length of Angus's tail. 'Lucas will be angry. But our baby will be all right, won't it?'

'Your baby will be fine, love.'

'Whatever happens?'

Rachel's hands moved rhythmically over Angus, her gaze never wavering from Harrie's, one bright blue eye and one almost black eye boring into her, staring into her soul, digging out the truth and dragging it up into the space between them. Harrie felt a spider of profound unease crawl up her spine.

'What do you mean?'

'What if I'm not here to take care of it?'

'But you *will* be here, sweetie. Stop talking nonsense.'

Rachel's left hand flew out and clutched at Harrie's wrist; Harrie could feel the tremor in it, the weakness that was becoming more pronounced every day. 'But if I'm *not*, Harrie. Will you care for it? Will you promise?'

'Of course I promise. But you will be here. I promise that, too.'

Rachel's hand dropped away and she made a sound that was nearly but not quite a sigh.

'I love you, Harrie. And I love Friday and Sarah, too. You'll tell them that, won't you?'

Willie died some time during the early hours of the sixteenth day of February, not in the hospital but in the first-class dormitory sleeping next to Janie and Rosie. In the morning he was blue about the mouth but his still, wasted little face looked, for the first time in months, relaxed and at peace. Mr Sharpe entered 'death by tuberculous meningitis' on his death certificate, his opinion being that the child had suffered a convulsion in the night and swallowed his tongue, thereby suffocating. He was buried in St John's cemetery.

Harrie and Janie never spoke of it but, as their mattresses were side by side, Harrie knew that Janie slept with both babies very close to her. Had Willie suffered a convulsion, both women would have been aware of it. Something else had finally put an end to his horrible torment, and Harrie could only be glad.

Twenty

Friday, 5 March 1830, Parramatta Female Factory

'I've got a funny feeling in my belly.'

Harrie, instantly alert, looked across at Rachel, who was sitting cross-legged on their mattress, patting Angus. The young cat was supposed to be outside murdering rats, the only reason he'd been allowed into the Factory, but as usual he had crept inside and up the stairs and was settling in for the evening. At one or two o'clock he would slink out to do his job, leaving mangled and headless corpses lying about in the yard to be discovered in the morning, but for now he was deeply content where he was.

'What sort of funny? Cramps, do you mean?'

'A dragging feeling.'

'Painful?'

'Sort of. Not really.'

'Have they just started?'

'No, this afternoon, just after dinner.'

Harrie felt a flash of irritation. Rachel had been grumpy for several days, and not very communicative. 'Rachel! You should have told me!'

'Why? I said it's only sort of sore. My back's worse.'

Harrie went in search of Mary Ann Neale, who was in the hospital attending to another woman lying-in. Harrie waited until she was free.

'She's due in a week or two, isn't she?' Mary Ann said.

Harrie said yes. She and Mary Ann had talked about what they might do if Rachel were ill when she went into labour. The idea of dosing her heavily with laudanum was a bad one — she wouldn't be able to push or help with the delivery in any way. Without the drug, of course, she might suffer a severe headache, and perhaps a fit, and have to be physically restrained. Both options risked the lives of mother and baby. But there had been no fits for over a month and only a few headaches, and as long as the actual delivery didn't set her off, both Mary Ann and Mr Sharpe thought the birth should proceed smoothly, despite the fact she was so underweight.

'Have her waters broken?'

'Not as far as I know,' Harrie replied.

'Then it's early days yet, but we'd better find somewhere to squeeze her in here.'

'Tonight?'

'The morning will do, unless things change. You can keep an eye on her. Bring her over if anything does change. Your fancy doctor's not doing the birthing, is he?'

'Mr Downey? No.'

'A good thing, too. You'd have to send for him now and he'd not get here in time if she does turn out to be quick. That Parramatta Road can be right treacherous at night.'

'Rachel's asked me to help with the birthing, but I'm not a midwife, I've only assisted with a few deliveries. I'd rather you were doing it, Mary Ann. I'm feeling quite sick about it.'

'Well don't: I'll be here to help. She knows you and it'll calm her nerves. The last thing we want is her pitching one of her fits. Don't worry, Harrie, we'll manage.'

When Rachel got up to use the bucket at four in the morning something slippery came out of her and, in the darkness, she thought she was bleeding. Wadding her shift between her legs she woke Harrie, who had only been dozing anyway.

'What is it, love?' she whispered.

Rachel tried to stifle her panic and failed, her voice loud in the relative quiet of the pre-dawn dormitory. 'I think something's wrong. I think it's coming out.'

Harrie rose to fetch the single lamp near the doorway.

Janie stirred and sat up, Rosie still fast asleep beside her. 'What's the matter?'

'I don't know!' Rachel sank to her knees on the mattress, clutching her belly. If she lost the baby now, Lucas would be utterly heartbroken. What would she say to him?

'Shut up, you lot!' a voice rasped from the shadowed darkness.

'Shut up yourself, you blind cow!' Janie shot back. 'Her baby's coming!'

'Then get her away t'hospital! We're tryna sleep!'

Harrie held the lamp high and thrust the slops bucket at Janie. 'What's that?'

Janie held her nose, looked, then patted Rachel's leg. 'You're all right, love. You've just had a show. It's the snotty bit that stops the babe from falling out before it should.'

Harrie inspected Rachel's shift for signs of blood, just to be sure. There was nothing she could see.

Rachel felt so weak with relief she wasn't sure she could stand. But her 'sort of' pains were turning into proper cramps now and she didn't want to be in the dormitory any more. She wanted to be in the hospital.

And there was another pain, too. A familiar one, inside her skull. A pinprick for now, but it would grow.

'Will you want help getting her across?' Janie asked.

Harrie touched Rachel's arm. 'Will you be all right, just me and you?'

Rachel looked at Janie; she would love both of them to take her to the hospital, but Lucas would expect her to be strong and she didn't want to disappoint him.

'Rosie's still asleep.'

But Janie had seen the expression on Rachel's face. 'Old sack-of-spuds Rosie?' Expertly she fashioned a sling from the cloth in which the baby was swaddled, tied it and Rosie around her torso, and stood. 'See, didn't even stir. Let's be off then.'

'Bleedin' hell, will you lot bugger off!'

'Jesus, blind *and* deaf! I just said we're goin'!' Janie retorted as she helped Harrie pull Rachel to her feet.

Outside, dawn wasn't far away. Overhead a ribbon of bats were on the wing, heading home after a night's feeding, gliding black and soundless through the moist summer air. Rachel came to a halt, her face tilted skywards to watch them, mesmerised. Wait for me, she called silently. Wait for me. Growing dizzy, she staggered, and Janie took a firmer grip on her arm.

'You and them bloody bats,' she said, shaking her head.

Mary Ann had managed to get Rachel a bed to herself in one of the smaller rooms, but as soon as she eased herself onto the mattress she had to get off it again to use the pot.

'I don't know if I've finished,' she said to Harrie as she climbed back onto the bed. 'What if I shit myself when the baby comes out?'

The room's other occupants, three women also lying-in and two recently delivered, burst into raucous laughter. Once — a long time ago — Rachel might have taken offence, but now she didn't care. She had peed and shat and vomited and been naked and wept and made a spectacle of herself in public so often now nothing like that mattered any more. Nothing.

Mary Ann laughed, too. 'We've seen it all before, love. It's only shite and it washes off. Don't worry.'

'Can I have Angus in here?' Rachel suddenly craved the silky feel of his fur and the low, soothing rumble of his purr.

'No you can't,' Harrie replied. 'He'll only be in the way.'

Rachel said nothing, but knew if she wheedled enough, Harrie would eventually let Angus in: she knew Angus always settled her.

While Harrie was off getting water in a basin, she massaged the back of her head, digging a thumb knuckle into the spot from which the pain radiated. It never stopped the headache, but did help to ease the tension a little. Another contraction squeezed down through her innards and she bent forwards and hugged her knees, groaning.

'Your first?' a woman opposite asked. She was hugely pregnant, but looked far more relaxed than Rachel felt.

Rachel nodded, puffing out her cheeks and leaning back.

'Well, just do as you're told and Mary Ann'll see you right. She's a good midwife, Mary Ann Neale.'

A shaft of pain drilled through Rachel's head and she put more pressure on the spot with her knuckle. She felt sick and bone weary already at the thought of the agony to come, not from the birth but from the rapidly worsening headache. But she'd made her decision; she wouldn't take laudanum for it even if they forced it down her throat. She would spew up the lining of her stomach before she swallowed a drop of it. If she did and the baby suffered, she could never face Lucas again.

Harrie returned and gave her a thorough wash with soap and water.

'How are you feeling, sweetie? No headache?'

'No headache.' But then she made the mistake of rubbing her eye with the heel of her hand.

'Let me see, love.' Harrie lifted her right eyelid and had a long look.

Rachel thought Harrie looked worried, which made *her* feel nervous. 'What?'

'Nothing, really. Your eye looks a bit red.' Harrie wrung out the cloth and draped it over the side of the basin. 'I might get

Mr Sharpe to have a look when he comes in. He'll be seeing you anyway, I expect.'

Mary Ann bustled in with several folded, worn towels and a small knitted blanket. Leaving them on the end of the bed she washed her hands in the basin.

'Let's have a look at you then, love.' Raising the hem of Rachel's shift, she peered between her raised knees. 'I'm just going to have a bit of a feel, all right?' She slid two fingers into Rachel and, her eyes fixed on the wall behind Rachel's head, felt about, then withdrew her hand and palpated Rachel's belly, gently pushing and prodding. 'It's the right way up, anyway,' she said brightly. 'That's a good start. But you've a few hours to go yet.'

Rachel's waters broke, not in a gush but in a series of trickles that collected beneath her on a square of oil cloth spread over the mattress. Janie came back, Rosie awake this time, to see how things were going, and obliged when Harrie asked her to fetch Angus. Matilda Bain, deemed too old and infirm to be assigned and still at the Factory, also visited, bringing Rachel a handful of raggedy greenery pinched from the garden in front of Mrs Gordon's apartment. Rachel liked Matilda, which was odd because no one else did. Even Harrie had little patience for her whining and endless petty complaints. Matilda, however, thought Rachel was a witch and Angus her familiar, and Harrie was sure she'd only come by in the hope of catching a glimpse of the birth of some sort of demon child, and so to curry supernatural favour.

What Matilda did catch a glimpse of, before Harrie sent her away, was Rachel crying, moaning and swearing like a drunken tar. At first Harrie assumed it was the birth pains, regular but not close together yet, but perhaps more vigorous and unpleasant than Rachel had been anticipating. She'd been that ill and confused over the past months she might not have contemplated the actual delivery at all, though Janie had gone to some lengths to explain to her what would happen.

But when Harrie noticed Rachel covering her eyes with her hands, her heart plummeted.

'Is it your head? Have you a headache coming on?'

Rachel turned her face away. 'No, it's just that the light hurts.'

This, Harrie knew, was a sure sign Rachel had a headache. When she'd looked before the sclera of her right eye had been shot with angry red veins, and now it was completely scarlet. It appeared grotesque, surrounding the black, fully dilated pupil, and looked extremely painful.

Rachel grimaced as another contraction rippled through her.

Harrie didn't know what to do. 'Is your head bad?'

More tears trickled down Rachel's face, but she remained silent, refusing to admit anything was wrong.

Mary Ann appeared at Harrie's elbow. 'Is something amiss?'

'She has a headache. A bad one.'

'Oh Lord. Mr Sharpe can probably give you a very small dose of tincture of opium, dear. A tiny one. Just to help a little bit.'

'No!' Rachel winced and clutched her head. 'No, I don't want anything! I'm not having it!'

Harrie and Mary Ann exchanged glances.

'She's getting into a state,' Mary Ann said. 'That isn't going to help.' She checked again to see how far along Rachel was. 'Another hour maybe? Mr Sharpe will be here by then.'

Harrie thought she looked relieved.

The surgeon did suggest a drachm or two of tincture of opium — a small enough dose to ease the pain in her head slightly but not enough to render her senseless — and Rachel had an almighty temper tantrum. Not one of her fits, but a spectacular show of bad behaviour all the same. Even though it sent waves of agony pounding through her skull, she screamed and swore and spat and wound herself into such a lather she vomited and all thoughts of administering any medicines were abandoned.

The women sharing the room with her were taken out and temporarily accommodated elsewhere in the hospital, though her shrieks and foul language could be heard as far away as the gatehouse and the top floor of the dormitory building. Angus relocated himself to an evacuated mattress, watching Rachel from across the room through unblinking eyes.

By the time she quietened, her contractions were occurring regularly and often, and Mary Ann expected the baby to arrive within the next thirty minutes. The neck of Rachel's womb had opened adequately, the baby was in the birth canal in the right position, and its heart still beating — the midwife could feel a pulse in a tiny vein on the top of its head. Harrie was hugely relieved to step aside and allow Mary Ann to take control; it made her far happier to sit on a stool and hold Rachel's hand.

Rachel, however, felt as though her head were being slowly and inexorably crushed in a blacksmith's vice. Each time she bore down the pain increased tenfold and an enormous, drilling pressure continued to build in her skull behind her bad eye. She kept thinking she was going to be sick again, and was, and she couldn't feel her hands and feet properly any more, and it was getting dark in the room.

Someone wiped her brow with a damp cloth. She was cold. She was freezing.

She could feel the baby lodged somewhere so far down her body she thought it must be nearly out. It was pressing on her spine down by her bum and it hurt … and then even that sensation began to fade.

'Another good hard push now, love,' someone said. 'Nearly there.'

Rachel looked at Lucas. He was smiling and holding her hand and she couldn't feel his touch.

She took a deep breath, closed her eyes and bore down as hard as she could.

A vicious, tearing sensation flared inside her head. There was a giddy moment of falling before her wings swept open and she righted herself. She banked, catching the breeze, and spiralled up and up into the great southern sky, lighter than the wind itself, higher than she'd ever flown before.

And this time she didn't come back.

Sunday, 7 March 1830, Parramatta Female Factory

James crossed the courtyard and entered the hospital, looking for Harrie. Under his arm he carried a parcel containing a small, good-quality winsey blanket, a gift for Rachel's infant, due, he knew, in the next week or so. He hadn't a clue what to buy but the woman in the shop had told him he couldn't go wrong with a blanket. He was sure she'd thought he was the father, especially when he'd mentioned the Female Factory, which had been rather embarrassing.

He couldn't see Harrie in the larger of the hospital rooms, but Sidney Sharpe, doing his rounds, would know where she was.

'Mr Sharpe, good afternoon.'

His fingers still pressed against the wrist of his patient, Sidney Sharpe nodded. He was counting, so James waited until he had finished.

'I'm looking for Harriet Clarke,' James said when he had.

'I believe she's in the storeroom.'

'Thank you.'

Mr Sharpe waved him closer. 'Just a moment, Mr Downey, before you speak with her I should tell you that her friend Rachel Winter died yesterday.'

James felt as though he'd been struck very hard in the face.

'During accouchement. I thought you should be aware.'

'I — yes — thank you.' James blinked, feeling a lump in his throat the size of an apple and hot tears behind his eyes. 'Cause of death?' he managed to ask.

Mr Sharpe shrugged, though not without sympathy. 'Not entirely sure. As usual I will be entering "childbirth" on the death certificate. Apoplexy, perhaps?'

Harrie was indeed in the storeroom, or what passed for the storeroom; James had noted during earlier visits there wasn't much in it. She was sitting on the floor rolling up laundered bandages. He knocked and when she looked up he was shocked at the state of her face. She had been crying so much her puffy eyes were half closed, her nose was bright red, a rash was developing beneath it, and even her mouth looked swollen.

His heart swelled painfully and instantly he was back sitting in the grubby chair in the foyer of the King Hotel, reading the letters from Beatrice and Victor. He knew how Harrie was feeling, but he didn't know what to do about it.

'Sidney Sharpe just told me,' he said at last.

Harrie nodded and returned to her bandage-rolling.

'I'm so very sorry, Harrie, I really am.'

Another nod.

'Do Sarah and Friday know yet?'

Quick shake of the head.

James wondered if he should just go. But there was something he had to know. 'The child: was it healthy otherwise?'

At last, a spark of life: Harrie gave a watery smile. 'Do you want to see her?'

James almost fainted — he'd just assumed! He felt an idiotic grin stretch across his face. 'I would very much like to see her, Harrie, thank you.'

Harrie led him through the hospital to a small room filled with pregnant women and new mothers. And there was Janie Braine, sitting on a chair with her child Rosie in a basket at her feet and a swaddled infant at her breast.

'Hello, Mr Downey,' she said. 'Come to see the little one?'

James noted that Janie's poor, unattractive face didn't look much brighter than Harrie's, but at least now she had a replacement for Willie, whom James had known she'd loved.

'Fancy a cuddle?' The infant's mouth made a popping noise as Janie disconnected her from her nipple and handed her up to James.

To a round of somewhat sarcastic applause from the other women, he settled the child in the crook of his arm, grateful he was accustomed to juggling Beatrice's children, and looked down at her. Given how beautiful her mother had been, she wasn't actually very pretty. She had large, round, protuberant eyes that were almost black, a tiny pursed mouth, a scrawny neck and a shock of wheat-coloured hair. In fact, she looked a lot like a pink-and-gold monkey.

'Beautiful, isn't she?' Harrie said.

'Very much so,' James agreed. 'Does she have a name yet?'

'Charlotte. That was Rachel's choice.' Harrie fiddled with the swaddling cloth around the baby's head. 'Or Lucas, if it was a boy. After his father.'

There was a flat silence.

Harrie said, 'In the end, Keegan did kill her, didn't he?'

'Where is the body now?' James asked.

Sidney Sharpe dried his hands on a towel. 'In the mortuary.'

'Will you be performing a post-mortem?'

'To what end?'

'I for one would be interested in knowing what actually caused her death. You said yourself you couldn't be sure.'

'I have never performed a post-mortem on a Factory patient. There has been the occasional inquest after a death, but to be frank those deaths have never attracted enough import to warrant a post-mortem examination.'

'Would you have any objections if I did?'

'A post-mortem? On Rachel Winter's body?'

'Yes.'

Mr Sharpe stared at James. 'Where would you do it?'

'In the mortuary, I suppose.'

'Then you'd better hurry up. The hearse is arriving at four o'clock.'

The Factory mortuary was located just inside the outer wall, a short distance from the gatehouse. The interior was very cool, as was intended, and dark, no windows having been built into the structure's walls. James lit all four lamps, as well as two borrowed from the gatehouse. The combined odour and smoke emitted in the airless environment was a little distracting, but helped to disguise the faint but distinct whiff of decomposition coming from the mortuary's three occupants.

In the centre of the chamber was a waist-high wooden bench on which to rest caskets when corpses were being collected. James had covered it with an oilcloth to collect any body fluids, though he was anticipating little mess, given that Rachel's heart had stopped beating almost twenty-four hours earlier.

He laid the body out, firmly reminding himself that this was simply a cadaver, an empty shell, that the bright, headstrong, troubled girl he had known as Rachel Winter had gone. The arms were crossed over the chest; as rigor mortis was still evident there was little he could do to alter that, but in any case he doubted he would have need to investigate the chest cavity.

The body was dressed in a clean, pressed shift and had been carefully washed, by Harrie no doubt, the jaw tied shut with a length of muslin knotted on top of the head. The eyes were closed but the pennies had slipped off and become caught up in the folds of the shroud. He would reposition them when he'd finished, although no doubt the undertakers would steal them before the body went into its grave.

James removed the muslin strip, gathered together the hair, still spectacular even in death, and arranged it so it all hung over the end of the bench, then draped a cloth over the body's neck and chest, tucking it beneath the shoulders. He opened Mr Sharpe's case of surgical implements and selected a scalpel. Working carefully but deftly he cut around the hairline from one side of the jaw to the other, the cold, waxy flesh parting bloodlessly, then pulled hard on the scalp, applying gentle pressure to muscles unwilling to relax, and flipped it back to expose the skull. Leaving the scalp still attached he scraped away the tissue covering the bone, reached for the drill and made a small indentation in the skull on the right side near the top. He then fitted the point of the centre-pin of Mr Sharpe's trephine into the dent, lowered the trephine's crown and started turning. It took him less than twenty minutes, but not operating on a live patient he wasn't having to employ any finesse. When he felt the teeth of the crown break through he removed it, picked out the round section of bone and put it aside. Moving a lamp closer he took a pair of long-handled tweezers and began to poke around.

As he left the mortuary the undertaker was just arriving, preparing to back his black wagon up to the door.

James remembered he'd left his gift in the storeroom and fetched it before he found Harrie again, this time kneeling in the kitchen garden collecting herbs for poultices.

'This is for Charlotte,' he said.

'Oh, I thought you'd gone. Thank you.'

'Harrie, I performed a quick post-mortem investigation of Rachel's body and —'

Slowly, Harrie stood up. 'You did what?'

Perhaps she didn't understand the terminology. 'A post-mortem. An internal investigation of the possible cause of death.'

Such an expression of revulsion crossed Harrie's face that James thought she was about to faint. He reached out to take her arm, but when she slapped him viciously away he realised her horror had suddenly turned into virulent hostility.

'You went into that ... charnel house, while she was all alone, and *cut into her*? That's *revolting*! How *could* you?! For God's sake, she's dead now, couldn't you have just left her alone?'

James had never seen Harrie so angry. Her face was as white as marble and her whole body shaking. She swung her basket of herbs at him and he only just managed to dodge it.

'You're as bad as Keegan! You're *disgusting*!' She burst into wild tears. 'Get away from me, go on! Get out!'

Stunned at how quickly everything had gone so terribly wrong, he turned and walked away, barely noticing Janie as she crossed his path, heading for the garden. His face burning, he made his way to the front courtyard to the internal gates, passed through and told the porter to fetch his horse. As he waited he heard the sound of running feet and whipped around, heart thudding, but it was only Janie.

'You're a bloody idiot, you are,' she said, and thrust a note at him. 'This is Harrie's letter to Friday and Sarah, about Rachel. There's no post today. The least you can do is deliver it yourself. Why couldn't you leave well enough alone?'

And as she marched off he asked himself the same question.

Friday sat in the visitor's room, staring down the turnkey. The mot had a moustache and could do with a good splash of arsenic and quicklime to get rid of it.

James Downey had come to Mrs Hislop's yesterday evening with Harrie's letter; Jack, the idiot, had sent him down the alleyway thinking he was a customer because he'd been asking for her. He'd stood in the reception room, his face all stiff and his hands shaking, and handed her the letter, and when she'd read it she'd nearly hit the deck. He'd grabbed her, sat her on the sofa, said he was sorry about ten times, told someone to get her a cup of tea, then buggered off.

The pain in her chest and throat had been so awful she'd thought she was going to die. She'd felt like she couldn't breathe, as though she were drowning on dry land. It had been like *daggers*. Mrs H had bunged her a full tumbler of brandy, given her a big, bosomy, perfumed hug and the night off, which had been really good of her, and she'd gone out and got on the gin. She couldn't remember much, but she knew she'd been round to see Sarah, climbing over the fence and banging on the back door and yelling her name. Sarah had come down and then that Adam and that Esther cow had come out and there'd been arguing and shouting and the next thing she'd been in the Bird-in-Hand and this morning she'd woken up in the stable behind the Siren next to young Jimmy Johnson, who'd got a hell of a fright. She'd had an almighty headache and felt sick, but gin in her tea had fixed that.

Sarah had arrived just before she'd set out this morning, breathless from running, red-eyed and spitting nails, to say Esther wouldn't give her the day off to go out to Parramatta to see Harrie, the baby or Rachel's body.

So Friday had had to come out by herself.

The door to the visitor's room opened and Harrie came in, looking as shattered as Friday expected. They hugged fiercely.

'You can go now,' Friday said to the turnkey.

'Not likely,' the woman said. 'It's not even a proper visiting day. You could be passing contraband.'

Friday opened her purse and offered a sovereign. The turnkey took it and left.

Sitting down at the table, Harrie reached for Friday's hands.

'Our beautiful girl,' Friday said, her voice cracking.

Harrie nodded and they held on tight, crying, not caring that they were being ugly and messy, because it was only them.

After a while, Friday blew her nose and cleared her throat. 'What happened?'

Harrie pulled her own handkerchief from her sleeve. 'She had one of her headaches, a bad one. Mr Sharpe doesn't really know but he thinks the strain of pushing ...' She gestured at her head. 'It may have been too much.'

'Was it quick?'

'Not really. She suffered, Friday, and there wasn't anything we could do and she refused the laudanum anyway and it went on for hours. I'm not even sure she was aware of the baby.'

They wept again at the thought of Rachel's pain.

'Were you allowed to lay her out?' Friday said at last.

Harrie shook her head. 'Not properly. All we could do was wash her and put her in her good shift, and tie her jaw and close her eyes. Janie helped. And then they took her away to the mortuary.'

Friday frowned. 'But what about ...?'

'Mrs Dick said the undertaker would do all that.'

'But that's *our* job! The people who love her.'

Fresh tears trickled hotly down Harrie's cheeks. 'I know it is, Friday. I *know* that.'

When Harrie's father, William, had died she had helped her mother lay out his body. They had bathed and shaved him, tied his jaw, plugged every orifice to prevent leakage, bound his elbows, wrists and ankles to keep his limbs straight, dressed him in his best clothes, laid him in his coffin and closed his eyes with pennies. There had been other essential tasks to see to as well. The clock had been stopped at the moment of his death to avoid bad luck, and Harrie had run down to the church to have the bell rung to announce his passing. The only looking glass they'd owned had been covered with black crepe to ensure her father's soul would not be trapped in the house and prevented from crossing to the other side, and the doors and windows had been unlocked for the same reason.

There had been the funeral feast to arrange, with a lot of help from neighbours, and Harrie and her mother had sat constantly with William Clarke's corpse in their tiny parlour for three days and three nights until the burial. When the time had come his coffin had been carried out of the house feet first to keep his spirit from looking back and enticing other family members into the grave.

But this time none of those precautions had been taken, and Harrie had been denied the chance to tend to Rachel's body in a way that might have helped to ease her grief.

'We should write to her family,' Friday said at last.

'I have.'

Friday nodded gratefully. 'I want to see her.'

'I don't think you do,' Harrie replied shortly, and told her what James Downey had done.

Friday was horrified. 'That's *awful*! That's ... Christ, I don't know what it is.'

They stared at each other.

Grief making her harsh, Harrie added, 'She'll be stinking by now, too. They say the mortuary isn't cold enough and the weather's been hot. They took her away yesterday. It won't be Rachel any more.'

'Well, can I see the baby?' Friday asked.

Harrie nodded. 'We named her Charlotte. Janie's bringing her soon. Could Sarah not come today?'

'Esther Green wouldn't let her. Sarah's roaring.'

'Poor Sarah, she only saw Rachel once after she left. She'll be heartbroken.'

'She is. She was desperate to say goodbye. I'm glad I'm not walking in Esther's shoes. Sarah harbours a mean grudge.'

Janie arrived with Charlotte and embraced Friday, almost squashing the baby between them.

As Friday took Charlotte and gazed down at her little features, her face crumpled again and fat tears plopped onto Charlotte's head. Quietly she began to sing a lullaby. She sang as tunelessly as ever, and couldn't remember all the words, and that only made it even more poignant.

Janie and Harrie exchanged a startled look.

'She reminds me,' Friday whispered.

Harrie touched the tattoo on Friday's left forearm that spelt out *Maria*. 'Of her?' she asked gently.

Friday nodded. She drew in a deep, shuddering breath. 'She was three months old. I left her alone while I went out to work. Just for an hour. When I got back she'd died. I don't know why.' She looked up at Harrie. 'We won't leave this one alone, will we?'

Harrie squeezed her hand. 'No. We won't.'

Although the day was warm, rain fell steadily and the skies were low and the colour of a dirty sixpence. From where Friday stood beneath the shelter of the lychgate to St John's Cemetery, Parramatta, she could see the mound of mud next to the open grave. She would, she expected, be the only mourner as Harrie and Janie couldn't leave the Factory and Sarah had again been denied time off.

Finally the black wagon bearing the coffin rattled down O'Connell Street and turned in through the gate. Friday stepped aside then followed it to the graveside where the chaplain waited, his damp vestments and cassock clinging.

The undertaker and his assistant unloaded the coffin with practised ease and manoeuvred it over the grave onto the straps, where it sat while the chaplain droned hurriedly through the short service.

Really, how *are* the dead raised up? Friday wondered idly, only half listening as rain dripped off the brim of her hat. Or do they never properly go to sleep?

She stared past the coffin into the watery grave, thinking about all the things Rachel had wanted. There would be no pretty dresses now, no cakes, and no Lucas. And no more laughing, darling, difficult Rachel.

Because of Gabriel Keegan.

The chaplain finished, closed his soggy bible and signalled for the coffin to be lowered. Friday dropped three white roses into the grave and turned to leave.

James Downey stood a short distance away, hat in hand, rain trickling down his face. He gave her a brief nod.

She stared at him for a moment then walked away.

Twenty-one

April 1830, Sydney Town

When Harrie informed Mrs Dick she refused to pay any more garnish to keep her position as a nurse in the Factory hospital, Mrs Dick told her she would lose it; there were plenty of other inmates willing. Harrie said fine, they could have it. They were welcome to the endless crooked dealings, too, and the desperate misery of the place, and the sad songs of home, and the furtive, night-time couplings in the dormitories — all of it. Harrie had had enough.

She was reassigned to George and Nora Barrett, who lived towards the Middlesex Lane end of Gloucester Street on the Rocks. It was slightly embarrassing, as their house wasn't far at all from the Overtons' grocery, and Harrie had already been sent in to buy a few things and Henry Overton had been behind the counter, but all he'd said was, 'Good morning, Harriet,' so she had said, 'Good morning, Mr Overton,' and that had been that.

It was a good assignment, Harrie thought. George Barrett was a tailor and made men's and boys' suits and shirts and had a shop on the ground floor below the house. His wife, Nora, was a sempstress of some renown and was supposed to be busy making the sort of dresses women with a bit of spare money could afford, but had her hands full with their children — Abigail, who was seven,

Hannah, five, and Samuel, three. And she was expecting again. Nora thought Harrie an utter miracle because she was good with children, had some experience as a midwife (Nora felt at thirty-six she was getting too long in the tooth for childbirth and wasn't looking forward to the arrival of number four) and could sew and embellish beautifully.

The Barretts were both ex-convicts, as were so many people who lived on the Rocks, and had built up their business together and were prospering. Harrie told them when she arrived she'd been transported for stealing silk and embroidery thread, and that she'd done it on the spur of the moment because she was desperate to start her own dressmaking business. She wanted to be honest from the outset but it sounded feeble once it was out, and she wondered if she'd made a mistake. But George had assured her the past was the past and as long as she didn't steal anything from them, they would all get along nicely. And so far they were. They'd even accepted Angus, busy earning his keep as a ratter.

Her days were full and she was grateful as there was little time to sit and mope about Rachel, though at night in her attic room she lay in bed, the twist of silver-white hair clutched in her hand, and wept. She knew Charlotte was safe with Janie. As long as Janie continued to receive a regular supply of money, she could give Charlotte — and Rosie — everything they needed for now. Harrie couldn't contribute the way Friday and Sarah did, not at present, but one day perhaps she would. In the meantime she had a position with a family she liked, at least half a day off every week, she was doing a little sewing again, and Friday and Sarah were nearby.

But things were still not right with the world.

'I know where he lives. I've known for a while.'

'How did you manage that?' Sarah pegged one shoulder of yet another of Esther's expensive lawn nightgowns to the drying line. 'Pass me another peg, will you?'

Friday obliged. A still, pale face looked down at them from an upstairs window. 'We're being watched.'

'Esther? She hates it when you come around. She doesn't think servants should have friends. Especially loud drunk ones.'

Friday puffed on her pipe. 'I got my boy Jimmy at the Siren to follow him, then I followed him myself. A couple of times. He's staying at a gentleman's boarding house in Phillip Street.'

'Where's that?'

'A couple of blocks that way on the other side of the stream.' Friday waved a hand vaguely over her shoulder.

Sarah selected another garment. 'Have you ordered the headstone yet?'

'Yes. It'll be a few weeks. Still quite soon, though, don't you think?'

'No, I don't. And neither does Harrie.'

They fell silent. Over the past month they'd said all they wanted to say about Rachel and any more talk of her death would be like jabbing at a raw and pus-filled wound. A small lizard darted out from behind the drying line pole and skittered across the cobbles, disappearing beneath a rock. Sarah hung up the last of the washing then turned to face Friday, eyes hard, her mouth a grim line.

'Will we, then?'

'I say yes.'

'When?'

'When can you get away?'

'I'd have to sneak out, so it doesn't really matter to me.'

'Monday then?'

Sarah looked at her hands, red from the washing. 'Will we tell Harrie?'

'I wasn't going to,' Friday said, 'but now I'm not so sure. She still feels very sad, and angry, about Rachel.'

Sarah grunted. They all did.

'She won't say so, though.' Friday shifted on the upturned pail she was sitting on. 'I'm wondering if it might, you know, help her settle.'

'Seeing justice served, you mean?'

Friday nodded. 'She wouldn't have to do anything.'

'She'll worry we'll get found out.'

The sash on the upstairs window rattled up and Esther Green's fair head emerged. 'Sarah!' she shouted down, 'I'll thank you to get back to work!' The sash slammed back into place.

'Bitch,' Sarah said. 'She was a lag herself, you know. Seven years for forgery.'

'We won't get found out,' Friday said. 'It's commonplace round here, just like it was commonplace at home. He'll be too shamed to complain about it and it's what he deserves.'

'And he's out and about every night?'

'Seems to be.'

'This Monday night?'

Friday stood and dusted off the back of her skirt. 'Monday.'

On her way back down towards the Rocks, Friday spied Bella Jackson's curricle travelling along Bridge Street, approaching the intersection with George. Galvanised into action, her heart thumping, she elbowed her way through a group of pedestrians gathering on the corner to cross the road.

Bella noticed her and said something to her driver, who had slowed the horses for the turn, and he suddenly sped up again. She was going to get away!

Friday was standing behind a man gripping the wooden handles of an enormous barrowful of fresh produce from the George Street markets. So she shoved him; he staggered out into the road, sending an avalanche of onions, squash and sweetcorn across the intersection. The horses, unnerved by the vegetables rolling in all directions, shied and reared, eliciting cries of alarm from onlookers, which only unsettled the animals further.

As they backed down the street, nostrils flaring, Friday lunged towards the curricle, jumped up onto the little iron foot step and grabbed hold of Bella's fashionably puffed silk sleeve.

'*Murderer!*' she screamed. '*Bloody stinking murderer!*'

She lashed out with her other hand and caught Bella across the side of the head, sending her hat flying.

'*Get off!*' Bella shrieked. '*Get the fuck off me!*'

She wrenched her arm away and retaliated with an enormous roundhouse punch to the jaw that knocked Friday off the step and sent her sprawling in the dust. The horses, still retreating in panic, responded to a fierce crack of the whip and leapt forwards, narrowly avoiding Friday, their hooves slashing and trampling the spilled produce. Onlookers scattered as a moment later the curricle cut the corner and turned onto George Street at speed.

Friday slowly got to her feet, gingerly feeling around her jaw for loose teeth. Everyone was looking at her, including the man with the barrow.

'What are you staring at?'

'You pushed me!'

'I did not.'

'What about my sweetcorn and my onions?'

'Oh, fuck your onions.'

Friday and Harrie stood on the corner of Bridge and George streets, Friday with a shawl draped over her head hiding her distinctive hair and Harrie wearing a plain bonnet.

Friday had gone to see her yesterday and told her what she and Sarah were going to do: it wasn't fair, she'd decided in the end, to leave her out. They were all in this together and had been from the very beginning — and Harrie should be able to choose whether she wanted to be involved or not. To Friday's surprise, Harrie had said straight away she was in. There had been no dithering, none of Harrie's usual 'what ifs', just a hard, flat, 'I'll be there.'

And she was, looking nervous but determined.

'You didn't have any trouble getting out of the house?' Friday asked.

'No, I didn't.' Harrie sounded surprised. 'I worried myself sick all last night and today about it, whether to pretend I was poorly and go to bed early and climb out of the window, or just disappear for a few hours and hope I wouldn't be too badly punished for it. But in the end I decided to say I had a sick friend and could I have an hour off to visit, and Mrs Barrett said yes. It was that easy and now I feel guilty.'

'Well, do something nice to make up for it tomorrow, then.' Friday waved an enormous mosquito away from her face. If that made Harrie feel guilty, how might she feel after tonight?

It was just on the cusp of true darkness when she spotted Keegan ambling along George Street, twirling his cane and lifting his hat to passersby. Ignoring her suddenly pounding heart, she pulled Harrie into the shadows and they waited until he'd crossed the road where it opened onto the plaza in front of St Philip's Church and turned down Bridge Street.

He didn't notice them. When he was roughly five yards ahead they stepped out and followed him, walking casually but confidently, two women out for an evening stroll. The moon was in its first quarter and partly occluded by scudding cloud and did little to help them avoid the potholes, and street-lamps were few and very far between, but tonight's activities were best performed in shadow.

At one point Keegan glanced over his shoulder, and raised his hat. 'Good evening, ladies!' he called. 'Pleasant night for a walk.'

'Good evening, sir,' Friday replied, almost crapping herself.

Still following him they turned into Bent Street and crossed the road where, to allay suspicion and catch their breaths after the steep incline, they stopped to admire a bush in a front garden.

Unfortunately there was a pig tethered beneath it: it grunted at them and they almost died of heart failure. Nerves and fear conspired to make them burst into snorts of hysterical, mirthless giggles.

Keegan had by now also crossed Bent Street and turned into Phillip Street.

Friday and Harrie, recovered, followed.

Ahead, a short distance along Phillip Street, a barely discernable figure materialised, the shape resolving itself into Sarah as she stepped out of the shadows.

Keegan strode on obliviously, houses and cottages on large plots lining both sides of this end of the street, interspersed with sheds, several small warehouses and a lumber yard. Weak lamplight glowed in several of the dwellings, but the commercial properties were dark and silent.

He raised his hat to Sarah, who nodded in reply, but as she passed him she swung around and struck him hard across the back of the head with the cosh she'd concealed at her side.

His hat flew off and he went down like a sack of spuds, knocked senseless.

'Quick,' Sarah urged, 'get him off the street.'

Harrie and Sarah took an arm each, Friday his feet, and together they hauled him down to the far end of an alleyway between a long shed and piles of stacked timber, and dumped him on the ground.

Where he immediately began to come around.

He moaned, his body curling up defensively and his hands going to the back of his head. He peered blearily up at them but it was clear he didn't recognise them. Friday lowered her shawl to give him a clue.

'You don't remember us?' she demanded.

'Should I? What the *fuck* do you think you're doing? I'll be reporting this straight to the police.' In the diluted moonlight his face was bleached of colour, and the blood on his hands looked black.

Friday felt a savage fury rise up in her. 'Go on, do it! And we'll report how you raped Rachel Winter, then shoved her off the foredeck of the *Isla* and nearly killed her!'

'Oh. That.'

'Yes,' Friday said, aiming a good, solid kick at his thigh, '*that*!'

He winced but replied, 'Do your best. No one will listen. Why would they? Whores and bitches, the lot of you.' He clutched the back of his head again and grimaced. 'Including your stupid little friend.'

Harrie moved closer and Friday could see she was almost incandescent with rage. 'Don't you call her that! She doesn't deserve that! Who the *hell* do you think you are?' Then she deliberately stepped behind Keegan and booted him in the kidneys. He arched backwards like a slater in a hot fire grate, his face contorted with pain.

Friday, to be honest, was shocked. She shot a look at Sarah, who gave the tiniest shake of her head. What did that mean? Let Harrie get on with it, or stop her?

While Keegan's spine was bent Sarah took the opportunity to kick him in the crotch. The impact made a satisfying thud. He whiplashed the other way, clamping his hands over his groin. Then he vomited.

He didn't shout for help, though. He was so bloody arrogant, Friday thought, he still didn't think he *needed* to shout for help.

He muttered something and Harrie leant in. 'What?'

'She was useless anyway.' He coughed and spat. 'I paid well over the odds.'

Friday yanked his head off the ground by the hair, her face inches from his. 'Who? Who did you pay?'

'The whoremonger.'

Harrie gave a small cry, as though she'd been physically hurt, then, her teeth bared, kicked Keegan again, this time in the chest. His hands flew up and he rolled into a ball.

'Harrie!' Friday grabbed her sleeve and yanked her away. 'Don't! What are you doing?'

Harrie jerked her arm out of Friday's grip. 'Paying him back!'

'No, this is for me and Sarah to do.'

'No, it's for all of us, because this is for Rachel, and she was ours. She'll *always* be ours.'

It was simple and it made sense: Friday stepped back and raised her hands in a gesture of surrender.

Harrie aimed another kick at Keegan: he'd attempted to crawl away and it landed against his ribs. She tried again, connecting solidly with his spine, and followed up with another to his shoulder.

And then they were all doing it, a flurry of boots driving into him, no noise except for muffled thuds that grew increasingly wet, and the occasional breathed-out grunt.

At last, long after he'd stopped moving, they stood back, panting and gazing down at him. He was on his side and his eyes were open. Or one was: the other was a mass of pulp. He stank like shit and his pale trousers were stained.

Then Sarah went out onto the street, fetched his hat and cane, and left them with the cosh beside his body.

There didn't seem to be much to say. Together they walked down Phillip Street and along Hunter Street, where they splashed in the stinking shallows of Tank Stream to wash the gore off their boots. Sarah veered off and followed the stream until she came to the rear of Adam Green's shop, and at the George Street intersection Friday and Harrie turned right and headed towards the Rocks.

Above them, a lone bat swooped and soared.

In the alleyway a bull ant crawled over Keegan's head, its feet sticking to the blood congealing in the hair and in the shattered hollows of the skull.

Candlelight suddenly flickered in the shed next door, a door opened and a figure descended the wooden steps. Crossing to

Keegan's body the woman prodded it with her boot, watching as it rolled part way over before flopping heavily onto its side again. She crouched, holding the candle close to the ruined face, examining it for signs of life and finding none.

Bella Jackson straightened, thought for a moment, picked up the cosh then walked away.

Sarah climbed stealthily over the fence at the rear of Adam Green's yard and, keeping to the shadows, crossed the rough cobbles to the back of the shop. There she removed her boots, sloshed them about in the overspill from the rain barrel, tied the laces together and slung them around her neck. She had always known Keegan would go unpunished by the authorities for what he had done to Rachel, but now that had been addressed. She had no regrets.

On her way out earlier in the evening she'd climbed down the drainpipe — now she spat on her hands for grip and began to climb back up. Curling her feet around the pipe, she worked her arm and shoulder muscles as her hands pulled upwards. It was easy going, especially now she was getting fit again, and certainly something she was familiar with, due to breaking into houses in London.

When she reached the level of her bedroom window she extended one foot to rest on the sill, a hand to grip the window frame, then launched herself across the two-foot gap and ducked through the open lower sash.

She landed with a light thump on the bare floorboards and remained still, listening for signs that her return had been detected, but nothing stirred in the house.

She checked to make sure her bedroom door was still locked — it was — set her boots on the floor by her bed then lit the candle. And that's when she saw them: a fancy drinking glass and a plate on her bedside cupboard. The plate contained three biscuits and the glass some sort of cordial. There was also a note. It read simply: *A*.

* * *

Harrie felt sick and light-headed; and coming up the stairs she'd been struck by the horrible notion there might be spots of blood — or worse — on her face or clothes.

It wasn't the right or wrong of what they'd done, or even the violence of it, because he'd deserved every painful second. She hadn't meant for him to die — she knew none of them had — but Rachel had died, so in a way he actually had paid a just price.

Still, she couldn't believe she'd done it.

She opened the door on the landing, hoping everyone had gone to bed and the parlour would be empty.

Rachel stared back at her from the sofa.

Harrie's knees buckled and she clung to the door knob.

Mrs Barrett said, 'Harrie? You look like you've seen a ghost.'

It was the hair, the hair and the big belly. Nora Barrett had honey-coloured hair streaked with grey and in the lamplight it looked silver-white.

'Harrie?'

Harrie closed the door behind her, moving on legs that felt like jelly.

'Are you all right? You don't look well.'

'I'm a little tired, but thank you.'

'Where are your boots and stockings?'

'Downstairs. I slipped in a drain.'

Mrs Barrett put aside her embroidery. 'How was your friend? Not suffering, I hope?'

'No,' Harrie replied. 'Not now.'

Friday didn't go straight home. She dropped her boots into the cesspit behind the Bird-in-Hand on Gloucester Street, then went inside and proceeded to get drunk.

Harrie's behaviour had shocked and frightened her. But, thinking about it, she realised this wasn't a new Harrie made hard and vicious by a year spent with felons, lunatics and London street dross, this was just a side of Harrie they'd never properly seen before. This was the side that had driven Harrie to work for a bitch of a boss for years just to keep her family fed, that had compelled her to steal a bolt of cloth against all her principles, and that had inspired her to care for Rachel so lovingly and so ferociously. This was the side that Keegan had finally pushed too far. And look what had happened. He'd pushed them *all* too far.

And so, it was clear now, had Bella Jackson.

After an hour or so she picked up a sailor and took him around the back and had sex with him against a wall, charging him a pound, which he thought was a bit pricey for a pub whore who could barely stand up. He paid it, though, because he liked her hair and she made him laugh. She did it not because she wanted the money or the sort of comfort a man could give, but because her own behaviour had frightened her and she needed to feel she was in charge of herself again, even if she was mashed.

At midnight she staggered back to the Siren's Arms, her bare feet filthy, reeking of alcohol and pipe smoke and missing her shawl and jacket.

Mrs Hislop fined her three pounds for coming home drunk.

May 1830, Sydney Town

Reading from the newspaper, Sarah said, 'Listen to this. *Foul Murder Remains Unsolved. Sydney constabulary regret to report that no arrest has yet been made regarding the disgraceful and cowardly murder of Gabriel Ambrose Redman Keegan, late of Knightsbridge, London, discovered bludgeoned to death in Phillip Street on 6th April. However, the Superintendent of Police has stated that Sydney's public may rest assured that robust inquiries will continue into this heinous crime for as long as necessary until the killer is safely behind bars.'*

Friday threw a piece of bun at the pair of crows loitering hopefully on the plaza. Soon, someone would come along and tell them they weren't allowed to sit on the steps of St Philip's Church on a Sunday afternoon, but until that happened it was a nice sunny spot. 'He'll be bloody busy.'

'Who?'

'The superintendent. There's been three murders since then.'

Harrie pulled her shawl closer around her shoulders. 'Will they have found anything, do you think? During their inquiries?'

'Hard to say,' Friday replied.

They watched the crows attempting to steal the bun off each other.

'Are you worried?' Harrie asked.

'A bit,' Sarah admitted.

'A bit?' Friday muttered. 'I'm crapping myself. Every time someone knocks on the door at Mrs Hislop's, I think it's the beaks.'

Harrie nodded. 'I am, too. I dream about it.'

'Well, don't,' Sarah said. 'It's not good for you. Take a sleeping draught or something. Look, there goes your Mr Downey.' She gestured towards James Downey as he walked up George Street on the far side of the plaza, head bowed, still traipsing around in mourning black.

'Stop *saying* that,' Harrie said sharply, deliberately not looking. 'I don't even want to hear his name.'

Anticipating her response, Sarah sighed. 'Go and say hello.'

'*No.*'

'For God's sake, Harrie, you'll have to one day. You're bound to run into him. Sydney's a small town.'

'No I won't.'

'You will. We're looking at him now!'

'I won't,' Harrie replied stubbornly.

Sarah shook her head. She knew Harrie liked James Downey very much. She also knew that what he'd done had hurt her deeply and that Harrie just couldn't forgive him. It was a prickly thing to watch, because she was clearly unhappy about the situation, but would not allow herself to change it. 'Shall we go and have a cup of tea?' she suggested, wishing now she'd let the subject lie.

'Not me,' Friday said. 'I have to start work soon.'

'I will,' Harrie said, 'if you promise to shut up about that man.' She finally dared to look in the direction Sarah had indicated, but James Downey had disappeared, swallowed by the afternoon's lengthening shadows.

Friday hurried down George Street past Middlesex Lane, the autumn wind gusting off the harbour, tangling her skirt around her legs and whipping her hair in all directions. At the sound of approaching hooves she moved onto the footway: the road wasn't wide, the ironstone surface badly potholed, and not really suitable for vehicles moving at speed.

The curricle rattled past. Then slowed. Then stopped.

Friday, of course, recognised it and the familiar acid of hatred flooded through her. But now was not the time for settling scores, not in full view of dozens of witnesses. She could say her piece, though. She had always said her piece.

Fists clenched, she strode towards the gig.

Bella's painted face was turned towards her, waiting. But before Friday could spit out a single word, the whoremonger gave a smirk of such reptilian triumph that Friday stopped dead. And then Bella slowly raised into view an object that at first Friday didn't recognise. When she did, her blood turned to ice.

It was Sarah's cosh.

Then, with a snap of the reins, the horses surged ahead, scattering loose ironstone with their hooves, and the curricle was gone.

Friday stood frozen, her heart racing, blood roaring in her ears, drowning out all other sounds.

Keegan was dead, but it wasn't over after all.

It had only just started.

Author's Notes

Behind this story

The characters in this story are all fictional, except for the ones already in the history books. The story itself is fictional, though aspects of it are based quite closely on the experiences of convict women of 1829 to 1830.

Some historical notes for those who quite rightly prefer their history to be one hundred per cent accurate. People who know their early- to mid-nineteenth-century law will be aware that most convicts were not usually transported for committing a first, or often even a second, offence, unless that offence was murder. In this story, two of my characters are transported for first offences. Please turn a blind eye: it works for their character arcs.

Unfortunately I wasn't able to discover whether the conveyance of convict women newly arrived in New South Wales between Sydney Cove and Parramatta in September of 1829 was by road or by river, so I've opted for the river route. In Judith Dunn's *Colonial Ladies: lovely, lively and lamentably loose: crime reports from the Sydney Herald relating to the Female Factory, Parramatta 1831– 1835* (Winston Hills, NSW, 2008), accounts suggest that road and river might both have been used from 1831 to 1835. For the purposes of this story, the river would have been the more realistic option, given the number of women involved.

With regard to the Parramatta Female Factory mortuary, it may not have existed in 1829, though in this story it does. It is mentioned in a description given by a visitor to the Factory dated 1836, situated near the gatehouse inside the outer wall, as I've described, but does not appear on a plan dated 1833, however that plan doesn't show the outer wall. The presence of a mortuary might be expected, given that there was a hospital, but perhaps in earlier days the undertaker came as soon as an inmate died.

Readers might be surprised by how literate the four main characters in the story are. Well, convict women were a reasonably literate lot. About sixty-five per cent of convict women could read and around half of those could also write. They were also quite numerate. Irish convict women, however, were overall less literate and numerate than English convict women. See Deborah Oxley, *Convict Maids: the forced migration of women to Australia* (Cambridge University Press, 1996). See also the fascinating thumbnail sketches of the convict women listed in the back of Babette Smith's *A Cargo of Women: Susannah Watson and the convicts of the Princess Royal* (Allen & Unwin, 2008).

The character Rachel Winter's arrest story is based on the experiences of the real 'Mary Rose' described in Sian Elias's fascinating book *The Floating Brothel: the extraordinary true story of female convicts bound for Botany Bay* (Hachette Australia, 2010).

And just a point on costume. In 1829 a petticoat wasn't only something you wore under your dress, it was also 'an outer garment for working women, like a skirt' (Margaret Maynard, *Fashioned from Penury: dress as cultural practice in colonial Australia*, Cambridge University Press, 1994). I've attempted to avoid confusion by using the term 'outer-petticoat'.

I'd also like to tip my hat to some family ghosts, whose lives inspired me to write this series. Thanks for rattling your chains, ladies and gentlemen, both supernatural and the ones the law put on you.

William Standley, marine (Private), arrived New South Wales aboard HMS *Sirius* on 26 January 1788.

In November 1791 he married ...

Mary Ann Anstey (Anster/Astey), convict, arrived New South Wales aboard *Lady Julian(a)* on 3 June 1790.

In August 1792 they became parents of Mary Standley, who, in September 1805, married ...

James Lowe (Low), convict, arrived New South Wales aboard *Minorca* on 14 December 1801.

In March 1806, they became parents of Anne Lowe, who, in September 1822, married Henry Atkins Bonney, son of ...

Joseph Bonney, convict, arrived New South Wales aboard *General Hewitt (Hewart)* on 7 February 1814, whose first wife and several children, including Henry Atkins Bonney, followed him from Suffolk, England.

In 1827, in Tasmania, Henry and Anne became parents of Christopher Bonney, and so on and so on until it was me.

Parramatta Female Factory Precinct

The original Parramatta Female Factory was located in two long, narrow rooms above Parramatta Gaol, a stone building constructed in 1802 in what is now Prince Alfred Park. There were no cooking facilities or beds, only the nine hand-looms on which the women wove linen, sailcloth and woollen fabrics. By 1818 up to two hundred women were crowded into an area sufficient for just sixty.

Governor Macquarie proposed the new Female Factory — the one which appears in this book — that opened in 1821 beside the Parramatta River. The Factory was built on land that has been significant to women of the Burramattagal clan of the Darug, or Eora, nation as a place of ceremony for thousands of years. From the outset it was never big enough to meet demand. By 1823 a two-storey sleeping quarters and yards were added for convict women serving time for crimes committed in the colony, or for inmates transgressing the Factory's rules.

During his tenure, Governor Darling introduced the three-class system: first-class women were those eligible for assignment plus 'blameless destitutes'; those of the second class were probationary; and third-class inmates were locally convicted criminals. The criteria for who should be classified as first or second class, however, appears to have blurred and changed over the years.

While waiting to be assigned, recuperating from illness or nursing their babies, first- and second-class women washed, spun and carded wool to be made into Parramatta cloth, a lightweight twill-weave, for clothing or to be sent to England — Australia's first manufactured export. Life in the Factory was harsh, and tainted with despair, homesickness and disease.

Transportation to New South Wales ceased in 1840 and, in an attempt to clear the Factory of children, the government built an orphanage on adjacent land. This became the Roman Catholic Orphan School when children from the Catholic orphanage at Waverley were transferred there in 1844. The Female Factory continued to accommodate convict women and, by 1846, female lunatics. By April of 1848, however, the institution was home to two hundred and forty male and female 'invalid and lunatic prisoners of the Crown'. In 1849 the institution was officially gazetted as the Parramatta Lunatic Asylum.

Three wards for the criminally insane were built between 1861 and 1869, all of which were demolished in 1960. Also during the 1860s, the third-class sleeping quarters was remodelled and a verandah built around three sides. A large new wing was added to the building in 1876; this remains standing today.

The main Female Factory building, designed by convict architect Francis Greenway, was approved for demolition in August 1883 and a new two-storey ward built in 1885, partly over the original construction and recycling sandstone and the clock from Greenway's building.

In 1886 the government evicted the Roman Catholic Orphan School to rehouse girls from Biloela Girls' Industrial School the following year. The first modification was a new nine-foot wall surrounding the compound.

For nearly ninety years Parramatta Girls Home, as it eventually became known, housed and trained girls up to age eighteen sent there via the Child Welfare and Crimes Acts. The girls were classified as either destitute, abandoned or orphaned and therefore not 'corrupt', or having tendencies towards criminal behaviour, but conditions in the institution were brutal for all. Isolation cells for punishment were built in 1897, with more added over the years. Riots over lack of food occurred; accounts of beatings, rape and deprivation were common.

In 1974, Parramatta Girls Home closed after accusations of abuse of inmates were raised, then reopened later the same year under a new name — Kamballa for the girls' facility, and now Taldree for boys. After the boys' facility moved to Werrington in 1980, the Department of Corrective Services acquired many of the old orphanage buildings and opened the Norma Parker Correctional Centre for women, where children under three could stay with their mothers in prison, an echo of the early Female Factory days. Kamballa closed three years later and the Norma Parker Correctional Centre in 2008.

In 2003 former Parramatta Girls Home inmates reunited for the first time, and the following year the Federal Senate's *Forgotten Australians: a report on Australians who experienced institutional or out-of-home care as children* was released. Much of this historical information and more can be viewed on the Parragirls website (www.parragirls.org.au).

What remains of the Parramatta Female Factory today lies in the grounds of Cumberland Hospital in Fleet Street, Parramatta, and is owned by the New South Wales Health Department. If you know what you're looking for, you'll recognise the Factory walls, the hospital building, the third-class dormitory and Matron's apartments. You might even encounter a few ghosts. Unfortunately you can't actually go there, because it's on private property.

When I first started writing this book in 2010 I contacted Bonney Djuric. Ms Djuric, together with Christina Green, Lynette Aitken and Sebastian Clark, a descendant of the Reverend Samuel Marsden, founded the Parramatta Female Factory Precinct Association. Established in 2006, the PFFPA is a community-based, non-government organisation that seeks to broaden understanding and awareness of the precinct's history and heritage, especially in relation to women and the generations of Australians who experienced institutional care as children — the Forgotten Australians — in the precinct's institutions.

In January of 2011 Bonney Djuric and I went to Cumberland Hospital to have a look at the remaining Factory buildings. At the time, the Health Department was in the middle of installing air conditioning units in the sandstone walls of the original 1823 third-class dormitory building so it could be used as a computer data room. There was a lot of protest by the PFFPA and others and media attention about it. Perhaps not unsurprisingly, we were told fairly bluntly to leave. Since then, because of that protest action, the work has stopped.

The PFFPA's campaign to have the Parramatta Female Factory Precinct recognised as a site of national heritage continues to gain momentum, but the greatest threat to the precinct's preservation is the disparity concerning women's history and heritage. Parramatta Female Factory was the first female convict factory to be built in Australia. Twenty per cent of Australians are descended from the women who went through those Factory gates. Approximately thirty thousand girls spent time in the Parramatta Girls Home. The precinct has immense historical and cultural value to Australians. It should be preserved as a place of memory and of conscience.

If you'd like to get involved with the campaign, visit the above website. See also www.heritageparramatta.org

Thank you very much to Bonney Djuric and her team for the time and research material contributed to this book and future volumes in this series. Much appreciated.

Bibliography

Some useful primary sources have been: the descriptions of trial procedures, and actual trial transcripts, available online at www.oldbaileyonline.org; the journals of Royal Navy medical officers serving on navy, convict and emigrant ships available online via the (British) National Archives at www.nationalarchives.gov.uk/surgeonsatsea/; Susannah Place Museum, 58–64 Gloucester Street, The Rocks — four working-class terrace houses and a corner shop built in 1844, preserved to showcase different historical periods (www.hht.net.au/museums/susannah_place_museum); the Australian National Maritime Museum also had loads of fascinating ship-type resources, not least the replica HMB *Endeavour*, which while not strictly like a convict ship because of the way her lower decks are arranged is similar in size to the *Isla* (www.anmm.gov.au); The Maritime Centre at Newcastle for similar material — thank you especially to researcher Peter Smith, who sent me some very helpful information (www.maritimecentrenewcastle.org.au/); and of course the collections in the New South Wales State and Mitchell libraries.

Some useful secondary sources have been: Jonathon Green, *Slang Down the Ages: the historical development of slang* (Kyle Cathie Ltd, 2005); *London's Underworld: being selections from 'Those That Will Not Work', the fourth volume of 'London*

Labour and the London Poor', by Henry Mayhew, edited by Peter Quennell (Spring Books, 1966); Catherine Arnold, *Necropolis: London and its dead* (Pocket Books, 2007), and *City of Sin: London and its vices* (Simon & Schuster, 2011); JJ Tobias, *Crime and Police in England 1700–1900* (Gill and Macmillan, 1979); Arthur Griffiths, *The Chronicles of Newgate* (Chapman and Hall, 1884); Charles Bateson, *The Convict Ships 1787–1868* (Library of Australian History, 1983); Robin Haines, *Life and Death in the Age of Sail: the passage to Australia* (University of New South Wales Press, 2003); Annette Salt, *These Outcast Women: the Parramatta Female Factory 1821–1848* (Hale & Iremonger Pty Ltd, 1984) — an indispensible source; Jordie Albiston, *Botany Bay Document: a poetic history of the women of Botany Bay* (Black Pepper, 2003) — enough to make you cry; Kay Daniels, *Convict Women* (Allen & Unwin, 1998); Grace Karskens, *Inside the Rocks: the archaeology of a neighbourhood* (Hale & Iremonger, 1999); John Birmingham, *Leviathan: the unauthorised biography of Sydney* (Vintage, 2000); and Robert Hughes, *The Fatal Shore: a history of the transportation of convicts to Australia 1787–1868* (Vintage, 2003).

Acknowledgments

Thank you to Anna Valdinger, commissioning editor and partner in crime at HarperCollins Australia, and freelance editor Kate O'Donnell for loads of encouragement, excellent ideas, lovely comments and fabulous manuscript-polishing skills. It's been fun. Thank you also to Shona Martyn, publishing director at HarperCollins Australia, for championing me. A big thanks, too, to my agent Clare Forster, for support, wise words and insightful comments. Also much deserved is a thank you to the team at HarperCollins New Zealand for their ongoing commitment, and one also for Kate Stone for the cheering up (and of course Mr Robinson), and to my writing group Hunter Romance Writers for the clever idea of switching the bit at the end around. The most heartfelt ta goes to my friends and family and to my husband Aaron Paul, for keeping me sane. More or less.

Girl of Shadows

BOOK TWO

Deborah Challinor

1830: Convict girls Friday Woolfe, Harriet Clarke and Sarah Morgan have been settled in Sydney for almost a year. Sarah has been assigned to jeweller Adam Green, Harriet is a maid for the Barrett family, and Friday is working as a prostitute in a brothel. Each of them is struggling to forget the brutal crime they committed.

But their fate is no longer theirs to control. Vicious underworld queen Bella Jackson holds the girls' futures in the palm of her hand, biding her time until she exacts payment for what she knows about their misdeeds — payment that will ruin them.

Harriet, racked with guilt and slowly losing her mind, is convinced that their lost friend is haunting them, and while Friday succumbs to the bottle, Sarah has to fight for everything she holds dear. Once again, the girls must join forces to save one of their own. But which one?

And in the background Bella Jackson waits and watches ...

Read on for a sneak peek at *Girl of Shadows* ...

September 1830, Sydney Town

As a lurid dawn broke over Sydney Harbour, the sun a slash of fire on the horizon, a handful of tardy bats straggled homewards across the shadowed land on a warm, salty breeze to seek dark shelter in trees and caves. Below them folk awoke — free men and women and convicts alike — stirred blearily in their houses, and set about preparing for the day ahead.

The weather promised to be fair after a week of almost constant pelting rain, and housewives and servants built fires beneath coppers for a long day of boiling mouldering laundry. Lags from Hyde Park Barracks looked forward to time outside the walls, even if it was only working on the roads or the tunnel from Lachlan Swamp, and ladies relished time in the shops unhampered by heavy capes and umbrellas. In paddocks horses squelched morosely in steaming puddles, while their better-heeled, more highly strung counterparts kicked out at stalls and ostlers' boys. After a quick breakfast, market gardeners out towards Parramatta rushed to check that their recently planted vegetables hadn't been washed right out of the ground.

Sydney Town was finally beginning to dry out, but at least everyone's water barrels were full, and the Tank Stream may have been cleansed of a *fraction* of its filth. The day that Mr Busby announced the completion of his water bore would be a day to celebrate indeed.

Those abroad by the time the sun hung free of the eastern horizon noted the change in the taste of the wind and agreed that spring had definitely arrived.

Sarah Morgan sat with her back against the sandstone wall, wrapped in a cloak of fear and gazing sightlessly at nothing, not even moving when she heard the rattle of keys.

There was little point. From outside came the clank and bang of the gallows being prepared: she knew very well who was coming for her.

The heavy door creaked open and the priest asked, 'Are you ready, Sarah?'

She didn't respond.

He tried again. 'Sarah, have you made your peace with God? Would you like to say a final prayer? It is not too late for redemption.'

Slowly, hearing her neck bones scrape as though her vertebrae had rusted, she moved her head to face him. 'I don't want redemption. I don't regret what I did. I'm glad I killed him.'

The turnkeys peering over the priest's shoulder stared at her.

As though he hadn't heard, the priest insisted, 'God will offer you forgiveness if you repent.'

'No. I refuse to. I hate spiders and that's what your God is.'

Shocked at her blasphemy, one of the turnkeys backed out of the cell, rapidly crossing himself. The other, evidently not so superstitious, fastened Sarah's hands behind her back with wrist-irons, then they were all in the corridor, their footsteps echoing hollowly off the flagstones. The passageway was cool and dim, and for several seconds a pair of sleek rats kept pace with them, scampering along the base of the wall, their pale faces those of the two young girls belonging to the reverend on the convict ship

Isla. What had been their names? Sarah struggled to remember: Eudora and Jennifer? No, Geneve, that was it. And then the rodents vanished.

She blinked rapidly.

'Those rats,' she said to the priest. 'Their faces, did you see them?'

'Yes, the Seaton girls,' he said. 'I know their father well.'

She stared at him in disbelief. Oh God, she was so frightened she was losing her mind.

Up ahead the door seemed to loom twelve feet tall. The priest, dwarfed, pulled it open and sunlight poured in, blinding Sarah. She squinted, shocked and confused by the noise until she realised it was the roar of the crowd gathered on Gallows Hill above the gaol, come to watch the day's hanging.

Beyond the door stood a column of soldiers, the scarlet and white of their jackets and trews glaringly bright. A drum began a slow, mournful beat as loud almost as her heart, and the troops set off towards the gallows across the yard. The turnkeys followed, gripping her elbows, while the priest trailed behind in his flapping black vestments, a tall, thin bat droning the funeral service under his breath: 'Jesus said unto her, I am the resurrection, and the life: he that believeth in me, though he were dead, yet he shall live. And whosoever liveth and believeth in me shall never die.'

A funeral service for *her*.

When her knees gave way the turnkeys simply jerked her upright again and dragged her along between them.

The good people of the Rocks cheered heartily.

She was hauled up the gallows's wooden steps and placed on a trapdoor beneath one of three rope nooses. Why were there three? She knew the number was profoundly important, but not *why* it was. If she closed her eyes and really concentrated it might come to her, but her terror and the drumming and the shouting and the rush of her own blood in her ears were all too much and she couldn't. Surrendering, she let her need to know float away.

From the gallows she could see over the high stone wall and into the Harrington Street crowd, and all the way up the hill to the houses and shops and pubs perched along Gloucester, Cambridge, Cumberland and even Princes streets. In the mob she fancied she recognised familiar faces. There was her master Adam in his sober black coat and hat, hands cupped around his mouth, shouting and shouting and shouting. What was he trying to tell her? She'd never hear him from here. Mrs Dick from the Female Factory had come, too, and James Downey, and, oh God, Bella Jackson, and Mr Skelton from the pawnshop. And there was Rachel, her long pale hair falling free and catching the sun, turning everything around her to silver. No, that couldn't be right: Rachel was dead.

She couldn't see Friday and Harrie, but didn't blame them at all for not coming to watch.

The door to the gaol swung open again; more manacled figures emerged and suddenly there they both were, shuffling into the sharp light.

'*No!*' Sarah shouted in horror, her cry echoing around the yard. '*No, not them!*'

Harrie and Friday barely glanced up.

But no matter how loudly Sarah screamed, Harrie and Friday continued to be escorted across the yard and up the steps to stand beside her. The drum beat on relentlessly, and overhead in the endless white sky crows wheeled and jeered.

Sarah blurted to Friday, 'But I confessed! I told them it was me!' Terror and panic conspired to make her feel dangerously light-headed, and she felt as though she might pass out. This was all horribly, horribly wrong.

Her copper hair shimmering in the sunlight, Friday shook her head sadly. 'You dobbed us in, Sarah.'

Sarah gasped. The shock almost stopped her heart and sent waves of confused dismay through her entire body. She hadn't, surely. Had she? She couldn't remember.

'It's for the best,' Harrie said in her lovely, kind voice. 'We'll be with Rachel soon. We'll all be together again.'

Sarah couldn't believe she could have done such a thing. 'I didn't! I know I didn't!'

Friday and Harrie would no longer meet her eye.

Then a great howl rose from the crowd as the hangman arrived. Clomping up the steps in an absurdly large pair of heavy black boots, a top hat, and a coat reaching his ankles, he creaked his way across the gallows platform.

'Tell him!' Sarah pleaded. 'Tell him you're innocent!'

But Harrie and Friday said nothing, standing as still as statues, their hair lifting slightly in the light breeze, not even blinking. Refusing to help themselves.

Desperate, Sarah cast her gaze back out over the crowd. Adam had moved closer, his hands still raised, still trying to call out to her.

She opened her mouth and shouted as loudly as she could, but nothing at all came out now. She tried again, straining until she thought her eyes might pop out of her head, and still nothing emerged, except perhaps for a tiny croak.

And the drum kept on beating, the crowd clapping in time now; a slow, gleeful, anticipatory cadence.

Behind her the hangman crouched, opened his leather case and removed three white hoods. He pulled one each over Harrie's and Friday's heads, and then Sarah's. The fabric smelled of lye soap and caught on her ear on the way down. The hangman then lowered the noose over Sarah's head, tightened it slightly and adjusted the knot so it sat just beneath her right ear.

She dragged in ragged, terrified breaths, the cloth of the hood drawing close against her mouth. 'Friday? Harrie?'

'Hush, girl.' The hangman stood back.

The drummer stopped drumming.

The priest intoned, 'For the wages of sin is death; but the gift of God is eternal life through Jesus Christ our Lord. Amen.'

The hangman yanked the trapdoor lever.

Sarah dropped like a stone.

She jerked upright, gasping, her shift plastered to her chest with sweat, her hand on her throat where she could still feel the rough scratch of rope. She sat for a few minutes, head bowed, until her heart slowed.

Her room was dark, though birds were starting up a racket in the tree in the backyard. She lit the candle on her nightstand and turned the miniature clock Adam had given her so Esther could never reprimand her for being late in the mornings. It was five-twenty — time to rise in a few minutes anyway.

Sarah threw back the bedclothes and set her feet on the floor. This was the fourth or fifth time she'd had the hanging dream, and every time she awoke feeling utterly hag-ridden, tormented and riddled with cold, greasy fear. They had murdered Gabriel Keegan five months ago and she had imagined the dread of being found out would have subsided a little by now, but it hadn't.

Thanks to Bella Jackson.

Sarah knelt and reached beneath the iron bed for the po and crouched over it, bunching her shift up around her waist and peeing for what felt like ages, then tossed the contents out of the open window. She crossed to the small chest of drawers and poured cold water from a jug into a bowl and scrubbed her face with a washcloth, then brushed most of the knots from her straight black hair and tied it up in a ponytail. Sniffing the armpits of the plain, sage-green dress she wore almost every day and deciding it would do, she shrugged it on over her head and fastened the buttons at the side. She cleaned her teeth with bicarbonate of soda and, after a cursory glance in the tiny looking glass on the wall, took the candle and went downstairs.

Her mistress Esther Green was, as usual, already in the kitchen; coiffed and corseted and wearing yet another new dress. Sarah knew she wore stays because she'd crept into Esther's room one day and had a good poke around, discovering a drawer full of good-quality demi-corsets. Being slender, Esther didn't *need* to wear one, but all women of class did, therefore Esther Green had to, even though she was hardly a toff, being an emancipated convict. But rather than ask for Sarah's assistance she'd bought demi-corsets, which she could — just — fasten herself. This suited Sarah: she would rather walk a mile over broken glass in bare feet than consent to lace Esther Green's stays.

Sarah deduced from the way she was banging the porridge spoon around that Esther was in a bad mood. As a rule she often was, and usually at her worst at breakfast time. 'Morning,' she muttered.

'Sarah,' Esther replied brusquely, without turning away from the fire.

Esther Green believed that instead of residing in a series of small rooms above her husband Adam's jewellery shop on George Street, and daily cooking in a detached kitchen — little more than a shed — just beyond the back door, she should be living in much grander style. That the kitchen was so located to prevent heat and cooking smells permeating the house and shop, particularly in summer, was, to her, irrelevant. Adam made good money as a manufacturing jeweller; if only he could be persuaded to work harder and sell more, then surely there must soon be the money to acquire a bigger and better appointed house, perhaps on Woolloomooloo Hill on the other side of Hyde Park where the smarter set were building. If not there, up on Princes Street would possibly do, though it was rather too close to the Rocks. Then she could have her modern indoor kitchen, with a big American cooking stove and room for enough sideboards to store her good crockery and cutlery and serving ware. She loved to cook: Adam knew that. It was the least he could do for her, considering. She could also take on more servants — proper domestics from England, not sluttish convict girls — and get rid of sly, nasty, wanton Sarah Morgan.

She set the wooden spoon back into the pot and turned around, wiping her hands on her flower-sprigged calico apron. 'Have you emptied the chamber pots yet?'

Sarah shook her head: it was a chore she hated. In the mornings Esther always crapped in hers — on purpose, Sarah suspected, so she would have to clean it out. Esther could easily use the privy in the backyard. Adam did. And why couldn't Esther call it by one of its usual names? What was wrong with pisspot? Or thunder mug? Or even just po? No one called it a chamber pot.

'Well, go and do it then!' Esther demanded.

Sarah left the kitchen and went inside, passing through the small dining room where she would claw a sliver of revenge when she sat down to breakfast with Adam and Esther. Adam insisted on it and it drove Esther wild — probably *because* Adam insisted on it — otherwise she would have to eat in her room, or outside, or standing in the kitchen or parlour.

She met Adam on the first-floor landing.

'Good morning, Sarah. And how is everything today?'

'Same as usual.'

By 'everything' Sarah knew he meant Esther and her mood. There were two bedrooms on the first floor and Adam and Esther often occupied one each, usually after a difference of opinion, which was a frequent occurrence. The following morning Adam always pretended nothing was amiss, as though Sarah couldn't possibly have heard Esther's carping demands and bitter accusations rising up through the floorboards of her tiny second-floor attic room. Sarah couldn't decide whether the pretence was a product of his embarrassment, or because he didn't want to admit to himself the bellicose state of his marriage.

After a year as an assigned servant to Adam and Esther Green, however, Sarah understood that Adam did genuinely care for his beautiful, bad-tempered wife; but she wasn't sure if he loved her. Yet who was she to say what form love took? She'd never been in love, and didn't care to be.

'Oh dear,' Adam said. 'What is it this morning?'

Sarah shrugged and thought, You should know; you were the one she was shouting at last night. He'd shaved already; the pale skin on his face was smooth and she could smell the toilet water he always wore, lightly fragranced with a hint of sandalwood and lime. This morning his dark hair, which had grown really rather long and well past his collar, was not tied back.

'Well, I expect I'll find out in due course,' he said.

Sarah nodded and went into Esther's bedroom. The pisspot sat on the floor near the bed draped with a piece of cloth, which was doing nothing to contain the stink. She picked up the pot by the handle and carried it downstairs, one hand pinching her nose shut, hoping she wouldn't meet Adam again. He knew Esther did this: it was embarrassing — for him and for Sarah. Obviously not for Esther though, or she wouldn't do it. Dirty cow.

Outside Sarah tipped the turd down the privy and rinsed the po in the overflow from the rain barrel, then washed her hands thoroughly with carbolic soap.

At breakfast she set a covered dish containing sausage and an egg each on the table, ladled the beautifully prepared porridge into three bowls, poured the tea, then sat down.

Esther glared at her; Sarah glared back. Adam concentrated on his porridge.

Sarah knew that if Esther had her way, she would be sent back to the Parramatta Female Factory tomorrow. Esther had convinced herself that she, Sarah, was lifting her leg for Adam. She wasn't; she would never take such a pointless and unrewarding risk. Aside from having to endure Esther, she liked her position. Adam was a kind, intelligent and, at times, quite amusing boss, and she delighted in working with jewellery again. She was crafting her own designs now and they were selling well, and her jewels were bringing new customers into the shop and increasing Adam's profits. Which was a good thing because she was still pilfering from him every chance she got.

And there was another reason she wanted to stay. When dear, precious Rachel had died six months ago, Esther had deliberately denied her leave to visit Rachel's body or attend her funeral. Poor little Rachel, whom Sarah, Friday and Harrie had tried so hard to protect and care for, and whose baby, Charlotte, they were now all working to support. That had really hurt, and had lodged in her like the broken-off barb of an arrow, festering ever since.

Now Sarah wanted revenge.